THE HAUNTED HOTEL
and other Strange Tales

THE HAUNTED HOTEL

HOTEL

and other Strange Tales

Wilkie Collins

with an Introduction by
DAVID STUART DAVIES

WORDSWORTH EDITIONS

For my husband
ANTHONY JOHN RANSON
with love from your wife, the publisher
Eternally grateful for your
unconditional love

Readers who are interested in other titles from
Wordsworth Editions are invited to visit our
website at www.wordsworth-editions.com

First published 2006 by Wordsworth Editions Limited
8B East Street, Ware, Hertfordshire SG12 9HJ

ISBN 978 1 84022 533 4

Wordsworth Editions is
the company founded in 1987 by
MICHAEL TRAYLER

Typeset in Great Britain by Roperford Editorial
Printed and bound by Clays Ltd, Elcograf S.p.A.

CONTENTS

INTRODUCTION

'Ask yourself if there is any explanation of the mystery of your
own life and death.'

'The Haunted Hotel'

The Victorians were fascinated by the dead. During the nineteenth
century there was an increasing curiosity concerning what actually
happened after one had passed over from this life into the world
beyond. It was during this period that the clairvoyant, the spiritualist
and other oddly named communicators with the dead rose to prom-
inence. Séances became fashionable and the eager, gullible public
flocked to these meetings to receive the sort of messages from the
grave that Hamlet received from his father. No novelist worth his
or her salt writing in the nineteenth century failed to explore the
intriguing idea of the dead interfering for good or ill in the affairs of
mortal man. At some point in their writing careers Charles Dickens,
Charlotte and Emily Brontë, Thomas Hardy, Arthur Conan Doyle,
Robert Louis Stevenson, Elizabeth Gaskell and Henry James – to
name a few – all penned tales concerning this subject or presented
scenes featuring the spirit world in their novels. And so did Wilkie
Collins. And he did so in a very individualistic and original fashion, a
manner epitomised in 'The Haunted Hotel', which is a brilliant
example of a realistic mystery/detective story laced with unnerving
elements of the supernatural. These elements are not gratuitously
shoe-horned into the narrative merely to spice up the story, they
are there to add that suggestion of danger and confusion which
spill out into life when the moral rules are broken and when evil
is committed.

In many ways this novella reflects the character of Collins himself:
dark and surprising. He was a member of the respected literati of the
time, a close friend of Charles Dickens, and yet his own personal and
social life was somewhat recherché. Collins was an odd mix of the
practical and the bohemian, the prudent and the daring. When he

first left home, at the ripe old age of thirty-two, it was to set up house with his mistress, Caroline Graves, a woman in her early twenties who already had a daughter, and apparently also a husband somewhere. Although this bold move shocked his family, friends and society, he was not the least concerned by their censure. He cared for Caroline – that was all that mattered to him. However, although he had been contemplating this action for some time, he did not make a move until he was sure that he was financially capable of supporting his new ménage. Although he fathered several children by her, he never married Caroline. This contrasting mixture of romanticism and realism were the hallmarks of Collins's fiction, too. In the preface to his second novel, *Basil* (1852), the author stressed the difference between the Ideal and the Actual, observing that 'the more of the Actual I could garner up as a text to speak from, the more certain I might feel of the genuineness of the Ideal which was sure to spring out of it.' This clever use of realism, the Actual to use his phrase, especially with characterisation, helps to give a sense of believability to the sensational, highly melodramatic elements – the Ideal – in his plots. It is this formula of the exciting and at times a fanciful plot tinged with the supernatural but peopled by wholly credible and engaging characters that makes 'The Haunted Hotel – A Mystery of Modern Venice' such a fascinating read. In essence Collins's ideas, themes and motifs introduced in earlier works are streamlined and concentrated here into this tight novella.

There is an emphasis on physical horrors that contrasts with his avoidance of such elements in his more famous novels. The visible and olfactory presences are described in grisly detail. It was as though Collins were trying to show that he could throw off the shackles of subtlety and restraint if necessary to shock and frighten. It was his last great work and there are echoes within the text of Collins's most celebrated novel *The Woman in White* – the substitution plot in particular – but nevertheless it is an individual piece, effectively and excitingly handled.

However, the sensations within 'The Haunted Hotel' are not all unbridled and presented at full throttle, for in describing Venice, the backdrop of the drama, Collins slips back into his more teasing mode. Venice, a city he knew well, is shown as one possessing dark corners and elusive shadows where what is real and what is imagined or conjured is not clear. He was one of the first writers to explore the strange, hypnotic power of this mysterious city resting on the seething waters of the Adriatic Sea. Collins loved Venice and it becomes a character within the novel. Here mystery seems to be endemic and all is not what it seems. The wicked brother and sister may or may not be lovers, or perhaps are not siblings. On the other hand, perhaps the victim may be thoroughly deserving of his fate. Can we be sure that the manifestations, seen only by the relatives of the murdered man, are not merely hysterical hallucinations? The villainess invites discovery and retribution by writing the truth in the form of a play which trails off into incoherence as she becomes increasingly demented. All these ambiguities raise doubts in the reader as to the truth and are a device by which Collins creates suspense while mixing in the supernatural ingredient to create a full-bodied concoction. As in all his work, Collins drives the reader along at such a pace and presents such interesting scenery that we are hardly aware of the potholes of coincidence and contrivance.

The Countess Narona is one of Collins' cosmopolitan enchantresses: she acts but as the tool of her doom. T.S. Eliot wrote:

In this story, as the chief character is internally melodramatic, the story itself ceases to be melodramatic, and partakes of true drama . . . The principal character, the fatal woman, is herself obsessed by the idea of fatality: her motives are melodramatic: she therefore compels the coincidences to occur, feeling that she is compelled to compel them.

Collins relieves the tension with some wry characterisations and ironies: the theatrics are sustained. Indeed, theatrical motifs figure prominently, Collins himself being much involved with the stage at that period. 'The Haunted Hotel' appears to be loosely based on a case from the annals of French crime, as was *The Woman in White* – a case of reality touched with imagination converted into engrossing fiction.

'The Haunted Hotel' was serialised in *Belgravia* magazine in six monthly parts, from June to November 1878. Though the story was very popular, Collins was only paid fifty pounds for each part, which reflects to some extent the short-sighted view the publishing world took of the author at this time. He was generally regarded as having passed his prime. In reading the story, you will judge, I am sure, that this was not the case. However, 'The Haunted Hotel' was the last significant work of this great writer before ill health and opium drained his powers.

* * *

The remaining stories in this volume of strange tales are collected here for the first time and further reveal Collins's ability to create effective, unusual and disturbing narratives, usually with a super-natural theme. 'The Dream Woman' (1855) is a classic ghost story. It was G. K. Chesterton who wrote of Charles Dickens and Wilkie Collins: 'They were two men who could not be exceeded at telling a ghost story.' 'The Dream Woman' is a slow-burn tale of a haunting, told in a Thomas Hardyesque fashion. The simplicity of the language and the deliberately undramatic manner in which the supernatural elements are introduced actually increase the sense of horror and unease, making the haunting seem all the more real. We follow the fortunes of Isaac Scatchard as he tries to find work but encounters a homicidal ghost instead. What is so appealing about the story is the leisured fashion in which it is related. Collins teases his readers, leading us to expect one certain obvious outcome to Scatchard's troubles, but then surprises us with an unexpected denouement. His unresolved dilemma is perhaps the most chilling aspect of this well-formed narrative.

If 'Mrs Zant and the Ghost' (first published as 'The Ghost's Touch' in 1885) were a television programme, we would call it a docu-drama. The style that Collins adapts in presenting the story is that of a historian dramatising a factual incident. We follow events at a distance, almost like scientific observers. Even the two central charac-ters, Mrs Zant and Rayburn, are not given first names. The clever paradox of this approach is that the reader becomes drawn into the very subtle drama which unfolds. Rather like 'The Haunted Hotel', the story involves an element of mystery/detective fiction as Ray-burn investigates the strange dilemma of Mrs Zant. The brilliance of Collins's characterisation is seen in his presentation of the villainous chiropodist, John Zant. When we first encounter him, there is little to tell us that this is a man not to be trusted. Indeed, on the surface he seems the most charming and obliging fellow and yet Collins creates – almost out of thin air – an impression that this is not the case. The reader shares the misgivings of Rayburn: 'Is that man a scoundrel, was Mr Rayburn's first thought, after he had left the hotel. His moral sense set all hesitation at rest – and answered. 'You're a fool if you doubt it.' In keeping with this subtlety, the ghostly influence is delicately handled in this story, gracing it with a ring of truth.

While there is a trace of romance in 'Mrs Zant and the Ghost', the following story, 'Miss Jéromette and the Clergyman' (1875), deals with a full-blown tragic and doomed love affair. Told in the first person, the story appears to be constructed in two disparate halves, one concerning the storyteller's passion for an enigmatic French girl and the other taking place some time later and detailing the strange behaviour of his troubled religious pupil. However, Collins cleverly binds the parts together in a chilling finale which features a murder and a spectral pillar of mist which predicts and illustrates the crime. Yet again the simplicity of the language, more relaxed here in the first-person mode, actually works in favour of emphasising the horror.

A nightmarish ambience is achieved effectively in 'A Terribly Strange Bed' (1852), one of Collins's most famous short stories. The tale begins casually enough: the narrator, a young Englishman who has finished his formal education, seeks excitement in one of the gambling houses of Paris, another favourite city of Collins. The student does not want the artificial glamour of the more fashionable up-market establishments, but prefers the appeal of the rough and ready houses where 'they don't mind letting a man in with a ragged coat'. However, in rejecting one form of artificiality, he is lured into accepting another and suffers as a result. He persuades his friend to accompany him and we know as soon as they enter the lowly gambling house that things are not as they should be. By the cunning descriptions of the place and the unwholesome characters the two young men encounter there, Collins creates a mood of unease and strangeness that both intrigues and repels the reader. We know now that the narrator is in peril but we cannot fathom what form it will take until it is almost too late. Collins dares us to keep on reading to discover the exact nature of the danger which threatens the hero. The oddness of the situation, the apparent innocence of the storyteller and the sense of claustrophobic menace draw the reader into this surreal tale until he is completely engrossed. Ideas on the nature of friendship, risk and gullibility are all explored in this deceptively simple but unsettling story.

On the face of it, 'The Dead Hand' (1857) is a domestic melodrama, featuring an illegitimate son, strange coincidences and the cruel hand of fate. Indeed, it has been suggested that the story was based on a real incident that Collins had heard about. However, the basic plot is only a structure on which Wilkie Collins hangs one of his most chilling set pieces. This is where his central character, Arthur, has to spend the night in a darkened room with the dead body of a stranger. The description of Arthur's rapidly changing emotions as he lies in the gloom, conscious of the corpse close by him, is a psychological *tour de force*. Collins charts with unerring accuracy the frantic thoughts of this young man who has had no previous experience of death in his life. As the solitary candle burns down to near extinction, the dial of terror is turned up a notch when Arthur notices that the dead man's hand has moved! In the end his frightening and bizarre predicament is the prelude to the unravelling of a family tragedy, but the horrors of that night stay in the mind long after the story has been read.

'Blow up with the Brig!' (1859) was originally titled 'The Ghost in the Cupboard'. Neither title really gives a hint of the nature of the plot which features a near-death experience that haunts the narrator for the rest of his life. Again the effectiveness of the tale is in the way Collins is able to create and maintain the suspense.

'Nine o'Clock' is an early story which was originally published anonymously in 1852. The reason for this is probably because it is based on an anonymous German tale, 'The Fatal Hour', that was often anthologised in England. It concerns a curse that causes members of a certain French family to die at the hour of nine o'clock. Collins has great fun with the concept, particularly with the predictable but very satisfying dénouement.

We finish in keeping with the title of this collection with 'The Devil's Spectacles', which is a strange tale indeed. This is an atypical foray for Wilkie Collins into the realms of fantasy, with touches of genuine horror involving cannibalism. The gruesome details of Septimus Notman's experiences at the North Pole still have the power to make one shudder, even in these brutalised times. It is true to say that Collins was not too happy with this story and after it had appeared in several periodicals in 1879 he locked it away, refusing to see it published in book form. It was probably the tone and subject-matter of the story, so different from Collins's usual style, which dissatisfied him. This is a shame because the story is a fascinating one. There is a certain irony in that at the time he wrote it Collins's own eyesight had deteriorated greatly. He must have longed for the clarity of vision granted by the Devil's spectacles, to say nothing of the magic qualities which allowed the wearer to be aware of the true motives and sentiments behind the lies that people tell.

Although his literary output was considerable, Wilkie Collins will be forever remembered as the author of *The Moonstone* and *The Woman in White*. As a result, his other works have suffered neglect. They deserve greater recognition than they currently receive. It is very much to be hoped that this collection will help to redress the balance a little, for, as it demonstrates, Collins's strange stories still have the power to entertain, stimulate and thrill. It is a great delight for me to bring them to your attention.

DAVID STUART DAVIES

THE HAUNTED HOTEL
and other Strange Tales

The Haunted Hotel

A Mystery of Modern Venice

THE FIRST PART

Chapter 1

In the year 1860, the reputation of Doctor Wybrow as a London physician reached its highest point. It was reported on good authority that he was in receipt of one of the largest incomes derived from the practice of medicine in modern times.

One afternoon, towards the close of the London season, the Doctor had just taken his luncheon after a specially hard morning's work in his consulting-room, and with a formidable list of visits to patients at their own houses to fill up the rest of his day – when the servant announced that a lady wished to speak to him.

'Who is she?' the Doctor asked. 'A stranger?'

'Yes, sir.'

'I see no strangers out of consulting-hours. Tell her what the hours are, and send her away.'

'I have told her, sir.'

'Well?'

'And she won't go.'

'Won't go?' The Doctor smiled as he repeated the words. He was a humorist in his way; and there was an absurd side to the situation which rather amused him. 'Has this obstinate lady given you her name?' he enquired.

'No, sir. She refused to give any name – she said she wouldn't keep you five minutes, and the matter was too important to wait till tomorrow. There she is in the consulting-room; and how to get her out again is more than I know.'

Doctor Wybrow considered for a moment. His knowledge of women (professionally speaking) rested on the ripe experience of more than thirty years; he had met with them in all their varieties – especially the variety which knows nothing of the value of time, and never hesitates at sheltering itself behind the privileges of its sex. A glance at his watch informed him that he must soon begin his rounds among the patients who were waiting for him at their own houses. He decided forthwith on taking the only wise course that was open under the circumstances. In other words, he decided on taking to flight.

'Is the carriage at the door?' he asked.

'Yes, sir.'

'Very well. Open the house-door for me without making any noise, and leave the lady in undisturbed possession of the consulting-room. When she gets tired of waiting, you know what to tell her. If she asks when I am expected to return, say that I dine at my club, and spend the evening at the theatre. Now then, softly, Thomas! If your shoes creak, I am a lost man.'

He noiselessly led the way into the hall, followed by the servant on tiptoe.

Did the lady in the consulting-room suspect him? Or did Thomas's shoes creak, and was her sense of hearing unusually keen? Whatever the explanation may be, the event that actually happened was beyond all doubt. Exactly as Doctor Wybrow passed his consulting-room, the door opened – the lady appeared on the threshold – and laid her hand on his arm.

'I entreat you, sir, not to go away without letting me speak to you first.'

The accent was foreign; the tone was low and firm. Her fingers closed gently, and yet resolutely, on the Doctor's arm.

Neither her language nor her action had the slightest effect in inclining him to grant her request. The influence that instantly stopped him, on the way to his carriage, was the silent influence of her face. The startling contrast between the corpse-like pallor of her complexion and the overpowering life and light, the glittering metallic brightness in her large black eyes, held him literally spellbound. She was dressed in dark colours, with perfect taste; she was of middle height, and (apparently) of middle age – say a year or two over thirty. Her lower features – the nose, mouth, and chin – possessed the fineness and delicacy of form which is oftener seen among women of foreign races than among women of English birth. She was unquestionably a handsome person – with the one serious drawback of her ghastly complexion, and with the less noticeable defect of a total want of tenderness in the expression of her eyes. Apart from his first emotion of surprise, the feeling she produced in the Doctor may be described as an overpowering feeling of professional curiosity. The case might prove to be something entirely new in his professional experience. 'It looks like it,' he thought; 'and it's worth waiting for.'

She perceived that she had produced a strong impression of some kind upon him, and dropped her hold on his arm.

'You have comforted many miserable women in your time,' she said. 'Comfort one more, today.'

Without waiting to be answered, she led the way back into the room.

The Doctor followed her, and closed the door. He placed her in the patients' chair, opposite the windows. Even in London the sun, on that summer afternoon, was dazzlingly bright. The radiant light flowed in on her. Her eyes met it unflinchingly, with the steely steadiness of the eyes of an eagle. The smooth pallor of her unwrinkled skin looked more fearfully white than ever. For the first time, for many a long year past, the Doctor felt his pulse quicken its beat in the presence of a patient.

Having possessed herself of his attention, she appeared, strangely enough, to have nothing to say to him. A curious apathy seemed to have taken possession of this resolute woman. Forced to speak first, the Doctor merely enquired, in the conventional phrase, what he could do for her.

The sound of his voice seemed to rouse her. Still looking straight at the light, she said abruptly: 'I have a painful question to ask.'

'What is it?'

Her eyes travelled slowly from the window to the Doctor's face. Without the slightest outward appearance of agitation, she put the 'painful question' in these extraordinary words: 'I want to know, if you please, whether I am in danger of going mad?'

Some men might have been amused, and some might have been alarmed. Doctor Wybrow was only conscious of a sense of disappointment. Was this the rare case that he had anticipated, judging rashly by appearances? Was the new patient only a hypochondriacal woman, whose malady was a disordered stomach and whose misfortune was a weak brain? 'Why do you come to me?' he asked sharply. 'Why don't you consult a doctor whose special employment is the treatment of the insane?'

She had her answer ready on the instant. 'I don't go to a doctor of that sort,' she said, 'for the very reason that he is a specialist: he has the fatal habit of judging everybody by lines and rules of his own laying down. I come to you, because my case is outside of all lines and rules, and because you are famous in your profession for the discovery of mysteries in disease. Are you satisfied?'

He was more than satisfied – his first idea had been the right idea, after all. Besides, she was correctly informed as to his professional position. The capacity which had raised him to fame and fortune was his capacity (unrivalled among his brethren) for the discovery of remote disease.

'I am at your disposal,' he answered. 'Let me try if I can find out what is the matter with you.'

He put his medical questions. They were promptly and plainly answered; and they led to no other conclusion than that the strange lady was, mentally and physically, in excellent health. Not satisfied with questions, he carefully examined the great organs of life. Neither his hand nor his stethoscope could discover anything that was amiss. With the admirable patience and devotion to his art which had distinguished him from the time when he was a student, he still subjected her to one test after another. The result was always the same. Not only was there no tendency to brain disease – there was not even a perceptible derangement of the nervous system. 'I can find nothing the matter with you,' he said. 'I can't even account for the extraordinary pallor of your complexion. You completely puzzle me.'

'The pallor of my complexion is nothing,' she answered a little impatiently. 'In my early life I had a narrow escape from death by poisoning. I have never had a complexion since – and my skin is so delicate, I cannot paint without producing a hideous rash. But that is of no importance. I wanted your opinion given positively. I believed in you, and you have disappointed me.' Her head dropped on her breast. 'And so it ends!' she said to herself bitterly.

The Doctor's sympathies were touched. Perhaps it might be more correct to say that his professional pride was a little hurt. 'It may end in the right way yet,' he remarked, 'if you choose to help me.'

She looked up again with flashing eyes, 'Speak plainly,' she said. 'How can I help you?'

'Plainly, madam, you come to me as an enigma, and you leave me to make the right guess by the unaided efforts of my art. My art will do much, but not all. For example, something must have occurred –

something quite unconnected with the state of your bodily health – to frighten you about yourself, or you would never have come here to consult me. Is that true?'

She clasped her hands in her lap. 'That is true!' she said eagerly. 'I begin to believe in you again.'

'Very well. You can't expect me to find out the moral cause which has alarmed you. I can positively discover that there is no physical cause of alarm; and (unless you admit me to your confidence) I can do no more.'

She rose, and took a turn in the room. 'Suppose I tell you?' she said. 'But, mind, I shall mention no names!'

'There is no need to mention names. The facts are all I want.'

'The facts are nothing,' she rejoined. 'I have only my own impressions to confess – and you will very likely think me a fanciful fool when you hear what they are. No matter. I will do my best to content you – I will begin with the facts that you want. Take my word for it, they won't do much to help you.'

She sat down again. In the plainest possible words, she began the strangest and wildest confession that had ever reached the Doctor's ears.

Chapter 2

'It is one fact, sir, that I am a widow,' she said. 'It is another fact, that I am going to be married again.'

There she paused, and smiled at some thought that occurred to her. Doctor Wybrow was not favourably impressed by her smile – there was something at once sad and cruel in it. It came slowly, and it went away suddenly. He began to doubt whether he had been wise in acting on his first impression. His mind reverted to the commonplace patients and the discoverable maladies that were waiting for him, with a certain tender regret.

The lady went on.

'My approaching marriage,' she said, 'has one embarrassing circumstance connected with it. The gentleman whose wife I am to be, was engaged to another lady when he happened to meet with me, abroad: that lady, mind, being of his own blood and family, related to him as his cousin. I have innocently robbed her of her lover, and destroyed her prospects in life. Innocently, I say – because he told me nothing of his engagement until after I had accepted him. When we next met in England – and when there was danger, no doubt, of the affair coming to my knowledge – he told me the truth. I was naturally indignant. He had his excuse ready; he showed me a letter from the lady herself, releasing him from his engagement. A more noble, a more high-minded letter, I never read in my life. I cried over it – I who have no tears in me for sorrows of my own! If the letter had left him any hope of being forgiven, I would have positively refused to marry him. But the firmness of it – without anger, without a word of reproach, with heartfelt wishes even for his happiness – the firmness of it, I say, left him no hope. He appealed to my compassion; he appealed to his love for me. You know what women are. I too was soft-hearted – I said, Very well: yes! In a week more (I tremble as I think of it) we are to be married.'

She did really tremble – she was obliged to pause and compose herself, before she could go on. The Doctor, waiting for more facts, began to fear that he stood committed to a long story. 'Forgive me for reminding you that I have suffering persons waiting to see me,' he said. 'The sooner you can come to the point, the better for my patients and for me.'

The strange smile – at once so sad and so cruel – showed itself again on the lady's lips. 'Every word I have said is to the point,' she answered. 'You will see it yourself in a moment more.'

She resumed her narrative.

'Yesterday – you need fear no long story, sir; only yesterday – I was among the visitors at one of your English luncheon parties. A lady, a perfect stranger to me, came in late – after we had left the table, and had retired to the drawing-room. She happened to take a chair near me; and we were presented to each other. I knew her by name, as she knew me. It was the woman whom I had robbed of her lover, the woman who had written the noble letter. Now listen! You were impatient with me for not interesting you in what I said just now. I said it to satisfy your mind that I had no enmity of feeling towards the lady, on my side. I admired her, I felt for her – I had no cause to reproach myself. This is very important, as you will presently see. On her side, I have reason to be assured that the circumstances had been truly explained to her, and that she understood I was in no way to blame. Now, knowing all these necessary things as you do, explain to me, if you can, why, when I rose and met that woman's eyes looking at me, I turned cold from head to foot, and shuddered, and shivered, and knew what a deadly panic of fear was, for the first time in my life.'

The Doctor began to feel interested at last.

'Was there anything remarkable in the lady's personal appearance?' he asked.

'Nothing whatever!' was the vehement reply. 'Here is the true description of her – the ordinary English lady; the clear cold blue eyes, the fine rosy complexion, the inanimately polite manner, the large good-humoured mouth, the too plump cheeks and chin: these, and nothing more.'

'Was there anything in her expression, when you first looked at her, that took you by surprise?'

'There was natural curiosity to see the woman who had been preferred to her; and perhaps some astonishment also, not to see a more engaging and more beautiful person; both those feelings restrained within the limits of good breeding, and both not lasting for more than a few moments – so far as I could see. I say "so far", because the horrible agitation that she communicated to me disturbed my judgement. If I could have got to the door, I would have run out of the room, she frightened me so! I was not even able to stand up – I sank back in my chair; I stared horror-struck at the calm blue eyes that were only looking at me with a gentle surprise. To say they affected me like the eyes of a serpent is to say nothing. I felt her soul in them, looking into mine – looking, if such a thing can be, unconsciously to her own mortal self. I tell you my impression, in all its horror and in all its folly! That woman is destined (without knowing it herself) to be the evil genius of my life. Her innocent eyes saw hidden capabilities of wickedness in me that I was not aware of myself, until I felt them stirring under her look. If I commit faults in my life to come – if I am even guilty of crimes – she will bring the retribution, without (as I firmly believe) any conscious exercise of her own will. In one indescribable moment I felt all this – and I suppose my face showed it. The good artless creature was inspired by a sort of gentle alarm for me. "I am afraid the heat of the room is too much for you; will you try my smelling bottle?" I heard her say those kind words; and I remember nothing else – I fainted. When I recovered my senses, the company had all gone; only the lady of the house was with me. For the moment I could say nothing to her; the dreadful impression that I have tried to describe to you came back to me with the coming back of my life. As soon I could speak, I implored her to tell me the whole truth about the woman whom I had supplanted. You see, I had a faint hope that her good character might not really be deserved, that her noble letter was a skilful piece of hypocrisy – in short, that she secretly hated me, and was cunning enough to hide it. No! The lady had been her friend from her girlhood, was as familiar with her as if they had been sisters – knew her positively to be as good, as innocent, as incapable of hating anybody, as the greatest saint that ever lived. My one last hope, that I had only felt an ordinary forewarning of danger in the presence of an ordinary enemy, was a hope destroyed for ever. There was one more effort I could make, and I made it. I went next to the man whom I am to marry. I implored him to release me from my promise. He refused. I declared I would break my engagement. He showed me letters from his sisters, letters from his brothers, and his dear friends – all entreating him to think again before he made me his wife; all repeating reports of me in Paris, Vienna, and London, which are so many vile lies. "If you refuse to marry me," he said, "you admit that these reports are true – you admit that you are afraid to face society in the character of my wife." What could I answer? There was no contradicting him – he was plainly right: if I persisted in my refusal, the utter destruction of my reputation would be the result. I consented to let the wedding take place as we had arranged it – and left him. The night has passed. I am here, with my fixed conviction – that innocent woman is ordained to have a fatal influence over my life. I am here with my one question to put, to the one man who can answer it. For the last time, sir, what am I – a demon who has seen the avenging angel? Or only a poor mad woman, misled by the delusion of a deranged mind?'

Doctor Wybrow rose from his chair, determined to close the interview.

He was strongly and painfully impressed by what he had heard. The longer he had listened to her, the more irresistibly the conviction of the woman's wickedness had forced itself on him. He tried vainly to think of her as a person to be pitied – a person with a morbidly sensitive imagination, conscious of the capacities for evil which lie dormant in us all, and striving earnestly to open her heart to the counter-influence of her own better nature; the effort was beyond him. A perverse instinct in him said, as if in words, Beware how you believe in her!

'I have already given you my opinion,' he said. 'There is no sign of your intellect being deranged, or being likely to be deranged, that medical science can discover – as *I* understand it. As for the impressions you have confided to me, I can only say that yours is a case (as I venture to think) for spiritual rather than for medical advice. Of one thing be assured: what you have said to me in this room shall not pass out of it. Your confession is safe in my keeping.'

She heard him, with a certain dogged resignation, to the end.

'Is that all?' she asked.

'That is all,' he answered.

She put a little paper packet of money on the table. 'Thank you, sir. There is your fee.'

With those words she rose. Her wild black eyes looked upward, with an expression of despair so defiant and so horrible in its silent agony that the Doctor turned away his head, unable to endure the sight of it. The bare idea of taking anything from her – not money only, but anything even that she had touched – suddenly revolted him. Still without looking at her, he said, 'Take it back; I don't want my fee.'

She neither heeded nor heard him. Still looking upward, she said slowly to herself, 'Let the end come. I have done with the struggle: I submit.'

She drew her veil over her face, bowed to the Doctor, and left the room.

He rang the bell, and followed her into the hall. As the servant closed the door on her, a sudden impulse of curiosity – utterly unworthy of him, and at the same time utterly irresistible – sprang up in the Doctor's mind. Blushing like a boy, he said to the servant, 'Follow her home, and find out her name.' For one moment the man looked at his master, doubting if his own ears had not deceived him. Doctor Wybrow looked back at him in silence. The submissive servant knew what that silence meant – he took his hat and hurried into the street.

The Doctor went back to the consulting-room. A sudden revulsion of feeling swept over his mind. Had the woman left an infection of wickedness in the house, and had he caught it? What devil had possessed him to degrade himself in the eyes of his own servant? He had behaved infamously – he had asked an honest man, a man who had served him faithfully for years, to turn spy! Stung by the bare thought of it, he ran out into the hall again, and opened the door. The servant had disappeared; it was too late to call him back. But one refuge from his contempt for himself was now open to him – the refuge of work. He got into his carriage and went his rounds among his patients.

If the famous physician could have shaken his own reputation, he would have done it that afternoon. Never before had he made himself so little welcome at the bedside. Never before had he put off until tomorrow the prescription which ought to have been written, the opinion which ought to have been given, today. He went home earlier than usual – unutterably dissatisfied with himself.

The servant had returned. Dr Wybrow was ashamed to question him. The man reported the result of his errand, without waiting to be asked.

'The lady's name is the Countess Narona. She lives at – '

Without waiting to hear where she lived, the Doctor acknowledged the all-important discovery of her name by a silent bend of the head, and entered his consulting-room. The fee that he had vainly refused still lay in its little white paper covering on the table. He sealed it up in an envelope; addressed it to the 'Poor-box' of the nearest police-court; and, calling the servant in, directed him to take it to the magistrate the next morning. Faithful to his duties, the servant waited to ask the customary question, 'Do you dine at home today, sir?'

After a moment's hesitation he said, 'No: I shall dine at the club.'

The most easily deteriorated of all the moral qualities is the quality called 'conscience'. In one state of a man's mind, his conscience is the severest judge that can pass sentence on him. In another state, he and his conscience are on the best possible terms with each other in the comfortable capacity of accomplices. When Doctor Wybrow left his house for the second time, he did not even attempt to conceal from himself that his sole object, in dining at the club, was to hear what the world said of the Countess Narona.

Chapter 3

There was a time when a man in search of the pleasures of gossip sought the society of ladies. The man knows better now. He goes to the smoking-room of his club.

Doctor Wybrow lit his cigar, and looked round him at his brethren in social conclave assembled. The room was well filled; but the flow of talk was still languid. The Doctor innocently applied the stimulant that was wanted. When he enquired if anybody knew the Countess Narona, he was answered by something like a shout of astonishment. Never (the conclave agreed) had such an absurd question been asked before! Every human creature, with the slightest claim to a place in society, knew the Countess Narona. An adventuress with a European reputation of the blackest possible colour – such was the general description of the woman with the deathlike complexion and the glittering eyes.

Descending to particulars, each member of the club contributed his own little stock of scandal to the memoirs of the Countess. It was doubtful whether she was really, what she called herself, a Dalmatian lady. It was doubtful whether she had ever been married to the Count whose widow she assumed to be. It was doubtful whether the man who accompanied her in her travels (under the name of Baron Rivar, and in the character of her brother) was her brother at all. Report pointed to the Baron as a gambler at every 'table' on the Continent. Report whispered that his so-called sister had narrowly escaped being implicated in a famous trial for poisoning at Vienna – that she had been known at Milan as a spy in the interests of Austria – that her 'apartment' in Paris had been denounced to the police as nothing less than a private gambling-house – and that her present appearance in England was the natural result of the discovery. Only one member of the assembly in the smoking-room took the part of this much-abused woman, and declared that her character had been most cruelly and most unjustly assailed. But as the man was a lawyer, his interference went for nothing: it was naturally attributed to the spirit of contradiction inherent in his profession. He was asked derisively what he thought of the circumstances under which the Countess had become engaged to be married; and he made the characteristic answer, that he thought the circumstances highly creditable to both parties, and that he looked on the lady's future husband as a most enviable man.

Hearing this, the Doctor raised another shout of astonishment by enquiring the name of the gentleman whom the Countess was about to marry.

His friends in the smoking-room decided unanimously that the celebrated physician must be a second 'Rip-van-Winkle,' and that he had just awakened from a supernatural sleep of twenty years. It was all very well to say that he was devoted to his profession, and that he had neither time nor inclination to pick up fragments of gossip at dinner-parties and balls. A man who did not know that the Countess Narona had borrowed money at Homburg of no less a person than Lord Montbarry, and had then deluded him into making her a proposal of marriage, was a man who had probably never heard of Lord Montbarry himself. The younger members of the club, humouring the joke, sent a waiter for the 'Peerage'; and read aloud the memoir of the nobleman in question, for the Doctor's benefit – with illustrative morsels of information interpolated by themselves.

'Herbert John Westwick. First Baron Montbarry, of Montbarry, King's County, Ireland. Created a Peer for distinguished military services in India. Born, 1812. Forty-eight years old, Doctor, at the present time. Not married. Will be married next week, Doctor, to the delightful creature we have been talking about. Heir presumptive, his lordship's next brother, Stephen Robert, married to Ella, youngest daughter of the Reverend Silas Marden, Rector of Runnigate, and has issue, three daughters. Younger brothers of his lordship, Francis and Henry, unmarried. Sisters of his lordship, Lady Barville, married to Sir Theodore Barville, Bart.; and Anne, widow of the late Peter Norbury, Esq., of Norbury Cross. Bear his lordship's relations well in mind, Doctor. Three brothers Westwick, Stephen, Francis, and Henry; and two sisters, Lady Barville and Mrs Norbury. Not one of the five will be present at the marriage; and not one of the five will leave a stone unturned to stop it, if the Countess will only give them a chance. Add to these hostile members of the family another offended relative not mentioned in the 'Peerage', a young lady – '

A sudden outburst of protest in more than one part of the room stopped the coming disclosure, and released the Doctor from further persecution.

'Don't mention the poor girl's name; it's too bad to make a joke of that part of the business; she has behaved nobly under shameful provocation; there is but one excuse for Montbarry – he is either a madman or a fool.' In these terms the protest expressed itself on all sides. Speaking confidentially to his next neighbour, the Doctor discovered that the lady referred to was already known to him (through the Countess's confession) as the lady deserted by Lord Montbarry. Her name was Agnes Lockwood. She was described as being the superior of the Countess in personal attraction, and as being also by some years the younger woman of the two. Making all allowance for the follies that men committed every day in their relations with women, Montbarry's delusion was still the most monstrous delusion on record. In this expression of opinion every man present agreed – the lawyer even included. Not one of them could call to mind the innumerable instances in which the sexual influence has proved irresistible in the persons of women without even the pretension to beauty. The very members of the club whom the Countess (in spite of her personal disadvantages) could have most easily fascinated, if she had thought it worth her while, were the members who wondered most loudly at Montbarry's choice of a wife.

While the topic of the Countess's marriage was still the one topic of conversation, a member of the club entered the smoking-room whose appearance instantly produced a dead silence. Doctor Wybrow's next neighbour whispered to him, 'Montbarry's brother – Henry Westwick!'

The newcomer looked round him slowly, with a bitter smile.

'You are all talking of my brother,' he said. 'Don't mind me. Not one of you can despise him more heartily than I do. Go on, gentlemen – go on!'

But one man present took the speaker at his word. That man was the lawyer who had already undertaken the defence of the Countess.

'I stand alone in my opinion,' he said, 'and I am not ashamed of repeating it in anybody's hearing. I consider the Countess Narona to be a cruelly-treated woman. Why shouldn't she be Lord Montbarry's wife? Who can say she has a mercenary motive in marrying him?'

Montbarry's brother turned sharply on the speaker. 'I say it!' he answered.

The reply might have shaken some men. The lawyer stood on his ground as firmly as ever.

'I believe I am right,' he rejoined, 'in stating that his lordship's income is not more than sufficient to support his station in life; also that it is an income derived almost entirely from landed property in Ireland, every acre of which is entailed.'

Montbarry's brother made a sign, admitting that he had no objection to offer so far.

'If his lordship dies first,' the lawyer proceeded, 'I have been informed that the only provision he can make for his widow consists in a rent-charge on the property of no more than four hundred a year. His retiring pension and allowances, it is well known, die with him. Four hundred a year is therefore all that he can leave to the Countess, if he leaves her a widow.'

'Four hundred a year is not all,' was the reply to this. 'My brother has insured his life for ten thousand pounds; and he has settled the whole of it on the Countess, in the event of his death.'

This announcement produced a strong sensation. Men looked at each other, and repeated the three startling words, 'Ten thousand pounds!' Driven fairly to the wall, the lawyer made a last effort to defend his position.

'May I ask who made that settlement a condition of the marriage?' he said. 'Surely it was not the Countess herself?'

Henry Westwick answered, 'it was the Countess's brother'; and added, 'which comes to the same thing'.

After that, there was no more to be said – so long, at least, as Montbarry's brother was present. The talk flowed into other channels; and the Doctor went home.

But his morbid curiosity about the Countess was not set at rest yet. In his leisure moments he found himself wondering whether Lord Montbarry's family would succeed in stopping the marriage after all. And more than this, he was conscious of a growing desire to see the infatuated man himself. Every day during the brief interval before the wedding, he looked in at the club, on the chance of hearing some news. Nothing had happened, so far as the club knew. The Countess's position was secure; Montbarry's resolution to be her husband was unshaken. They were both Roman Catholics, and they were to be married at the chapel in Spanish Place. So much the Doctor discovered about them – and no more.

On the day of the wedding, after a feeble struggle with himself, he actually sacrificed his patients and their guineas, and slipped away secretly to see the marriage. To the end of his life, he was angry with anybody who reminded him of what he had done on that day!

The wedding was strictly private. A close carriage stood at the church door; a few people, mostly of the lower class, and mostly old women, were scattered about the interior of the building. Here and there Doctor Wybrow detected the faces of some of his brethren of the club, attracted by curiosity, like himself. Four persons only stood before the altar – the bride and bridegroom and their two witnesses. One of these last was an elderly woman, who might have been the Countess's companion or maid; the other was undoubtedly her brother, Baron Rivar. The bridal party (the bride herself included) wore their ordinary morning costume. Lord Montbarry, personally viewed, was a middle-aged military man of the ordinary type: nothing in the least remarkable distinguished him either in face or figure. Baron Rivar, again, in his way was another conventional representative of another well-known type. One sees his finely-pointed moustache, his bold eyes, his crisply-curling hair, and his dashing carriage of the head, repeated hundreds of times over on the Boulevards of Paris. The only noteworthy point about him was of the negative sort – he was not in the least like his sister. Even the officiating priest was only a harmless, humble-looking old man, who

went through his duties resignedly, and felt visible rheumatic difficulties every time he bent his knees. The one remarkable person,
the Countess herself, only raised her veil at the beginning of the
ceremony, and presented nothing in her plain dress that was worth a
second look. Never, on the face of it, was there a less interesting and
less romantic marriage than this. From time to time the Doctor
glanced round at the door or up at the galleries, vaguely anticipating
the appearance of some protesting stranger, in possession of some
terrible secret, commissioned to forbid the progress of the service.
Nothing in the shape of an event occurred – nothing extraordinary,
nothing dramatic. Bound fast together as man and wife, the two
disappeared, followed by their witnesses, to sign the registers; and
still Doctor Wybrow waited, and still he cherished the obstinate
hope that something worth seeing must certainly happen yet.

The interval passed, and the married couple, returning to the
church, walked together down the nave to the door. Doctor Wybrow
drew back as they approached. To his confusion and surprise, the
Countess discovered him. He heard her say to her husband, 'One
moment; I see a friend.' Lord Montbarry bowed and waited. She
stepped up to the Doctor, took his hand, and wrung it hard. He felt
her overpowering black eyes looking at him through her veil. 'One
step more, you see, on the way to the end!' She whispered those
strange words, and returned to her husband. Before the Doctor
could recover himself and follow her, Lord and Lady Montbarry had
stepped into their carriage, and had driven away.

Outside the church door stood the three or four members of the
club who, like Doctor Wybrow, had watched the ceremony out of
curiosity. Near them was the bride's brother, waiting alone. He was
evidently bent on seeing the man whom his sister had spoken to, in
broad daylight. His bold eyes rested on the Doctor's face, with a
momentary flash of suspicion in them. The cloud suddenly cleared
away; the Baron smiled with charming courtesy, lifted his hat to his
sister's friend, and walked off.

The members constituted themselves into a club conclave on
the church steps. They began with the Baron. 'Damned ill-looking
rascal!' They went on with Montbarry. 'Is he going to take that
horrid woman with him to Ireland?' 'Not he! He can't face the
tenantry; they know about Agnes Lockwood.' 'Well, but where is he
going?' 'To Scotland.' 'Does she like that?' 'It's only for a fortnight;
they come back to London, and go abroad.' 'And they will never
return to England, eh?' 'Who can tell? Did you see how she looked

at Montbarry, when she had to lift her veil at the beginning of the service? In his place, I should have bolted. Did you see her, Doctor?' By this time, Doctor Wybrow had remembered his patients, and had heard enough of the club gossip. He followed the example of Baron Rivar, and walked off.

'One step more, you see, on the way to the end,' he repeated to himself, on his way home. 'What end?'

Chapter 4

On the day of the marriage Agnes Lockwood sat alone in the little drawing-room of her London lodgings, burning the letters which had been written to her by Montbarry in the bygone time.

The Countess's maliciously smart description of her, addressed to Doctor Wybrow, had not even hinted at the charm that most distinguished Agnes – the artless expression of goodness and purity which instantly attracted everyone who approached her. She looked by many years younger than she really was. With her fair complexion and her shy manner, it seemed only natural to speak of her as 'a girl', although she was now really advancing towards thirty years of age. She lived alone with an old nurse devoted to her, on a modest little income which was just enough to support the two. There were none of the ordinary signs of grief in her face, as she slowly tore the letters of her false lover in two, and threw the pieces into the small fire which had been lit to consume them. Unhappily for herself, she was one of those women who feel too deeply to find relief in tears. Pale and quiet, with cold trembling fingers, she destroyed the letters one by one without daring to read them again. She had torn the last of the series, and was still shrinking from throwing it after the rest into the swiftly destroying flame, when the old nurse came in, and asked if she would see 'Master Henry' – meaning that youngest member of the Westwick family, who had publicly declared his contempt for his brother in the smoking-room of the club.

Agnes hesitated. A faint tinge of colour stole over her face.

There had been a long past time when Henry Westwick had owned that he loved her. She had made her confession to him, acknowledging that her heart was given to his eldest brother. He had submitted to his disappointment; and they had met thenceforth as cousins and friends. Never before had she associated the idea of him with embarrassing recollections. But now, on the very day when his brother's marriage to another woman had consummated his brother's treason towards her, there was something vaguely repellent in the prospect of seeing him. The old nurse (who remembered them both in their cradles) observed her hesitation; and sympathising of course with the man, put in a timely word for Henry. 'He says, he's going away, my dear; and he only wants to shake hands, and say goodbye.' This plain statement of the case had its effect. Agnes decided on receiving her cousin.

He entered the room so rapidly that he surprised her in the act of throwing the fragments of Montbarry's last letter into the fire. She hurriedly spoke first.

'You are leaving London very suddenly, Henry. Is it business? Or pleasure?'

Instead of answering her, he pointed to the flaming letter, and to some black ashes of burnt paper lying lightly in the lower part of the fireplace.

'Are you burning letters?'

'Yes.'

'*His* letters?'

'Yes.'

He took her hand gently. 'I had no idea I was intruding on you, at a time when you must wish to be alone. Forgive me, Agnes – I shall see you when I return.'

She signed to him, with a faint smile, to take a chair.

'We have known one another since we were children,' she said. 'Why should I feel a foolish pride about myself in your presence? Why should I have any secrets from you? I sent back all your brother's gifts to me some time ago. I have been advised to do more, to keep nothing that can remind me of him – in short, to burn his letters. I have taken the advice; but I own I shrank a little from destroying the last of the letters. No – not because it was the last, but because it had this in it.' She opened her hand, and showed him a lock of Montbarry's hair, tied with a morsel of golden cord. 'Well! Well! Let it go with the rest.'

She dropped it into the flame. For a while, she stood with her back to Henry, leaning on the mantel-piece, and looking into the fire. He took the chair to which she had pointed, with a strange contradiction of expression in his face: the tears were in his eyes, while the brows above were knit close in an angry frown. He muttered to himself, 'Damn him!'

She rallied her courage, and looked at him again when she spoke. 'Well, Henry, and why are you going away?'

'I am out of spirits, Agnes, and I want a change.'

She paused before she spoke again. His face told her plainly that he was thinking of *her* when he made that reply. She was grateful to him, but her mind was not with him: her mind was still with the man who had deserted her. She turned round again to the fire.

'Is it true,' she asked, after a long silence, 'that they have been married today?'

He answered ungraciously in the one necessary word: 'Yes.'

'Did you go to the church?'

He resented the question with an expression of indignant surprise. 'Go to the church?' he repeated. 'I would as soon go to – ' He checked himself there. 'How can you ask?' he added in lower tones. 'I have never spoken to Montbarry, I have not even seen him, since he treated you like the scoundrel and the fool that he is.'

She looked at him suddenly, without saying a word. He understood her, and begged her pardon. But he was still angry. 'The reckoning comes to some men,' he said, 'even in this world. He will live to rue the day when he married that woman!'

Agnes took a chair by his side, and looked at him with a gentle surprise.

'Is it quite reasonable to be so angry with her, because your brother preferred her to me?' she asked.

Henry turned on her sharply. 'Do *you* defend the Countess, of all the people in the world?'

'Why not?' Agnes answered. 'I know nothing against her. On the only occasion when we met, she appeared to be a singularly timid, nervous person, looking dreadfully ill; and *being* indeed so ill that she fainted under the heat of my room. Why should we not do her justice? We know that she was innocent of any intention to wrong me; we know that she was not aware of my engagement – '

Henry lifted his hand impatiently, and stopped her. 'There is such a thing as being *too* just and *too* forgiving!' he interposed. 'I can't bear to hear you talk in that patient way, after the scandalously cruel manner in which you have been treated. Try to forget them both, Agnes. I wish to God I could help you to do it!'

Agnes laid her hand on his arm. 'You are very good to me, Henry; but you don't quite understand me. I was thinking of myself and my trouble in quite a different way, when you came in. I was wondering whether anything which has so entirely filled my heart, and so absorbed all that is best and truest in me, as my feeling for your brother, can really pass away as if it had never existed. I have destroyed the last visible things that remind me of him. In this world I shall see him no more. But is the tie that once bound us completely broken? Am I as entirely parted from the good and evil fortune of his life as if we had never met and never loved? What do you think, Henry? I can hardly believe it.'

'If you could bring the retribution on him that he has deserved,' Henry Westwick answered sternly, 'I might be inclined to agree with you.'

As that reply passed his lips, the old nurse appeared again at the door, announcing another visitor.

'I'm sorry to disturb you, my dear. But here is little Mrs Ferrari wanting to know when she may say a few words to you.'

Agnes turned to Henry, before she replied. 'You remember Emily Bidwell, my favourite pupil years ago at the village school, and afterwards my maid? She left me, to marry an Italian courier, named Ferrari – and I am afraid it has not turned out very well. Do you mind my having her in here for a minute or two?'

Henry rose to take his leave. 'I should be glad to see Emily again at any other time,' he said. 'But it is best that I should go now. My mind is disturbed, Agnes; I might say things to you, if I stayed here any longer, which – which are better not said now. I shall cross the Channel by the mail tonight, and see how a few weeks' change will help me.' He took her hand. 'Is there anything in the world that I can do for you?' he asked very earnestly. She thanked him, and tried to release her hand. He held it with a tremulous lingering grasp. 'God bless you, Agnes!' he said in faltering tones, with his eyes on the ground. Her face flushed again, and the next instant turned paler than ever; she knew his heart as well as he knew it himself – she was too distressed to speak. He lifted her hand to his lips, kissed it fervently, and, without looking at her again, left the room. The nurse hobbled after him to the head of the stairs: she had not forgotten the time when the younger brother had been the unsuccessful rival of the elder for the hand of Agnes. 'Don't be downhearted, Master Henry,' whispered the old woman, with the unscrupulous common sense of persons in the lower rank of life. 'Try her again, when you come back!'

Left alone for a few moments, Agnes took a turn in the room, trying to compose herself. She paused before a little watercolour drawing on the wall, which had belonged to her mother: it was her own portrait when she was a child. 'How much happier we should be,' she thought to herself sadly, 'if we never grew up!'

The courier's wife was shown in – a little meek melancholy woman, with white eyelashes, and watery eyes, who curtseyed deferentially and was troubled with a small chronic cough. Agnes shook hands with her kindly. 'Well, Emily, what can I do for you?'

The courier's wife made rather a strange answer: 'I'm afraid to tell you, Miss.'

'Is it such a very difficult favour to grant? Sit down, and let me hear how you are going on. Perhaps the petition will slip out while we are talking. How does your husband behave to you?'

Emily's light grey eyes looked more watery than ever. She shook her head and sighed resignedly. 'I have no positive complaint to make against him, Miss. But I'm afraid he doesn't care about me; and he seems to take no interest in his home – I may almost say he's tired of his home. It might be better for both of us, Miss, if he went travelling for a while – not to mention the money, which is beginning to be wanted sadly.' She put her handkerchief to her eyes, and sighed again more resignedly than ever.

'I don't quite understand,' said Agnes. 'I thought your husband had an engagement to take some ladies to Switzerland and Italy?'

'That was his ill-luck, Miss. One of the ladies fell ill – and the others wouldn't go without her. They paid him a month's salary as compensation. But they had engaged him for the autumn and winter – and the loss is serious.'

'I am sorry to hear it, Emily. Let us hope he will soon have another chance.'

'It's not his turn, Miss, to be recommended when the next applications come to the couriers' office. You see, there are so many of them out of employment just now. If he could be privately recommended – ' She stopped, and left the unfinished sentence to speak for itself.

Agnes understood her directly. 'You want my recommendation,' she rejoined. 'Why couldn't you say so at once?'

Emily blushed. 'It would be such a chance for my husband,' she answered confusedly. 'A letter, enquiring for a good courier (a six months' engagement, Miss!) came to the office this morning. It's another man's turn to be chosen – and the secretary will recommend him. If my husband could only send his testimonials by the same post – with just a word in your name, Miss – it might turn the scale, as they say. A private recommendation between gentlefolks goes so far.' She stopped again, and sighed again, and looked down at the carpet, as if she had some private reason for feeling a little ashamed of herself.

Agnes began to be rather weary of the persistent tone of mystery in which her visitor spoke. 'If you want my interest with any friend of mine,' she said, 'why can't you tell me the name?'

The courier's wife began to cry. 'I'm ashamed to tell you, Miss.'

For the first time, Agnes spoke sharply. 'Nonsense, Emily! Tell me the name directly – or drop the subject – whichever you like best.'

Emily made a last desperate effort. She wrung her handkerchief hard in her lap, and let off the name as if she had been letting off a loaded gun: 'Lord Montbarry!'

Agnes rose and looked at her.

'You have disappointed me,' she said very quietly, but with a look which the courier's wife had never seen in her face before. 'Knowing what you know, you ought to be aware that it is impossible for me to communicate with Lord Montbarry. I always supposed you had some delicacy of feeling. I am sorry to find that I have been mistaken.'

Weak as she was, Emily had spirit enough to feel the reproof. She walked in her meek noiseless way to the door. 'I beg your pardon, Miss. I am not quite so bad as you think me. But I beg your pardon, all the same.'

She opened the door. Agnes called her back. There was something in the woman's apology that appealed irresistibly to her just and generous nature. 'Come,' she said; 'we must not part in this way. Let me not misunderstand you. What is it that you expected me to do?'

Emily was wise enough to answer this time without any reserve. 'My husband will send his testimonials, Miss, to Lord Montbarry in Scotland. I only wanted you to let him say in his letter that his wife has been known to you since she was a child, and that you feel some little interest in his welfare on that account. I don't ask it now, Miss. You have made me understand that I was wrong.'

Had she really been wrong? Past remembrances, as well as present troubles, pleaded powerfully with Agnes for the courier's wife. 'It seems only a small favour to ask,' she said, speaking under the impulse of kindness which was the strongest impulse in her nature. 'But I am not sure that I ought to allow my name to be mentioned in your husband's letter. Let me hear again exactly what he wishes to say.' Emily repeated the words – and then offered one of those suggestions which have a special value of their own to persons unaccustomed to the use of their pens. 'Suppose you try, Miss, how it looks in writing?' Childish as the idea was, Agnes tried the experiment. 'If I let you mention me,' she said, 'we must at least decide what you are to say.' She wrote the words in the briefest and plainest form: 'I venture to state that my wife has been known from her childhood to Miss Agnes Lockwood, who feels some little interest in my welfare on that account.' Reduced to this one sentence, there was surely nothing in the reference to her name which implied that Agnes had permitted it, or that she was even aware of it. After a last struggle with herself, she handed the written paper to Emily. 'Your husband must copy it exactly, without altering anything,' she stipulated. 'On that condition, I grant your request.' Emily was not only thankful – she was really touched. Agnes hurried the little woman out of the room. 'Don't give me time to repent and take it back again,' she said. Emily vanished.

'Is the tie that once bound us completely broken? Am I as entirely parted from the good and evil fortune of his life as if we had never met and never loved?' Agnes looked at the clock on the mantelpiece. Not ten minutes since, those serious questions had been on her lips. It almost shocked her to think of the commonplace manner in which they had already met with their reply. The mail of that night would appeal once more to Montbarry's remembrance of her – in the choice of a servant.

Two days later, the post brought a few grateful lines from Emily. Her husband had got the place. Ferrari was engaged, for six months certain, as Lord Montbarry's courier.

THE SECOND PART

Chapter 5

After only one week of travelling in Scotland, my lord and my lady returned unexpectedly to London. Introduced to the mountains and lakes of the Highlands, her ladyship positively declined to improve her acquaintance with them. When she was asked for her reason, she answered with a Roman brevity, 'I have seen Switzerland.'

For a week more, the newly-married couple remained in London, in the strictest retirement. On one day in that week the nurse returned in a state of most uncustomary excitement from an errand on which Agnes had sent her. Passing the door of a fashionable dentist, she had met Lord Montbarry himself just leaving the house. The good woman's report described him, with malicious pleasure, as looking wretchedly ill. 'His cheeks are getting hollow, my dear, and his beard is turning grey. I hope the dentist hurt him!'

Knowing how heartily her faithful old servant hated the man who had deserted her, Agnes made due allowance for a large infusion of exaggeration in the picture presented to her. The main impression produced on her mind was an impression of nervous uneasiness. If she trusted herself in the streets by daylight while Lord Montbarry remained in London, how could she be sure that his next chance-meeting might not be a meeting with herself? She waited at home, privately ashamed of her own undignified conduct, for the next two days. On the third day the fashionable intelligence of the newspapers announced the departure of Lord and Lady Montbarry for Paris, on their way to Italy.

Mrs Ferrari, calling the same evening, informed Agnes that her husband had left her with all reasonable expression of conjugal kindness; his temper being improved by the prospect of going abroad. But one other servant accompanied the travellers – Lady Montbarry's maid, rather a silent, unsociable woman, so far as Emily had heard. Her ladyship's brother, Baron Rivar, was already on the Continent. It had been arranged that he was to meet his sister and her husband at Rome.

One by one the dull weeks succeeded each other in the life of Agnes. She faced her position with admirable courage, seeing her friends, keeping herself occupied in her leisure hours with reading and drawing, leaving no means untried of diverting her mind from the melancholy remembrance of the past. But she had loved too faithfully, she had been wounded too deeply, to feel in any adequate degree the influence of the moral remedies which she employed. Persons who met with her in the ordinary relations of life, deceived by her outward serenity of manner, agreed that 'Miss Lockwood seemed to be getting over her disappointment'. But an old friend and school companion who happened to see her during a brief visit to London, was inexpressibly distressed by the change that she detected in Agnes. This lady was Mrs Westwick, the wife of that brother of Lord Montbarry who came next to him in age, and who was described in the 'Peerage' as presumptive heir to the title. He was then away, looking after his interests in some mining property which he possessed in America. Mrs Westwick insisted on taking Agnes back with her to her home in Ireland. 'Come and keep me company while my husband is away. My three little girls will make you their playfellow, and the only stranger you will meet is the governess, whom I answer for your liking beforehand. Pack up your things, and I will call for you tomorrow on my way to the train.' In those hearty terms the invitation was given. Agnes thankfully accepted it. For three happy months she lived under the roof of her friend. The girls hung round her in tears at her departure; the youngest of them wanted to go back with Agnes to London. Half in jest, half in earnest, she said to her old friend at parting, 'If your governess leaves you, keep the place open for me.' Mrs Westwick laughed. The wiser children took it seriously, and promised to let Agnes know.

On the very day when Miss Lockwood returned to London, she was recalled to those associations with the past which she was most anxious to forget. After the first kissings and greetings were over, the old nurse (who had been left in charge at the lodgings) had some startling information to communicate, derived from the courier's wife.

'Here has been little Mrs Ferrari, my dear, in a dreadful state of mind, enquiring when you would be back. Her husband has left

Lord Montbarry, without a word of warning – and nobody knows what has become of him.'

Agnes looked at her in astonishment. 'Are you sure of what you are saying?' she asked.

The nurse was quite sure. 'Why, Lord bless you! The news comes from the couriers' office in Golden Square – from the secretary, Miss Agnes, the secretary himself!' Hearing this, Agnes began to feel alarmed as well as surprised. It was still early in the evening. She at once sent a message to Mrs Ferrari, to say that she had returned.

In an hour more the courier's wife appeared, in a state of agitation which it was not easy to control. Her narrative, when she was at last able to speak connectedly, entirely confirmed the nurse's report of it.

After hearing from her husband with tolerable regularity from Paris, Rome, and Venice, Emily had twice written to him afterwards – and had received no reply. Feeling uneasy, she had gone to the office in Golden Square, to enquire if he had been heard of there. The post of the morning had brought a letter to the secretary from a courier then at Venice. It contained startling news of Ferrari. His wife had been allowed to take a copy of it, which she now handed to Agnes to read.

The writer stated that he had recently arrived in Venice. He had previously heard that Ferrari was with Lord and Lady Montbarry, at one of the old Venetian palaces which they had hired for a term. Being a friend of Ferrari, he had gone to pay him a visit. Ringing at the door that opened on the canal, and failing to make anyone hear him, he had gone round to a side entrance opening on one of the narrow lanes of Venice. Here, standing at the door (as if she was waiting for him to try that way next), he found a pale woman with magnificent dark eyes, who proved to be no other than Lady Montbarry herself.

She asked, in Italian, what he wanted. He answered that he wanted to see the courier Ferrari, if it was quite convenient. She at once informed him that Ferrari had left the palace, without assigning any reason, and without even leaving an address at which his monthly salary (then due to him) could be paid. Amazed at this reply, the courier enquired if any person had offended Ferrari, or quarrelled with him. The lady answered, 'To my knowledge, certainly not. I am Lady Montbarry; and I can positively assure you that Ferrari was treated with the greatest kindness in this house. We are as much astonished as you are at his extraordinary disappearance. If you should hear of him, pray let us know, so that we may at least pay him the money which is due.'

After one or two more questions (quite readily answered) relating to the date and the time of day at which Ferrari had left the palace, the courier took his leave.

He at once entered on the necessary investigations – without the slightest result so far as Ferrari was concerned. Nobody had seen him. Nobody appeared to have been taken into his confidence. Nobody knew anything (that is to say, anything of the slightest importance) even about persons so distinguished as Lord and Lady Montbarry. It was reported that her ladyship's English maid had left her, before the disappearance of Ferrari, to return to her relatives in her own country, and that Lady Montbarry had taken no steps to supply her place. His lordship was described as being in delicate health. He lived in the strictest retirement – nobody was admitted to him, not even his own countrymen. A stupid old woman was discovered who did the housework at the palace, arriving in the morning and going away again at night. She had never seen the lost courier – she had never even seen Lord Montbarry, who was then confined to his room. Her ladyship, 'a most gracious and adorable mistress', was in constant attendance on her noble husband. There was no other servant then in the house (so far as the old woman knew) but herself. The meals were sent in from a restaurant. My lord, it was said, disliked strangers. My lord's brother-in-law, the Baron, was generally shut up in a remote part of the palace, occupied (the gracious mistress said) with experiments in chemistry. The experiments sometimes made a nasty smell. A doctor had latterly been called in to his lordship – an Italian doctor, long resident in Venice. Enquiries being addressed to this gentleman (a physician of undoubted capacity and respectability), it turned out that he also had never seen Ferrari, having been summoned to the palace (as his memorandum book showed) at a date subsequent to the courier's disappearance. The doctor described Lord Montbarry's malady as bronchitis. So far, there was no reason to feel any anxiety, though the attack was a sharp one. If alarming symptoms should appear, he had arranged with her ladyship to call in another physician. For the rest, it was impossible to speak too highly of my lady; night and day, she was at her lord's bedside.

With these particulars began and ended the discoveries made by

Ferrari's courier-friend. The police were on the lookout for the lost man – and that was the only hope which could be held forth for the present, to Ferrari's wife.

'What do you think of it, Miss?' the poor woman asked eagerly. 'What would you advise me to do?'

Agnes was at a loss how to answer her; it was an effort even to listen to what Emily was saying. The references in the courier's letter to Montbarry – the report of his illness, the melancholy picture of his secluded life – had reopened the old wound. She was not even thinking of the lost Ferrari; her mind was at Venice, by the sick man's bedside.

'I hardly know what to say,' she answered. 'I have had no experience in serious matters of this kind.'

'Do you think it would help you, Miss, if you read my husband's letters to me? There are only three of them – they won't take long to read.'

Agnes compassionately read the letters.

They were not written in a very tender tone. 'Dear Emily', and 'Yours affectionately' – these conventional phrases were the only phrases of endearment which they contained. In the first letter, Lord Montbarry was not very favourably spoken of: 'We leave Paris tomorrow. I don't much like my lord. He is proud and cold, and, between ourselves, stingy in money matters. I have had to dispute such trifles as a few centimes in the hotel bill; and twice already, some sharp remarks have passed between the newly-married couple, in consequence of her ladyship's freedom in purchasing pretty tempting things at the shops in Paris. "I can't afford it; you must keep to your allowance." She has had to hear those words already. For my part, I like her. She has the nice, easy foreign manners – she talks to me as if I was a human being like herself.'

The second letter was dated from Rome.

My lord's caprices (Ferrari wrote) 'have kept us perpetually on the move. He is becoming incurably restless. I suspect he is uneasy in his mind. Painful recollections, I should say – I find him constantly reading old letters, when her ladyship is not present. We were to have stopped at Genoa, but he hurried us on. The same thing at Florence. Here, at Rome, my lady insists on resting. Her brother has met us at this place. There has been a quarrel already (the lady's maid tells me) between my lord and the Baron. The latter wanted to borrow money of the former. His lordship refused in language which offended Baron Rivar. My lady pacified them, and made them shake hands.

The third, and last letter, was from Venice.

More of my lord's economy! Instead of staying at the hotel, we have hired a damp, mouldy, rambling old palace. My lady insists on having the best suites of rooms wherever we go – and the palace comes cheaper for a two months' term. My lord tried to get it for longer; he says the quiet of Venice is good for his nerves. But a foreign speculator has secured the palace, and is going to turn it into an hotel. The Baron is still with us, and there have been more disagreements about money matters. I don't like the Baron – and I don't find the attractions of my lady grow on me. She was much nicer before the Baron joined us. My lord is a punctual paymaster; it's a matter of honour with him; he hates parting with his money, but he does it because he has given his word. I receive my salary regularly at the end of each month – not a franc extra, though I have done many things which are not part of a courier's proper work. Fancy the Baron trying to borrow money of me! He is an inveterate gambler. I didn't believe it when my lady's maid first told me so – but I have seen enough since to satisfy me that she was right. I have seen other things besides, which – well! which don't increase my respect for my lady and the Baron. The maid says she means to give warning to leave. She is a respectable British female, and doesn't take things quite so easily as I do. It is a dull life here. No going into company – no company at home – not a creature sees my lord – not even the consul, or the banker. When he goes out, he goes alone, and generally towards nightfall. Indoors, he shuts himself up in his own room with his books, and sees as little of his wife and the Baron as possible. I fancy things are coming to a crisis here. If my lord's suspicions are once awakened, the consequences will be terrible. Under certain provocations, the noble Montbarry is a man who would stick at nothing. However, the pay is good – and I can't afford to talk of leaving the place, like my lady's maid.'

Agnes handed back the letters – so suggestive of the penalty paid already for his own infatuation by the man who had deserted her! – with feelings of shame and distress, which made her no fit counsellor for the helpless woman who depended on her advice.

'The one thing I can suggest,' she said, after first speaking some kind words of comfort and hope, 'is that we should consult a person of greater experience than ours. Suppose I write and ask my lawyer (who is also my friend and trustee) to come and advise us tomorrow after his business hours?'

Emily eagerly and gratefully accepted the suggestion. An hour was arranged for the meeting on the next day; the correspondence was left under the care of Agnes; and the courier's wife took her leave.

Weary and heartsick, Agnes lay down on the sofa, to rest and compose herself. The careful nurse brought in a reviving cup of tea. Her quaint gossip about herself and her occupations while Agnes had been away, acted as a relief to her mistress's overburdened mind. They were still talking quietly, when they were startled by a loud knock at the house door. Hurried footsteps ascended the stairs. The door of the sitting-room was thrown open violently; the courier's wife rushed in like a mad woman. 'He's dead! They've murdered him!' Those wild words were all she could say. She dropped on her knees at the foot of the sofa – held out her hand with something clasped in it – and fell back in a swoon.

The nurse, signing to Agnes to open the window, took the necessary measures to restore the fainting woman. 'What's this?' she exclaimed. 'Here's a letter in her hand. See what it is, Miss.'

The open envelope was addressed (evidently in a feigned handwriting) to 'Mrs Ferrari'. The post-mark was 'Venice'. The contents of the envelope were a sheet of foreign notepaper, and a folded enclosure.

On the notepaper, one line only was written. It was again in a feigned handwriting, and it contained these words: '*To console you for the loss of your husband.*'

Agnes opened the enclosure next.

It was a Bank of England note for a thousand pounds.

Chapter 6

The next day, the friend and legal adviser of Agnes Lockwood, Mr Troy, called on her by appointment in the evening.

Mrs Ferrari – still persisting in the conviction of her husband's death – had sufficiently recovered to be present at the consultation.

Assisted by Agnes, she told the lawyer the little that was known relating to Ferrari's disappearance, and then produced the correspondence connected with that event. Mr Troy read (first) the three letters addressed by Ferrari to his wife; (secondly) the letter written by Ferrari's courier-friend, describing his visit to the palace and his interview with Lady Montbarry; and (thirdly) the one line of anonymous writing which had accompanied the extraordinary gift of a thousand pounds to Ferrari's wife.

Well known, at a later period, as the lawyer who acted for Lady Lydiard, in the case of theft generally described as the case of 'My Lady's Money', Mr Troy was not only a man of learning and experience in his profession – he was also a man who had seen something of society at home and abroad. He possessed a keen eye for character, a quaint humour, and a kindly nature which had not been deteriorated even by a lawyer's professional experience of mankind. With all these personal advantages, it is a question, nevertheless, whether he was the fittest adviser whom Agnes could have chosen under the circumstances. Little Mrs Ferrari, with many domestic merits, was an essentially commonplace woman. Mr Troy was the last person living who was likely to attract her sympathies – he was the exact opposite of a commonplace man.

'She looks very ill, poor thing!' In these words the lawyer opened the business of the evening, referring to Mrs Ferrari as unceremoniously as if she had been out of the room.

'She has suffered a terrible shock,' Agnes answered.

Mr Troy turned to Mrs Ferrari, and looked at her again, with the interest due to the victim of a shock. He drummed absently with his fingers on the table. At last he spoke to her.

'My good lady, you don't really believe that your husband is dead?'

Mrs Ferrari put her handkerchief to her eyes. The word 'dead' was ineffectual to express her feelings. 'Murdered!' she said sternly, behind her handkerchief.

'Why? And by whom?' Mr Troy asked.

Mrs Ferrari seemed to have some difficulty in answering. 'You have read my husband's letters, sir,' she began. 'I believe he discovered – ' She got as far as that, and there she stopped.

'What did he discover?'

There are limits to human patience – even the patience of a bereaved wife. This cool question irritated Mrs Ferrari into expressing herself plainly at last.

'He discovered Lady Montbarry and the Baron!' she answered,

with a burst of hysterical vehemence. 'The Baron is no more that vile woman's brother than I am. The wickedness of those two wretches came to my poor dear husband's knowledge. The lady's maid left her place on account of it. If Ferrari had gone away too, he would have been alive at this moment. They have killed him. I say they have killed him, to prevent it from getting to Lord Montbarry's ears.' So, in short sharp sentences, and in louder and louder accents, Mrs Ferrari stated her opinion of the case.

Still keeping his own view in reserve, Mr Troy listened with an expression of satirical approval.

'Very strongly stated, Mrs Ferrari,' he said. 'You build up your sentences well; you clinch your conclusions in a workmanlike manner. If you had been a man, you would have made a good lawyer – you would have taken juries by the scruff of their necks. Complete the case, my good lady – complete the case. Tell us next who sent you this letter, enclosing the bank-note. The "two wretches" who murdered Mr Ferrari would hardly put their hands in their pockets and send you a thousand pounds. Who is it – eh? I see the post-mark on the letter is "Venice". Have you any friend in that interesting city, with a large heart, and a purse to correspond, who has been let into the secret and who wishes to console you anonymously?'

It was not easy to reply to this. Mrs Ferrari began to feel the first inward approaches of something like hatred towards Mr Troy. 'I don't understand you, sir,' she answered. 'I don't think this is a joking matter.'

Agnes interfered, for the first time. She drew her chair a little nearer to her legal counsellor and friend.

'What is the most probable explanation, in your opinion?' she asked.

'I shall offend Mrs Ferrari if I tell you,' Mr Troy answered.

'No, sir, you won't!' cried Mrs Ferrari, hating Mr Troy undisguisedly by this time.

The lawyer leaned back in his chair. 'Very well,' he said, in his most good-humoured manner. 'Let's have it out. Observe, madam, I don't dispute your view of the position of affairs at the palace in Venice. You have your husband's letters to justify you; and you have also the significant fact that Lady Montbarry's maid did really leave the house. We will say, then, that Lord Montbarry has presumably been made the victim of a foul wrong – that Mr Ferrari was the first to find it out – and that the guilty persons had reason to fear, not only that he would acquaint Lord Montbarry with his discovery, but that he would be a principal witness against them if the scandal was made public in a court of law. Now mark! Admitting all this, I draw a totally different conclusion from the conclusion at which you have arrived. Here is your husband left in this miserable household of three, under very awkward circumstances for him. What does he do? But for the bank-note and the written message sent to you with it, I should say that he had wisely withdrawn himself from association with a disgraceful discovery and exposure, by taking secretly to flight. The money modifies this view – unfavourably so far as Mr Ferrari is concerned. I still believe he is keeping out of the way. But I now say he is paid for keeping out of the way – and that bank-note there on the table is the price of his absence, sent by the guilty persons to his wife.'

Mrs Ferrari's watery grey eyes brightened suddenly; Mrs Ferrari's dull drab-coloured complexion became enlivened by a glow of brilliant red.

'It's false!' she cried. 'It's a burning shame to speak of my husband in that way!'

'I told you I should offend you!' said Mr Troy.

Agnes interposed once more – in the interests of peace. She took the offended wife's hand; she appealed to the lawyer to reconsider that side of his theory which reflected harshly on Ferrari. While she was still speaking, the servant interrupted her by entering the room with a visiting-card. It was the card of Henry Westwick; and there was an ominous request written on it in pencil. 'I bring bad news. Let me see you for a minute downstairs.' Agnes immediately left the room.

Alone with Mrs Ferrari, Mr Troy permitted his natural kindness of heart to show itself on the surface at last. He tried to make his peace with the courier's wife.

'You have every claim, my good soul, to resent a reflection cast upon your husband,' he began. 'I may even say that I respect you for speaking so warmly in his defence. At the same time, remember, that I am bound, in such a serious matter as this, to tell you what is really in my mind. I can have no intention of offending you, seeing that I am a total stranger to you and to Mr Ferrari. A thousand pounds is a large sum of money; and a poor man may excusably be tempted by it to do nothing worse than to keep out of the way for a while. My only interest, acting on your behalf, is to get at the truth. If you will give me time, I see no reason to despair of finding your husband yet.'

Ferrari's wife listened, without being convinced: her narrow little mind, filled to its extreme capacity by her unfavourable opinion of Mr Troy, had no room left for the process of correcting its first impression. 'I am much obliged to you, sir,' was all she said. Her eyes were more communicative – her eyes added, in their language, 'You may say what you please; I will never forgive you to my dying day.'

Mr Troy gave it up. He composedly wheeled his chair around, put his hands in his pockets, and looked out of window.

After an interval of silence, the drawing-room door was opened.

Mr Troy wheeled round again briskly to the table, expecting to see Agnes. To his surprise there appeared, in her place, a perfect stranger to him – a gentleman, in the prime of life, with a marked expression of pain and embarrassment on his handsome face. He looked at Mr Troy, and bowed gravely.

'I am so unfortunate as to have brought news to Miss Agnes Lockwood which has greatly distressed her,' he said. 'She has retired to her room. I am requested to make her excuses, and to speak to you in her place.'

Having introduced himself in those terms, he noticed Mrs Ferrari, and held out his hand to her kindly. 'It is some years since we last met, Emily,' he said. 'I am afraid you have almost forgotten the "Master Henry" of old times.' Emily, in some little confusion, made her acknowledgments, and begged to know if she could be of any use to Miss Lockwood. 'The old nurse is with her,' Henry answered; 'they will be better left together.' He turned once more to Mr Troy. 'I ought to tell you,' he said, 'that my name is Henry Westwick. I am the younger brother of the late Lord Montbarry.'

'The late Lord Montbarry!' Mr Troy exclaimed.

'My brother died at Venice yesterday evening. There is the telegram.' With that startling answer, he handed the paper to Mr Troy. The message was in these words:

LADY MONTBARRY, VENICE. TO STEPHEN ROBERT WESTWICK, NEW-BURY'S HOTEL, LONDON. IT IS USELESS TO TAKE THE JOURNEY. LORD MONTBARRY DIED OF BRONCHITIS, AT 8.40 THIS EVENING. ALL NEEDFUL DETAILS BY POST.

'Was this expected, sir?' the lawyer asked.

'I cannot say that it has taken us entirely by surprise, Henry answered. 'My brother Stephen (who is now the head of the family) received a telegram three days since, informing him that alarming symptoms had declared themselves, and that a second physician had been called in. He telegraphed back to say that he had left Ireland for London, on his way to Venice, and to direct that any further message might be sent to his hotel. The reply came in a second telegram. It announced that Lord Montbarry was in a state of insensibility, and that, in his brief intervals of consciousness, he recognised nobody. My brother was advised to wait in London for later information. The third telegram is now in your hands. That is all I know, up to the present time.'

Happening to look at the courier's wife, Mr Troy was struck by the expression of blank fear which showed itself in the woman's face.

'Mrs Ferrari,' he said, 'have you heard what Mr Westwick has just told me?'

'Every word of it, sir.'

'Have you any questions to ask?'

'No, sir.'

'You seem to be alarmed,' the lawyer persisted. 'Is it still about your husband?'

'I shall never see my husband again, sir. I have thought so all along, as you know. I feel sure of it now.'

'Sure of it, after what you have just heard?'

'Yes, sir.'

'Can you tell me why?'

'No, sir. It's a feeling I have. I can't tell why.'

'Oh, a feeling?' Mr Troy repeated, in a tone of compassionate contempt. 'When it comes to feelings, my good soul – !' He left the sentence unfinished, and rose to take his leave of Mr Westwick. The truth is, he began to feel puzzled himself, and he did not choose to let Mrs Ferrari see it. 'Accept the expression of my sympathy, sir,' he said to Mr Westwick politely. 'I wish you good-evening.'

Henry turned to Mrs Ferrari as the lawyer closed the door. 'I have heard of your trouble, Emily, from Miss Lockwood. Is there anything I can do to help you?'

'Nothing, sir, thank you. Perhaps, I had better go home after what has happened? I will call tomorrow, and see if I can be of any use to Miss Agnes. I am very sorry for her.' She stole away, with her formal curtsey, her noiseless step, and her obstinate resolution to take the gloomiest view of her husband's case.

Henry Westwick looked round him in the solitude of the little drawing-room. There was nothing to keep him in the house, and yet he lingered in it. It was something to be even near Agnes – to see the things belonging to her that were scattered about the room.

There, in the corner, was her chair, with her embroidery on the work-table by its side. On the little easel near the window was her last drawing, not quite finished yet. The book she had been reading lay on the sofa, with her tiny pencil-case in it to mark the place at which she had left off. One after another, he looked at the objects that reminded him of the woman whom he loved – took them up tenderly – and laid them down again with a sigh. Ah, how far, how unattainably far from him, she was still! 'She will never forget Montbarry,' he thought to himself as he took up his hat to go. 'Not one of us feels his death as she feels it. Miserable, miserable wretch – how she loved him!'

In the street, as Henry closed the house-door, he was stopped by a passing acquaintance – a wearisome inquisitive man – doubly unwelcome to him, at that moment. 'Sad news, Westwick, this about your brother. Rather an unexpected death, wasn't it? We never heard at the club that Montbarry's lungs were weak. What will the insurance offices do?'

Henry started; he had never thought of his brother's life insurance. What could the offices do but pay? A death by bronchitis, certified by two physicians, was surely the least disputable of all deaths. 'I wish you hadn't put that question into my head!' he broke out irritably. 'Ah!' said his friend, 'you think the widow will get the money? So do I! So do I!'

Chapter 7

Some days later, the insurance offices (two in number) received the formal announcement of Lord Montbarry's death, from her lady-ship's London solicitors. The sum insured in each office was five thousand pounds – on which one year's premium only had been paid. In the face of such a pecuniary emergency as this, the Directors thought it desirable to consider their position. The medical advisers of the two offices, who had recommended the insurance of Lord Montbarry's life, were called into council over their own reports. The result excited some interest among persons connected with the business of life insurance. Without absolutely declining to pay the money, the two offices (acting in concert) decided on sending a commission of inquiry to Venice, 'for the purpose of obtaining further information'.

Mr Troy received the earliest intelligence of what was going on. He wrote at once to communicate his news to Agnes; adding, what he considered to be a valuable hint, in these words:

You are intimately acquainted, I know, with Lady Barville, the late Lord Montbarry's eldest sister. The solicitors employed by her husband are also the solicitors to one of the two insurance offices. There may possibly be something in the report of the commission of inquiry touching on Ferrari's disappearance. Ordinary persons would not be permitted, of course, to see such a document. But a sister of the late lord is so near a relative as to be an exception to general rules. If Sir Theodore Barville puts it on that footing, the lawyers, even if they do not allow his wife to look at the report, will at least answer any discreet questions she may ask referring to it. Let me hear what you think of this suggestion, at your earliest convenience.

The reply was received by return of post. Agnes declined to avail herself of Mr Troy's proposal.

My interference, innocent as it was, (she wrote) has already been productive of such deplorable results, that I cannot and dare not stir any further in the case of Ferrari. If I had not consented to let that unfortunate man refer to me by name, the late Lord Montbarry would never have engaged him, and his wife would have been spared the misery and suspense from which she is suffering now. I would not even look at the report to which you allude if it was placed in my hands – I have heard more than enough already of that hideous life in the palace at Venice. If Mrs Ferrari chooses to address herself to Lady Barville (with your assistance), that is of course quite another thing. But, even in this case, I must make it a positive condition that my name shall not be mentioned. Forgive me, dear Mr Troy! I am very unhappy, and very unreasonable – but I am only a woman, and you must not expect too much from me.'

Foiled in this direction, the lawyer next advised making the attempt to discover the present address of Lady Montbarry's English maid. This excellent suggestion had one drawback: it could only be carried out by spending money – and there was no money to spend. Mrs Ferrari shrank from the bare idea of making any use of the thousand-pound note. It had been deposited in the safe keeping of a bank. If it was even mentioned in her hearing, she shuddered and referred to it, with melodramatic fervour, as 'my husband's blood-money!'

So, under stress of circumstances, the attempt to solve the mystery of Ferrari's disappearance was suspended for a while.

It was the last month of the year 1860. The commission of inquiry was already at work, having begun its investigations on December 6. On the 10th, the term for which the late Lord Montbarry had hired the Venetian palace, expired. News by telegram reached the insurance offices that Lady Montbarry had been advised by her lawyers to leave for London with as little delay as possible. Baron Rivar, it was believed, would accompany her to England, but would not remain in that country, unless his services were absolutely required by her ladyship. The Baron, 'well known as an enthusiastic student of chemistry', had heard of certain recent discoveries in connection with that science in the United States, and was anxious to investigate them personally.

These items of news, collected by Mr Troy, were duly communicated to Mrs Ferrari, whose anxiety about her husband made her a frequent, a too frequent, visitor at the lawyer's office. She attempted to relate what she had heard to her good friend and protectress. Agnes steadily refused to listen, and positively forbade any further conversation relating to Lord Montbarry's wife, now that Lord Montbarry was no more. 'You have Mr Troy to advise you,' she said; 'and you are welcome to what little money I can spare, if money is wanted. All I ask in return is that you will not distress me. I am trying to separate myself from remembrances – ' her voice faltered; she paused to control herself – 'from remembrances,' she resumed, 'which are sadder than ever since I have heard of Lord Montbarry's death. Help me by your silence to recover my spirits, if I can. Let me hear nothing more, until I can rejoice with you that your husband is found.'

Time advanced to the 13th of the month; and more information of the interesting sort reached Mr Troy. The labours of the insurance commission had come to an end – the report had been received from Venice on that day.

Chapter 8

On the 14th the Directors and their legal advisers met for the reading of the report, with closed doors. These were the terms in which the Commissioners related the results of their inquiry:

Private and confidential
We have the honour to inform our Directors that we arrived in Venice on December 6, 1860. On the same day we proceeded to the palace inhabited by Lord Montbarry at the time of his last illness and death.

We were received with all possible courtesy by Lady Montbarry's brother, Baron Rivar. 'My sister was her husband's only attendant throughout his illness,' the Baron informed us. 'She is overwhelmed by grief and fatigue – or she would have been here to receive you personally. What are your wishes, gentlemen? And what can I do for you in her ladyship's place?'

In accordance with our instructions, we answered that the death and burial of Lord Montbarry abroad made it desirable to obtain more complete information relating to his illness, and to the circumstances which had attended it, than could be conveyed in writing. We explained that the law provided for the lapse of a certain interval of time before the payment of the sum assured, and we expressed our wish to conduct the inquiry with the most respectful consideration for her ladyship's feelings, and for the convenience of any other members of the family inhabiting the house.

To this the Baron replied, 'I am the only member of the family living here, and I and the palace are entirely at your disposal.' From first to last we found this gentleman perfectly straightforward, and most amiably willing to assist us.

With the one exception of her ladyship's room, we went over the whole of the palace the same day. It is an immense place only partially furnished. The first floor and part of the second floor were the portions of it that had been inhabited by Lord Montbarry and the members of the household. We saw the bedchamber, at one extremity of the palace, in which his lordship died, and the small room communicating with it, which he used as a study. Next to this was a large apartment or hall, the doors of which he habitually kept locked, his object being (as we were informed) to pursue his studies uninterruptedly in perfect solitude. On the other side of the large hall were the bedchamber occupied by her ladyship, and the dressing-room in which the maid slept previous to her departure for England. Beyond these were the dining and reception rooms, opening into an antechamber, which gave access to the grand staircase of the palace.

The only inhabited rooms on the second floor were the sitting-room and bedroom occupied by Baron Rivar, and another room at some distance from it, which had been the bedroom of the courier Ferrari.

The rooms on the third floor and on the basement were completely unfurnished, and in a condition of great neglect. We enquired if there was anything to be seen below the basement – and we were at once informed that there were vaults beneath, which we were at perfect liberty to visit.

We went down, so as to leave no part of the palace unexplored. The vaults were, it was believed, used as dungeons in the old times – say, some centuries since. Air and light were only partially admitted to these dismal places by two long shafts of winding construction, which communicated with the back yard of the palace, and the openings of which, high above the ground, were protected by iron gratings. The stone stairs leading down into the vaults could be closed at will by a heavy trap-door in the back hall, which we found open. The Baron himself led the way down the stairs. We remarked that it might be awkward if that trap-door fell down and closed the opening behind us. The Baron smiled at the idea. 'Don't be alarmed, gentlemen,' he said; 'the door is safe. I had an interest in seeing to it myself, when we first inhabited the palace. My favourite study is the study of experimental chemistry – and my workshop, since we have been in Venice, is down here.'

These last words explained a curious smell in the vaults, which we noticed the moment we entered them. We can only describe the smell by saying that it was of a twofold sort – faintly aromatic, as it were, in its first effect, but with some after-odour very sickening in our nostrils. The Baron's furnaces and retorts, and other things, were all there to speak for themselves, together with some packages of chemicals, having the name and address of the person who had supplied them plainly visible on their labels. 'Not a pleasant place for study,' Baron Rivar observed, 'but my sister is timid. She has a horror of chemical smells and explosions – and she has banished me to these lower regions, so that my experiments may neither be smelt nor heard.' He held out his hands, on which we had noticed that he wore gloves in the house. 'Accidents will happen sometimes,' he said, 'no matter how careful a man may be. I burnt my hands severely in trying a new combination the other day, and they are only recovering now.'

We mention these otherwise unimportant incidents, in order to show that our exploration of the palace was not impeded by any attempt at concealment. We were even admitted to her ladyship's own room – on a subsequent occasion, when she went out to take the air. Our instructions recommended us to examine his lordship's residence, because the extreme privacy of his life at Venice, and the remarkable departure of the only two servants in the house, might have some suspicious connection with the nature of his death. We found nothing to justify suspicion.

As to his lordship's retired way of life, we have conversed on the subject with the consul and the banker – the only two strangers who held any communication with him. He called once at the bank to obtain money on his letter of credit, and excused himself from accepting an invitation to visit the banker at his private residence, on the ground of delicate health. His lordship wrote to the same effect on sending his card to the consul, to excuse himself from personally returning that gentleman's visit to the palace. We have seen the letter, and we beg to offer the following copy of it. 'Many years passed in India have injured my constitution. I have ceased to go into society; the one occupation of my life now is the study of Oriental literature. The air of Italy is better for me than the air of England, or I should never have left home. Pray accept the apologies of a student and an invalid. The active part of my life is at an end.' The self-seclusion of his lordship seems to us to be explained in these brief lines. We have not, however, on that account spared our enquiries in other directions. Nothing to excite a suspicion of anything wrong has come to our knowledge.

As to the departure of the lady's maid, we have seen the woman's receipt for her wages, in which it is expressly stated that she left Lady Montbarry's service because she disliked the Continent, and wished to get back to her own country. This is not an uncommon result of taking English servants to foreign parts. Lady Montbarry has informed us that she abstained from engaging another maid in consequence of the extreme dislike which his lordship expressed to having strangers in the house, in the state of his health at that time.

The disappearance of the courier Ferrari is, in itself, unquestionably a suspicious circumstance. Neither her ladyship nor the Baron can explain it; and no investigation that we could make has thrown the smallest light on this event, or has justified us in associating it, directly or indirectly, with the object of our inquiry. We have even gone the length of examining the portmanteau which Ferrari left behind him. It contains nothing but clothes and linen – no money, and not even a scrap of paper in the pockets of the clothes. The portmanteau remains in charge of the police.

We have also found opportunities of speaking privately to the old woman who attends to the rooms occupied by her ladyship and the Baron. She was recommended to fill this situation by the keeper of the restaurant who has supplied the meals to the family throughout the period of their residence at the palace. Her character is most favourably spoken of. Unfortunately, her limited intelligence makes her of no value as a witness. We were patient and careful in questioning her, and we found her perfectly willing to answer us; but we could elicit nothing which is worth including in the present report.

On the second day of our enquiries, we had the honour of an interview with Lady Montbarry. Her ladyship looked miserably worn and ill, and seemed to be quite at a loss to understand what we wanted with her. Baron Rivar, who introduced us, explained the nature of our errand in Venice, and took pains to assure her that it was a purely formal duty on which we were engaged. Having satisfied her ladyship on this point, he discreetly left the room.

The questions which we addressed to Lady Montbarry related mainly, of course, to his lordship's illness. The answers, given with great nervousness of manner, but without the slightest appearance of reserve, informed us of the facts that follow:

Lord Montbarry had been out of order for some time past – nervous and irritable. He first complained of having taken cold on November 13 last; he passed a wakeful and feverish night, and remained in bed the next day. Her ladyship proposed sending for medical advice. He refused to allow her to do this, saying that he could quite easily be his own doctor in such a trifling matter as a cold. Some hot lemonade was made at his request, with a view to producing perspiration. Lady Montbarry's maid having left her at that time, the courier Ferrari (then the only servant in the house) went out to buy the lemons. Her ladyship made the drink with her own hands. It was successful in producing perspiration – and Lord

Montbarry had some hours of sleep afterwards. Later in the day, having need of Ferrari's services, Lady Montbarry rang for him. The bell was not answered. Baron Rivar searched for the man, in the palace and out of it, in vain. From that time forth not a trace of Ferrari could be discovered. This happened on November 14.

On the night of the 14th, the feverish symptoms accompanying his lordship's cold returned. They were in part perhaps attributable to the annoyance and alarm caused by Ferrari's mysterious disappearance. It had been impossible to conceal the circumstance, as his lordship rang repeatedly for the courier; insisting that the man should relieve Lady Montbarry and the Baron by taking their places during the night at his bedside.

On the 15th (the day on which the old woman first came to do the housework), his lordship complained of sore throat, and of a feeling of oppression on the chest. On this day, and again on the 16th, her ladyship and the Baron entreated him to see a doctor. He still refused. 'I don't want strange faces about me; my cold will run its course, in spite of the doctor' – that was his answer. On the 17th he was so much worse that it was decided to send for medical help whether he liked it or not. Baron Rivar, after enquiry at the consul's, secured the services of Doctor Bruno, well known as an eminent physician in Venice; with the additional recommendation of having resided in England, and having made himself acquainted with English forms of medical practice.

Thus far our account of his lordship's illness has been derived from statements made by Lady Montbarry. The narrative will now be most fitly continued in the language of the doctor's own report, herewith subjoined.

'My medical diary informs me that I first saw the English Lord Montbarry, on November 17. He was suffering from a sharp attack of bronchitis. Some precious time had been lost, through his obstinate objection to the presence of a medical man at his bedside. Generally speaking, he appeared to be in a delicate state of health. His nervous system was out of order – he was at once timid and contradictory. When I spoke to him in English, he answered in Italian; and when I tried him in Italian, he went back to English. It mattered little – the malady had already made such progress that he could only speak a few words at a time, and those in a whisper.

'I at once applied the necessary remedies. Copies of my prescriptions (with translation into English) accompany the present statement, and are left to speak for themselves.

'For the next three days I was in constant attendance on my patient. He answered to the remedies employed – improving slowly, but decidedly. I could conscientiously assure Lady Montbarry that no danger was to be apprehended thus far. She was indeed a most devoted wife. I vainly endeavoured to induce her to accept the services of a competent nurse; she would allow nobody to attend on her husband but herself. Night and day this estimable woman was at his bedside. In her brief intervals of repose, her brother watched the sick man in her place. This brother was, I must say, very good company, in the intervals when we had time for a little talk. He dabbled in chemistry, down in the horrid underwater vaults of the palace; and he wanted to show me some of his experiments. I have enough of chemistry in writing prescriptions – and I declined. He took it quite good-humouredly.

'I am straying away from my subject. Let me return to the sick lord.

'Up to the 20th, then, things went well enough. I was quite unprepared for the disastrous change that showed itself, when I paid Lord Montbarry my morning visit on the 21st. He had relapsed, and seriously relapsed. Examining him to discover the cause, I found symptoms of pneumonia – that is to say, in unmedical language, inflammation of the substance of the lungs. He breathed with difficulty, and was only partially able to relieve himself by coughing. I made the strictest enquiries, and was assured that his medicine had been administered as carefully as usual, and that he had not been exposed to any changes of temperature. It was with great reluctance that I added to Lady Montbarry's distress; but I felt bound, when she suggested a consultation with another physician, to own that I too thought there was really need for it.

'Her ladyship instructed me to spare no expense, and to get the best medical opinion in Italy. The best opinion was happily within our reach. The first and foremost of Italian physicians is Torello of Padua. I sent a special messenger for the great man. He arrived on the evening of the 21st, and confirmed my opinion that pneumonia had set in, and that our patient's life was in danger. I told him what my treatment of the case had been, and he approved of it in every particular. He made some valuable suggestions, and (at Lady

Montbarry's express request) he consented to defer his return to Padua until the following morning.

'We both saw the patient at intervals in the course of the night. The disease, steadily advancing, set our utmost resistance at defiance. In the morning Doctor Torello took his leave. "I can be of no further use," he said to me. "The man is past all help – and he ought to know it."

'Later in the day I warned my lord, as gently as I could, that his time had come. I am informed that there are serious reasons for my stating what passed between us on this occasion, in detail, and without any reserve. I comply with the request.

'Lord Montbarry received the intelligence of his approaching death with becoming composure, but with a certain doubt. He signed to me to put my ear to his mouth. He whispered faintly, "Are you sure?" It was no time to deceive him; I said, "Positively sure." He waited a little, gasping for breath, and then he whispered again, "Feel under my pillow." I found under his pillow a letter, sealed and stamped, ready for the post. His next words were just audible and no more – "Post it yourself." I answered, of course, that I would do so – and I did post the letter with my own hand. I looked at the address. It was directed to a lady in London. The street I cannot remember. The name I can perfectly recall: it was an Italian name – "Mrs Ferrari".

'That night my lord nearly died of asphyxia. I got him through it for the time; and his eyes showed that he understood me when I told him, the next morning, that I had posted the letter. This was his last effort of consciousness. When I saw him again he was sunk in apathy. He lingered in a state of insensibility, supported by stimulants, until the 25th, and died (unconscious to the last) on the evening of that day.

'As to the cause of his death, it seems (if I may be excused for saying so) simply absurd to ask the question. Bronchitis, terminating in pneumonia – there is no more doubt that this, and this only, was the malady of which he expired, than that two and two make four. Doctor Torello's own note of the case is added here to a duplicate of my certificate, in order (as I am informed) to satisfy some English offices in which his lordship's life was insured. The English offices must have been founded by that celebrated saint and doubter, mentioned in the New Testament, whose name was Thomas!'

Doctor Bruno's evidence ends here.

Reverting for a moment to our enquiries addressed to Lady Montbarry, we have to report that she can give us no information on the subject of the letter which the doctor posted at Lord Montbarry's request. When his lordship wrote it? What it contained? Why he kept it a secret from Lady Montbarry (and from the Baron also); and why he should write at all to the wife of his courier? These are questions to which we find it simply impossible to obtain any replies. It seems even useless to say that the matter is open to suspicion. Suspicion implies conjecture of some kind – and the letter under my lord's pillow baffles all conjecture. Application to Mrs Ferrari may perhaps clear up the mystery. Her residence in London will be easily discovered at the Italian Couriers' Office, Golden Square.

Having arrived at the close of the present report, we have now to draw your attention to the conclusion which is justified by the results of our investigation.

The plain question before our Directors and ourselves appears to be this: has the inquiry revealed any extraordinary circumstances which render the death of Lord Montbarry open to suspicion? The inquiry has revealed extraordinary circumstances beyond all doubt – such as the disappearance of Ferrari, the remarkable absence of the customary establishment of servants in the house, and the mysterious letter which his lordship asked the doctor to post. But where is the proof that any one of these circumstances is associated – suspiciously and directly associated – with the only event which concerns us, the event of Lord Montbarry's death? In the absence of any such proof, and in the face of the evidence of two eminent physicians, it is impossible to dispute the statement on the certificate that his lordship died a natural death. We are bound, therefore, to report, that there are no valid grounds for refusing the payment of the sum for which the late Lord Montbarry's life was assured.

We shall send these lines to you by the post of tomorrow, December 10; leaving time to receive your further instructions (if any), in reply to our telegram of this evening announcing the conclusion of the inquiry.

Chapter 9

'Now, my good creature, whatever you have to say to me, out with it at once! I don't want to hurry you needlessly; but these are business hours, and I have other people's affairs to attend to besides yours.'

Addressing Ferrari's wife, with his usual blunt good-humour, in these terms, Mr Troy registered the lapse of time by a glance at the watch on his desk, and then waited to hear what his client had to say to him.

'It's something more, sir, about the letter with the thousand-pound note,' Mrs Ferrari began. 'I have found out who sent it to me.'

Mr Troy started. 'This is news indeed!' he said. 'Who sent you the letter?'

'Lord Montbarry sent it, sir.'

It was not easy to take Mr Troy by surprise. But Mrs Ferrari threw him completely off his balance. For a while he could only look at her in silent surprise. 'Nonsense!' he said, as soon as he had recovered himself. 'There is some mistake – it can't be!'

'There is no mistake,' Mrs Ferrari rejoined, in her most positive manner. 'Two gentlemen from the insurance offices called on me this morning, to see the letter. They were completely puzzled – especially when they heard of the bank-note inside. But they know who sent the letter. His lordship's doctor in Venice posted it at his lordship's request. Go to the gentlemen yourself, sir, if you don't believe me. They were polite enough to ask if I could account for Lord Montbarry's writing to me and sending me the money. I gave them my opinion directly – I said it was like his lordship's kindness.'

'Like his lordship's kindness?' Mr Troy repeated, in blank amazement.

'Yes, sir! Lord Montbarry knew me, like all the other members of his family, when I was at school on the estate in Ireland. If he could have done it, he would have protected my poor dear husband. But he was helpless himself in the hands of my lady and the Baron – and the only kind thing he could do was to provide for me in my widowhood, like the true nobleman he was!'

'A very pretty explanation!' said Mr Troy. 'What did your visitors from the insurance offices think of it?'

'They asked if I had any proof of my husband's death.'

'And what did you say?'

'I said, "I give you better than proof, gentlemen; I give you my positive opinion." '

'That satisfied them, of course?'

'They didn't say so in words, sir. They looked at each other – and wished me good-morning.'

'Well, Mrs Ferrari, unless you have some more extraordinary news for me, I think I shall wish you good-morning too. I can take a note of your information (very startling information, I own); and, in the absence of proof, I can do no more.'

'I can provide you with proof, sir – if that is all you want,' said Mrs Ferrari, with great dignity. 'I only wish to know, first, whether the law justifies me in doing it. You may have seen in the fashionable intelligence of the newspapers, that Lady Montbarry has arrived in London, at Newbury's Hotel. I propose to go and see her.'

'The deuce you do! May I ask for what purpose?'

Mrs Ferrari answered in a mysterious whisper. 'For the purpose of catching her in a trap! I shan't send in my name – I shall announce myself as a person on business, and the first words I say to her will be these: "I come, my lady, to acknowledge the receipt of the money sent to Ferrari's widow." Ah! You may well start, Mr Troy! It almost takes you off your guard, doesn't it? Make your mind easy, sir; I shall find the proof that everybody asks me for in her guilty face. Let her only change colour by the shadow of a shade – let her eyes only drop for half an instant – I shall discover her! The one thing I want to know is, does the law permit it?'

'The law permits it,' Mr Troy answered gravely; 'but whether her ladyship will permit it, is quite another question. Have you really courage enough, Mrs Ferrari, to carry out this notable scheme of yours? You have been described to me, by Miss Lockwood, as rather a nervous, timid sort of person – and, if I may trust my own observation, I should say you justify the description.'

'If you had lived in the country, sir, instead of living in London,' Mrs Ferrari replied, 'you would sometimes have seen even a sheep turn on a dog. I am far from saying that I am a bold woman – quite the reverse. But when I stand in that wretch's presence, and think of my murdered husband, the one of us two who is likely to be frightened is not me. I am going there now, sir. You shall hear how it ends. I wish you good-morning.'

With those brave words the courier's wife gathered her mantle about her, and walked out of the room.

Mr Troy smiled – not satirically, but compassionately. 'The little simpleton!' he thought to himself. 'If half of what they say of Lady Montbarry is true, Mrs Ferrari and her trap have but a poor prospect before them. I wonder how it will end?'

All Mr Troy's experience failed to forewarn him of how it *did* end.

Chapter 10

In the meantime, Mrs Ferrari held to her resolution. She went straight from Mr Troy's office to Newbury's Hotel.

Lady Montbarry was at home, and alone. But the authorities of the hotel hesitated to disturb her when they found that the visitor declined to mention her name. Her ladyship's new maid happened to cross the hall while the matter was still in debate. She was a Frenchwoman, and, on being appealed to, she settled the question in the swift, easy, rational French way. 'Madame's appearance was perfectly respectable. Madame might have reasons for not mentioning her name which Miladi might approve. In any case, there being no orders forbidding the introduction of a strange lady, the matter clearly rested between Madame and Miladi. Would Madame, therefore, be good enough to follow Miladi's maid up the stairs?'

In spite of her resolution, Mrs Ferrari's heart beat as if it would burst out of her bosom, when her conductress led her into an anteroom, and knocked at a door opening into a room beyond. But it is remarkable that persons of sensitively-nervous organisation are the very persons who are capable of forcing themselves (apparently by the exercise of a spasmodic effort of will) into the performance of acts of the most audacious courage. A low, grave voice from the inner room said, 'Come in.' The maid, opening the door, announced, 'A person to see you, Miladi, on business,' and immediately retired. In the one instant while these events passed, timid little Mrs Ferrari mastered her own throbbing heart; stepped over the threshold, conscious of her clammy hands, dry lips, and burning head; and stood in the presence of Lord Montbarry's widow, to all outward appearance as supremely self-possessed as her ladyship herself.

It was still early in the afternoon, but the light in the room was dim. The blinds were drawn down. Lady Montbarry sat with her back to the windows, as if even the subdued daylight were disagreeable to her. She had altered sadly for the worse in her personal appearance, since the memorable day when Doctor Wybrow had seen her in his consulting-room. Her beauty was gone – her face had fallen away to mere skin and bone; the contrast between her ghastly complexion and her steely glittering black eyes was more startling than ever. Robed in dismal black, relieved only by the brilliant whiteness of her widow's cap – reclining in a panther-like suppleness of attitude on a little green sofa – she looked at the stranger who had intruded on her, with a moment's languid curiosity, then dropped her eyes again to the hand-screen which she held between her face and the fire. 'I don't know you,' she said. 'What do you want with me?'

Mrs Ferrari tried to answer. Her first burst of courage had already worn itself out. The bold words that she had determined to speak were living words still in her mind, but they died on her lips.

There was a moment of silence. Lady Montbarry looked round again at the speechless stranger. 'Are you deaf?' she asked. There was another pause. Lady Montbarry quietly looked back again at the screen, and put another question. 'Do you want money?'

'Money!' That one word roused the sinking spirit of the courier's wife. She recovered her courage; she found her voice. 'Look at me, my lady, if you please,' she said, with a sudden outbreak of audacity.

Lady Montbarry looked round for the third time. The fatal words passed Mrs Ferrari's lips.

'I come, my lady, to acknowledge the receipt of the money sent to Ferrari's widow.'

Lady Montbarry's glittering black eyes rested with steady attention on the woman who had addressed her in those terms. Not the faintest expression of confusion or alarm, not even a momentary flutter of interest stirred the deadly stillness of her face. She reposed as quietly, she held the screen as composedly, as ever. The test had been tried, and had utterly failed.

There was another silence. Lady Montbarry considered with herself. The smile that came slowly and went away suddenly – the smile at once so sad and so cruel – showed itself on her thin lips. She lifted her screen, and pointed with it to a seat at the farther end of the room. 'Be so good as to take that chair,' she said.

Helpless under her first bewildering sense of failure – not knowing what to say or what to do next – Mrs Ferrari mechanically obeyed. Lady Montbarry, rising on the sofa for the first time, watched her with undisguised scrutiny as she crossed the room – then sank back into a reclining position once more. 'No,' she said to herself, 'the woman walks steadily; she is not intoxicated – the only other possibility is that she may be mad.'

She had spoken loud enough to be heard. Stung by the insult, Mrs Ferrari instantly answered her: 'I am no more drunk or mad than you are!'

'No?' said Lady Montbarry. 'Then you are only insolent? The ignorant English mind (I have observed) is apt to be insolent in the exercise of unrestrained English liberty. This is very noticeable to us foreigners among you people in the streets. Of course I can't be insolent to you, in return. I hardly know what to say to you. My maid was imprudent in admitting you so easily to my room. I suppose your respectable appearance misled her. I wonder who you are? You mentioned the name of a courier who left us very strangely. Was he married by any chance? Are you his wife? And do you know where he is?'

Mrs Ferrari's indignation burst its way through all restraints. She advanced to the sofa; she feared nothing, in the fervour and rage of her reply.

'I am his widow – and you know it, you wicked woman! Ah! It was an evil hour when Miss Lockwood recommended my husband to be his lordship's courier – !'

Before she could add another word, Lady Montbarry sprang from the sofa with the stealthy suddenness of a cat – seized her by both shoulders – and shook her with the strength and frenzy of a madwoman. 'You lie! You lie! You lie!' She dropped her hold at the third repetition of the accusation, and threw up her hands wildly with a gesture of despair. 'Oh, Jesu Maria! Is it possible?' she cried. 'Can the courier have come to me through that woman?' She turned like lightning on Mrs Ferrari, and stopped her as she was escaping from the room. 'Stay here, you fool – stay here, and answer me! If you cry out, as sure as the heavens are above you, I'll strangle you with my own hands. Sit down again – and fear nothing. Wretch! It is I who am frightened – frightened out of my senses. Confess that you lied, when you used Miss Lockwood's name just now! No! I don't believe you on your oath; I will believe nobody but Miss Lockwood herself. Where does she live? Tell me that, you noxious stinging little insect – and you may go.' Terrified as she was, Mrs Ferrari hesitated. Lady Montbarry lifted her hands threateningly, with the long, lean, yellow-white fingers outspread and crooked at the tips. Mrs Ferrari shrank at the sight of them, and gave the address. Lady Montbarry pointed contemptuously to the door – then changed her mind. 'No! Not yet! You will tell Miss Lockwood what has happened, and she may refuse to see me. I will go there at once, and you shall go with me. As far as the house – not inside of it. Sit down again. I am going to ring for my maid. Turn your back to the door – your cowardly face is not fit to be seen!'

She rang the bell. The maid appeared.

'My cloak and bonnet – instantly!'

The maid produced the cloak and bonnet from the bedroom.

'A cab at the door – before I can count ten!'

The maid vanished. Lady Montbarry surveyed herself in the glass, and wheeled round again, with her cat-like suddenness, to Mrs Ferrari.

'I look more than half dead already, don't I?' she said with a grim outburst of irony. 'Give me your arm.'

She took Mrs Ferrari's arm, and left the room. 'You have nothing to fear, so long as you obey,' she whispered, on the way downstairs. 'You leave me at Miss Lockwood's door, and never see me again.'

In the hall they were met by the landlady of the hotel. Lady Montbarry graciously presented her companion. 'My good friend Mrs Ferrari; I am so glad to have seen her.' The landlady accompanied them to the door. The cab was waiting. 'Get in first, good Mrs Ferrari,' said her ladyship; 'and tell the man where to go.'

They were driven away. Lady Montbarry's variable humour changed again. With a low groan of misery, she threw herself back in the cab. Lost in her own dark thoughts, as careless of the woman whom she had bent to her iron will as if no such person sat by her side, she preserved a sinister silence, until they reached the house where Miss Lockwood lodged. In an instant, she roused herself to action. She opened the door of the cab, and closed it again on Mrs Ferrari, before the driver could get off his box.

'Take that lady a mile farther on her way home!' she said, as she paid the man his fare. The next moment she had knocked at the house-door. 'Is Miss Lockwood at home?' 'Yes, ma'am.' She stepped over the threshold – the door closed on her.

'Which way, ma'am?' asked the driver of the cab.

Mrs Ferrari put her hand to her head, and tried to collect her thoughts. Could she leave her friend and benefactress helpless at Lady Montbarry's mercy? She was still vainly endeavouring to decide on the course that she ought to follow – when a gentleman, stopping at Miss Lockwood's door, happened to look towards the cab-window, and saw her.

'Are you going to call on Miss Agnes too?' he asked.

It was Henry Westwick. Mrs Ferrari clasped her hands in gratitude as she recognised him.

'Go in, sir!' she cried. 'Go in, directly. That dreadful woman is with Miss Agnes. Go and protect her!'

'What woman?' Henry asked.

The answer literally struck him speechless. With amazement and indignation in his face, he looked at Mrs Ferrari as she pronounced the hated name of 'Lady Montbarry'. 'I'll see to it,' was all he said. He knocked at the house-door; and he too, in his turn, was let in.

Chapter 11

'Lady Montbarry, Miss.'

Agnes was writing a letter, when the servant astonished her by announcing the visitor's name. Her first impulse was to refuse to see the woman who had intruded on her. But Lady Montbarry had taken care to follow close on the servant's heels. Before Agnes could speak, she had entered the room.

'I beg to apologise for my intrusion, Miss Lockwood. I have a question to ask you, in which I am very much interested. No one can answer me but yourself.' In low hesitating tones, with her glittering black eyes bent modestly on the ground, Lady Montbarry opened the interview in those words.

Without answering, Agnes pointed to a chair. She could do this, and, for the time, she could do no more. All that she had read of the hidden and sinister life in the palace at Venice; all that she had heard of Montbarry's melancholy death and burial in a foreign land; all that she knew of the mystery of Ferrari's disappearance, rushed into her mind, when the black-robed figure confronted her, standing just inside the door. The strange conduct of Lady Montbarry added a new perplexity to the doubts and misgivings that troubled her. There stood the adventuress whose character had left its mark on society all over Europe – the Fury who had terrified Mrs Ferrari at the hotel – inconceivably transformed into a timid, shrinking woman! Lady Montbarry had not once ventured to look at Agnes since she had made her way into the room. Advancing to take the chair that had been pointed out to her, she hesitated, put her hand on the rail to support herself, and still remained standing. 'Please give me a moment to compose myself,' she said faintly. Her head sank on her bosom: she stood before Agnes like a conscious culprit before a merciless judge.

The silence that followed was, literally, the silence of fear on both sides. In the midst of it, the door was opened once more – and Henry Westwick appeared.

He looked at Lady Montbarry with a moment's steady attention – bowed to her with formal politeness – and passed on in silence. At the sight of her husband's brother, the sinking spirit of the woman sprang to life again. Her drooping figure became erect. Her eyes met Westwick's look, brightly defiant. She returned his bow with an icy smile of contempt.

Henry crossed the room to Agnes.

'Is Lady Montbarry here by your invitation?' he asked quietly.

'No.'

'Do you wish to see her?'

'It is very painful to me to see her.'

He turned and looked at his sister-in-law. 'Do you hear that?' he asked coldly.

'I hear it,' she answered, more coldly still.

'Your visit is, to say the least of it, ill-timed.'

'Your interference is, to say the least of it, out of place.'

With that retort, Lady Montbarry approached Agnes. The presence of Henry Westwick seemed at once to relieve and embolden her. 'Permit me to ask my question, Miss Lockwood,' she said, with graceful courtesy. 'It is nothing to embarrass you. When the courier Ferrari applied to my late husband for employment, did you – ' Her resolution failed her, before she could say more. She sank trembling into the nearest chair, and, after a moment's struggle, composed herself again. 'Did you permit Ferrari,' she resumed, 'to make sure of being chosen for our courier by using your name?'

Agnes did not reply with her customary directness. Trifling as it was, the reference to Montbarry, proceeding from that woman of all others, confused and agitated her.

'I have known Ferrari's wife for many years,' she began. 'And I take an interest – '

Lady Montbarry abruptly lifted her hands with a gesture of

entreaty. 'Ah, Miss Lockwood, don't waste time by talking of his wife! Answer my plain question, plainly!'

'Let me answer her,' Henry whispered. 'I will undertake to speak plainly enough.'

Agnes refused by a gesture. Lady Montbarry's interruption had roused her sense of what was due to herself. She resumed her reply in plainer terms.

'When Ferrari wrote to the late Lord Montbarry,' she said, 'he did certainly mention my name.'

Even now, she had innocently failed to see the object which her visitor had in view. Lady Montbarry's impatience became ungovernable. She started to her feet, and advanced to Agnes.

'Was it with your knowledge and permission that Ferrari used your name?' she asked. 'The whole soul of my question is in that. For God's sake answer me – Yes, or No!'

'Yes.'

That one word struck Lady Montbarry as a blow might have struck her. The fierce life that had animated her face the instant before, faded out of it suddenly, and left her like a woman turned to stone. She stood, mechanically confronting Agnes, with a stillness so rapt and perfect that not even the breath she drew was perceptible to the two persons who were looking at her.

Henry spoke to her roughly. 'Rouse yourself,' he said. 'You have received your answer.'

She looked round at him. 'I have received my Sentence,' she rejoined – and turned slowly to leave the room.

To Henry's astonishment, Agnes stopped her. 'Wait a moment, Lady Montbarry. I have something to ask on my side. You have spoken of Ferrari. I wish to speak of him too.'

Lady Montbarry bent her head in silence. Her hand trembled as she took out her handkerchief, and passed it over her forehead. Agnes detected the trembling, and shrank back a step. 'Is the subject painful to you?' she asked timidly.

Still silent, Lady Montbarry invited her by a wave of the hand to go on. Henry approached, attentively watching his sister-in-law. Agnes went on.

'No trace of Ferrari has been discovered in England,' she said. 'Have you any news of him? And will you tell me (if you have heard anything), in mercy to his wife?'

Lady Montbarry's thin lips suddenly relaxed into their sad and cruel smile.

'Why do you ask me about the lost courier?' she said. 'You will know what has become of him, Miss Lockwood, when the time is ripe for it.'

Agnes started. 'I don't understand you,' she said. 'How shall I know? Will someone tell me?'

'Someone will tell you.'

Henry could keep silence no longer. 'Perhaps, your ladyship may be the person?' he interrupted with ironical politeness.

She answered him with contemptuous ease. 'You may be right, Mr Westwick. One day or another, I may be the person who tells Miss Lockwood what has become of Ferrari, if – ' She stopped; with her eyes fixed on Agnes.

'If what?' Henry asked.

'If Miss Lockwood forces me to it.'

Agnes listened in astonishment. 'Force you to it?' she repeated. 'How can I do that? Do you mean to say my will is stronger than yours?'

'Do you mean to say that the candle doesn't burn the moth, when the moth flies into it?' Lady Montbarry rejoined. 'Have you ever heard of such a thing as the fascination of terror? I am drawn to you by a fascination of terror. I have no right to visit you, I have no wish to visit you: you are my enemy. For the first time in my life, against my own will, I submit to my enemy. See! I am waiting because you told me to wait – and the fear of you (I swear it!) creeps through me while I stand here. Oh, don't let me excite your curiosity or your pity! Follow the example of Mr Westwick. Be hard and brutal and unforgiving, like him. Grant me my release. Tell me to go.'

The frank and simple nature of Agnes could discover but one intelligible meaning in this strange outbreak.

'You are mistaken in thinking me your enemy,' she said. 'The wrong you did me when you gave your hand to Lord Montbarry was not intentionally done. I forgave you my sufferings in his lifetime. I forgive you even more freely now that he has gone.'

Henry heard her with mingled emotions of admiration and distress. 'Say no more!' he exclaimed. 'You are too good to her; she is not worthy of it.'

The interruption passed unheeded by Lady Montbarry. The simple words in which Agnes had replied seemed to have absorbed the whole attention of this strangely-changeable woman. As she listened, her face settled slowly into an expression of hard and tearless sorrow.

There was a marked change in her voice when she spoke next. It expressed that last worst resignation which has done with hope.

'You good innocent creature,' she said, 'what does your amiable forgiveness matter? What are your poor little wrongs, in the reckoning for greater wrongs which is demanded of me? I am not trying to frighten you, I am only miserable about myself. Do you know what it is to have a firm presentiment of calamity that is coming to you – and yet to hope that your own positive conviction will not prove true? When I first met you, before my marriage, and first felt your influence over me, I had that hope. It was a starveling sort of hope that lived a lingering life in me until today. You struck it dead, when you answered my question about Ferrari.'

'How have I destroyed your hopes?' Agnes asked. 'What connection is there between my permitting Ferrari to use my name to Lord Montbarry, and the strange and dreadful things you are saying to me now?'

'The time is near, Miss Lockwood, when you will discover that for yourself. In the meanwhile, you shall know what my fear of you is, in the plainest words I can find. On the day when I took your hero from you and blighted your life – I am firmly persuaded of it! – you were made the instrument of the retribution that my sins of many years had deserved. Oh, such things have happened before today! One person has, before now, been the means of innocently ripening the growth of evil in another. You have done that already – and you have more to do yet. You have still to bring me to the day of discovery, and to the punishment that is my doom. We shall meet again – here in England, or there in Venice where my husband died – and meet for the last time.'

In spite of her better sense, in spite of her natural superiority to superstitions of all kinds, Agnes was impressed by the terrible earnestness with which those words were spoken. She turned pale as she looked at Henry. 'Do you understand her?' she asked.

'Nothing is easier than to understand her,' he replied contemptuously. 'She knows what has become of Ferrari; and she is confusing you in a cloud of nonsense, because she daren't own the truth. Let her go!'

If a dog had been under one of the chairs, and had barked, Lady Montbarry could not have proceeded more impenetrably with the last words she had to say to Agnes.

'Advise your interesting Mrs Ferrari to wait a little longer,' she said. 'You will know what has become of her husband, and you will tell her. There will be nothing to alarm you. Some trifling event will bring us together the next time – as trifling, I dare say, as the engagement of Ferrari. Sad nonsense, Mr Westwick, is it not? But you make allowances for women; we all talk nonsense. Good morning, Miss Lockwood.'

She opened the door – suddenly, as if she was afraid of being called back for the second time – and left them.

Chapter 12

'Do you think she is mad?' Agnes asked.

'I think she is simply wicked. False, superstitious, inveterately cruel – but not mad. I believe her main motive in coming here was to enjoy the luxury of frightening you.'

'She has frightened me. I am ashamed to own it – but so it is.'

Henry looked at her, hesitated for a moment, and seated himself on the sofa by her side.

'I am very anxious about you, Agnes,' he said. 'But for the fortunate chance which led me to call here today – who knows what that vile woman might not have said or done, if she had found you alone? My dear, you are leading a sadly unprotected solitary life. I don't like to think of it; I want to see it changed – especially after what has happened today. No! No! It is useless to tell me that you have your old nurse. She is too old; she is not in your rank of life – there is no sufficient protection in the companionship of such a person for a lady in your position. Don't mistake me, Agnes! What I say, I say in the sincerity of my devotion to you.' He paused, and took her hand. She made a feeble effort to withdraw it – and yielded. 'Will the day never come,' he pleaded, 'when the privilege of protecting you may be mine? When you will be the pride and joy of my life, as long as my life lasts?' He pressed her hand gently. She made no reply. The colour came and went on her face; her eyes were turned away from him. 'Have I been so unhappy as to offend you?' he asked.

She answered that – she said, almost in a whisper, 'No.'

'Have I distressed you?'

'You have made me think of the sad days that are gone.' She said no more; she only tried to withdraw her hand from his for the second time. He still held it; he lifted it to his lips.

'Can I never make you think of other days than those – of the happier days to come? Or, if you must think of the time that is passed, can you not look back to the time when I first loved you?'

She sighed as he put the question. 'Spare me, Henry,' she answered sadly. 'Say no more!'

The colour again rose in her cheeks; her hand trembled in his. She looked lovely, with her eyes cast down and her bosom heaving gently. At that moment he would have given everything he had in the world to take her in his arms and kiss her. Some mysterious sympathy, passing from his hand to hers, seemed to tell her what was in his mind. She snatched her hand away, and suddenly looked up at him. The tears were in her eyes. She said nothing; she let her eyes speak for her. They warned him – without anger, without unkindness – but still they warned him to press her no further that day.

'Only tell me that I am forgiven,' he said, as he rose from the sofa.

'Yes,' she answered quietly, 'you are forgiven.'

'I have not lowered myself in your estimation, Agnes?'

'Oh, no!'

'Do you wish me to leave you?'

She rose, in her turn, from the sofa, and walked to her writing-table before she replied. The unfinished letter which she had been writing when Lady Montbarry interrupted her, lay open on the blotting-book. As she looked at the letter, and then looked at Henry, the smile that charmed everybody showed itself in her face.

'You must not go just yet,' she said: 'I have something to tell you. I hardly know how to express it. The shortest way perhaps will be to let you find it out for yourself. You have been speaking of my lonely unprotected life here. It is not a very happy life, Henry – I own that.' She paused, observing the growing anxiety of his expression as he looked at her, with a shy satisfaction that perplexed him. 'Do you know that I have anticipated your idea?' she went on. 'I am going to make a great change in my life – if your brother Stephen and his wife will only consent to it.' She opened the desk of the writing-table while she spoke, took a letter out, and handed it to Henry.

He received it from her mechanically. Vague doubts, which he hardly understood himself, kept him silent. It was impossible that the 'change in her life' of which she had spoken could mean that she was about to be married – and yet he was conscious of a perfectly unreasonable reluctance to open the letter. Their eyes met; she smiled again. 'Look at the address,' she said. 'You ought to know the handwriting – but I dare say you don't.'

He looked at the address. It was in the large, irregular, uncertain writing of a child. He opened the letter instantly.

DEAR AUNT AGNES – Our governess is going away. She has had money left to her, and a house of her own. We have had cake and wine to drink her health. You promised to be our governess if we wanted another. We want you. Mamma knows nothing about this. Please come before Mamma can get another governess.

YOUR LOVING LUCY, who writes this.

Clara and Blanche have tried to write too. But they are too young to do it. They blot the paper.

'Your eldest niece,' Agnes explained, as Henry looked at her in amazement. 'The children used to call me aunt when I was staying with their mother in Ireland, in the autumn. The three girls were my inseparable companions – they are the most charming children I know. It is quite true that I offered to be their governess, if they ever wanted one, on the day when I left them to return to London. I was writing to propose it to their mother, just before you came.'

'Not seriously!' Henry exclaimed.

Agnes placed her unfinished letter in his hand. Enough of it had been written to show that she did seriously propose to enter the household of Mr and Mrs Stephen Westwick as governess to their children! Henry's bewilderment was not to be expressed in words.

'They won't believe you are in earnest,' he said.

'Why not?' Agnes asked quietly.

'You are my brother Stephen's cousin; you are his wife's old friend.'

'All the more reason, Henry, for trusting me with the charge of their children.'

'But you are their equal; you are not obliged to get your living by teaching. There is something absurd in your entering their service as a governess!'

'What is there absurd in it? The children love me; the mother loves me; the father has shown me innumerable instances of his true friendship and regard. I am the very woman for the place – and, as to my education, I must have completely forgotten it indeed, if I am not fit to teach three children the eldest of whom is only eleven years old. You say I am their equal. Are there no other women who serve as governesses, and who are the equals of the persons whom they serve? Besides, I don't know that I am their equal. Have I not heard that your brother Stephen was the next heir to the title? Will he not be the new lord? Never mind answering me! We won't dispute whether

I am right or wrong in turning governess – we will wait the event. I am weary of my lonely useless existence here, and eager to make my life more happy and more useful, in the household of all others in which I should like most to have a place. If you will look again, you will see that I have these personal considerations still to urge before I finish my letter. You don't know your brother and his wife as well as I do, if you doubt their answer. I believe they have courage enough and heart enough to say Yes.'

Henry submitted without being convinced.

He was a man who disliked all eccentric departures from custom and routine; and he felt especially suspicious of the change proposed in the life of Agnes. With new interests to occupy her mind, she might be less favourably disposed to listen to him, on the next occasion when he urged his suit. The influence of the 'lonely useless existence' of which she complained, was distinctly an influence in his favour. While her heart was empty, her heart was accessible. But with his nieces in full possession of it, the clouds of doubt overshadowed his prospects. He knew the sex well enough to keep these purely selfish perplexities to himself. The waiting policy was especially the policy to pursue with a woman as sensitive as Agnes. If he once offended her delicacy he was lost. For the moment he wisely controlled himself and changed the subject.

'My little niece's letter has had an effect,' he said, 'which the child never contemplated in writing it. She has just reminded me of one of the objects that I had in calling on you today.'

Agnes looked at the child's letter. 'How does Lucy do that?' she asked.

'Lucy's governess is not the only lucky person who has had money left her,' Henry answered. 'Is your old nurse in the house?'

'You don't mean to say that nurse has got a legacy?'

'She has got a hundred pounds. Send for her, Agnes, while I show you the letter.'

He took a handful of letters from his pocket, and looked through them, while Agnes rang the bell. Returning to him, she noticed a printed letter among the rest, which lay open on the table. It was a 'prospectus', and the title of it was 'Palace Hotel Company of Venice (Limited)'. The two words, 'Palace' and 'Venice', instantly recalled her mind to the unwelcome visit of Lady Montbarry. 'What is that?' she asked, pointing to the title.

Henry suspended his search, and glanced at the prospectus. 'A really promising speculation,' he said. 'Large hotels always pay well, if they are well managed. I know the man who is appointed to be manager of this hotel when it is opened to the public; and I have such entire confidence in him that I have become one of the shareholders of the Company.'

The reply did not appear to satisfy Agnes. 'Why is the hotel called the "Palace Hotel"?' she enquired.

Henry looked at her, and at once penetrated her motive for asking the question. 'Yes,' he said, 'it is the palace that Montbarry hired at Venice; and it has been purchased by the Company to be changed into an hotel.'

Agnes turned away in silence, and took a chair at the farther end of the room. Henry had disappointed her. His income as a younger son stood in need, as she well knew, of all the additions that he could make to it by successful speculation. But she was unreasonable enough, nevertheless, to disapprove of his attempting to make money already out of the house in which his brother had died. Incapable of understanding this purely sentimental view of a plain matter of business, Henry returned to his papers, in some perplexity at the sudden change in the manner of Agnes towards him. Just as he found the letter of which he was in search, the nurse made her appearance. He glanced at Agnes, expecting that she would speak first. She never even looked up when the nurse came in. It was left to Henry to tell the old woman why the bell had summoned her to the drawing-room.

'Well, nurse,' he said, 'you have had a windfall of luck. You have had a legacy left you of a hundred pounds.'

The nurse showed no outward signs of exultation. She waited a little to get the announcement of the legacy well settled in her mind – and then she said quietly, 'Master Henry, who gives me that money, if you please?'

'My late brother, Lord Montbarry, gives it to you.' (Agnes instantly looked up, interested in the matter for the first time. Henry went on.) 'His will leaves legacies to the surviving old servants of the family. There is a letter from his lawyers, authorising you to apply to them for the money.'

In every class of society, gratitude is the rarest of all human virtues. In the nurse's class it is extremely rare. Her opinion of the man who had deceived and deserted her mistress remained the same opinion still, perfectly undisturbed by the passing circumstance of the legacy.

'I wonder who reminded my lord of the old servants?' she said. 'He would never have heart enough to remember them himself!'

Agnes suddenly interposed. Nature, always abhorring monotony, institutes reserves of temper as elements in the composition of the gentlest women living. Even Agnes could, on rare occasions, be angry. The nurse's view of Montbarry's character seemed to have provoked her beyond endurance.

'If you have any sense of shame in you,' she broke out, 'you ought to be ashamed of what you have just said! Your ingratitude disgusts me. I leave you to speak with her, Henry – *you* won't mind it!' With this significant intimation that he too had dropped out of his customary place in her good opinion, she left the room.

The nurse received the smart reproof administered to her with every appearance of feeling rather amused by it than not. When the door had closed, this female philosopher winked at Henry.

'There's a power of obstinacy in young women,' she remarked. 'Miss Agnes wouldn't give my lord up as a bad one, even when he jilted her. And now she's sweet on him after he's dead. Say a word against him, and she fires up as you see. All obstinacy! It will wear out with time. Stick to her, Master Henry – stick to her!'

'She doesn't seem to have offended you,' said Henry.

'She?' the nurse repeated in amazement – 'she offend me? I like her in her tantrums; it reminds me of her when she was a baby. Lord bless you! When I go to bid her good-night, she'll give me a big kiss, poor dear – and say, Nurse, I didn't mean it! About this money, Master Henry? If I was younger I should spend it in dress and jewellery. But I'm too old for that. What shall I do with my legacy when I have got it?'

'Put it out at interest,' Henry suggested. 'Get so much a year for it, you know.'

'How much shall I get?' the nurse asked.

'If you put your hundred pounds into the Funds, you will get between three and four pounds a year.'

The nurse shook her head. 'Three or four pounds a year? That won't do! I want more than that. Look here, Master Henry. I don't care about this bit of money – I never did like the man who has left it to me, though he was your brother. If I lost it all tomorrow, I shouldn't break my heart; I'm well enough off, as it is, for the rest of my days. They say you're a speculator. Put me in for a good thing, there's a dear! Neck-or-nothing – and that for the Funds!' She snapped her fingers to express her contempt for security of investment at three per cent.

Henry produced the prospectus of the Venetian Hotel Company. 'You're a funny old woman,' he said. 'There, you dashing speculator –

there is neck-or-nothing for you! You must keep it a secret from Miss Agnes, mind. I'm not at all sure that she would approve of my helping you to this investment.'

The nurse took out her spectacles. 'Six per cent. guaranteed,' she read; 'and the Directors have every reason to believe that ten per cent., or more, will be ultimately realised to the shareholders by the hotel.' 'Put me into that, Master Henry! And, wherever you go, for Heaven's sake recommend the hotel to your friends!'

So the nurse, following Henry's mercenary example, had her pecuniary interest, too, in the house in which Lord Montbarry had died.

Three days passed before Henry was able to visit Agnes again. In that time, the little cloud between them had entirely passed away. Agnes received him with even more than her customary kindness. She was in better spirits than usual. Her letter to Mrs Stephen Westwick had been answered by return of post; and her proposal had been joyfully accepted, with one modification. She was to visit the Westwicks for a month – and, if she really liked teaching the children, she was then to be governess, aunt, and cousin, all in one – and was only to go away in an event which her friends in Ireland persisted in contemplating, the event of her marriage.

'You see I was right,' she said to Henry.

He was still incredulous. 'Are you really going?' he asked.

'I am going next week.'

'When shall I see you again?'

'You know you are always welcome at your brother's house. You can see me when you like.' She held out her hand. 'Pardon me for leaving you – I am beginning to pack up already.'

Henry tried to kiss her at parting. She drew back directly.

'Why not? I am your cousin,' he said.

'I don't like it,' she answered.

Henry looked at her, and submitted. Her refusal to grant him his privilege as a cousin was a good sign – it was indirectly an act of encouragement to him in the character of her lover.

On the first day in the new week, Agnes left London on her way to Ireland. As the event proved, this was not destined to be the end of her journey. The way to Ireland was only the first stage on a roundabout road – the road that led to the palace at Venice.

THE THIRD PART

Chapter 13

In the spring of the year 1861, Agnes was established at the country seat of her two friends – now promoted (on the death of the first lord, without offspring) to be the new Lord and Lady Montbarry. The old nurse was not separated from her mistress. A place, suited to her time of life, had been found for her in the pleasant Irish household. She was perfectly happy in her new sphere; and she spent her first half-year's dividend from the Venice Hotel Company, with characteristic prodigality, in presents for the children.

Early in the year, also, the Directors of the life insurance offices submitted to circumstances, and paid the ten thousand pounds. Immediately afterwards, the widow of the first Lord Montbarry (otherwise, the dowager Lady Montbarry) left England, with Baron Rivar, for the United States. The Baron's object was announced, in the scientific columns of the newspapers, to be investigation into the present state of experimental chemistry in the great American republic. His sister informed enquiring friends that she accompanied him in the hope of finding consolation in change of scene after the bereavement that had fallen on her. Hearing this news from Henry Westwick (then paying a visit at his brother's house), Agnes was conscious of a certain sense of relief. 'With the Atlantic between us,' she said, 'surely I have done with that terrible woman now!'

Barely a week passed after those words had been spoken, before an event happened which reminded Agnes of 'the terrible woman' once more.

On that day, Henry's engagements had obliged him to return to London. He had ventured, on the morning of his departure, to press his suit once more on Agnes; and the children, as he had anticipated, proved to be innocent obstacles in the way of his success. On the other hand, he had privately secured a firm ally in his sister-in-law.

'Have a little patience,' the new Lady Montbarry had said, 'and leave me to turn the influence of the children in the right direction. If they can persuade her to listen to you – they shall!'

The two ladies had accompanied Henry, and some other guests who went away at the same time, to the railway station, and had just driven back to the house, when the servant announced that 'a person of the name of Rolland was waiting to see her ladyship'.

'Is it a woman?'

'Yes, my lady.'

Young Lady Montbarry turned to Agnes.

'This is the very person,' she said, 'whom your lawyer thought likely to help him, when he was trying to trace the lost courier.'

'You don't mean the English maid who was with Lady Montbarry at Venice?'

'My dear! Don't speak of Montbarry's horrid widow by the name which is my name now. Stephen and I have arranged to call her by her foreign title, before she was married. I am "Lady Montbarry", and she is "the Countess". In that way there will be no confusion – Yes, Mrs Rolland was in my service before she became the Countess's maid. She was a perfectly trustworthy person, with one defect that obliged me to send her away – a sullen temper which led to perpetual complaints of her in the servants' hall. Would you like to see her?'

Agnes accepted the proposal, in the faint hope of getting some information for the courier's wife. The complete defeat of every attempt to trace the lost man had been accepted as final by Mrs Ferrari. She had deliberately arrayed herself in widow's mourning; and was earning her livelihood in an employment which the unwearied kindness of Agnes had procured for her in London. The last chance of penetrating the mystery of Ferrari's disappearance seemed to rest now on what Ferrari's former fellow-servant might be able to tell. With highly-wrought expectations, Agnes followed her friend into the room in which Mrs Rolland was waiting.

A tall bony woman, in the autumn of life, with sunken eyes and iron-grey hair, rose stiffly from her chair, and saluted the ladies with stern submission as they opened the door. A person of unblemished character, evidently – but not without visible drawbacks. Big bushy eyebrows, an awfully deep and solemn voice, a harsh unbending manner, a complete absence in her figure of the undulating lines characteristic of the sex, presented Virtue in this excellent person under its least alluring aspect. Strangers, on a first introduction to her, were accustomed to wonder why she was not a man.

'Are you pretty well, Mrs Rolland?'

'I am as well as I can expect to be, my lady, at my time of life.'

'Is there anything I can do for you?'

'Your ladyship can do me a great favour, if you will please speak to my character while I was in your service. I am offered a place, to wait on an invalid lady who has lately come to live in this neighbourhood.'

'Ah, yes – I have heard of her. A Mrs Carbury, with a very pretty niece I am told. But, Mrs Rolland, you left my service some time ago. Mrs Carbury will surely expect you to refer to the last mistress by whom you were employed.'

A flash of virtuous indignation irradiated Mrs Rolland's sunken eyes. She coughed before she answered, as if her 'last mistress' stuck in her throat.

'I have explained to Mrs Carbury, my lady, that the person I last served – I really cannot give her her title in your ladyship's presence! – has left England for America. Mrs Carbury knows that I quitted the person of my own free will, and knows why, and approves of my conduct so far. A word from your ladyship will be amply sufficient to get me the situation.'

'Very well, Mrs Rolland, I have no objection to be your reference, under the circumstances. Mrs Carbury will find me at home to-morrow until two o'clock.'

'Mrs Carbury is not well enough to leave the house, my lady. Her niece, Miss Haldane, will call and make the enquiries, if your lady-ship has no objection.'

'I have not the least objection. The pretty niece carries her own welcome with her. Wait a minute, Mrs Rolland. This lady is Miss Lockwood – my husband's cousin, and my friend. She is anxious to speak to you about the courier who was in the late Lord Montbarry's service at Venice.'

Mrs Rolland's bushy eyebrows frowned in stern disapproval of the new topic of conversation. 'I regret to hear it, my lady,' was all she said.

'Perhaps you have not been informed of what happened after you left Venice?' Agnes ventured to add. 'Ferrari left the palace secretly; and he has never been heard of since.'

Mrs Rolland mysteriously closed her eyes – as if to exclude some vision of the lost courier which was of a nature to disturb a respect-able woman. 'Nothing that Mr Ferrari could do would surprise me,' she replied in her deepest bass tones.

'You speak rather harshly of him,' said Agnes.

Mrs Rolland suddenly opened her eyes again. 'I speak harshly of nobody without reason,' she said. 'Mr Ferrari behaved to me, Miss Lockwood, as no man living has ever behaved – before or since.'

'What did he do?'

Mrs Rolland answered, with a stony stare of horror: 'He took liberties with me.'

Young Lady Montbarry suddenly turned aside, and put her hand-kerchief over her mouth in convulsions of suppressed laughter.

Mrs Rolland went on, with a grim enjoyment of the bewilderment which her reply had produced in Agnes: 'And when I insisted on an apology, Miss, he had the audacity to say that the life at the palace was dull, and he didn't know how else to amuse himself!'

'I am afraid I have hardly made myself understood,' said Agnes. 'I am not speaking to you out of any interest in Ferrari. Are you aware that he is married?'

'I pity his wife,' said Mrs Rolland.

'She is naturally in great grief about him,' Agnes proceeded.

'She ought to thank God she is rid of him,' Mrs Rolland interposed.

Agnes still persisted. 'I have known Mrs Ferrari from her child-hood, and I am sincerely anxious to help her in this matter. Did you notice anything, while you were at Venice, that would account for her husband's extraordinary disappearance? On what sort of terms, for instance, did he live with his master and mistress?'

'On terms of familiarity with his mistress,' said Mrs Rolland, 'which were simply sickening to a respectable English servant. She used to encourage him to talk to her about all his affairs – how he got on with his wife, and how pressed he was for money, and suchlike – just as if they were equals. Contemptible – that's what I call it.'

'And his master?' Agnes continued. 'How did Ferrari get on with Lord Montbarry?'

'My lord used to live shut up with his studies and his sorrows,' Mrs Rolland answered, with a hard solemnity expressive of respect for his lordship's memory. Mr Ferrari got his money when it was due; and he cared for nothing else. "If I could afford it, I would leave the place too; but I can't afford it." Those were the last words he said to me, on the morning when I left the palace. I made no reply. After what had happened (on that other occasion) I was naturally not on speaking terms with Mr Ferrari.'

'Can you really tell me nothing which will throw any light on this matter?'

'Nothing,' said Mrs Rolland, with an undisguised relish of the disappointment that she was inflicting.

'There was another member of the family at Venice,' Agnes resumed, determined to sift the question to the bottom while she had the chance. 'There was Baron Rivar.'

Mrs Rolland lifted her large hands, covered with rusty black gloves, in mute protest against the introduction of Baron Rivar as a subject of enquiry. 'Are you aware, Miss,' she began, 'that I left my place in consequence of what I observed – ?'

Agnes stopped her there. 'I only wanted to ask,' she explained, 'if anything was said or done by Baron Rivar which might account for Ferrari's strange conduct.'

'Nothing that I know of,' said Mrs Rolland. 'The Baron and Mr Ferrari (if I may use such an expression) were "birds of a feather", so far as I could see – I mean, one was as unprincipled as the other. I am a just woman; and I will give you an example. Only the day before I left, I heard the Baron say (through the open door of his room while I was passing along the corridor), "Ferrari, I want a thousand pounds. What would you do for a thousand pounds?" And I heard Mr Ferrari answer, "Anything, sir, as long as I was not found out." And then they both burst out laughing. I heard no more than that. Judge for yourself, Miss.'

Agnes reflected for a moment. A thousand pounds was the sum that had been sent to Mrs Ferrari in the anonymous letter. Was that enclosure in any way connected, as a result, with the conversation between the Baron and Ferrari? It was useless to press any more enquiries on Mrs Rolland. She could give no further information which was of the slightest importance to the object in view. There was no alternative but to grant her dismissal. One more effort had been made to find a trace of the lost man, and once again the effort had failed.

They were a family party at the dinner-table that day. The only guest left in the house was a nephew of the new Lord Montbarry – the eldest son of his sister, Lady Barrville. Lady Montbarry could not resist telling the story of the first (and last) attack made on the virtue of Mrs Rolland, with a comically-exact imitation of Mrs Rolland's deep and dismal voice. Being asked by her husband what was the object which had brought that formidable person to the house, she naturally mentioned the expected visit of Miss Haldane. Arthur Barville, unusually silent and pre-occupied so far, suddenly struck into the conversation with a burst of enthusiasm. 'Miss Haldane is the most charming girl in all Ireland!' he said. 'I caught sight of her yesterday, over the wall of her garden, as I was riding by. What time is she coming tomorrow? Before two? I'll look into the drawing-room by accident – I am dying to be introduced to her!'

Agnes was amused by his enthusiasm. 'Are you in love with Miss Haldane already?' she asked.

Arthur answered gravely, 'It's no joking matter. I have been all day at the garden wall, waiting to see her again! It depends on Miss Haldane to make me the happiest or the wretchedest man living.'

'You foolish boy! How can you talk such nonsense?'

He was talking nonsense undoubtedly. But, if Agnes had only known it, he was doing something more than that. He was innocently leading her another stage nearer on the way to Venice.

Chapter 14

As the summer months advanced, the transformation of the Venetian palace into the modern hotel proceeded rapidly towards completion.

The outside of the building, with its fine Palladian front looking on the canal, was wisely left unaltered. Inside, as a matter of necessity, the rooms were almost rebuilt – so far at least as the size and the arrangement of them were concerned. The vast saloons were partitioned off into 'apartments' containing three or four rooms each. The broad corridors in the upper regions afforded spare space enough for rows of little bedchambers, devoted to servants and to travellers with limited means. Nothing was spared but the solid floors and the finely-carved ceilings. These last, in excellent preservation as to workmanship, merely required cleaning, and regilding here and there, to add greatly to the beauty and importance of the best rooms in the hotel. The only exception to the complete reorganisation of the interior was at one extremity of the edifice, on the first and second floors. Here there happened, in each case, to be rooms of such comparatively moderate size, and so attractively decorated, that the architect suggested leaving them as they were. It was afterwards discovered that these were no other than the apartments formerly occupied by Lord Montbarry (on the first floor), and by Baron Rivar (on the second). The room in which Montbarry had died was still fitted up as a bedroom, and was now distinguished as

Number Fourteen. The room above it, in which the Baron had slept, took its place on the hotel-register as Number Thirty-Eight. With the ornaments on the walls and ceilings cleaned and brightened up, and with the heavy old-fashioned beds, chairs, and tables replaced by bright, pretty, and luxurious modern furniture, these two promised to be at once the most attractive and the most comfortable bed-chambers in the hotel. As for the once-desolate and disused ground floor of the building, it was now transformed, by means of splendid dining-rooms, reception-rooms, billiard-rooms, and smoking-rooms, into a palace by itself. Even the dungeon-like vaults beneath, now lighted and ventilated on the most approved modern plan, had been turned as if by magic into kitchens, servants' offices, ice-rooms and wine cellars, worthy of the splendour of the grandest hotel in Italy, in the now bygone period of seventeen years since.

Passing from the lapse of the summer months at Venice, to the lapse of the summer months in Ireland, it is next to be recorded that Mrs Rolland obtained the situation of attendant on the invalid Mrs Carbury; and that the fair Miss Haldane, like a female Caesar, came, saw, and conquered, on her first day's visit to the new Lord Montbarry's house.

The ladies were as loud in her praises as Arthur Barville himself. Lord Montbarry declared that she was the only perfectly pretty woman he had ever seen who was really unconscious of her own attractions. The old nurse said she looked as if she had just stepped out of a picture, and wanted nothing but a gilt frame round her to make her complete. Miss Haldane, on her side, returned from her first visit to the Montbarrys charmed with her new acquaintances. Later on the same day, Arthur called with an offering of fruit and flowers for Mrs Carbury, and with instructions to ask if she was well enough to receive Lord and Lady Montbarry and Miss Lockwood on the morrow. In a week's time, the two households were on the friendliest terms. Mrs Carbury, confined to the sofa by a spinal malady, had been hitherto dependent on her niece for one of the few pleasures she could enjoy, the pleasure of having the best new novels read to her as they came out. Discovering this, Arthur volunteered to relieve Miss Haldane, at intervals, in the office of reader. He was clever at mechanical contrivances of all sorts, and he introduced improvements in Mrs Carbury's couch, and in the means of convey-ing her from the bedchamber to the drawing-room, which alleviated the poor lady's sufferings and brightened her gloomy life. With these claims on the gratitude of the aunt, aided by the personal advantages which he unquestionably possessed, Arthur advanced rapidly in the favour of the charming niece. She was, it is needless to say, perfectly well aware that he was in love with her, while he was himself modestly reticent on the subject – so far as words went. But she was not equally quick in penetrating the nature of her own feelings towards Arthur. Watching the two young people with keen powers of observation, necessarily concentrated on them by the complete seclusion of her life, the invalid lady discovered signs of roused sensibility in Miss Haldane, when Arthur was present, which had never yet shown themselves in her social relations with other admirers eager to pay their addresses to her. Having drawn her own conclusions in private, Mrs Carbury took the first favourable opportunity (in Arthur's interests) of putting them to the test.

'I don't know what I shall do,' she said one day, 'when Arthur goes away.'

Miss Haldane looked up quickly from her work. 'Surely he is not going to leave us!' she exclaimed.

'My dear! He has already stayed at his uncle's house a month longer than he intended. His father and mother naturally expect to see him at home again.'

Miss Haldane met this difficulty with a suggestion which could only have proceeded from a judgement already disturbed by the ravages of the tender passion. 'Why can't his father and mother go and see him at Lord Montbarry's?' she asked. 'Sir Theodore's place is only thirty miles away, and Lady Barville is Lord Montbarry's sister. They needn't stand on ceremony.'

'They may have other engagements,' Mrs Carbury remarked.

'My dear aunt, we don't know that! Suppose you ask Arthur?'

'Suppose you ask him?'

Miss Haldane bent her head again over her work. Suddenly as it was done, her aunt had seen her face – and her face betrayed her.

When Arthur came the next day, Mrs Carbury said a word to him in private, while her niece was in the garden. The last new novel lay neglected on the table. Arthur followed Miss Haldane into the garden. The next day he wrote home, enclosing in his letter a photograph of Miss Haldane. Before the end of the week, Sir Theodore and Lady Barville arrived at Lord Montbarry's, and formed their own judgement of the fidelity of the portrait. They had themselves married early in life – and, strange to say, they did not object on principle to the early marriages of other people. The question of age being thus disposed of, the course of true love had no other obstacles to encounter. Miss Haldane was an only child, and was possessed of an ample fortune. Arthur's career at the university had been creditable, but certainly not brilliant enough to present his withdrawal in the light of a disaster. As Sir Theodore's eldest son, his position was already made for him. He was two-and-twenty years of age; and the young lady was eighteen. There was really no producible reason for keeping the lovers waiting, and no excuse for deferring the wedding-day beyond the first week in September. In the interval, while the bride and bridegroom would be necessarily absent on the inevitable tour abroad, a sister of Mrs Carbury volunteered to stay with her during the temporary separation from her niece. On the conclusion of the honeymoon, the young couple were to return to Ireland, and were to establish themselves in Mrs Carbury's spacious and comfortable house.

These arrangements were decided upon early in the month of August. About the same date, the last alterations in the old palace at Venice were completed. The rooms were dried by steam; the cellars were stocked; the manager collected round him his army of skilled servants; and the new hotel was advertised all over Europe to open in October.

Chapter 15

[*Miss Agnes Lockwood to Mrs Ferrari*]

I promised to give you some account, dear Emily, of the marriage of Mr Arthur Barville and Miss Haldane. It took place ten days since. But I have had so many things to look after in the absence of the master and mistress of this house, that I am only able to write to you today.

The invitations to the wedding were limited to members of the families on either side, in consideration of the ill-health of Miss Haldane's aunt. On the side of the Montbarry family, there were present, besides Lord and Lady Montbarry, Sir Theodore and Lady Barville; Mrs Norbury (whom you may remember as his lordship's second sister); and Mr Francis Westwick, and Mr Henry Westwick. The three children and I attended the ceremony as bridesmaids. We were joined by two young ladies, cousins of the bride and very agreeable girls. Our dresses were white, trimmed with green in honour of Ireland; and we each had a handsome gold bracelet given to us as a present from the bridegroom. If you add to the persons whom I have already mentioned, the elder members of Mrs Carbury's family, and the old servants in both houses – privileged to drink the healths of the married pair at the lower end of the room – you will have the list of the company at the wedding-breakfast complete.

The weather was perfect, and the ceremony (with music) was beautifully performed. As for the bride, no words can describe how lovely she looked, or how well she went through it all. We were very merry at the breakfast, and the speeches went off on the whole quite well enough. The last speech, before the party broke up, was made by Mr Henry Westwick, and was the best of all. He offered a happy suggestion, at the end, which has produced a very unexpected change in my life here.

As well as I remember, he concluded in these words: 'On one point, we are all agreed – we are sorry that the parting hour is near, and we should be glad to meet again. Why should we not meet again? This is the autumn time of the year; we are most of us leaving home for the holidays. What do you say (if you have no engagements that will prevent it) to joining our young married friends before the close of their tour, and renewing the social success of this delightful breakfast by another festival in honour of the honeymoon? The bride and bridegroom are going to Germany and the Tyrol, on their way to Italy. I propose that we allow them a month to themselves, and that we arrange to meet them afterwards in the North of Italy – say at Venice.'

This proposal was received with great applause, which was changed into shouts of laughter by no less a person than my dear old nurse. The moment Mr Westwick pronounced the word 'Venice', she started up among the servants at the lower end of the room, and called out at the top of her voice, 'to our hotel, ladies and gentlemen! We get six per cent. on our money already; and if you will only crowd the place and call for the best of everything, it will be ten per cent in our pockets in no time. Ask Master Henry!'

Appealed to in this irresistible manner, Mr Westwick had no choice but to explain that he was concerned as a shareholder in a new Hotel Company at Venice, and that he had invested a small sum of money for the nurse (not very considerately, as I think) in the speculation. Hearing this, the company, by way of humouring the joke, drank a new toast: 'Success to the nurse's hotel, and a speedy rise in the dividend!'

When the conversation returned in due time to the more serious question of the proposed meeting at Venice, difficulties began to present themselves, caused of course by invitations for the autumn which many of the guests had already accepted. Only two members of Mrs Carbury's family were at liberty to keep the proposed appointment. On our side we were more at leisure to do as we pleased. Mr Henry Westwick decided to go to Venice in advance of the rest, to test the accommodation of the new hotel on the opening day. Mrs Norbury and Mr Francis Westwick volunteered to follow him; and, after some persuasion, Lord and Lady Montbarry consented to a species of compromise. His lordship could not conveniently spare time enough for the journey to Venice, but he and Lady Montbarry arranged to accompany Mrs Norbury and Mr Francis Westwick as far on their way to Italy as Paris. Five days since, they took their departure to meet their travelling companions in London; leaving me here in charge of the three dear children. They begged hard, of course, to be taken with papa and mamma. But it was thought better not to interrupt the progress of their education, and not to expose them (especially the two younger girls) to the fatigues of travelling.

I have had a charming letter from the bride, this morning, dated Cologne. You cannot think how artlessly and prettily she assures me of her happiness. Some people, as they say in Ireland, are born to good luck – and I think Arthur Barville is one of them.

When you next write, I hope to hear that you are in better health and spirits, and that you continue to like your employment. Believe me, sincerely your friend – A. L.

Agnes had just closed and directed her letter, when the eldest of her three pupils entered the room with the startling announcement that Lord Montbarry's travelling-servant had arrived from Paris! Alarmed by the idea that some misfortune had happened, she ran out to meet the man in the hall. Her face told him how seriously he had frightened her, before she could speak. 'There's nothing wrong, Miss,' he hastened to say. 'My lord and my lady are enjoying themselves at Paris. They only want you and the young ladies to be with them.' Saying these amazing words, he handed to Agnes a letter from Lady Montbarry.

DEAREST AGNES (she read), I am so charmed with the delightful change in my life – it is six years, remember, since I last travelled on the Continent – that I have exerted all my fascinations to persuade Lord Montbarry to go on to Venice. And, what is more to the purpose, I have actually succeeded! He has just gone to his room to write the necessary letters of excuse in time for the post to England. May you have as good a husband, my dear, when your time comes! In the meanwhile, the one thing wanting now to make my happiness complete, is to have you and the darling children with us. Montbarry is just as miserable without them as I am – though he doesn't confess it so freely. You will have no difficulties to trouble you. Louis will deliver these hurried lines, and will take care of you on the journey to Paris. Kiss the children for me a thousand times – and never mind their education for the present! Pack up instantly, my dear, and I will be fonder of you than ever. Your affectionate friend, ADELA MONTBARRY.

Agnes folded up the letter; and, feeling the need of composing herself, took refuge for a few minutes in her own room.

Her first natural sensations of surprise and excitement at the prospect of going to Venice were succeeded by impressions of a less agreeable kind. With the recovery of her customary composure came the unwelcome remembrance of the parting words spoken to her by Montbarry's widow: 'We shall meet again – here in England, or there in Venice where my husband died – and meet for the last time.'

It was an odd coincidence, to say the least of it, that the march of events should be unexpectedly taking Agnes to Venice, after those words had been spoken! Was the woman of the mysterious warnings and the wild black eyes still thousands of miles away in America? Or was the march of events taking her unexpectedly, too, on the journey to Venice? Agnes started out of her chair, ashamed of even the momentary concession to superstition which was implied by the mere presence of such questions as these in her mind.

She rang the bell, and sent for her little pupils, and announced their approaching departure to the household. The noisy delight of the children, the inspiriting effort of packing up in a hurry, roused all her energies. She dismissed her own absurd misgivings from consideration, with the contempt that they deserved. She worked as only women can work, when their hearts are in what they do. The travellers reached Dublin that day, in time for the boat to England. Two days later, they were with Lord and Lady Montbarry at Paris.

THE FOURTH PART

Chapter 16

It was only the twentieth of September, when Agnes and the children reached Paris. Mrs Norbury and her brother Francis had then already started on their journey to Italy – at least three weeks before the date at which the new hotel was to open for the reception of travellers.

The person answerable for this premature departure was Francis Westwick.

Like his younger brother Henry, he had increased his pecuniary resources by his own enterprise and ingenuity; with this difference, that his speculations were connected with the Arts. He had made money, in the first instance, by a weekly newspaper; and he had then invested his profits in a London theatre. This latter enterprise, admirably conducted, had been rewarded by the public with steady and liberal encouragement. Pondering over a new form of theatrical attraction for the coming winter season, Francis had determined to revive the languid public taste for the ballet by means of an entertainment of his own invention, combining dramatic interest with dancing. He was now, accordingly, in search of the best dancer (possessed of the indispensable personal attractions) who was to be found in the theatres of the Continent. Hearing from his foreign correspondents of two women who had made successful first appearances, one at Milan and one at Florence, he had arranged to visit those cities, and to judge of the merits of the dancers for himself, before he joined the bride and bridegroom. His widowed sister, having friends at Florence whom she was anxious to see, readily accompanied him. The Montbarrys remained at Paris, until it was time to present themselves at the family meeting in Venice. Henry found them still in the French capital, when he arrived from London on his way to the opening of the new hotel.

Against Lady Montbarry's advice, he took the opportunity of renewing his addresses to Agnes. He could hardly have chosen a more unpropitious time for pleading his cause with her. The gaieties of Paris (quite incomprehensibly to herself as well as to everyone about her) had a depressing effect on her spirits. She had no illness to complain of; she shared willingly in the ever-varying succession of amusements offered to strangers by the ingenuity of the liveliest people in the world – but nothing roused her: she remained persistently dull and weary through it all. In this frame of mind and body, she was in no humour to receive Henry's ill-timed addresses with favour, or even with patience: she plainly and positively refused to listen to him. 'Why do you remind me of what I have suffered?' she asked petulantly. 'Don't you see that it has left its mark on me for life?'

'I thought I knew something of women by this time,' Henry said, appealing privately to Lady Montbarry for consolation. 'But Agnes completely puzzles me. It is a year since Montbarry's death; and she remains as devoted to his memory as if he had died faithful to her – she still feels the loss of him, as none of us feel it!'

'She is the truest woman that ever breathed the breath of life,' Lady Montbarry answered. 'Remember that, and you will understand her. Can such a woman as Agnes give her love or refuse it, according to circumstances? Because the man was unworthy of her, was he less the man of her choice? The truest and best friend to him (little as he deserved it) in his lifetime, she naturally remains the truest and best friend to his memory now. If you really love her, wait; and trust to your two best friends – to time and to me. There is my advice; let your own experience decide whether it is not the best advice that I can offer. Resume your journey to Venice tomorrow; and when you take leave of Agnes, speak to her as cordially as if nothing had happened.'

Henry wisely followed this advice. Thoroughly understanding him, Agnes made the leave-taking friendly and pleasant on her side. When he stopped at the door for a last look at her, she hurriedly turned her head so that her face was hidden from him. Was that a good sign? Lady Montbarry, accompanying Henry down the stairs, said, 'Yes, decidedly! Write when you get to Venice. We shall wait here to receive letters from Arthur and his wife, and we shall time our departure for Italy accordingly.'

A week passed, and no letter came from Henry. Some days later, a telegram was received from him. It was despatched from Milan, instead of from Venice; and it brought this strange message: I HAVE LEFT THE HOTEL. WILL RETURN ON THE ARRIVAL OF ARTHUR AND HIS WIFE. ADDRESS MEANWHILE, ALBERGO REALE, MILAN.

Preferring Venice before all other cities of Europe, and having arranged to remain there until the family meeting took place, what unexpected event had led Henry to alter his plans? And why did he state the bare fact, without adding a word of explanation? Let the narrative follow him – and find the answer to those questions at Venice.

Chapter 17

The Palace Hotel, appealing for encouragement mainly to English and American travellers, celebrated the opening of its doors, as a matter of course, by the giving of a grand banquet, and the delivery of a long succession of speeches.

Delayed on his journey, Henry Westwick only reached Venice in time to join the guests over their coffee and cigars. Observing the splendour of the reception rooms, and taking note especially of the artful mixture of comfort and luxury in the bedchambers, he began to share the old nurse's view of the future, and to contemplate seriously the coming dividend of ten per cent. The hotel was beginning well, at all events. So much interest in the enterprise had been aroused, at home and abroad, by profuse advertising, that the whole accommodation of the building had been secured by travellers of all nations for the opening night. Henry only obtained one of the small rooms on the upper floor, by a lucky accident – the absence of the gentleman who had written to engage it. He was quite satisfied, and was on his way to bed, when another accident altered his prospects for the night, and moved him into another and a better room.

Ascending on his way to the higher regions as far as the first floor of the hotel, Henry's attention was attracted by an angry voice protesting, in a strong New England accent, against one of the greatest hardships that can be inflicted on a citizen of the United States – the hardship of sending him to bed without gas in his room.

The Americans are not only the most hospitable people to be found on the face of the earth – they are (under certain conditions) the most patient and good-tempered people as well. But they are human; and the limit of American endurance is found in the obsolete institution of a bedroom candle. The American traveller, in the present case, declined to believe that his bedroom was in a complete finished state without a gas-burner. The manager pointed to the fine antique decorations (renewed and regilt) on the walls and the ceiling, and explained that the emanations of burning gas-light would certainly spoil them in the course of a few months. To this the traveller replied that it was possible, but that he did not understand decorations. A bedroom with gas in it was what he was used to, was what he wanted, and was what he was determined to have. The compliant manager volunteered to ask some other gentleman, housed on the inferior upper storey (which was lit throughout with gas), to change rooms. Hearing this, and being quite willing to exchange a small bedchamber for a large one, Henry volunteered to be the other gentleman. The excellent American shook hands with him on the spot. 'You are a cultured person, sir,' he said; 'and *you* will no doubt understand the decorations.'

Henry looked at the number of the room on the door as he opened it. The number was Fourteen.

Tired and sleepy, he naturally anticipated a good night's rest. In the thoroughly healthy state of his nervous system, he slept as well in a bed abroad as in a bed at home. Without the slightest assignable reason, however, his just expectations were disappointed. The luxurious bed, the well-ventilated room, the delicious tranquillity of Venice by night, all were in favour of his sleeping well. He never slept at all. An indescribable sense of depression and discomfort kept him waking through darkness and daylight alike. He went down to the coffee-room as soon as the hotel was astir, and ordered some breakfast. Another unaccountable change in himself appeared with the appearance of the meal. He was absolutely without appetite. An excellent omelette, and cutlets cooked to perfection, he sent away untasted – he, whose appetite never failed him, whose digestion was still equal to any demands on it!

The day was bright and fine. He sent for a gondola, and was rowed to the Lido.

Out on the airy Lagoon, he felt like a new man. He had not left the hotel ten minutes before he was fast asleep in the gondola. Waking, on reaching the landing-place, he crossed the Lido, and enjoyed a morning's swim in the Adriatic. There was only a poor restaurant on the island, in those days; but his appetite was now ready for anything; he ate whatever was offered to him, like a famished man.

He could hardly believe, when he reflected on it, that he had sent away untasted his excellent breakfast at the hotel.

Returning to Venice, he spent the rest of the day in the picture-galleries and the churches. Towards six o'clock his gondola took him back, with another fine appetite, to meet some travelling acquaintances with whom he had engaged to dine at the table d'hote.

The dinner was deservedly rewarded with the highest approval by every guest in the hotel but one. To Henry's astonishment, the appetite with which he had entered the house mysteriously and completely left him when he sat down to table. He could drink some wine, but he could literally eat nothing. 'What in the world is the matter with you?' his travelling acquaintances asked. He could honestly answer, 'I know no more than you do.'

When night came, he gave his comfortable and beautiful bedroom another trial. The result of the second experiment was a repetition of the result of the first. Again he felt the all-pervading sense of depression and discomfort. Again he passed a sleepless night. And once more, when he tried to eat his breakfast, his appetite completely failed him!

This personal experience of the new hotel was too extraordinary to be passed over in silence. Henry mentioned it to his friends in the public room, in the hearing of the manager. The manager, naturally zealous in defence of the hotel, was a little hurt at the implied reflection cast on Number Fourteen. He invited the travellers present to judge for themselves whether Mr Westwick's bedroom was to blame for Mr Westwick's sleepless nights; and he especially appealed to a grey-headed gentleman, a guest at the breakfast-table of an English traveller, to take the lead in the investigation. 'This is Doctor Bruno, our first physician in Venice,' he explained. 'I appeal to him to say if there are any unhealthy influences in Mr Westwick's room.'

Introduced to Number Fourteen, the doctor looked round him with a certain appearance of interest which was noticed by everyone present. 'The last time I was in this room,' he said, 'was on a melancholy occasion. It was before the palace was changed into an hotel. I was in professional attendance on an English nobleman who died here.' One of the persons present enquired the name of the nobleman. Doctor Bruno answered (without the slightest suspicion that he was speaking before a brother of the dead man), 'Lord Montbarry.'

Henry quietly left the room, without saying a word to anybody.

He was not, in any sense of the term, a superstitious man. But he felt, nevertheless, an insurmountable reluctance to remaining in the hotel. He decided on leaving Venice. To ask for another room would be, as he could plainly see, an offence in the eyes of the manager. To remove to another hotel, would be to openly abandon an establishment in the success of which he had a pecuniary interest. Leaving a note for Arthur Barville, on his arrival in Venice, in which he merely mentioned that he had gone to look at the Italian lakes, and that a line addressed to his hotel at Milan would bring him back again, he took the afternoon train to Padua – and dined with his usual appetite, and slept as well as ever that night.

The next day, a gentleman and his wife (perfect strangers to the Montbarry family), returning to England by way of Venice, arrived at the hotel and occupied Number Fourteen.

Still mindful of the slur that had been cast on one of his best bedchambers, the manager took occasion to ask the travellers the next morning how they liked their room. They left him to judge for himself how well they were satisfied, by remaining a day longer in Venice than they had originally planned to do, solely for the purpose of enjoying the excellent accommodation offered to them by the new hotel. 'We have met with nothing like it in Italy,' they said; 'you may rely on our recommending you to all our friends.'

On the day when Number Fourteen was again vacant, an English lady travelling alone with her maid arrived at the hotel, saw the room, and at once engaged it.

The lady was Mrs Norbury. She had left Francis Westwick at Milan, occupied in negotiating for the appearance at his theatre of the new dancer at the Scala. Not having heard to the contrary, Mrs Norbury supposed that Arthur Barville and his wife had already arrived at Venice. She was more interested in meeting the young married couple than in awaiting the result of the hard bargaining which delayed the engagement of the new dancer; and she volunteered to make her brother's apologies, if his theatrical business caused him to be late in keeping his appointment at the honeymoon festival.

Mrs Norbury's experience of Number Fourteen differed entirely from her brother Henry's experience of the room.

Failing asleep as readily as usual, her repose was disturbed by a succession of frightful dreams; the central figure in every one of them being the figure of her dead brother, the first Lord Montbarry. She saw him starving in a loathsome prison; she saw him pursued by assassins, and dying under their knives; she saw him drowning in immeasurable depths of dark water; she saw him in a bed on fire, burning to death in the flames; she saw him tempted by a shadowy creature to drink, and dying of the poisonous draught. The reiterated horror of these dreams had such an effect on her that she rose with the dawn of day, afraid to trust herself again in bed. In the old times, she had been noted in the family as the one member of it who lived on affectionate terms with Montbarry. His other sister and his brothers were constantly quarrelling with him. Even his mother owned that her eldest son was of all her children the child whom she least liked. Sensible and resolute woman as she was, Mrs Norbury shuddered with terror as she sat at the window of her room, watching the sunrise, and thinking of her dreams.

She made the first excuse that occurred to her, when her maid came in at the usual hour, and noticed how ill she looked. The woman was of so superstitious a temperament that it would have been in the last degree indiscreet to trust her with the truth. Mrs Norbury merely remarked that she had not found the bed quite to her liking, on account of the large size of it. She was accustomed at home, as her maid knew, to sleep in a small bed. Informed of this objection later in the day, the manager regretted that he could only offer to the lady the choice of one other bedchamber, numbered Thirty-eight, and situated immediately over the bedchamber which she desired to leave. Mrs Norbury accepted the proposed change of quarters. She was now about to pass her second night in the room occupied in the old days of the palace by Baron Rivar.

Once more, she fell asleep as usual. And, once more, the frightful dreams of the first night terrified her, following each other in the same succession. This time her nerves, already shaken, were not equal to the renewed torture of terror inflicted on them. She threw on her dressing-gown, and rushed out of her room in the middle of the night. The porter, alarmed by the banging of the door, met her hurrying headlong down the stairs, in search of the first human being she could find to keep her company. Considerably surprised at this last new manifestation of the famous 'English eccentricity', the man looked at the hotel register, and led the lady upstairs again to the room occupied by her maid. The maid was not asleep, and, more wonderful still, was not even undressed. She received her mistress quietly. When they were alone, and when Mrs Norbury had, as a matter of necessity, taken her attendant into her confidence, the woman made a very strange reply.

'I have been asking about the hotel, at the servants' supper to-night,' she said. 'The valet of one of the gentlemen staying here has heard that the late Lord Montbarry was the last person who lived in the palace, before it was made into an hotel. The room he died in, ma'am, was the room you slept in last night. Your room tonight is the room just above it. I said nothing for fear of frightening you. For my own part, I have passed the night as you see, keeping my light on, and reading my Bible. In my opinion, no member of your family can hope to be happy or comfortable in this house.'

'What do you mean?'

'Please to let me explain myself, ma'am. When Mr Henry West-wick was here (I have this from the valet, too) he occupied the room his brother died in (without knowing it), like you. For two nights he never closed his eyes. Without any reason for it (the valet heard him tell the gentlemen in the coffee-room) he could not sleep; he felt so low and so wretched in himself. And what is more, when daytime came, he couldn't even eat while he was under this roof. You may laugh at me, ma'am – but even a servant may draw her own conclusions. It's my conclusion that something happened to my lord, which we none of us know about, when he died in this house. His ghost walks in torment until he can tell it – and the living persons related to him are the persons who feel he is near them. Those persons may yet see him in the time to come. Don't, pray don't stay any longer in this dreadful place! I wouldn't stay another night here myself – no, not for anything that could be offered me!'

Mrs Norbury at once set her servant's mind at ease on this last point.

'I don't think about it as you do,' she said gravely. 'But I should like to speak to my brother of what has happened. We will go back to Milan.'

Some hours necessarily elapsed before they could leave the hotel, by the first train in the forenoon.

In that interval, Mrs Norbury's maid found an opportunity of confidentially informing the valet of what had passed between her mistress and herself. The valet had other friends to whom he related the circumstances in his turn. In due course of time, the narrative, passing from mouth to mouth, reached the ears of the manager. He instantly saw that the credit of the hotel was in danger, unless something was done to retrieve the character of the room numbered Fourteen. English travellers, well acquainted with the peerage of their native country, informed him that Henry Westwick and Mrs

Norbury were by no means the only members of the Montbarry family. Curiosity might bring more of them to the hotel, after hearing what had happened. The manager's ingenuity easily hit on the obvious means of misleading them, in this case. The numbers of all the rooms were enamelled in blue, on white china plates, screwed to the doors. He ordered a new plate to be prepared, bearing the number, '13 A'; and he kept the room empty, after its tenant for the time being had gone away, until the plate was ready. He then renumbered the room; placing the removed Number Fourteen on the door of his own room (on the second floor), which, not being to let, had not previously been numbered at all. By this device, Number Fourteen disappeared at once and for ever from the books of the hotel, as the number of a bedroom to let.

Having warned the servants to beware of gossiping with travellers on the subject of the changed numbers, under penalty of being dismissed, the manager composed his mind with the reflection that he had done his duty to his employers. 'Now,' he thought to himself, with an excusable sense of triumph, 'let the whole family come here if they like! The hotel is a match for them.'

Chapter 18

Before the end of the week, the manager found himself in relations with 'the family' once more. A telegram from Milan announced that Mr Francis Westwick would arrive in Venice on the next day; and would be obliged if Number Fourteen, on the first floor, could be reserved for him, in the event of its being vacant at the time.

The manager paused to consider, before he issued his directions.

The re-numbered room had been last let to a French gentleman. It would be occupied on the day of Mr Francis Westwick's arrival, but it would be empty again on the day after. Would it be well to reserve the room for the special occupation of Mr Francis? And when he had passed the night unsuspiciously and comfortably in 'No. 13A', to ask him in the presence of witnesses how he liked his bedchamber? In this case, if the reputation of the room happened to be called in question again, the answer would vindicate it, on the evidence of a member of the very family which had first given Number Fourteen a bad name. After a little reflection, the manager decided on trying the experiment, and directed that '13A' should be reserved accordingly.

On the next day, Francis Westwick arrived in excellent spirits.

He had signed agreements with the most popular dancer in Italy; he had transferred the charge of Mrs Norbury to his brother Henry, who had joined him in Milan; and he was now at full liberty to amuse himself by testing in every possible way the extraordinary influence exercised over his relatives by the new hotel. When his brother and sister first told him what their experience had been, he instantly declared that he would go to Venice in the interest of his theatre. The circumstances related to him contained invaluable hints for a ghost-drama. The title occurred to him in the railway: 'The Haunted Hotel'. Post that in red letters six feet high, on a black ground, all over London – and trust the excitable public to crowd into the theatre!

Received with the politest attention by the manager, Francis met with a disappointment on entering the hotel. 'Some mistake, sir. No such room on the first floor as Number Fourteen. The room bearing that number is on the second floor, and has been occupied by me, from the day when the hotel opened. Perhaps you meant Number 13a, on the first floor? It will be at your service tomorrow – a charming room. In the meantime, we will do the best we can for you, tonight.'

A man who is the successful manager of a theatre is probably the last man in the civilised universe who is capable of being impressed with favourable opinions of his fellow-creatures. Francis privately set the manager down as a humbug, and the story about the numbering of the rooms as a lie.

On the day of his arrival, he dined by himself in the restaurant, before the hour of the table d'hote, for the express purpose of questioning the waiter, without being overheard by anybody. The answer led him to the conclusion that '13A' occupied the situation in the hotel which had been described by his brother and sister as the situation of '14'. He asked next for the Visitors' List; and found that the French gentleman who then occupied '13A', was the proprietor of a theatre in Paris, personally well known to him. Was the gentleman then in the hotel? He had gone out, but would certainly return for the table d'hote. When the public dinner was over, Francis entered the room, and was welcomed by his Parisian colleague, literally, with open arms. 'Come and have a cigar in my room,' said the friendly Frenchman. 'I want to hear whether you have really engaged that woman at Milan or not.' In this easy way, Francis found his opportunity of comparing the interior of the room with the description which he had heard of it at Milan.

Arriving at the door, the Frenchman bethought himself of his travelling-companion. 'My scene-painter is here with me,' he said, 'on the look-out for materials. An excellent fellow, who will take it as a kindness if we ask him to join us. I'll tell the porter to send him up when he comes in.' He handed the key of his room to Francis. 'I will be back in a minute. It's at the end of the corridor – 13A.'

Francis entered the room alone. There were the decorations on the walls and the ceiling, exactly as they had been described to him! He had just time to perceive this at a glance, before his attention was diverted to himself and his own sensations, by a grotesquely disagreeable occurrence which took him completely by surprise.

He became conscious of a mysteriously offensive odour in the room, entirely new in his experience of revolting smells. It was composed (if such a thing could be) of two mingling exhalations, which were separately-discoverable exhalations nevertheless. This strange blending of odours consisted of something faintly and unpleasantly aromatic, mixed with another underlying smell, so unutterably sickening that he threw open the window, and put his head out into the fresh air, unable to endure the horribly infected atmosphere for a moment longer.

The French proprietor joined his English friend, with his cigar already lit. He started back in dismay at a sight terrible to his countrymen in general – the sight of an open window. 'You English people are perfectly mad on the subject of fresh air!' he exclaimed. 'We shall catch our deaths of cold.'

Francis turned, and looked at him in astonishment. 'Are you really not aware of the smell there is in the room?' he asked.

'Smell!' repeated his brother-manager. 'I smell my own good cigar. Try one yourself. And for Heaven's sake shut the window!'

Francis declined the cigar by a sign. 'Forgive me,' he said. 'I will leave you to close the window. I feel faint and giddy – I had better go out.' He put his handkerchief over his nose and mouth, and crossed the room to the door.

The Frenchman followed the movements of Francis, in such a state of bewilderment that he actually forgot to seize the opportunity of shutting out the fresh air. 'Is it so nasty as that?' he asked, with a broad stare of amazement.

'Horrible!' Francis muttered behind his handkerchief. 'I never smelt anything like it in my life!'

There was a knock at the door. The scene-painter appeared. His employer instantly asked him if he smelt anything.

'I smell your cigar. Delicious! Give me one directly!'

'Wait a minute. Besides my cigar, do you smell anything else – vile, abominable, overpowering, indescribable, never-never-never-smelt before?'

The scene-painter appeared to be puzzled by the vehement energy of the language addressed to him. 'The room is as fresh and sweet as a room can be,' he answered. As he spoke, he looked back with astonishment at Francis Westwick, standing outside in the corridor, and eyeing the interior of the bedchamber with an expression of undisguised disgust.

The Parisian director approached his English colleague, and looked at him with grave and anxious scrutiny.

'You see, my friend, here are two of us, with as good noses as yours, who smell nothing. If you want evidence from more noses, look there!' He pointed to two little English girls, at play in the corridor. 'The door of my room is wide open – and you know how fast a smell can travel. Now listen, while I appeal to these innocent noses, in the language of their own dismal island. My little loves, do you sniff a nasty smell here – ha?' The children burst out laughing, and answered emphatically, 'No.' 'My good Westwick,' the Frenchman resumed, in his own language, 'the conclusion is surely plain? There is something wrong, very wrong, with your own nose. I recommend you to see a medical man.'

Having given that advice, he returned to his room, and shut out the horrid fresh air with a loud exclamation of relief. Francis left the hotel, by the lanes that led to the Square of St Mark. The night-breeze soon revived him. He was able to light a cigar, and to think quietly over what had happened.

Chapter 19

Avoiding the crowd under the colonnades, Francis walked slowly up and down the noble open space of the square, bathed in the light of the rising moon.

Without being aware of it himself, he was a thorough materialist. The strange effect produced on him by the room – following on the other strange effects produced on the other relatives of his dead brother – exercised no perplexing influence over the mind of this sensible man. 'Perhaps,' he reflected, 'my temperament is more imaginative than I supposed it to be – and this is a trick played on me by my own fancy? Or, perhaps, my friend is right; something is physically amiss with me? I don't feel ill, certainly. But that is no safe criterion sometimes. I am not going to sleep in that abominable room tonight – I can well wait till tomorrow to decide whether I shall speak to a doctor or not. In the meantime, the hotel doesn't seem likely to supply me with the subject of a piece. A terrible smell from an invisible ghost is a perfectly new idea. But it has one drawback. If I realise it on the stage, I shall drive the audience out of the theatre.'

As his strong common sense arrived at this facetious conclusion, he became aware of a lady, dressed entirely in black, who was observing him with marked attention. 'Am I right in supposing you to be Mr Francis Westwick?' the lady asked, at the moment when he looked at her.

'That is my name, madam. May I enquire to whom I have the honour of speaking?'

'We have only met once,' she answered a little evasively, 'when your late brother introduced me to the members of his family. I wonder if you have quite forgotten my big black eyes and my hideous complexion?' She lifted her veil as she spoke, and turned so that the moonlight rested on her face.

Francis recognised at a glance the woman of all others whom he most cordially disliked – the widow of his dead brother, the first Lord Montbarry. He frowned as he looked at her. His experience on the stage, gathered at innumerable rehearsals with actresses who had sorely tried his temper, had accustomed him to speak roughly to women who were distasteful to him. 'I remember you,' he said. 'I thought you were in America!'

She took no notice of his ungracious tone and manner; she simply stopped him when he lifted his hat, and turned to leave her.

'Let me walk with you for a few minutes,' she quietly replied. 'I have something to say to you.'

He showed her his cigar. 'I am smoking,' he said.

'I don't mind smoking.'

After that, there was nothing to be done (short of downright brutality) but to yield. He did it with the worst possible grace. 'Well?' he resumed. 'What do you want of me?'

'You shall hear directly, Mr Westwick. Let me first tell you what my position is. I am alone in the world. To the loss of my husband has now been added another bereavement, the loss of my companion in America, my brother – Baron Rivar.'

The reputation of the Baron, and the doubt which scandal had thrown on his assumed relationship to the Countess, were well known to Francis. 'Shot in a gambling-saloon?' he asked brutally.

'The question is a perfectly natural one on your part,' she said, with the impenetrably ironical manner which she could assume on certain occasions. 'As a native of horse-racing England, you belong to a nation of gamblers. My brother died no extraordinary death, Mr Westwick. He sank, with many other unfortunate people, under a fever prevalent in a Western city which we happened to visit. The calamity of his loss made the United States unendurable to me. I left by the first steamer that sailed from New York – a French vessel which brought me to Havre. I continued my lonely journey to the South of France. And then I went on to Venice.'

'What does all this matter to me?' Francis thought to himself. She paused, evidently expecting him to say something. 'So you have come to Venice?' he said carelessly. 'Why?'

'Because I couldn't help it,' she answered.

Francis looked at her with cynical curiosity. 'That sounds odd,' he remarked. 'Why couldn't you help it?'

'Women are accustomed to act on impulse,' she explained. 'Suppose we say that an impulse has directed my journey? And yet, this is the last place in the world that I wish to find myself in. Associations that I detest are connected with it in my mind. If I had a will of my own, I would never see it again. I hate Venice. As you see, however, I am here. When did you meet with such an unreasonable woman before? Never, I am sure!' She stopped, eyed him for a moment, and suddenly altered her tone. 'When is Miss Agnes Lockwood expected to be in Venice?' she asked.

It was not easy to throw Francis off his balance, but that extraordinary question did it. 'How the devil did you know that Miss Lockwood was coming to Venice?' he exclaimed.

She laughed – a bitter mocking laugh. 'Say, I guessed it!'

Something in her tone, or perhaps something in the audacious defiance of her eyes as they rested on him, roused the quick temper that was in Francis Warwick. 'Lady Montbarry – !' he began.

'Stop there!' she interposed. 'Your brother Stephen's wife calls herself Lady Montbarry now. I share my title with no woman. Call me by my name before I committed the fatal mistake of marrying your brother. Address me, if you please, as Countess Narona.'

'Countess Narona,' Francis resumed, 'if your object in claiming my acquaintance is to mystify me, you have come to the wrong man. Speak plainly, or permit me to wish you good-evening.'

'If your object is to keep Miss Lockwood's arrival in Venice a secret,' she retorted, 'speak plainly, Mr Westwick, on *your* side, and say so.'

Her intention was evidently to irritate him; and she succeeded. 'Nonsense!' he broke out petulantly. 'My brother's travelling arrangements are secrets to nobody. He brings Miss Lockwood here, with Lady Montbarry and the children. As you seem so well informed, perhaps you know why she is coming to Venice?'

The Countess had suddenly become grave and thoughtful. She made no reply. The two strangely associated companions, having reached one extremity of the square, were now standing before the church of St Mark. The moonlight was bright enough to show the architecture of the grand cathedral in its wonderful variety of detail. Even the pigeons of St Mark were visible, in dark closely-packed rows, roosting in the archways of the great entrance doors.

'I never saw the old church look so beautiful by moonlight,' the Countess said quietly; speaking, not to Francis, but to herself. 'Good-bye, St Mark's by moonlight! I shall not see you again.'

She turned away from the church, and saw Francis listening to her with wondering looks. 'No,' she resumed, placidly picking up the lost thread of the conversation, 'I don't know why Miss Lockwood is coming here, I only know that we are to meet in Venice.'

'By previous appointment?'

'By Destiny,' she answered, with her head on her breast, and her eyes on the ground. Francis burst out laughing. 'Or, if you like it better,' she instantly resumed, 'by what fools call Chance.' Francis answered easily, out of the depths of his strong common sense. 'Chance seems to be taking a queer way of bringing the meeting about,' he said. 'We have all arranged to meet at the Palace Hotel. How is it that your name is not on the Visitors' List? Destiny ought to have brought you to the Palace Hotel too.'

She abruptly pulled down her veil. 'Destiny may do that yet!' she said. 'The Palace Hotel?' she repeated, speaking once more to herself. 'The old hell, transformed into the new purgatory. The place itself! Jesu Maria! The place itself!' She paused and laid her hand on her companion's arm. 'Perhaps Miss Lockwood is not going there with the rest of you?' she burst out with sudden eagerness. 'Are you positively sure she will be at the hotel?'

'Positively! Haven't I told you that Miss Lockwood travels with Lord and Lady Montbarry? And don't you know that she is a member of the family? You will have to move, Countess, to our hotel.'

She was perfectly impenetrable to the bantering tone in which he spoke. 'Yes,' she said faintly, 'I shall have to move to your hotel.' Her hand was still on his arm – he could feel her shivering from head to foot while she spoke. Heartily as he disliked and distrusted her, the common instinct of humanity obliged him to ask if she felt cold.

'Yes,' she said. 'Cold and faint.'

'Cold and faint, Countess, on such a night as this?'

'The night has nothing to do with it, Mr Westwick. How do you suppose the criminal feels on the scaffold, while the hangman is putting the rope around his neck? Cold and faint, too, I should think. Excuse my grim fancy. You see, Destiny has got the rope round my neck – and *I* feel it.'

She looked about her. They were at that moment close to the famous cafe known as 'Florian's'. 'Take me in there,' she said; 'I must have something to revive me. You had better not hesitate. You are interested in reviving me. I have not said what I wanted to say to you yet. It's business, and it's connected with your theatre.'

Wondering inwardly what she could possibly want with his theatre, Francis reluctantly yielded to the necessities of the situation, and took her into the cafe. He found a quiet corner in which they could take their places without attracting notice. 'What will you have?' he enquired resignedly. She gave her own orders to the waiter, without troubling him to speak for her.

'Maraschino. And a pot of tea.'

The waiter stared; Francis stared. The tea was a novelty (in connection with maraschino) to both of them. Careless whether she surprised them or not, she instructed the waiter, when her directions had been complied with, to pour a large wineglassfull of the liqueur into a tumbler, and to fill it up from the teapot. 'I can't do it for myself,' she remarked, 'my hand trembles so.' She drank the strange mixture eagerly, hot as it was. 'Maraschino punch – will you taste some of it?' she said. 'I inherit the discovery of this drink. When your English Queen Caroline was on the Continent, my mother was attached to her Court. That much-injured Royal Person invented, in her happier hours, maraschino punch. Fondly attached to her gracious mistress, my mother shared her tastes. And I, in my turn, learnt from my mother. Now,

Mr Westwick, suppose I tell you what my business is. You are manager of a theatre. Do you want a new play?'

'I always want a new play – provided it's a good one.'

'And you pay, if it's a good one?'

'I pay liberally – in my own interests.'

'If *I* write the play, will you read it?'

Francis hesitated. 'What has put writing a play into your head?' he asked.

'Mere accident,' she answered. 'I had once occasion to tell my late brother of a visit which I paid to Miss Lockwood, when I was last in England. He took no interest in what happened at the interview, but something struck him in my way of relating it. He said, "You describe what passed between you and the lady with the point and contrast of good stage dialogue. You have the dramatic instinct – try if you can write a play. You might make money." That put it into my head.'

Those last words seemed to startle Francis. 'Surely you don't want money!' he exclaimed.

'I always want money. My tastes are expensive. I have nothing but my poor little four hundred a year – and the wreck that is left of the other money: about two hundred pounds in circular notes – no more.'

Francis knew that she was referring to the ten thousand pounds paid by the insurance offices. 'All those thousands gone already!' he exclaimed.

She blew a little puff of air over her fingers. 'Gone like that!' she answered coolly.

'Baron Rivar?'

She looked at him with a flash of anger in her hard black eyes.

'My affairs are my own secret, Mr Westwick. I have made you a proposal – and you have not answered me yet. Don't say No, without thinking first. Remember what a life mine has been. I have seen more of the world than most people, playwrights included. I have had strange adventures; I have heard remarkable stories; I have observed; I have remembered. Are there no materials, here in my head, for writing a play – if the opportunity is granted to me?' She waited a moment, and suddenly repeated her strange question about Agnes.

'When is Miss Lockwood expected to be in Venice?'

'What has that to do with your new play, Countess?'

The Countess appeared to feel some difficulty in giving that question its fit reply. She mixed another tumbler full of maraschino punch, and drank one good half of it before she spoke again.

'It has everything to do with my new play,' was all she said. 'Answer me.' Francis answered her.

'Miss Lockwood may be here in a week. Or, for all I know to the contrary, sooner than that.'

'Very well. If I am a living woman and a free woman in a week's time – or if I am in possession of my senses in a week's time (don't interrupt me; I know what I am talking about) – I shall have a sketch or outline of my play ready, as a specimen of what I can do. Once again, will you read it?'

'I will certainly read it. But, Countess, I don't understand – '

She held up her hand for silence, and finished the second tumbler of maraschino punch.

'I am a living enigma – and you want to know the right reading of me,' she said. 'Here is the reading, as your English phrase goes, in a nutshell. There is a foolish idea in the minds of many persons that the natives of the warm climates are imaginative people. There never was a greater mistake. You will find no such unimaginative people anywhere as you find in Italy, Spain, Greece, and the other Southern countries. To anything fanciful, to anything spiritual, their minds are deaf and blind by nature. Now and then, in the course of centuries, a great genius springs up among them; and he is the exception which proves the rule. Now see! I, though I am no genius – I am, in my little way (as I suppose), an exception too. To my sorrow, I have some of that imagination which is so common among the English and the Germans – so rare among the Italians, the Spaniards, and the rest of them! And what is the result? I think it has become a disease in me. I am filled with presentiments which make this wicked life of mine one long terror to me. It doesn't matter, just now, what they are. Enough that they absolutely govern me – they drive me over land and sea at their own horrible will; they are in me, and torturing me, at this moment! Why don't I resist them? Ha! but I do resist them. I am trying (with the help of the good punch) to resist them now. At intervals I cultivate the difficult virtue of common sense. Sometimes, sound sense makes a hopeful woman of me. At one time, I had the hope that what seemed reality to me was only mad delusion, after all – I even asked the question of an English doctor! At other times, other sensible doubts of myself beset me. Never mind dwelling on them now – it always ends in the old terrors and superstitions taking possession of me again. In a week's time, I shall know whether Destiny does indeed decide my future for me, or whether I decide it for myself. In the last case, my resolution is to absorb this self-tormenting fancy of mine in the occupation that I have told you of already. Do you understand me a little better now? And, our business being settled, dear Mr Westwick, shall we get out of this hot room into the nice cool air again?'

They rose to leave the cafe. Francis privately concluded that the maraschino punch offered the only discoverable explanation of what the Countess had said to him.

Chapter 20

'Shall I see you again?' she asked, as she held out her hand to take leave. 'It is quite understood between us, I suppose, about the play?'

Francis recalled his extraordinary experience of that evening in the re-numbered room. 'My stay in Venice is uncertain,' he replied. 'If you have anything more to say about this dramatic venture of yours, it may be as well to say it now. Have you decided on a subject already? I know the public taste in England better than you do – I might save you some waste of time and trouble, if you have not chosen your subject wisely.'

'I don't care what subject I write about, so long as I write,' she answered carelessly. 'If *you* have got a subject in your head, give it to me. I answer for the characters and the dialogue.'

'You answer for the characters and the dialogue,' Francis repeated. 'That's a bold way of speaking for a beginner! I wonder if I should shake your sublime confidence in yourself, if I suggested the most ticklish subject to handle which is known to the stage? What do you say, Countess, to entering the lists with Shakespeare, and trying a drama with a ghost in it? A true story, mind! Founded on events in this very city in which you and I are interested.'

She caught him by the arm, and drew him away from the crowded colonnade into the solitary middle space of the square. 'Now tell me!' she said eagerly. 'Here, where nobody is near us. How am I interested in it? How? How?'

Still holding his arm, she shook him in her impatience to hear the coming disclosure. For a moment he hesitated. Thus far, amused by her ignorant belief in herself, he had merely spoken in jest. Now, for the first time, impressed by her irresistible earnestness, he began to consider what he was about from a more serious point of view. With her knowledge of all that had passed in the old palace, before its transformation into an hotel, it was surely possible that she might suggest some explanation of what had happened to his brother, and sister, and himself. Or, failing to do this, she might accidentally reveal some event in her own experience which, acting as a hint to a competent dramatist, might prove to be the making of a play. The prosperity of his theatre was his one serious object in life. 'I may be on the trace of another *Corsican Brothers*,' he thought. 'A new piece of that sort would be ten thousand pounds in my pocket, at least.'

With these motives (worthy of the single-hearted devotion to dramatic business which made Francis a successful manager) he related, without further hesitation, what his own experience had been, and what the experience of his relatives had been, in the haunted hotel. He even described the outbreak of superstitious terror which had escaped Mrs Norbury's ignorant maid. 'Sad stuff, if you look at it reasonably,' he remarked. 'But there is something dramatic in the notion of the ghostly influence making itself felt by the relations in succession, as they one after another enter the fatal room – until the one chosen relative comes who will see the Unearthly Creature, and know the terrible truth. Material for a play, Countess – first-rate material for a play!'

There he paused. She neither moved nor spoke. He stooped and looked closer at her.

What impression had he produced? It was an impression which his utmost ingenuity had failed to anticipate. She stood by his side – just as she had stood before Agnes when her question about Ferrari was plainly answered at last – like a woman turned to stone. Her eyes were vacant and rigid; all the life in her face had faded out of it. Francis took her by the hand. Her hand was as cold as the pavement that they were standing on. He asked her if she was ill.

Not a muscle in her moved. He might as well have spoken to the dead.

'Surely,' he said, 'you are not foolish enough to take what I have been telling you seriously?'

Her lips moved slowly. As it seemed, she was making an effort to speak to him.

'Louder,' he said. 'I can't hear you.'

She struggled to recover possession of herself. A faint light began to soften the dull cold stare of her eyes. In a moment more she spoke so that he could hear her.

'I never thought of the other world,' she murmured, in low dull tones, like a woman talking in her sleep.

Her mind had gone back to the day of her last memorable interview with Agnes; she was slowly recalling the confession that had escaped her, the warning words which she had spoken at that past time. Necessarily incapable of understanding this, Francis looked at her in perplexity. She went on in the same dull vacant tone, steadily following out her own train of thought, with her heedless eyes on his face, and her wandering mind far away from him.

'I said some trifling event would bring us together the next time. I was wrong. No trifling event will bring us together. I said I might be the person who told her what had become of Ferrari, if she forced me to it. Shall I feel some other influence than hers? Will *he* force me to it? When *she* sees him, shall *I* see him too?'

Her head sank a little; her heavy eyelids dropped slowly; she heaved a long low weary sigh. Francis put her arm in his, and made an attempt to rouse her.

'Come, Countess, you are weary and overwrought. We have had enough talking tonight. Let me see you safe back to your hotel. Is it far from here?'

She started when he moved, and obliged her to move with him, as if he had suddenly awakened her out of a deep sleep.

'Not far,' she said faintly. 'The old hotel on the quay. My mind's in a strange state; I have forgotten the name.'

'Danieli's?'

'Yes!'

He led her on slowly. She accompanied him in silence as far as the end of the Piazzetta. There, when the full view of the moonlit Lagoon revealed itself, she stopped him as he turned towards the Riva degli Schiavoni. 'I have something to ask you. I want to wait and think.'

She recovered her lost idea, after a long pause.

'Are you going to sleep in the room tonight?' she asked.

He told her that another traveller was in possession of the room that night. 'But the manager has reserved it for me tomorrow,' he added, 'if I wish to have it.'

'No,' she said. 'You must give it up.'

'To whom?'

'To me!'

He started. 'After what I have told you, do you really wish to sleep in that room tomorrow night?'

'I must sleep in it.'

'Are you not afraid?'

'I am horribly afraid.'

'So I should have thought, after what I have observed in you tonight. Why should you take the room? You are not obliged to occupy it, unless you like.'

'I was not obliged to go to Venice, when I left America,' she answered. 'And yet I came here. I must take the room, and keep the room, until – ' She broke off at those words. 'Never mind the rest,' she said. 'It doesn't interest you.'

It was useless to dispute with her. Francis changed the subject. 'We can do nothing tonight,' he said. 'I will call on you tomorrow morning, and hear what you think of it then.'

They moved on again to the hotel. As they approached the door, Francis asked if she was staying in Venice under her own name.

She shook her head. 'As your brother's widow, I am known here. As Countess Narona, I am known here. I want to be unknown, this time, to strangers in Venice; I am travelling under a common English name.' She hesitated, and stood still. 'What has come to me?' she muttered to herself. 'Some things I remember; and some I forget. I forgot Danieli's – and now I forget my English name.' She drew him hurriedly into the hall of the hotel, on the wall of which hung a list of visitors' names. Running her finger slowly down the list, she pointed to the English name that she had assumed: 'Mrs James'.

'Remember that when you call tomorrow,' she said. 'My head is heavy. Good night.'

Francis went back to his own hotel, wondering what the events of the next day would bring forth. A new turn in his affairs had taken place in his absence. As he crossed the hall, he was requested by one of the servants to walk into the private office. The manager was waiting there with a gravely pre-occupied manner, as if he had something serious to say. He regretted to hear that Mr Francis Westwick had, like other members of the family, discovered serious sources of discomfort in the new hotel. He had been informed in strict confidence of Mr Westwick's extraordinary objection to the atmosphere of the bedroom upstairs. Without presuming to discuss the matter, he must beg to be excused from reserving the room for Mr Westwick after what had happened.

Francis answered sharply, a little ruffled by the tone in which the manager had spoken to him. 'I might, very possibly, have declined to sleep in the room, if you *had* reserved it,' he said. 'Do you wish me to leave the hotel?'

The manager saw the error that he had committed, and hastened to repair it. 'Certainly not, sir! We will do our best to make you comfortable while you stay with us. I beg your pardon, if I have said anything to offend you. The reputation of an establishment like this is a matter of very serious importance. May I hope that you will do us the great favour to say nothing about what has happened upstairs? The two French gentlemen have kindly promised to keep it a secret.'

This apology left Francis no polite alternative but to grant the manager's request. 'There is an end to the Countess's wild scheme,' he thought to himself, as he retired for the night. 'So much the better for the Countess!'

He rose late the next morning. Enquiring for his Parisian friends, he was informed that both the French gentlemen had left for Milan. As he crossed the hall, on his way to the restaurant, he noticed the head porter chalking the numbers of the rooms on some articles of luggage which were waiting to go upstairs. One trunk attracted his attention by the extraordinary number of old travelling labels left on it. The porter was marking it at the moment – and the number was '13A'. Francis instantly looked at the card fastened on the lid. It bore the common English name, 'Mrs James'! He at once enquired about the lady. She had arrived early that morning, and she was then in the Reading Room. Looking into the room, he discovered a lady in it alone. Advancing a little nearer, he found himself face to face with the Countess.

She was seated in a dark corner, with her head down and her arms crossed over her bosom. 'Yes,' she said, in a tone of weary impatience, before Francis could speak to her. 'I thought it best not to wait for you – I determined to get here before anybody else could take the room.'

'Have you taken it for long?' Francis asked.

'You told me Miss Lockwood would be here in a week's time. I have taken it for a week.'

'What has Miss Lockwood to do with it?'

'She has everything to do with it – she must sleep in the room. I shall give the room up to her when she comes here.'

Francis began to understand the superstitious purpose that she had in view. 'Are you (an educated woman) really of the same opinion as my sister's maid!' he exclaimed. 'Assuming your absurd superstition to be a serious thing, you are taking the wrong means to prove it true. If I and my brother and sister have seen nothing, how should Agnes Lockwood discover what was not revealed to us? She is only distantly related to the Montbarrys – she is only our cousin.'

'She was nearer to the heart of the Montbarry who is dead than any of you,' the Countess answered sternly. 'To the last day of his life, my miserable husband repented his desertion of her. She will see what none of you have seen – she shall have the room.'

Francis listened, utterly at a loss to account for the motives that animated her. 'I don't see what interest you have in trying this extraordinary experiment,' he said.

'It is my interest *not* to try it! It is my interest to fly from Venice, and never set eyes on Agnes Lockwood or any of your family again!'

'What prevents you from doing that?'

She started to her feet and looked at him wildly. 'I know no more what prevents me than you do!' she burst out. 'Some will that is stronger than mine drives me on to my destruction, in spite of my own self!' She suddenly sat down again, and waved her hand for him to go. 'Leave me,' she said. 'Leave me to my thoughts.'

Francis left her, firmly persuaded by this time that she was out of her senses. For the rest of the day, he saw nothing of her. The night, so far as he knew, passed quietly. The next morning he breakfasted early, determining to wait in the restaurant for the appearance of the Countess. She came in and ordered her breakfast quietly, looking dull and worn and self-absorbed, as she had looked when he last saw her. He hastened to her table, and asked if anything had happened in the night.

'Nothing,' she answered.

'You have rested as well as usual?'

'Quite as well as usual. Have you had any letters this morning? Have you heard when she is coming?'

'I have had no letters. Are you really going to stay here? Has your experience of last night not altered the opinion which you expressed to me yesterday?'

'Not in the least.'

The momentary gleam of animation which had crossed her face when she questioned him about Agnes, died out of it again when he answered her. She looked, she spoke, she ate her breakfast, with a vacant resignation, like a woman who had done with hopes, done with interests, done with everything but the mechanical movements and instincts of life.

Francis went out, on the customary travellers' pilgrimage to the shrines of Titian and Tintoret. After some hours of absence, he found a letter waiting for him when he got back to the hotel. It was written by his brother Henry, and it recommended him to return to Milan immediately. The proprietor of a French theatre, recently arrived from Venice, was trying to induce the famous dancer whom Francis had engaged to break faith with him and accept a higher salary.

Having made this startling announcement, Henry proceeded to inform his brother that Lord and Lady Montbarry, with Agnes and the children, would arrive in Venice in three days more. 'They know nothing of our adventures at the hotel,' Henry wrote; 'and they have telegraphed to the manager for the accommodation that they want. There would be something absurdly superstitious in our giving them a warning which would frighten the ladies and children out of the best hotel in Venice. We shall be a strong party this time – too strong a party for ghosts! I shall meet the travellers on their arrival, of course, and try my luck again at what you call the Haunted Hotel. Arthur Barville and his wife have already got as far on their way as Trent; and two of the lady's relations have arranged to accompany them on the journey to Venice.'

Naturally indignant at the conduct of his Parisian colleague, Francis made his preparations for returning to Milan by the train of that day.

On his way out, he asked the manager if his brother's telegram had been received. The telegram had arrived, and, to the surprise of Francis, the rooms were already reserved. 'I thought you would refuse to let any more of the family into the house,' he said satirically. The manager answered (with the due dash of respect) in the same tone. 'Number 13A is safe, sir, in the occupation of a stranger. I am the servant of the Company; and I dare not turn money out of the hotel.'

Hearing this, Francis said goodbye – and said nothing more. He was ashamed to acknowledge it to himself, but he felt an irresistible curiosity to know what would happen when Agnes arrived at the hotel. Besides, 'Mrs James' had reposed a confidence in him. He got into his gondola, respecting the confidence of 'Mrs James'.

Towards evening on the third day, Lord Montbarry and his travelling companions arrived, punctual to their appointment.

'Mrs James', sitting at the window of her room watching for them, saw the new Lord land from the gondola first. He handed his wife to the steps. The three children were next committed to his care. Last of all, Agnes appeared in the little black doorway of the gondola cabin, and, taking Lord Montbarry's hand, passed in her turn to the steps. She wore no veil. As she ascended to the door of the hotel, the Countess (eyeing her through an opera-glass) noticed that she paused to look at the outside of the building, and that her face was very pale.

Chapter 21

Lord and Lady Montbarry were received by the housekeeper, the manager being absent for a day or two on business connected with the affairs of the hotel.

The rooms reserved for the travellers on the first floor were three in number; consisting of two bedrooms opening into each other, and communicating on the left with a drawing-room. Complete so far, the arrangements proved to be less satisfactory in reference to the third bedroom required for Agnes and for the eldest daughter of Lord Montbarry, who usually slept with her on their travels. The bedchamber on the right of the drawing-room was already occupied by an English widow lady. Other bedchambers at the other end of the corridor were also let in every case. There was accordingly no alternative but to place at the disposal of Agnes a comfortable room on the second floor. Lady Montbarry vainly complained of this separation of one of the members of her travelling party from the rest. The housekeeper politely hinted that it was impossible for her to ask other travellers to give up their rooms. She could only express her regret, and assure Miss Lockwood that her bedchamber on the second floor was one of the best rooms in that part of the hotel.

On the retirement of the housekeeper, Lady Montbarry noticed that Agnes had seated herself apart, feeling apparently no interest in the question of the bedrooms. Was she ill? No; she felt a little unnerved by the railway journey, and that was all. Hearing this, Lord Montbarry proposed that she should go out with him, and try the experiment of half an hour's walk in the cool evening air. Agnes gladly accepted the suggestion. They directed their steps towards the square of St Mark, so as to enjoy the breeze blowing over the lagoon. It was the first visit of Agnes to Venice. The fascination of the wonderful city of the waters exerted its full influence over her sensitive nature. The proposed half-hour of the walk had passed away, and was fast expanding to half an hour more, before Lord Montbarry could persuade his companion to remember that dinner was waiting for them. As they returned, passing under the colonnade, neither of them noticed a lady in deep mourning, loitering in the open space of the square. She started as she recognised Agnes walking with the new Lord Montbarry – hesitated for a moment – and then followed them, at a discreet distance, back to the hotel.

Lady Montbarry received Agnes in high spirits – with news of an event which had happened in her absence.

She had not left the hotel more than ten minutes, before a little note in pencil was brought to Lady Montbarry by the housekeeper. The writer proved to be no less a person than the widow lady who occupied the room on the other side of the drawing-room, which her ladyship had vainly hoped to secure for Agnes. Writing under the name of Mrs James, the polite widow explained that she had heard from the housekeeper of the disappointment experienced by Lady Montbarry in the matter of the rooms. Mrs James was quite alone; and as long as her bedchamber was airy and comfortable, it mattered nothing to her whether she slept on the first or the second floor of the house. She had accordingly much pleasure in proposing to change rooms with Miss Lockwood. Her luggage had already been removed, and Miss Lockwood had only to take possession of the room (Number 13A), which was now entirely at her disposal.

'I immediately proposed to see Mrs James,' Lady Montbarry continued, 'and to thank her personally for her extreme kindness. But I was informed that she had gone out, without leaving word at what hour she might be expected to return. I have written a little note of thanks, saying that we hope to have the pleasure of personally expressing our sense of Mrs James's courtesy tomorrow. In the meantime, Agnes, I have ordered your boxes to be removed downstairs. Go! – and judge for yourself, my dear, if that good lady has not given up to you the prettiest room in the house!'

With those words, Lady Montbarry left Miss Lockwood to make a hasty toilet for dinner.

The new room at once produced a favourable impression on Agnes. The large window, opening into a balcony, commanded an admirable view of the canal. The decorations on the walls and ceiling were skilfully copied from the exquisitely graceful designs of Raphael in the Vatican. The massive wardrobe possessed compartments of unusual size, in which double the number of dresses that Agnes possessed might have been conveniently hung at full length. In the inner corner of the room, near the head of the bedstead, there was a recess which had been turned into a little dressing-room, and which opened by a second door on the inferior staircase of the hotel, commonly used by the servants. Noticing these aspects of the room at a glance, Agnes made the necessary change in her dress, as quickly as possible. On her way back to the drawing-room she was addressed by a chambermaid in the corridor who asked for her key. 'I will put your room tidy for the night, Miss,' the woman said, 'and I will then bring the key back to you in the drawing-room.'

While the chambermaid was at her work, a solitary lady, loitering about the corridor of the second storey, was watching her over the banisters. After a while, the maid appeared, with her pail in her hand, leaving the room by way of the dressing-room and the back stairs. As she passed out of sight, the lady on the second floor (no other, it is needless to add, than the Countess herself) ran swiftly down the stairs, entered the bedchamber by the principal door, and hid herself in the empty side compartment of the wardrobe. The chambermaid returned, completed her work, locked the door of the dressing-room on the inner side, locked the principal entrance-door on leaving the room, and returned the key to Agnes in the drawing-room.

The travellers were just sitting down to their late dinner, when one of the children noticed that Agnes was not wearing her watch. Had she left it in her bedchamber in the hurry of changing her dress? She rose from the table at once in search of her watch, Lady Montbarry advising her, as she went out, to see to the security of her bedchamber, in the event of there being thieves in the house. Agnes found her watch, forgotten on the toilet table, as she had anticipated. Before leaving the room again she acted on Lady Montbarry's advice, and tried the key in the lock of the dressing-room door. It was properly secured. She left the bedchamber, locking the main door behind her.

Immediately on her departure, the Countess, oppressed by the confined air in the wardrobe, ventured on stepping out of her hiding place into the empty room.

Entering the dressing-room, she listened at the door, until the silence outside informed her that the corridor was empty. Upon this, she unlocked the door, and, passing out, closed it again softly; leaving it to all appearance (when viewed on the inner side) as carefully secured as Agnes had seen it when she tried the key in the lock with her own hand.

While the Montbarrys were still at dinner, Henry Westwick joined them, arriving from Milan.

When he entered the room, and again when he advanced to shake hands with her, Agnes was conscious of a latent feeling which secretly reciprocated Henry's unconcealed pleasure on meeting her again. For a moment only, she returned his look; and in that moment her own observation told her that she had silently encouraged him to hope. She saw it in the sudden glow of happiness which overspread his face; and she confusedly took refuge in the usual conventional enquiries relating to the relatives whom he had left at Milan.

Taking his place at the table, Henry gave a most amusing account of the position of his brother Francis between the mercenary opera-dancer on one side, and the unscrupulous manager of the French theatre on the other. Matters had proceeded to such extremities, that the law had been called on to interfere, and had decided the dispute in favour of Francis. On winning the victory the English manager had at once left Milan, recalled to London by the affairs of his theatre. He was accompanied on the journey back, as he had been accompanied on the journey out, by his sister. Resolved, after passing two nights of terror in the Venetian hotel, never to enter it again, Mrs Norbury asked to be excused from appearing at the family festival, on the ground of ill-health. At her age, travelling fatigued her, and she was glad to take advantage of her brother's escort to return to England.

While the talk at the dinner-table flowed easily onward, the evening-time advanced to night – and it became necessary to think of sending the children to bed.

As Agnes rose to leave the room, accompanied by the eldest girl, she observed with surprise that Henry's manner suddenly changed. He looked serious and preoccupied; and when his niece wished him good-night, he abruptly said to her, 'Marian, I want to know what part of the hotel you sleep in?' Marian, puzzled by the question, answered that she was going to sleep, as usual, with 'Aunt Agnes'. Not satisfied with that reply, Henry next enquired whether the bedroom was near the rooms occupied by the other members of the travelling party. Answering for the child, and wondering what Henry's object could possibly be, Agnes mentioned the polite sacrifice made to her convenience by Mrs James. 'Thanks to that lady's kindness,' she said, 'Marian and I are only on the other side of the drawing-room.' Henry made no remark; he looked incomprehensibly discontented as he opened the door for Agnes and her companion to pass out. After wishing them good-night, he waited in the corridor until he saw them enter the fatal corner-room – and then he called abruptly to his brother, 'Come out, Stephen, and let us smoke!'

As soon as the two brothers were at liberty to speak together privately, Henry explained the motive which had led to his strange enquiries about the bedrooms. Francis had informed him of the meeting with the Countess at Venice, and of all that had followed it; and Henry now carefully repeated the narrative to his brother in all its details. 'I am not satisfied,' he added, 'about that woman's purpose in giving up her room. Without alarming the ladies by telling them what I have just told you, can you not warn Agnes to be careful in securing her door?'

Lord Montbarry replied, that the warning had been already given by his wife, and that Agnes might be trusted to take good care of herself and her little bed-fellow. For the rest, he looked upon the story of the Countess and her superstitions as a piece of theatrical exaggeration, amusing enough in itself, but unworthy of a moment's serious attention.

While the gentlemen were absent from the hotel, the room which had been already associated with so many startling circumstances, became the scene of another strange event in which Lady Montbarry's eldest child was concerned.

Little Marian had been got ready for bed as usual, and had (so far) taken hardly any notice of the new room. As she knelt down to say her prayers, she happened to look up at that part of the ceiling above her which was just over the head of the bed. The next instant she alarmed Agnes, by starting to her feet with a cry of terror, and pointing to a small brown spot on one of the white panelled spaces of the carved ceiling. 'It's a spot of blood!' the child exclaimed. 'Take me away! I won't sleep here!'

Seeing plainly that it would be useless to reason with her while she was in the room, Agnes hurriedly wrapped Marian in a dressing-gown, and carried her back to her mother in the drawing-room. Here, the ladies did their best to soothe and reassure the trembling girl. The effort proved to be useless; the impression that had been produced on the young and sensitive mind was not to be removed by persuasion. Marian could give no explanation of the panic of terror that had seized her. She was quite unable to say why the spot on the ceiling looked like the colour of a spot of blood. She only knew that she should die of terror if she saw it again. Under these circumstances, but one alternative was left. It was arranged that the child should pass the night in the room occupied by her two younger sisters and the nurse.

In half an hour more, Marian was peacefully asleep with her arm around her sister's neck. Lady Montbarry went back with Agnes to her room to see the spot on the ceiling which had so strangely frightened the child. It was so small as to be only just perceptible, and it had in all probability been caused by the carelessness of a workman, or by a dripping from water accidentally spilt on the floor of the room above.

'I really cannot understand why Marian should place such a shocking interpretation on such a trifling thing,' Lady Montbarry remarked.

'I suspect the nurse is in some way answerable for what has happened,' Agnes suggested. 'She may quite possibly have been telling Marian some tragic nursery story which has left its mischievous impression behind it. Persons in her position are sadly ignorant of the danger of exciting a child's imagination. You had better caution the nurse tomorrow.'

Lady Montbarry looked round the room with admiration. 'Is it not prettily decorated?' she said. 'I suppose, Agnes, you don't mind sleeping here by yourself.?'

Agnes laughed. 'I feel so tired,' she replied, 'that I was thinking of bidding you good-night, instead of going back to the drawing-room.'

Lady Montbarry turned towards the door. 'I see your jewel-case on the table,' she resumed. 'Don't forget to lock the other door there, in the dressing-room.'

'I have already seen to it, and tried the key myself,' said Agnes. 'Can I be of any use to you before I go to bed?'

'No, my dear, thank you; I feel sleepy enough to follow your example. Good night, Agnes – and pleasant dreams on your first night in Venice.'

Chapter 22

Having closed and secured the door on Lady Montbarry's departure, Agnes put on her dressing-gown, and, turning to her open boxes, began the business of unpacking. In the hurry of making her toilet for dinner, she had taken the first dress that lay uppermost in the trunk, and had thrown her travelling costume on the bed. She now opened the doors of the wardrobe for the first time, and began to hang her dresses on the hooks in the large compartment on one side.

After a few minutes only of this occupation, she grew weary of it, and decided on leaving the trunks as they were, until the next morning. The oppressive south wind, which had blown throughout the day, still prevailed at night. The atmosphere of the room felt close; Agnes threw a shawl over her head and shoulders, and, opening the window, stepped into the balcony to look at the view.

The night was heavy and overcast: nothing could be distinctly seen. The canal beneath the window looked like a black gulf; the opposite houses were barely visible as a row of shadows, dimly relieved against the starless and moonless sky. At long intervals, the warning cry of a belated gondolier was just audible, as he turned the corner of a distant canal, and called to invisible boats which might be approaching him in the darkness. Now and then, the nearer dip of an oar in the water told of the viewless passage of other gondolas bringing guests back to the hotel. Excepting these rare sounds, the mysterious night-silence of Venice was literally the silence of the grave.

Leaning on the parapet of the balcony, Agnes looked vacantly into the black void beneath. Her thoughts reverted to the miserable man who had broken his pledged faith to her, and who had died in that house. Some change seemed to have come over her since her arrival in Venice; some new influence appeared to be at work. For the first time in her experience of herself, compassion and regret were not the only emotions aroused in her by the remembrance of the dead Montbarry. A keen sense of the wrong that she had suffered, never yet felt by that gentle and forgiving nature, was felt by it now. She found herself thinking of the bygone days of her humiliation almost as harshly as Henry Westwick had thought of them – she who had rebuked him the last time he had spoken slightingly of his brother in her presence! A sudden fear and doubt of herself, startled her physically as well as morally. She turned from the shadowy abyss of the dark water as if the mystery and the gloom of it had been answerable for the emotions which had taken her by surprise. Abruptly closing the window, she threw aside her shawl, and lit the candles on the mantelpiece, impelled by a sudden craving for light in the solitude of her room.

The cheering brightness round her, contrasting with the black gloom outside, restored her spirits. She felt herself enjoying the light like a child!

Would it be well (she asked herself) to get ready for bed? No! The sense of drowsy fatigue that she had felt half an hour since was gone. She returned to the dull employment of unpacking her boxes. After a few minutes only, the occupation became irksome to her once more. She sat down by the table, and took up a guide-book. 'Suppose I inform myself,' she thought, 'on the subject of Venice?'

Her attention wandered from the book, before she had turned the first page of it.

The image of Henry Westwick was the presiding image in her memory now. Recalling the minutest incidents and details of the evening, she could think of nothing which presented him under other than a favourable and interesting aspect. She smiled to herself softly, her colour rose by fine gradations, as she felt the full luxury of dwelling on the perfect truth and modesty of his devotion to her. Was the depression of spirits from which she had suffered so persistently on her travels attributable, by any chance, to their long separation from each other – embittered perhaps by her own vain regret when she remembered her harsh reception of him in Paris? Suddenly conscious of this bold question, and of the self-abandonment which it implied, she returned mechanically to her book, distrusting the unrestrained liberty of her own thoughts. What lurking temptations to forbidden tenderness find their hiding-places in a woman's dressing-gown, when she is alone in her room at night! With her heart in the tomb of the dead Montbarry, could Agnes even think of another man, and think of love? How shameful! How unworthy of her! For the second time, she tried to interest herself in the guide-book – and once more she tried in vain. Throwing the book aside, she turned desperately to the one resource that was left, to her luggage – resolved to fatigue herself without mercy, until she was weary enough and sleepy enough to find a safe refuge in bed.

For some little time, she persisted in the monotonous occupation of transferring her clothes from her trunk to the wardrobe. The large clock in the hall, striking midnight, reminded her that it was getting late. She sat down for a moment in an armchair by the bedside, to rest.

The silence in the house now caught her attention, and held it – held it disagreeably. Was everybody in bed and asleep but herself? Surely it was time for her to follow the general example? With a certain irritable nervous haste, she rose again and undressed herself. 'I have lost two hours of rest,' she thought, frowning at the reflection of herself in the glass, as she arranged her hair for the night. 'I shall be good for nothing tomorrow!'

She lit the night-light, and extinguished the candles – with one exception, which she removed to a little table, placed on the side of the bed opposite to the side occupied by the armchair. Having put her travelling-box of matches and the guide-book near the candle, in case she might be sleepless and might want to read, she blew out the light, and laid her head on the pillow.

The curtains of the bed were looped back to let the air pass freely over her. Lying on her left side, with her face turned away from the table, she could see the armchair by the dim night-light. It had a chintz covering – representing large bunches of roses scattered over a pale green ground. She tried to weary herself into drowsiness by counting over and over again the bunches of roses that were visible from her point of view. Twice her attention was distracted from the counting, by sounds outside – by the clock chiming the half-hour past twelve; and then again, by the fall of a pair of boots on the upper floor, thrown out to be cleaned, with that barbarous disregard of the comfort of others which is observable in humanity when it inhabits an hotel. In the silence that followed these passing disturbances, Agnes went on counting the roses on the armchair, more and more slowly. Before long, she confused herself in the figures – tried to begin counting again – thought she would wait a little first – felt her eyelids drooping, and her head reclining lower and lower on the pillow – sighed faintly – and sank into sleep.

How long that first sleep lasted, she never knew. She could only remember, in the after-time, that she woke instantly.

Every faculty and perception in her passed the boundary line between insensibility and consciousness, so to speak, at a leap. Without knowing why, she sat up suddenly in the bed, listening for she knew not what. Her head was in a whirl; her heart beat furiously, without any assignable cause. But one trivial event had happened during the interval while she had been asleep. The night-light had gone out; and the room, as a matter of course, was in total darkness.

She felt for the match-box, and paused after finding it. A vague sense of confusion was still in her mind. She was in no hurry to light the match. The pause in the darkness was, for the moment, agreeable to her.

In the quieter flow of her thoughts during this interval, she could ask herself the natural question: what cause had awakened her so suddenly, and had so strangely shaken her nerves? Had it been the influence of a dream? She had not dreamed at all – or, to speak more correctly, she had no waking remembrance of having dreamed. The mystery was beyond her fathoming: the darkness began to oppress her. She struck the match on the box, and lit her candle.

As the welcome light diffused itself over the room, she turned from the table and looked towards the other side of the bed.

In the moment when she turned, the chill of a sudden terror gripped her round the heart, as with the clasp of an icy hand.

She was not alone in her room!

There – in the chair at the bedside – there, suddenly revealed under the flow of light from the candle, was the figure of a woman, reclining. Her head lay back over the chair. Her face, turned up to the ceiling, had the eyes closed, as if she was wrapped in a deep sleep.

The shock of the discovery held Agnes speechless and helpless. Her first conscious action, when she was in some degree mistress of herself again, was to lean over the bed, and to look closer at the woman who had so incomprehensibly stolen into her room in the dead of night. One glance was enough: she started back with a cry of amazement. The person in the chair was no other than the widow of the dead Montbarry – the woman who had warned her that they were to meet again, and that the place might be Venice!

Her courage returned to her, stung into action by the natural sense of indignation which the presence of the Countess provoked.

'Wake up!' she called out. 'How dare you come here? How did you get in? Leave the room – or I will call for help!'

She raised her voice at the last words. It produced no effect. Leaning farther over the bed, she boldly took the Countess by the shoulder and shook her. Not even this effort succeeded in rousing the sleeping woman. She still lay back in the chair, possessed by a torpor like the torpor of death – insensible to sound, insensible to touch. Was she really sleeping? Or had she fainted?

Agnes looked closer at her. She had not fainted. Her breathing was audible, rising and falling in deep heavy gasps. At intervals she ground her teeth savagely. Beads of perspiration stood thickly on her forehead. Her clenched hands rose and fell slowly from time to time on her lap. Was she in the agony of a dream? Or was she spiritually conscious of something hidden in the room?

The doubt involved in that last question was unendurable. Agnes determined to rouse the servants who kept watch in the hotel at night.

The bell-handle was fixed to the wall, on the side of the bed by which the table stood.

She raised herself from the crouching position which she had assumed in looking close at the Countess; and, turning towards the other side of the bed, stretched out her hand to the bell. At the same instant, she stopped and looked upward. Her hand fell helplessly at her side. She shuddered, and sank back on the pillow.

What had she seen?

She had seen another intruder in her room.

Midway between her face and the ceiling, there hovered a human head – severed at the neck, like a head struck from the body by the guillotine.

Nothing visible, nothing audible, had given her any intelligible warning of its appearance. Silently and suddenly, the head had taken its place above her. No supernatural change had passed over the room, or was perceptible in it now. The dumbly-tortured figure in the chair; the broad window opposite the foot of the bed, with the black night beyond it; the candle burning on the table – these, and all other objects in the room, remained unaltered. One object more, unutterably horrid, had been added to the rest. That was the only change – no more, no less.

By the yellow candlelight she saw the head distinctly, hovering in mid-air above her. She looked at it steadfastly, spell-bound by the terror that held her.

The flesh of the face was gone. The shrivelled skin was darkened in hue, like the skin of an Egyptian mummy – except at the neck. There it was of a lighter colour; there it showed spots and splashes of the hue of that brown spot on the ceiling, which the child's fanciful terror had distorted into the likeness of a spot of blood. Thin remains of a discoloured moustache and whiskers, hanging over the upper lip, and over the hollows where the cheeks had once been, made the head just recognisable as the head of a man. Over all the features death and time had done their obliterating work. The eyelids were closed. The hair on the skull, discoloured like the hair on the face, had been burnt away in places. The bluish lips, parted in a fixed grin, showed the double row of teeth. By slow degrees, the hovering head (perfectly still when she first saw it) began to descend towards Agnes as she lay beneath. By slow degrees, that strange doubly-blended odour, which the Commissioners had discovered in the vaults of the old palace – which had sickened Francis Westwick in the bedchamber of the new hotel – spread its fetid exhalations over the room. Downward and downward the hideous apparition made its slow progress, until it stopped close over Agnes – stopped, and turned slowly, so that the face of it confronted the upturned face of the woman in the chair.

There was a pause. Then, a supernatural movement disturbed the rigid repose of the dead face.

The closed eyelids opened slowly. The eyes revealed themselves, bright with the glassy film of death – and fixed their dreadful look on the woman in the chair.

Agnes saw that look; saw the eyelids of the living woman open slowly like the eyelids of the dead; saw her rise, as if in obedience to some silent command – and saw no more.

Her next conscious impression was of the sunlight pouring in at the window; of the friendly presence of Lady Montbarry at the bedside; and of the children's wondering faces peeping in at the door.

Chapter 23

' . . . You have some influence over Agnes. Try what you can do, Henry, to make her take a sensible view of the matter. There is really nothing to make a fuss about. My wife's maid knocked at her door early in the morning, with the customary cup of tea. Getting no answer, she went round to the dressing-room – found the door on that side unlocked – and discovered Agnes on the bed in a fainting fit. With my wife's help, they brought her to herself again; and she told the extraordinary story which I have just repeated to you. You must have seen for yourself that she has been over-fatigued, poor thing, by our long railway journeys: her nerves are out of order – and she is just the person to be easily terrified by a dream. She obstinately refuses, however, to accept this rational view. Don't suppose that I have been severe with her! All that a man can do to humour her I have done. I have written to the Countess (in her assumed name) offering to restore the room to her. She writes back, positively declining to return to it. I have accordingly arranged (so as not to have the thing known in the hotel) to occupy the room for one or two nights, and to leave Agnes to recover her spirits under my wife's care. Is there anything more that I can do? Whatever questions Agnes has asked of me I have answered to the best of my ability; she knows all that you told me about Francis and the Countess last night. But try as I may I can't quiet her mind. I have given up the attempt in despair, and left her in the drawing-room. Go, like a good fellow, and try what you can do to compose her.'

In those words, Lord Montbarry stated the case to his brother from the rational point of view. Henry made no remark, he went straight to the drawing-room.

He found Agnes walking rapidly backwards and forwards, flushed and excited. 'If you come here to say what your brother has been saying to me,' she broke out, before he could speak, 'spare yourself the trouble. I don't want common sense – I want a true friend who will believe in me.'

'I am that friend, Agnes,' Henry answered quietly, 'and you know it.'

'You really believe that I am not deluded by a dream?'

'I know that you are not deluded – in one particular, at least.'

'In what particular?'

'In what you have said of the Countess. It is perfectly true – '

Agnes stopped him there. 'Why do I only hear this morning that the Countess and Mrs James are one and the same person?' she asked distrustfully. 'Why was I not told of it last night?'

'You forget that you had accepted the exchange of rooms before I reached Venice,' Henry replied. 'I felt strongly tempted to tell you, even then – but your sleeping arrangements for the night were all made; I should only have inconvenienced and alarmed you. I waited till the morning, after hearing from my brother that you had yourself seen to your security from any intrusion. How that intrusion was accomplished it is impossible to say. I can only declare that the Countess's presence by your bedside last night was no dream of yours. On her own authority I can testify that it was a reality.'

'On her own authority?' Agnes repeated eagerly. 'Have you seen her this morning?'

'I have seen her not ten minutes since.'

'What was she doing?'

She was busily engaged in writing. I could not even get her to look at me until I thought of mentioning your name.'

'She remembered me, of course?'

'She remembered you with some difficulty. Finding that she wouldn't answer me on any other terms, I questioned her as if I had come direct from you. Then she spoke. She not only admitted that she had the same superstitious motive for placing you in that room which she had acknowledged to Francis – she even owned that she had been by your bedside, watching through the night, "to see what you saw", as she expressed it. Hearing this, I tried to persuade her to tell me how she got into the room. Unluckily, her manuscript on the table caught her eye; she returned to her writing. "The Baron wants money," she said; "I must get on with my play." What she saw or dreamed while she was in your room last night, it is at present impossible to discover. But judging by my brother's account of her, as well as by what I remember of her myself, some recent influence has been at work which has produced a marked change in this wretched woman for the worse. Her mind (since last night, perhaps) is partially deranged. One proof of it is that she spoke to me of the Baron as if he were still a living man. When Francis saw her, she declared that the Baron was dead, which is the truth. The United States Consul at Milan showed us the announcement of the death in an American newspaper. So far as I can see, such sense as she still possesses seems to be entirely absorbed in one absurd idea – the idea of writing a play for Francis to bring out at his theatre. He admits that he encouraged her to hope she might get money in this way. I think he did wrong. Don't you agree with me?'

Without heeding the question, Agnes rose abruptly from her chair.

'Do me one more kindness, Henry,' she said. 'Take me to the Countess at once.'

Henry hesitated. 'Are you composed enough to see her, after the shock that you have suffered?' he asked.

She trembled, the flush on her face died away, and left it deadly pale. But she held to her resolution. 'You have heard of what I saw last night?' she said faintly.

'Don't speak of it!' Henry interposed. 'Don't uselessly agitate yourself.'

'I must speak! My mind is full of horrid questions about it. I know I can't identify it – and yet I ask myself over and over again, in whose likeness did it appear? Was it in the likeness of Ferrari? Or was it – ?' she stopped, shuddering. 'The Countess knows, I must see the Countess!' she resumed vehemently. 'Whether my courage fails me or not, I must make the attempt. Take me to her before I have time to feel afraid of it!'

Henry looked at her anxiously. 'If you are really sure of your own resolution,' he said, 'I agree with you – the sooner you see her the better. You remember how strangely she talked of your influence over her, when she forced her way into your room in London?'

'I remember it perfectly. Why do you ask?'

'For this reason. In the present state of her mind, I doubt if she will be much longer capable of realising her wild idea of you as the avenging angel who is to bring her to a reckoning for her evil deeds. It may be well to try what your influence can do while she is still capable of feeling it.'

He waited to hear what Agnes would say. She took his arm and led him in silence to the door.

They ascended to the second floor, and, after knocking, entered the Countess's room.

She was still busily engaged in writing. When she looked up from the paper, and saw Agnes, a vacant expression of doubt was the only expression in her wild black eyes. After a few moments, the lost remembrances and associations appeared to return slowly to her mind. The pen dropped from her hand. Haggard and trembling, she looked closer at Agnes, and recognised her at last. 'Has the time come already?' she said in low awe-struck tones. 'Give me a little longer respite, I haven't done my writing yet!'

She dropped on her knees, and held out her clasped hands entreatingly. Agnes was far from having recovered, after the shock that she had suffered in the night: her nerves were far from being equal to the strain that was now laid on them. She was so startled by the change in the Countess, that she was at a loss what to say or to do next. Henry was obliged to speak to her. 'Put your questions while you have the chance,' he said, lowering his voice. 'See! The vacant look is coming over her face again.'

Agnes tried to rally her courage. 'You were in my room last night – ' she began. Before she could add a word more, the Countess lifted her hands, and wrung them above her head with a low moan of horror. Agnes shrank back, and turned as if to leave the room. Henry stopped her, and whispered to her to try again. She obeyed him after an effort. 'I slept last night in the room that you gave up to me,' she resumed. 'I saw – '

The Countess suddenly rose to her feet. 'No more of that,' she cried. 'Oh, Jesu Maria! Do you think I want to be told what you saw? Do you think I don't know what it means for you and for me? Decide for yourself, Miss. Examine your own mind. Are you well assured that the day of reckoning has come at last? Are you ready to follow me back, through the crimes of the past, to the secrets of the dead?'

She returned again to the writing-table, without waiting to be answered. Her eyes flashed; she looked like her old self once more as she spoke. It was only for a moment. The old ardour and impetuosity were nearly worn out. Her head sank; she sighed heavily as she unlocked a desk which stood on the table. Opening a drawer in the desk, she took out a leaf of vellum, covered with faded writing. Some ragged ends of silken thread were still attached to the leaf, as if it had been torn out of a book.

'Can you read Italian?' she asked, handing the leaf to Agnes.

Agnes answered silently by an inclination of her head.

'The leaf,' the Countess proceeded, 'once belonged to a book in the old library of the palace, while this building was still a palace. By whom it was torn out you have no need to know. For what purpose it was torn out you may discover for yourself, if you will. Read it first – at the fifth line from the top of the page.'

Agnes felt the serious necessity of composing herself. 'Give me a chair,' she said to Henry; 'and I will do my best.' He placed himself behind her chair so that he could look over her shoulder and help her to understand the writing on the leaf. Rendered into English, it ran as follows:

I have now completed my literary survey of the first floor of the palace. At the desire of my noble and gracious patron, the lord of this glorious edifice, I next ascend to the second floor, and continue my catalogue or description of the pictures, decorations, and other treasures of art therein contained. Let me begin with the corner room at the western extremity of the palace, called the Room of the Caryatides, from the statues which support the mantelpiece. This work is of comparatively recent execution: it dates from the eighteenth century only, and reveals the corrupt taste of the period in every part of it. Still, there is a certain interest which attaches to the mantelpiece: it conceals a cleverly constructed hiding-place, between the floor of the room and the ceiling of the room beneath, which was made during the last evil days of the Inquisition in Venice, and which is reported to have saved an ancestor of my gracious lord pursued by that terrible tribunal. The machinery of this curious place of concealment has been kept in good order by the present lord, as a species of curiosity. He condescended to show me the method of working it. Approaching the two Caryatides, rest your hand on the forehead (midway between the eyebrows) of the figure which is on your left as you stand opposite to the fireplace, then press the head inwards as if you were pushing it against the wall behind. By doing this, you set in motion the hidden machinery in the wall which turns the hearthstone on a pivot, and discloses the hollow place below. There is room enough in it for a man to lie easily at full length. The method of closing the cavity again is equally simple. Place both your hands on the temples of the figures; pull as if you were pulling it towards you – and the hearthstone will revolve into its proper position again.

'You need read no farther,' said the Countess. 'Be careful to remember what you have read.'

She put back the page of vellum in her writing-desk, locked it, and led the way to the door.

'Come!' she said; 'and see what the mocking Frenchman called "The beginning of the end". '

Agnes was barely able to rise from her chair; she trembled from head to foot. Henry gave her his arm to support her. 'Fear nothing,' he whispered; 'I shall be with you.'

The Countess proceeded along the westward corridor, and stopped at the door numbered Thirty-eight. This was the room which had been inhabited by Baron Rivar in the old days of the palace: it was situated immediately over the bedchamber in which Agnes had passed the night. For the last two days the room had been empty. The absence of luggage in it, when they opened the door, showed that it had not yet been let.

'You see?' said the Countess, pointing to the carved figure at the fireplace; 'and you know what to do. Have I deserved that you should temper justice with mercy?' she went on in lower tones. 'Give me a few hours more to myself. The Baron wants money – I must get on with my play.'

She smiled vacantly, and imitated the action of writing with her right hand as she pronounced the last words. The effort of concentrating her weakened mind on other and less familiar topics than the constant want of money in the Baron's lifetime, and the vague prospect of gain from the still unfinished play, had evidently exhausted her poor reserves of strength. When her request had been granted, she addressed no expressions of gratitude to Agnes; she only said, 'Feel no fear, miss, of my attempting to escape you. Where you are, there I must be till the end comes.'

Her eyes wandered round the room with a last weary and stupefied look. She returned to her writing with slow and feeble steps, like the steps of an old woman.

Chapter 24

Henry and Agnes were left alone in the Room of the Caryatides.

The person who had written the description of the palace – probably a poor author or artist – had correctly pointed out the defects of the mantelpiece. Bad taste, exhibiting itself on the most costly and splendid scale, was visible in every part of the work. It was nevertheless greatly admired by ignorant travellers of all classes; partly on account of its imposing size, and partly on account of the number of variously-coloured marbles which the sculptor had contrived to introduce into his design. Photographs of the mantelpiece were exhibited in the public rooms, and found a ready sale among English and American visitors to the hotel.

Henry led Agnes to the figure on the left as they stood facing the empty fireplace. 'Shall I try the experiment,' he asked, 'or will you?' She abruptly drew her arm away from him, and turned back to the door. 'I can't even look at it,' she said. 'That merciless marble face frightens me!'

Henry put his hand on the forehead of the figure. 'What is there to alarm you, my dear, in this conventionally classical face?' he asked jestingly. Before he could press the head inwards, Agnes hurriedly opened the door. 'Wait till I am out of the room!' she cried. 'The bare idea of what you may find there horrifies me!' She looked back into the room as she crossed the threshold. 'I won't leave you altogether,' she said, 'I will wait outside.'

She closed the door. Left by himself, Henry lifted his hand once more to the marble forehead of the figure.

For the second time, he was checked on the point of setting the machinery of the hiding-place in motion. On this occasion, the interruption came from an outbreak of friendly voices in the corridor. A woman's voice exclaimed, 'Dearest Agnes, how glad I am to see you again!' A man's voice followed, offering to introduce some friend to 'Miss Lockwood'. A third voice (which Henry recognised as the voice of the manager of the hotel) became audible next, directing the housekeeper to show the ladies and gentlemen the vacant apartments at the other end of the corridor. 'If more accommodation is wanted,' the manager went on, 'I have a charming room to let here.' He opened the door as he spoke, and found himself face to face with Henry Westwick.

'This is indeed an agreeable surprise, sir!' said the manager cheer-fully. 'You are admiring our famous chimney-piece, I see. May I ask, Mr Westwick, how you find yourself in the hotel, this time? Have the supernatural influences affected your appetite again?'

'The supernatural influences have spared me, this time,' Henry answered. 'Perhaps you may yet find that they have affected some other member of the family.' He spoke gravely, resenting the familiar tone in which the manager had referred to his previous visit to the hotel. 'Have you just returned?' he asked, by way of changing the topic.

'Just this minute, sir. I had the honour of travelling in the same train with friends of yours who have arrived at the hotel – Mr and Mrs Arthur Barville, and their travelling companions. Miss Lockwood is with them, looking at the rooms. They will be here before long, if they find it convenient to have an extra room at their disposal.'

This announcement decided Henry on exploring the hiding-place before the interruption occurred. It had crossed his mind, when Agnes left him, that he ought perhaps to have a witness, in the not very probable event of some alarming discovery taking place. The too-familiar manager, suspecting nothing, was there at his disposal. He turned again to the Caryan figure, maliciously resolving to make the manager his witness.

'I am delighted to hear that our friends have arrived at last,' he said. 'Before I shake hands with them, let me ask you a question about this queer work of art here. I see photographs of it downstairs. Are they for sale?'

'Certainly, Mr Westwick!'

'Do you think the chimney-piece is as solid as it looks?' Henry proceeded. 'When you came in, I was just wondering whether this figure here had not accidentally got loosened from the wall behind it.' He laid his hand on the marble forehead, for the third time. 'To my eye, it looks a little out of the perpendicular. I almost fancied I could jog the head just now, when I touched it.' He pressed the head inwards as he said those words.

A sound of jarring iron was instantly audible behind the wall. The solid hearthstone in front of the fire-place turned slowly at the feet of the two men, and disclosed a dark cavity below. At the same moment, the strange and sickening combination of odours, hitherto associated with the vaults of the old palace and with the bedchamber beneath, now floated up from the open recess, and filled the room.

The manager started back. 'Good God, Mr Westwick!' he exclaimed, 'what does this mean?'

Remembering, not only what his brother Francis had felt in the room beneath, but what the experience of Agnes had been on the previous night, Henry was determined to be on his guard. 'I am as much surprised as you are,' was his only reply.

'Wait for me one moment, sir,' said the manager. 'I must stop the ladies and gentlemen outside from coming in.'

He hurried away – not forgetting to close the door after him. Henry opened the window, and waited there breathing the purer air. Vague apprehensions of the next discovery to come, filled his mind for the first time. He was doubly resolved, now, not to stir a step in the investigation without a witness.

The manager returned with a wax taper in his hand, which he lighted as soon as he entered the room.

'We need fear no interruption now,' he said. 'Be so kind, Mr Westwick, as to hold the light. It is my business to find out what this extraordinary discovery means.'

Henry held the taper. Looking into the cavity, by the dim and flickering light, they both detected a dark object at the bottom of it. 'I think I can reach the thing,' the manager remarked, 'if I lie down, and put my hand into the hole.'

He knelt on the floor – and hesitated. 'Might I ask you, sir, to give me my gloves?' he said. 'They are in my hat, on the chair behind you.'

Henry gave him the gloves. 'I don't know what I may be going to take hold of,' the manager explained, smiling rather uneasily as he put on his right glove.

He stretched himself at full length on the floor, and passed his right arm into the cavity. 'I can't say exactly what I have got hold of,' he said. 'But I have got it.'

Half raising himself, he drew his hand out.

The next instant, he started to his feet with a shriek of terror. A human head dropped from his nerveless grasp on the floor, and rolled to Henry's feet. It was the hideous head that Agnes had seen hovering above her, in the vision of the night!

The two men looked at each other, both struck speechless by the same emotion of horror. The manager was the first to control himself. 'See to the door, for God's sake!' he said. 'Some of the people outside may have heard me.'

Henry moved mechanically to the door.

Even when he had his hand on the key, ready to turn it in the lock in case of necessity, he still looked back at the appalling object on the floor. There was no possibility of identifying those decayed and distorted features with any living creature whom he had seen – and, yet, he was conscious of feeling a vague and awful doubt which shook him to the soul. The questions which had tortured the mind of Agnes, were now *his* questions too. *He* asked himself, 'In whose likeness might I have recognised it before the decay set in? The likeness of Ferrari? Or the likeness of – ?' He paused trembling, as Agnes had paused trembling before him. Agnes! The name, of all women's names the dearest to him, was a terror to him now! What was he to say to her? What might be the consequence if he trusted her with the terrible truth?

No footsteps approached the door; no voices were audible outside. The travellers were still occupied in the rooms at the eastern end of the corridor.

In the brief interval that had passed, the manager had sufficiently recovered himself to be able to think once more of the first and foremost interests of his life – the interests of the hotel. He approached Henry anxiously.

'If this frightful discovery becomes known,' he said, 'the closing of the hotel and the ruin of the Company will be the inevitable results. I feel sure that I can trust your discretion, sir, so far?'

'You can certainly trust me,' Henry answered. 'But surely discretion has its limits,' he added, 'after such a discovery as we have made?'

The manager understood that the duty which they owed to the community, as honest and law-abiding men, was the duty to which Henry now referred. 'I will at once find the means,' he said, 'of conveying the remains privately out of the house, and I will myself place them in the care of the police authorities. Will you leave the room with me? Or do you not object to keep watch here, and help me when I return?'

While he was speaking, the voices of the travellers made themselves heard again at the end of the corridor. Henry instantly consented to wait in the room. He shrank from facing the inevitable meeting with Agnes if he showed himself in the corridor at that moment.

The manager hastened his departure, in the hope of escaping notice. He was discovered by his guests before he could reach the head of the stairs. Henry heard the voices plainly as he turned the key. While the terrible drama of discovery was in progress on one side of the door, trivial questions about the amusements of Venice, and facetious discussions on the relative merits of French and Italian cookery, were proceeding on the other. Little by little, the sound of the talking grew fainter. The visitors, having arranged their plans of amusement for the day, were on their way out of the hotel. In a minute or two, there was silence once more.

Henry turned to the window, thinking to relieve his mind by looking at the bright view over the canal. He soon grew wearied of the familiar scene. The morbid fascination which seems to be exercised by all horrible sights, drew him back again to the ghastly object on the floor.

Dream or reality, how had Agnes survived the sight of it? As the question passed through his mind, he noticed for the first time something lying on the floor near the head. Looking closer, he perceived a thin little plate of gold, with three false teeth attached to it, which had apparently dropped out (loosened by the shock) when the manager let the head fall on the floor.

The importance of this discovery, and the necessity of not too readily communicating it to others, instantly struck Henry. Here surely was a chance – if any chance remained – of identifying the shocking relic of humanity which lay before him, the dumb witness of a crime! Acting on this idea, he took possession of the teeth, purposing to use them as a last means of enquiry when other attempts at investigation had been tried and had failed.

He went back again to the window: the solitude of the room began to weigh on his spirits. As he looked out again at the view, there was a soft knock at the door. He hastened to open it – and checked himself in the act. A doubt occurred to him. Was it the manager who had knocked? He called out, 'Who is there?'

The voice of Agnes answered him. 'Have you anything to tell me, Henry?'

He was hardly able to reply. 'Not just now,' he said, confusedly. 'Forgive me if I don't open the door. I will speak to you a little later.'

The sweet voice made itself heard again, pleading with him piteously. 'Don't leave me alone, Henry! I can't go back to the happy people downstairs.'

How could he resist that appeal? He heard her sigh – he heard the rustling of her dress as she moved away in despair. The very thing that he had shrunk from doing but a few minutes since was the thing that he did now! He joined Agnes in the corridor. She turned as she heard him, and pointed, trembling, in the direction of the closed room. 'Is it so terrible as that?' she asked faintly.

He put his arm round her to support her. A thought came to him as he looked at her, waiting in doubt and fear for his reply. 'You shall know what I have discovered,' he said, 'if you will first put on your hat and cloak, and come out with me.'

She was naturally surprised. 'Can you tell me your object in going out?' she asked.

He owned what his object was unreservedly. 'I want, before all things,' he said, 'to satisfy your mind and mine, on the subject of Montbarry's death. I am going to take you to the doctor who attended him in his illness, and to the consul who followed him to the grave.'

Her eyes rested on Henry gratefully. 'Oh, how well you understand me!' she said. The manager joined them at the same moment, on his way up the stairs. Henry gave him the key of the room, and then called to the servants in the hall to have a gondola ready at the steps. 'Are you leaving the hotel?' the manager asked. 'In search of evidence,' Henry whispered, pointing to the key. 'If the authorities want me, I shall be back in an hour.'

Chapter 25

The day had advanced to evening. Lord Montbarry and the bridal party had gone to the Opera. Agnes alone, pleading the excuse of fatigue, remained at the hotel. Having kept up appearances by accompanying his friends to the theatre, Henry Westwick slipped away after the first act, and joined Agnes in the drawing-room.

'Have you thought of what I said to you earlier in the day?' he asked, taking a chair at her side. 'Do you agree with me that the one dreadful doubt which oppressed us both is at least set at rest?'

Agnes shook her head sadly. 'I wish I could agree with you, Henry – I wish I could honestly say that my mind is at ease.'

The answer would have discouraged most men. Henry's patience (where Agnes was concerned) was equal to any demands on it.

'If you will only look back at the events of the day,' he said, 'you must surely admit that we have not been completely baffled. Remember how Dr Bruno disposed of our doubts: "After thirty years of medical practice, do you think I am likely to mistake the symptoms of death by bronchitis?" If ever there was an unanswerable question, there it is! Was the consul's testimony doubtful in any part of it?

He called at the palace to offer his services, after hearing of Lord Montbarry's death; he arrived at the time when the coffin was in the house; he himself saw the corpse placed in it, and the lid screwed down. The evidence of the priest is equally beyond dispute. He remained in the room with the coffin, reciting the prayers for the dead, until the funeral left the palace. Bear all these statements in mind, Agnes, and how can you deny that the question of Montbarry's death and burial is a question set at rest? We have really but one doubt left: we have still to ask ourselves whether the remains which I discovered are the remains of the lost courier, or not. There is the case, as I understand it. Have I stated it fairly?'

Agnes could not deny that he had stated it fairly.

"Then what prevents you from experiencing the same sense of relief that I feel?' Henry asked.

'What I saw last night prevents me,' Agnes answered. 'When we spoke of this subject, after our enquiries were over, you reproached me with taking what you called the superstitious view. I don't quite admit that – but I do acknowledge that I should find the superstitious view intelligible if I heard it expressed by some other person. Remembering what your brother and I once were to each other in the bygone time, I can understand the apparition making itself visible to me, to claim the mercy of Christian burial, and the vengeance due to a crime. I can even perceive some faint possibility of truth in the explanation which you described as the mesmeric theory – that what I saw might be the result of magnetic influence communicated to me, as I lay between the remains of the murdered husband above me and the guilty wife suffering the tortures of remorse at my bedside. But what I do not understand is, that I should have passed through that dreadful ordeal, having no previous knowledge of the murdered man in his lifetime, or only knowing him (if you suppose that I saw the apparition of Ferrari) through the interest which I took in his wife. I can't dispute your reasoning, Henry. But I feel in my heart of hearts that you are deceived. Nothing will shake my belief that we are still as far from having discovered the dreadful truth as ever.'

Henry made no further attempt to dispute with her. She had impressed him with a certain reluctant respect for her own opinion, in spite of himself.

'Have you thought of any better way of arriving at the truth?' he asked. 'Who is to help us? No doubt there is the Countess, who has the clue to the mystery in her own hands. But, in the present state of her mind, is her testimony to be trusted – even if she were willing to speak? Judging by my own experience, I should say decidedly not.'

'You don't mean that you have seen her again?' Agnes eagerly interposed.

'Yes. I disturbed her once more over her endless writing; and I insisted on her speaking out plainly.'

'Then you told her what you found when you opened the hiding-place?'

'Of course I did!' Henry replied. 'I said that I held her responsible for the discovery, though I had not mentioned her connection with it to the authorities as yet. She went on with her writing as if I had spoken in an unknown tongue! I was equally obstinate, on my side. I told her plainly that the head had been placed under the care of the police, and that the manager and I had signed our declarations and given our evidence. She paid not the slightest heed to me. By way of tempting her to speak, I added that the whole investigation was to be kept a secret, and that she might depend on my discretion. For the moment I thought I had succeeded. She looked up from her writing with a passing flash of curiosity, and said, "What are they going to do with it?" – meaning, I suppose, the head. I answered that it was to be privately buried, after photographs of it had first been taken. I even went the length of communicating the opinion of the surgeon con-sulted, that some chemical means of arresting decomposition had been used and had only partially succeeded – and I asked her point-blank if the surgeon was right? The trap was not a bad one – but it completely failed. She said in the coolest manner, "Now you are here, I should like to consult you about my play; I am at a loss for some new incidents." Mind! There was nothing satirical in this. She was really eager to read her wonderful work to me – evidently supposing that I took a special interest in such things, because my brother is the manager of a theatre! I left her, making the first excuse that occurred to me. So far as I am concerned, I can do nothing with her. But it is possible that your influence may succeed with her again, as it has succeeded already. Will you make the attempt, to satisfy your own mind? She is still upstairs; and I am quite ready to accompany you.'

Agnes shuddered at the bare suggestion of another interview with the Countess.

'I can't! I daren't!' she exclaimed. 'After what has happened in that horrible room, she is more repellent to me than ever. Don't ask me to do it, Henry! Feel my hand – you have turned me as cold as death only with talking of it!'

She was not exaggerating the terror that possessed her. Henry hastened to change the subject.

'Let us talk of something more interesting,' he said. 'I have a question to ask you about yourself. Am I right in believing that the sooner you get away from Venice the happier you will be?'

'Right?' she repeated excitedly. 'You are more than right! No words can say how I long to be away from this horrible place. But you know how I am situated – you heard what Lord Montbarry said at dinner-time?'

'Suppose he has altered his plans, since dinner-time?' Henry suggested.

Agnes looked surprised. 'I thought he had received letters from England which obliged him to leave Venice tomorrow,' she said.

'Quite true,' Henry admitted. 'He had arranged to start for England tomorrow, and to leave you and Lady Montbarry and the children to enjoy your holiday in Venice, under my care. Circumstances have occurred, however, which have forced him to alter his plans. He must take you all back with him tomorrow because I am not able to assume the charge of you. I am obliged to give up my holiday in Italy, and return to England too.'

Agnes looked at him in some little perplexity: she was not quite sure whether she understood him or not.

'Are you really obliged to go back?' she asked.

Henry smiled as he answered her. 'Keep the secret,' he said, 'or Montbarry will never forgive me!'

She read the rest in his face. 'Oh!' she exclaimed, blushing brightly, 'you have not given up your pleasant holiday in Italy on my account?'

'I shall go back with you to England, Agnes. That will be holiday enough for me.'

She took his hand in an irrepressible outburst of gratitude. 'How good you are to me!' she murmured tenderly. 'What should I have done in the troubles that have come to me, without your sympathy? I can't tell you, Henry, how I feel your kindness.'

She tried impulsively to lift his hand to her lips. He gently stopped her. 'Agnes,' he said, 'are you beginning to understand how truly I love you?'

That simple question found its own way to her heart. She owned the whole truth, without saying a word. She looked at him – and then looked away again.

He drew her nearer to him. 'My own darling!' he whispered – and kissed her. Softly and tremulously, the sweet lips lingered, and touched his lips in return. Then her head drooped. She put her arms round his neck, and hid her face on his bosom. They spoke no more.

The charmed silence had lasted but a little while, when it was mercilessly broken by a knock at the door.

Agnes started to her feet. She placed herself at the piano; the instrument being opposite to the door, it was impossible, when she seated herself on the music-stool, for any person entering the room to see her face. Henry called out irritably, 'Come in.'

The door was not opened. The person on the other side of it asked a strange question.

'Is Mr Henry Westwick alone?'

Agnes instantly recognised the voice of the Countess. She hurried to a second door, which communicated with one of the bedrooms. 'Don't let her come near me!' she whispered nervously. 'Good-night, Henry! Good-night!'

If Henry could, by an effort of will, have transported the Countess to the uttermost ends of the earth, he would have made the effort without remorse. As it was, he only repeated, more irritably than ever, 'Come in!'

She entered the room slowly with her everlasting manuscript in her hand. Her step was unsteady; a dark flush appeared on her face, in place of its customary pallor; her eyes were bloodshot and widely dilated. In approaching Henry, she showed a strange incapability of calculating her distances – she struck against the table near which he happened to be sitting. When she spoke, her articulation was confused, and her pronunciation of some of the longer words was hardly intelligible. Most men would have suspected her of being under the influence of some intoxicating liquor. Henry took a truer view – he said, as he placed a chair for her, 'Countess, I am afraid you have been working too hard: you look as if you wanted rest.'

She put her hand to her head. 'My invention has gone,' she said. 'I can't write my fourth act. It's all a blank – all a blank!'

Henry advised her to wait till the next day. 'Go to bed,' he suggested; and try to sleep.'

She waved her hand impatiently. 'I must finish the play,' she answered. 'I only want a hint from you. You must know something about plays. Your brother has got a theatre. You must often have heard him talk about fourth and fifth acts – you must have seen rehearsals, and all the rest of it.' She abruptly thrust the manuscript into Henry's hand. 'I can't read it to you,' she said; 'I feel giddy when I look at my own writing. Just run your eye over it, there's a good fellow – and give me a hint.'

Henry glanced at the manuscript. He happened to look at the list of the persons of the drama. As he read the list he started and turned abruptly to the Countess, intending to ask her for some explanation. The words were suspended on his lips. It was but too plainly useless to speak to her. Her head lay back on the rail of the chair. She seemed to be half asleep already. The flush on her face had deepened: she looked like a woman who was in danger of having a fit.

He rang the bell, and directed the man who answered it to send one of the chambermaids upstairs. His voice seemed to partially rouse the Countess; she opened her eyes in a slow drowsy way. 'Have you read it?' she asked.

It was necessary as a mere act of humanity to humour her. 'I will read it willingly,' said Henry, 'if you will go upstairs to bed. You shall hear what I think of it tomorrow morning. Our heads will be clearer, we shall be better able to make the fourth act in the morning.'

The chambermaid came in while he was speaking. 'I am afraid the lady is ill,' Henry whispered. 'Take her up to her room.' The woman looked at the Countess and whispered back, 'Shall we send for a doctor, sir?'

Henry advised taking her upstairs first, and then asking the manager's opinion. There was great difficulty in persuading her to rise, and accept the support of the chambermaid's arm. It was only by reiterated promises to read the play that night, and to make the fourth act in the morning, that Henry prevailed on the Countess to return to her room.

Left to himself, he began to feel a certain languid curiosity in relation to the manuscript. He looked over the pages, reading a line here and a line there. Suddenly he changed colour as he read – and looked up from the manuscript like a man bewildered. 'Good God! What does this mean?' he said to himself.

His eyes turned nervously to the door by which Agnes had left him. She might return to the drawing-room, she might want to see what the Countess had written. He looked back again at the passage which had startled him – considered with himself for a moment – and, snatching up the unfinished play, suddenly and softly left the room.

Chapter 26

Entering his own room on the upper floor, Henry placed the manuscript on his table, open at the first leaf. His nerves were unquestionably shaken; his hand trembled as he turned the pages, he started at chance noises on the staircase of the hotel.

The scenario, or outline, of the Countess's play began with no formal prefatory phrases. She presented herself and her work with the easy familiarity of an old friend.

'Allow me, dear Mr Francis Westwick, to introduce to you the persons in my proposed Play. Behold them, arranged symmetrically in a line.

'My Lord. The Baron. The Courier. The Doctor. The Countess.

'I don't trouble myself, you see, to invent fictitious family names. My characters are sufficiently distinguished by their social titles, and by the striking contrast which they present one with another.

'The First Act opens –

'No! Before I open the First Act, I must announce, in justice to myself, that this Play is entirely the work of my own invention. I scorn to borrow from actual events; and, what is more extraordinary still, I have not stolen one of my ideas from the Modern French drama. As the manager of an English theatre, you will naturally refuse to believe this. It doesn't matter. Nothing matters – except the opening of my first act.

'We are at Homburg, in the famous Salon d'Or, at the height of the season. The Countess (exquisitely dressed) is seated at the green table. Strangers of all nations are standing behind the players, venturing their money or only looking on. My Lord is among the strangers. He is struck by the Countess's personal appearance, in which beauties and defects are fantastically mingled in the most attractive manner. He watches the Countess's game, and places his money where he sees her deposit her own little stake. She looks round at him, and says, "Don't trust to my colour; I have been unlucky the whole evening. Place your stake on the other colour, and you may have a chance of winning." My Lord (a true Englishman) blushes, bows, and obeys. The Countess proves to be a prophet. She loses again. My Lord wins twice the sum that he has risked.

'The Countess rises from the table. She has no more money, and she offers my Lord her chair.

'Instead of taking it, he politely places his winnings in her hand, and begs her to accept the loan as a favour to himself. The Countess stakes again, and loses again. My Lord smiles superbly, and presses a second loan on her. From that moment her luck turns. She wins, and wins largely. Her brother, the Baron, trying his fortune in another room, hears of what is going on, and joins my Lord and the Countess.

'Pay attention, if you please, to the Baron. He is delineated as a remarkable and interesting character.

'This noble person has begun life with a single-minded devotion to the science of experimental chemistry, very surprising in a young and handsome man with a brilliant future before him. A profound knowledge of the occult sciences has persuaded the Baron that it is possible to solve the famous problem called the "Philosopher's Stone". His own pecuniary resources have long since been exhausted by his costly experiments. His sister has next supplied him with the small fortune at her disposal: reserving only the family jewels, placed in the charge of her banker and friend at Frankfort. The Countess's fortune also being swallowed up, the Baron has in a fatal moment sought for new supplies at the gaming table. He proves, at starting on his perilous career, to be a favourite of fortune; wins largely, and, alas! profanes his noble enthusiasm for science by yielding his soul to the all-debasing passion of the gamester.

'At the period of the Play, the Baron's good fortune has deserted him. He sees his way to a crowning experiment in the fatal search after the secret of transmuting the baser elements into gold. But how is he to pay the preliminary expenses? Destiny, like a mocking echo, answers, How?

'Will his sister's winnings (with my Lord's money) prove large enough to help him? Eager for this result, he gives the Countess his advice how to play. From that disastrous moment the infection of his own adverse fortune spreads to his sister. She loses again, and again – loses to the last farthing.

'The amiable and wealthy Lord offers a third loan; but the scrupulous Countess positively refuses to take it. On leaving the table, she presents her brother to my Lord. The gentlemen fall into pleasant talk. My Lord asks leave to pay his respects to the Countess, the next morning, at her hotel. The Baron hospitably invites him to breakfast. My Lord accepts, with a last admiring glance at the Countess which does not escape her brother's observation, and takes his leave for the night.

'Alone with his sister, the Baron speaks out plainly. "Our affairs," he says, "are in a desperate condition, and must find a desperate remedy. Wait for me here, while I make enquiries about my Lord. You have evidently produced a strong impression on him. If we can turn that impression into money, no matter at what sacrifice, the thing must be done."

'The Countess now occupies the stage alone, and indulges in a soliloquy which develops her character.

'It is at once a dangerous and attractive character. Immense capacities for good are implanted in her nature, side by side with equally remarkable capacities for evil. It rests with circumstances to develop either the one or the other. Being a person who produces a sensation wherever she goes, this noble lady is naturally made the subject of all sorts of scandalous reports. To one of these reports (which falsely and abominably points to the Baron as her lover instead of her brother) she now refers with just indignation. She has just expressed her desire to leave Homburg, as the place in which the vile calumny first took its rise, when the Baron returns, overhears her last words, and says to her, "Yes, leave Homburg by all means, provided you leave it in the character of my Lord's betrothed wife!"

'The Countess is startled and shocked. She protests that she does not reciprocate my Lord's admiration for her. She even goes the length of refusing to see him again. The Baron answers, "I must positively have command of money. Take your choice, between marrying my Lord's income, in the interest of my grand discovery – or leave me to sell myself and my title to the first rich woman of low degree who is ready to buy me."

'The Countess listens in surprise and dismay. Is it possible that the Baron is in earnest? He is horribly in earnest. "The woman who will buy me," he says, "is in the next room to us at this moment. She is the wealthy widow of a Jewish usurer. She has the money I want to reach the solution of the great problem. I have only to be that woman's husband, and to make myself master of untold millions of gold. Take five minutes to consider what I have said to you, and tell me on my return which of us is to marry for the money I want, you or I."

'As he turns away, the Countess stops him.

'All the noblest sentiments in her nature are exalted to the highest pitch. "Where is the true woman," she exclaims, "who wants time to consummate the sacrifice of herself, when the man to whom she is devoted demands it? She does not want five minutes – she does not want five seconds – she holds out her hand to him, and she says, Sacrifice me on the altar of your glory! Take as stepping-stones on the way to your triumph, my love, my liberty, and my life!"

'On this grand situation the curtain falls. Judging by my first act, Mr Westwick, tell me truly, and don't be afraid of turning my head – Am I not capable of writing a good play?'

Henry paused between the First and Second Acts; reflecting, not on the merits of the play, but on the strange resemblance which the incidents so far presented to the incidents that had attended the disastrous marriage of the first Lord Montbarry.

Was it possible that the Countess, in the present condition of her mind, supposed herself to be exercising her invention when she was only exercising her memory?

The question involved considerations too serious to be made the subject of a hasty decision. Reserving his opinion, Henry turned the page, and devoted himself to the reading of the next act. The manuscript proceeded as follows:

'The Second Act opens at Venice. An interval of four months has elapsed since the date of the scene at the gambling table. The action now takes place in the reception-room of one of the Venetian palaces.

'The Baron is discovered, alone, on the stage. He reverts to the events which have happened since the close of the First Act. The Countess has sacrificed herself; the mercenary marriage has taken place – but not without obstacles, caused by difference of opinion on the question of marriage settlements.

'Private enquiries, instituted in England, have informed the Baron that my Lord's income is derived chiefly from what is called entailed property. In case of accidents, he is surely bound to do something for his bride? Let him, for example, insure his life, for a sum proposed by the Baron, and let him so settle the money that his widow shall have it, if he dies first.

'My Lord hesitates. The Baron wastes no time in useless discussion. "Let us by all means" (he says) "consider the marriage as broken off." My Lord shifts his ground, and pleads for a smaller sum than the sum proposed. The Baron briefly replies, "I never bargain." My lord is in love; the natural result follows – he gives way.

'So far, the Baron has no cause to complain. But my Lord's turn comes, when the marriage has been celebrated, and when the honeymoon is over. The Baron has joined the married pair at a palace which they have hired in Venice. He is still bent on solving the problem of the "Philosopher's Stone". His laboratory is set up in the vaults beneath the palace – so that smells from chemical experiments may not incommode the Countess, in the higher regions of the house. The one obstacle in the way of his grand discovery is, as usual, the want of money. His position at the present time has become truly critical. He owes debts of honour to gentlemen in his own rank of life, which must positively be paid; and he proposes, in his own friendly manner, to borrow the money of my Lord. My Lord positively refuses, in the rudest terms. The Baron applies to his sister to exercise her conjugal influence. She can only answer that her noble husband (being no longer distractedly in love with her) now appears in his true character, as one of the meanest men living. The sacrifice of the marriage has been made, and has already proved useless.

'Such is the state of affairs at the opening of the Second Act.

'The entrance of the Countess suddenly disturbs the Baron's reflections. She is in a state bordering on frenzy. Incoherent expressions of rage burst from her lips: it is some time before she can sufficiently control herself to speak plainly. She has been doubly insulted – first, by a menial person in her employment; secondly, by her husband. Her maid, an Englishwoman, has declared that she will serve the Countess no longer. She will give up her wages, and return at once to England. Being asked her reason for this strange proceeding, she insolently hints that the Countess's service is no service for an honest woman, since the Baron has entered the house. The Countess does, what any lady in her position would do; she indignantly dismisses the wretch on the spot.

'My Lord, hearing his wife's voice raised in anger, leaves the study in which he is accustomed to shut himself up over his books, and asks what this disturbance means. The Countess informs him of the outrageous language and conduct of her maid. My Lord not only declares his entire approval of the woman's conduct, but expresses his own abominable doubts of his wife's fidelity in language of such horrible brutality that no lady could pollute her lips by repeating it. "If I had been a man," the Countess says, "and if I had had a weapon in my hand, I would have struck him dead at my feet!"

'The Baron, listening silently so far, now speaks. "Permit me to finish the sentence for you," he says. "You would have struck your husband dead at your feet; and by that rash act, you would have deprived yourself of the insurance money settled on the widow – the very money which is wanted to relieve your brother from the unendurable pecuniary position which he now occupies!"

'The Countess gravely reminds the Baron that this is no joking matter. After what my Lord has said to her, she has little doubt that he will communicate his infamous suspicions to his lawyers in England. If nothing is done to prevent it, she may be divorced and disgraced, and thrown on the world, with no resource but the sale of her jewels to keep her from starving.

'At this moment, the Courier who has been engaged to travel with my Lord from England crosses the stage with a letter to take to the post. The Countess stops him, and asks to look at the address on the letter. She takes it from him for a moment, and shows it to her brother. The handwriting is my Lord's; and the letter is directed to his lawyers in London.

'The Courier proceeds to the post-office. The Baron and the Countess look at each other in silence. No words are needed. They thoroughly understand the position in which they are placed; they clearly see the terrible remedy for it. What is the plain alternative before them? Disgrace and ruin – or, my Lord's death and the insurance money!

'The Baron walks backwards and forwards in great agitation, talking to himself. The Countess hears fragments of what he is saying. He speaks of my Lord's constitution, probably weakened in India – of a cold which my Lord has caught two or three days since – of the remarkable manner in which such slight things as colds sometimes end in serious illness and death.

'He observes that the Countess is listening to him, and asks if she has anything to propose. She is a woman who, with many defects, has the great merit of speaking out. "Is there no such thing as a serious illness," she asks, "corked up in one of those bottles of yours in the vaults downstairs?"

'The Baron answers by gravely shaking his head. What is he afraid of? A possible examination of the body after death? No: he can set any post-mortem examination at defiance. It is the process of administering the poison that he dreads. A man so distinguished as my Lord cannot be taken seriously ill without medical attendance. Where there is a Doctor, there is always danger of discovery. Then, again, there is the Courier, faithful to my Lord as long as my Lord pays him. Even if the Doctor sees nothing suspicious, the Courier may discover something. The poison, to do its work with the necessary secrecy, must be repeatedly administered in graduated doses. One trifling miscalculation or mistake may rouse suspicion. The insurance offices may hear of it, and may refuse to pay the money. As things are, the Baron will not risk it, and will not allow his sister to risk it in his place.

'My Lord himself is the next character who appears. He has repeatedly rung for the Courier, and the bell has not been answered. "What does this insolence mean?"

'The Countess (speaking with quiet dignity – for why should her infamous husband have the satisfaction of knowing how deeply he has wounded her?) reminds my Lord that the Courier has gone to the post. My Lord asks suspiciously if she has looked at the letter. The Countess informs him coldly that she has no curiosity about his letters. Referring to the cold from which he is suffering, she enquires if he thinks of consulting a medical man. My Lord answers roughly that he is quite old enough to be capable of doctoring himself.

'As he makes this reply, the Courier appears, returning from the post. My Lord gives him orders to go out again and buy some lemons. He proposes to try hot lemonade as a means of inducing perspiration in bed. In that way he has formerly cured colds, and in that way he will cure the cold from which he is suffering now.

'The Courier obeys in silence. Judging by appearances, he goes very reluctantly on this second errand.

'My Lord turns to the Baron (who has thus far taken no part in the conversation) and asks him, in a sneering tone, how much longer he proposes to prolong his stay in Venice. The Baron answers quietly, "Let us speak plainly to one another, my Lord. If you wish me to leave your house, you have only to say the word, and I go." My Lord turns to his wife, and asks if she can support the calamity of her brother's absence – laying a grossly insulting emphasis on the word "brother". The Countess preserves her impenetrable composure; nothing in her betrays the deadly hatred with which she regards the titled ruffian who has insulted her. "You are master in this house, my Lord," is all she says. "Do as you please."

'My Lord looks at his wife; looks at the Baron – and suddenly alters his tone. Does he perceive in the composure of the Countess and her brother something lurking under the surface that threatens him? This is at least certain, he makes a clumsy apology for the language that he has used. (Abject wretch!)

'My Lord's excuses are interrupted by the return of the Courier with the lemons and hot water.

'The Countess observes for the first time that the man looks ill. His hands tremble as he places the tray on the table. My Lord orders his Courier to follow him, and make the lemonade in the bedroom. The Countess remarks that the Courier seems hardly capable of obeying his orders. Hearing this, the man admits that he is ill. He, too, is suffering from a cold; he has been kept waiting in a draught at the shop where he bought the lemons; he feels alternately hot and cold, and he begs permission to lie down for a little while on his bed.

'Feeling her humanity appealed to, the Countess volunteers to make the lemonade herself. My Lord takes the Courier by the arm, leads him aside, and whispers these words to him: "Watch her, and see that she puts nothing into the lemonade; then bring it to me with your own hands; and, then, go to bed, if you like."

'Without a word more to his wife, or to the Baron, my Lord leaves the room.

'The Countess makes the lemonade, and the Courier takes it to his master.

'Returning, on the way to his own room, he is so weak, and feels, he says, so giddy, that he is obliged to support himself by the backs of the chairs as he passes them. The Baron, always considerate to persons of low degree, offers his arm. "I am afraid, my poor fellow," he says, "that you are really ill." The Courier makes this extraordinary answer: "It's all over with me, Sir: I have caught my death."

'The Countess is naturally startled. "You are not an old man," she says, trying to rouse the Courier's spirits. "At your age, catching cold doesn't surely mean catching your death?" The Courier fixes his eyes despairingly on the Countess.

' "My lungs are weak, my Lady," he says; "I have already had two attacks of bronchitis. The second time, a great physician joined my own doctor in attendance on me. He considered my recovery almost in the light of a miracle. Take care of yourself," he said. "If you have a third attack of bronchitis, as certainly as two and two make four, you will be a dead man. I feel the same inward shivering, my Lady, that I felt on those two former occasions – and I tell you again, I have caught my death in Venice."

'Speaking some comforting words, the Baron leads him to his room. The Countess is left alone on the stage.

'She seats herself, and looks towards the door by which the Courier has been led out. "Ah! My poor fellow," she says, "if you could only change constitutions with my Lord, what a happy result would follow for the Baron and for me! If *you* could only get cured of a trumpery cold with a little hot lemonade, and if *he* could only catch his death in your place – !"

'She suddenly pauses – considers for a while – and springs to her feet, with a cry of triumphant surprise: the wonderful, the unparalleled idea has crossed her mind like a flash of lightning. Make the two men change names and places – and the deed is done! Where are the obstacles? Remove my Lord (by fair means or foul) from his room; and keep him secretly prisoner in the palace, to live or die as future necessity may determine. Place the Courier in the vacant bed, and call in the doctor to see him – ill, in my Lord's character, and (if he dies) dying under my Lord's name!'

The manuscript dropped from Henry's hands. A sickening sense of horror overpowered him. The question which had occurred to his mind at the close of the First Act of the Play assumed a new and terrible interest now. As far as the scene of the Countess's soliloquy, the incidents of the Second Act had reflected the events of his late brother's life as faithfully as the incidents of the First Act. Was the monstrous plot, revealed in the lines which he had just read, the offspring of the Countess's morbid imagination? Or had she, in this case also, deluded herself with the idea that she was inventing when she was really writing under the influence of her own guilty remembrances of the past? If the latter interpretation were the true one, he had just read the narrative of the contemplated murder of his brother, planned in cold blood by a woman who was at that moment inhabiting the same house with him. While, to make the fatality complete, Agnes herself had innocently provided the conspirators with the one man who was fitted to be the passive agent of their crime.

Even the bare doubt that it might be so was more than he could endure. He left his room, resolved to force the truth out of the Countess, or to denounce her before the authorities as a murderess at large.

Arrived at her door, he was met by a person just leaving the room. The person was the manager. He was hardly recognisable; he looked and spoke like a man in a state of desperation.

'Oh, go in, if you like!' he said to Henry. 'Mark this, sir! I am not a superstitious man; but I do begin to believe that crimes carry their own curse with them. This hotel is under a curse. What happens in the morning? We discover a crime committed in the old days of the palace. The night comes, and brings another dreadful event with it –

a death; a sudden and shocking death, in the house. Go in, and see for yourself! I shall resign my situation, Mr Westwick: I can't contend with the fatalities that pursue me here!'

Henry entered the room.

The Countess was stretched on her bed. The doctor on one side, and the chambermaid on the other, were standing looking at her. From time to time, she drew a heavy stertorous breath, like a person oppressed in sleeping. 'Is she likely to die?' Henry asked.

'She is dead,' the doctor answered. 'Dead of the rupture of a blood-vessel on the brain. Those sounds that you hear are purely mechanical – they may go on for hours.'

Henry looked at the chambermaid. She had little to tell. The Countess had refused to go to bed, and had placed herself at her desk to proceed with her writing. Finding it useless to remonstrate with her, the maid had left the room to speak to the manager. In the shortest possible time, the doctor was summoned to the hotel, and found the Countess dead on the floor. There was this to tell – and no more.

Looking at the writing-table as he went out, Henry saw the sheet of paper on which the Countess had traced her last lines of writing. The characters were almost illegible. Henry could just distinguish the words, 'First Act', and 'Persons of the Drama'. The lost wretch had been thinking of her Play to the last, and had begun it all over again!

Chapter 27

Henry returned to his room.

His first impulse was to throw aside the manuscript, and never to look at it again. The one chance of relieving his mind from the dreadful uncertainty that oppressed it, by obtaining positive evidence of the truth, was a chance annihilated by the Countess's death. What good purpose could be served, what relief could he anticipate, if he read more?

He walked up and down the room. After an interval, his thoughts took a new direction; the question of the manuscript presented itself under another point of view. Thus far, his reading had only informed him that the conspiracy had been planned. How did he know that the plan had been put in execution?

The manuscript lay just before him on the floor. He hesitated; then picked it up; and, returning to the table, read on as follows, from the point at which he had left off.

'While the Countess is still absorbed in the bold yet simple combination of circumstances which she has discovered, the Baron returns. He takes a serious view of the case of the Courier; it may be necessary, he thinks, to send for medical advice. No servant is left in the palace, now the English maid has taken her departure. The Baron himself must fetch the doctor, if the doctor is really needed.

' "Let us have medical help, by all means," his sister replies. "But wait and hear something that I have to say to you first." She then electrifies the Baron by communicating her idea to him. What danger of discovery have they to dread? My Lord's life in Venice has been a life of absolute seclusion: nobody but his banker knows him, even by personal appearance. He has presented his letter of credit as a perfect stranger; and he and his banker have never seen each other since that first visit. He has given no parties, and gone to no parties. On the few occasions when he has hired a gondola or taken a walk, he has always been alone. Thanks to the atrocious suspicion which makes him ashamed of being seen with his wife, he has led the very life which makes the proposed enterprise easy of accomplishment.

'The cautious Baron listens – but gives no positive opinion, as yet. "See what you can do with the Courier," he says; "and I will decide when I hear the result. One valuable hint I may give you before you go. Your man is easily tempted by money – if you only offer him enough. The other day, I asked him, in jest, what he would do for a thousand pounds. He answered, 'Anything.' Bear that in mind, and offer your highest bid without bargaining."

'The scene changes to the Courier's room, and shows the poor wretch with a photographic portrait of his wife in his hand, crying. The Countess enters.

'She wisely begins by sympathising with her contemplated accomplice. He is duly grateful; he confides his sorrows to his gracious mistress. Now that he believes himself to be on his deathbed, he feels remorse for his neglectful treatment of his wife. He could resign himself to die; but despair overpowers him when he remembers that he has saved no money, and that he will leave his widow, without resources, to the mercy of the world.

'On this hint, the Countess speaks. "Suppose you were asked to do a perfectly easy thing," she says; "and suppose you were rewarded for doing it by a present of a thousand pounds, as a legacy for your widow?"

'The Courier raises himself on his pillow, and looks at the Countess with an expression of incredulous surprise. She can hardly be cruel enough (he thinks) to joke with a man in his miserable plight. Will she say plainly what this perfectly easy thing is, the doing of which will meet with such a magnificent reward?

'The Countess answers that question by confiding her project to the Courier, without the slightest reserve.

'Some minutes of silence follow when she has done. The Courier is not weak enough yet to speak without stopping to think first. Still keeping his eyes on the Countess, he makes a quaintly insolent remark on what he has just heard. "I have not hitherto been a religious man; but I feel myself on the way to it. Since your ladyship has spoken to me, I believe in the Devil." It is the Countess's interest to see the humorous side of this confession of faith. She takes no offence. She only says, "I will give you half an hour by yourself, to think over my proposal. You are in danger of death. Decide, in your wife's interests, whether you will die worth nothing, or die worth a thousand pounds."

'Left alone, the Courier seriously considers his position – and decides. He rises with difficulty; writes a few lines on a leaf taken from his pocket-book; and, with slow and faltering steps, leaves the room.

'The Countess, returning at the expiration of the half-hour's interval, finds the room empty. While she is wondering, the Courier opens the door. What has he been doing out of his bed? He answers, "I have been protecting my own life, my lady, on the bare chance that I may recover from the bronchitis for the third time. If you or the Baron attempt to hurry me out of this world, or to deprive me of my thousand pounds reward, I shall tell the doctor where he will find a few lines of writing, which describe your ladyship's plot. I may not have strength enough, in the case supposed, to betray you by making a complete confession with my own lips; but I can employ my last breath to speak the half-dozen words which will tell the doctor where he is to look. Those words, it is needless to add, will be addressed to your Ladyship, if I find your engagements towards me faithfully kept."

'With this audacious preface, he proceeds to state the conditions on which he will play his part in the conspiracy, and die (if he does die) worth a thousand pounds.

'Either the Countess or the Baron are to taste the food and drink brought to his bedside, in his presence, and even the medicines which the doctor may prescribe for him. As for the promised sum of money, it is to be produced in one bank-note, folded in a sheet of paper, on which a line is to be written, dictated by the Courier. The two enclosures are then to be sealed up in an envelope, addressed to his wife, and stamped ready for the post. This done, the letter is to be placed under his pillow; the Baron or the Countess being at liberty to satisfy themselves, day by day, at their own time, that the letter remains in its place, with the seal unbroken, as long as the doctor has any hope of his patient's recovery. The last stipulation follows. The Courier has a conscience; and with a view to keeping it easy, insists that he shall be left in ignorance of that part of the plot which relates to the sequestration of my Lord. Not that he cares particularly what becomes of his miserly master – but he does dislike taking other people's responsibilities on his own shoulders.

'These conditions being agreed to, the Countess calls in the Baron, who has been waiting events in the next room.

'He is informed that the Courier has yielded to temptation; but he is still too cautious to make any compromising remarks. Keeping his back turned on the bed, he shows a bottle to the Countess. It is labelled "Chloroform". She understands that my Lord is to be removed from his room in a convenient state of insensibility. In what part of the palace is he to be hidden? As they open the door to go out, the Countess whispers that question to the Baron. The Baron whispers back, "In the vaults!" The curtain falls.'

Chapter 28

So the Second Act ended.

Turning to the Third Act, Henry looked wearily at the pages as he let them slip through his fingers. Both in mind and body, he began to feel the need of repose.

In one important respect, the later portion of the manuscript differed from the pages which he had just been reading. Signs of an overwrought brain showed themselves, here and there, as the outline of the play approached its end. The handwriting grew worse and worse. Some of the longer sentences were left unfinished. In the exchange of dialogue, questions and answers were not always attributed respectively to the right speaker. At certain intervals the writer's failing intelligence seemed to recover itself for a while, only to relapse again, and to lose the thread of the narrative more hopelessly than ever.

After reading one or two of the more coherent passages Henry recoiled from the ever-darkening horror of the story. He closed the manuscript, heartsick and exhausted, and threw himself on his bed to rest. The door opened almost at the same moment. Lord Montbarry entered the room.

'We have just returned from the Opera,' he said; 'and we have heard the news of that miserable woman's death. They say you spoke to her in her last moments; and I want to hear how it happened.'

'You shall hear how it happened,' Henry answered; 'and more than that. You are now the head of the family, Stephen; and I feel bound, in the position which oppresses me, to leave you to decide what ought to be done.'

With those introductory words, he told his brother how the Countess's play had come into his hands. 'Read the first few pages,' he said. 'I am anxious to know whether the same impression is produced on both of us.'

Before Lord Montbarry had got halfway through the First Act, he stopped, and looked at his brother. 'What does she mean by boasting of this as her own invention?' he asked. 'Was she too crazy to remember that these things really happened?'

This was enough for Henry: the same impression had been produced on both of them. 'You will do as you please,' he said. 'But if you will be guided by me, spare yourself the reading of those pages to come, which describe our brother's terrible expiation of his heartless marriage.'

'Have you read it all, Henry?'

'Not all. I shrank from reading some of the latter part of it. Neither you nor I saw much of our elder brother after we left school; and, for my part, I felt, and never scrupled to express my feeling, that he behaved infamously to Agnes. But when I read that unconscious confession of the murderous conspiracy to which he fell a victim, I remembered, with something like remorse, that the same mother bore us. I have felt for him tonight, what I am ashamed to think I never felt for him before.'

Lord Montbarry took his brother's hand.

'You are a good fellow, Henry,' he said; 'but are you quite sure that you have not been needlessly distressing yourself? Because some of this crazy creature's writing accidentally tells what we know to be the truth, does it follow that all the rest is to be relied on to the end?'

'There is no possible doubt of it,' Henry replied.

'No possible doubt?' his brother repeated. 'I shall go on with my reading, Henry – and see what justification there may be for that confident conclusion of yours.'

He read on steadily, until he had reached the end of the Second Act. Then he looked up.

'Do you really believe that the mutilated remains which you discovered this morning are the remains of our brother?' he asked. 'And do you believe it on such evidence as this?'

Henry answered silently by a sign in the affirmative.

Lord Montbarry checked himself – evidently on the point of entering an indignant protest.

'You acknowledge that you have not read the later scenes of the piece,' he said. 'Don't be childish, Henry! If you persist in pinning your faith on such stuff as this, the least you can do is to make yourself thoroughly acquainted with it. Will you read the Third Act? No? Then I shall read it to you.'

He turned to the Third Act, and ran over those fragmentary passages which were clearly enough written and expressed to be intelligible to the mind of a stranger.

'Here is a scene in the vaults of the palace,' he began. 'The victim of the conspiracy is sleeping on his miserable bed; and the Baron and the Countess are considering the position in which they stand. The Countess (as well as I can make it out) has raised the money that is wanted by borrowing on the security of her jewels at Frankfort; and the Courier upstairs is still declared by the Doctor to have a chance of recovery. What are the conspirators to do, if the man does recover? The cautious Baron suggests setting the prisoner free. If he ventures to appeal to the law, it is easy to declare that he is subject to insane delusion, and to call his own wife as witness. On the other hand, if the Courier dies, how is the sequestrated and unknown nobleman to be put out of the way? Passively, by letting him starve in his prison? No: the Baron is a man of refined tastes; he dislikes needless cruelty. The active policy remains – say, assassination by the knife of a hired bravo? The Baron objects to trusting an accomplice; also to spending money on anyone but himself. Shall they drop their prisoner into the canal? The Baron declines to trust water; water will show him on the surface. Shall they set his bed on fire? An excellent idea; but the smoke might be seen. No: the circumstances being now entirely altered, poisoning him presents the easiest way out of it. He has simply become a superfluous person. The cheapest poison will do. – Is it possible, Henry, that you believe this consultation really took place?'

Henry made no reply. The succession of the questions that had just been read to him, exactly followed the succession of the dreams that had terrified Mrs Norbury, on the two nights which she had passed in the hotel. It was useless to point out this coincidence to his brother. He only said, 'Go on.'

Lord Montbarry turned the pages until he came to the next intelligible passage.

'Here,' he proceeded, 'is a double scene on the stage – so far as I can understand the sketch of it. The Doctor is upstairs, innocently writing his certificate of my Lord's decease, by the dead Courier's bedside. Down in the vaults, the Baron stands by the corpse of the poisoned lord, preparing the strong chemical acids which are to reduce it to a heap of ashes – Surely, it is not worth while to trouble ourselves with deciphering such melodramatic horrors as these? Let us get on! Let us get on!'

He turned the leaves again; attempting vainly to discover the meaning of the confused scenes that followed. On the last page but one, he found the last intelligible sentences.

'The Third Act seems to be divided,' he said, 'into two Parts or Tableaux. I think I can read the writing at the beginning of the Second Part. The Baron and the Countess open the scene. The Baron's hands are mysteriously concealed by gloves. He has reduced the body to ashes by his own system of cremation, with the exception of the head – '

Henry interrupted his brother there. 'Don't read any more!' he exclaimed.

'Let us do the Countess justice,' Lord Montbarry persisted. 'There are not half a dozen lines more that I can make out! The accidental breaking of his jar of acid has burnt the Baron's hands severely. He is still unable to proceed to the destruction of the head – and the Countess is woman enough (with all her wickedness) to shrink from attempting to take his place – when the first news is received of the coming arrival of the commission of inquiry despatched by the insurance offices. The Baron feels no alarm. Enquire as the commission may, it is the natural death of the Courier (in my Lord's character) that they are blindly investigating. The head not being destroyed, the obvious alternative is to hide it – and the Baron is equal to the occasion. His studies in the old library have informed him of a safe place of concealment in the palace. The Countess may recoil from handling the acids and watching the process of cremation; but she can surely sprinkle a little disinfecting powder – '

'No more!' Henry reiterated. 'No more!'

'There is no more that can be read, my dear fellow. The last page looks like sheer delirium. She may well have told you that her invention had failed her!'

'Face the truth honestly, Stephen, and say her memory.'

Lord Montbarry rose from the table at which he had been sitting, and looked at his brother with pitying eyes.

'Your nerves are out of order, Henry,' he said. 'And no wonder, after that frightful discovery under the hearthstone. We won't dispute about it; we will wait a day or two until you are quite yourself again. In the meantime, let us understand each other on one point at least. You leave the question of what is to be done with these pages of writing to me, as the head of the family?'

'I do.'

Lord Montbarry quietly took up the manuscript, and threw it into the fire. 'Let this rubbish be of some use,' he said, holding the pages down with the poker. 'The room is getting chilly – the Countess's play will set some of these charred logs flaming again.' He waited a little at the fireplace, and returned to his brother. 'Now, Henry, I have a last word to say, and then I have done. I am ready to admit that you have stumbled, by an unlucky chance, on the proof of a crime committed in the old days of the palace, nobody knows how long ago. With that one concession, I dispute everything else. Rather than agree in the opinion you have formed, I won't believe anything that has happened. The supernatural influences that some of us felt when we first slept in this hotel – your loss of appetite, our sister's dreadful dreams, the smell that overpowered Francis, and the head that appeared to Agnes – I declare them all to be sheer delusions! I believe in nothing, nothing, nothing!' He opened the door to go out, and looked back into the room. 'Yes,' he resumed, 'there is one thing I believe in. My wife has committed a breach of confidence – I believe Agnes will marry you. Good night, Henry. We leave Venice the first thing tomorrow morning.

So Lord Montbarry disposed of the mystery of The Haunted Hotel.

Postscript

A last chance of deciding the difference of opinion between the two brothers remained in Henry's possession. He had his own idea of the use to which he might put the false teeth as a means of enquiry when he and his fellow-travellers returned to England.

The only surviving depositary of the domestic history of the family in past years, was Agnes Lockwood's old nurse. Henry took his first opportunity of trying to revive her personal recollections of the deceased Lord Montbarry. But the nurse had never forgiven the great man of the family for his desertion of Agnes; she flatly refused to consult her memory. 'Even the bare sight of my lord, when I last saw him in London,' said the old woman, 'made my fingernails itch to set their mark on his face. I was sent on an errand by Miss Agnes; and I met him coming out of his dentist's door – and, thank God, that's the last I ever saw of him!'

Thanks to the nurse's quick temper and quaint way of expressing herself, the object of Henry's enquiries was gained already! He ventured on asking if she had noticed the situation of the house. She had noticed, and still remembered the situation – did Master Henry suppose she had lost the use of her senses, because she happened to be nigh on eighty years old? The same day, he took the false teeth to the dentist, and set all further doubt (if doubt had still been possible) at rest for ever. The teeth had been made for the first Lord Montbarry.

Henry never revealed the existence of this last link in the chain of discovery to any living creature, his brother Stephen included. He carried his terrible secret with him to the grave.

There was one other event in the memorable past on which he preserved the same compassionate silence. Little Mrs Ferrari never knew that her husband had been – not, as she supposed, the Countess's victim – but the Countess's accomplice. She still believed that the late Lord Montbarry had sent her the thousand-pound note, and still recoiled from making use of a present which she persisted in declaring had 'the stain of her husband's blood on it'. Agnes, with the widow's entire approval, took the money to the Children's Hospital, and spent it in adding to the number of the beds.

In the spring of the new year, the marriage took place. At the special request of Agnes, the members of the family were the only persons present at the ceremony. There was no wedding breakfast –

and the honeymoon was spent in the retirement of a cottage on the banks of the Thames.

During the last few days of the residence of the newly married couple by the riverside, Lady Montbarry's children were invited to enjoy a day's play in the garden. The eldest girl overheard (and reported to her mother) a little conjugal dialogue which touched on the topic of The Haunted Hotel.

'Henry, I want you to give me a kiss.'

'There it is, my dear.'

'Now I am your wife, may I speak to you about something?'

'What is it?'

'Something that happened the day before we left Venice. You saw the Countess, during the last hours of her life. Won't you tell me whether she made any confession to you?'

'No conscious confession, Agnes – and therefore no confession that I need distress you by repeating.'

'Did she say nothing about what she saw or heard, on that dreadful night in my room?'

'Nothing. We only know that her mind never recovered from the terror of it.'

Agnes was not quite satisfied. The subject troubled her. Even her own brief intercourse with her miserable rival of other days suggested questions that perplexed her. She remembered the Countess's prediction. 'You have to bring me to the day of discovery, and to the punishment that is my doom.' Had the prediction simply faded, like other mortal prophecies? – or had it been fulfilled on the terrible night when she had seen the apparition, and when she had innocently tempted the Countess to watch her in her room?

Let it, however, be recorded, among the other virtues of Mrs Henry Westwick, that she never again attempted to persuade her husband into betraying his secrets. Other men's wives, hearing of this extraordinary conduct (and being trained in the modern school of morals and manners), naturally regarded her with compassionate contempt. They spoke of Agnes, from that time forth, as 'rather an old-fashioned person'.

Is that all?

That is all.

Is there no explanation of the mystery of The Haunted Hotel?

Ask yourself if there is any explanation of the mystery of your own life and death. – Farewell.

The Dream Woman

I

I had not been settled much more than six weeks in my country practice when I was sent for to a neighbouring town, to consult with the resident medical man there on a case of very dangerous illness.

My horse had come down with me at the end of a long ride the night before, and had hurt himself, luckily, much more than he had hurt his master. Being deprived of the animal's services, I started for my destination by the coach (there were no railways at that time), and I hoped to get back again, toward the afternoon, in the same way.

After the consultation was over, I went to the principal inn of the town to wait for the coach. When it came up it was full inside and out. There was no resource left me but to get home as cheaply as I could by hiring a gig. The price asked for this accommodation struck me as being so extortionate, that I determined to look out for an inn of inferior pretensions, and to try if I could not make a better bargain with a less prosperous establishment.

I soon found a likely-looking house, dingy and quiet, with an old-fashioned sign, that had evidently not been repainted for many years past. The landlord, in this case, was not above making a small profit, and as soon as we came to terms he rang the yard-bell to order the gig.

'Has Robert not come back from that errand?' asked the landlord, appealing to the waiter who answered the bell.

'No, sir, he hasn't.'

'Well, then, you must wake up Isaac.'

'Wake up Isaac!' I repeated; 'that sounds rather odd. Do your ostlers go to bed in the daytime?'

'This one does,' said the landlord, smiling to himself in rather a strange way.

'And dreams too,' added the waiter; 'I shan't forget the turn it gave me the first time I heard him.'

'Never you mind about that,' retorted the proprietor; 'you go and rouse Isaac up. The gentleman's waiting for his gig.'

The landlord's manner and the waiter's manner expressed a great deal more than they either of them said. I began to suspect that I might be on the trace of something professionally interesting to me as a medical man, and I thought I should like to look at the ostler before the waiter awakened him.

'Stop a minute,' I interposed; 'I have rather a fancy for seeing this man before you wake him up. I'm a doctor; and if this queer sleeping and dreaming of his comes from anything wrong in his brain, I may be able to tell you what to do with him.'

'I rather think you will find his complaint past all doctoring, sir,' said the landlord; 'but, if you would like to see him, you're welcome, I'm sure.'

He led the way across a yard and down a passage to the stables, opened one of the doors, and, waiting outside himself, told me to look in.

I found myself in a two-stall stable. In one of the stalls a horse was munching his corn; in the other an old man was lying asleep on the litter.

I stooped and looked at him attentively. It was a withered, woebegone face. The eyebrows were painfully contracted; the mouth was fast set, and drawn down at the corners. The hollow wrinkled cheeks, and the scantly grizzled hair, told their own tale of some past sorrow or suffering. He was drawing his breath convulsively when I first looked at him, and in a moment more he began to talk in his sleep.

'Wake up!' I heard him say, in a quick whisper, through his clenched teeth. 'Wake up there! Murder!'

He moved one lean arm slowly till it rested over his throat, shuddered a little, and turned on his straw. Then the arm left his throat, the hand stretched itself out, and clutched at the side toward which he had turned, as if he fancied himself to be grasping at the edge of something. I saw his lips move, and bent lower over him. He was still talking in his sleep.

'Light grey eyes,' he murmured, 'and a droop in the left eyelid; flaxen hair, with a gold-yellow streak in it – all right, mother – fair white arms, with a down on them – little lady's hand, with a reddish look under the finger nails. The knife – always the cursed knife – first on one side, then on the other. Aha! You she-devil, where's the knife?'

At the last word his voice rose, and he grew restless on a sudden. I saw him shudder on the straw; his withered face became distorted, and he threw up both his hands with a quick hysterical gasp. They struck against the bottom of the manger under which he lay, and the blow awakened him. I had just time to slip through the door and close it before his eyes were fairly open, and his senses his own again.

'Do you know anything about that man's past life?' I said to the landlord.

'Yes, sir, I know pretty well all about it,' was the answer, 'and an uncommon queer story it is. Most people don't believe it. It's true, though, for all that. Why, just look at him,' continued the landlord, opening the stable door again. 'Poor devil! He's so worn out with his restless nights that he's dropped back into his sleep already.'

'Don't wake him,' I said; 'I'm in no hurry for the gig. Wait till the other man comes back from his errand; and, in the meantime, suppose I have some lunch and a bottle of sherry, and suppose you come and help me to get through it?'

The heart of mine host, as I had anticipated, warmed to me over his own wine. He soon became communicative on the subject of the man asleep in the stable, and by little and little I drew the whole story out of him. Extravagant and incredible as the events must appear to everybody, they are related here just as I heard them and just as they happened.

2

Some years ago there lived in the suburbs of a large seaport town on the west coast of England a man in humble circumstances, by name Isaac Scatchard. His means of subsistence were derived from any employment that he could get as an ostler, and occasionally, when times went well with him, from temporary engagements in service as stable-helper in private houses. Though a faithful, steady, and honest man, he got on badly in his calling. His ill-luck was proverbial among his neighbours. He was always missing good opportunities by no fault of his own, and always living longest in service with amiable people who were not punctual payers of wages. 'Unlucky Isaac' was his nickname in his own neighbourhood, and no one could say that he did not richly deserve it.

With far more than one man's fair share of adversity to endure, Isaac had but one consolation to support him, and that was of the dreariest and most negative kind. He had no wife and children to increase his anxieties and add to the bitterness of his various failures in life. It might have been from mere insensibility, or it might have been from generous unwillingness to involve another in his own unlucky destiny; but the fact undoubtedly was, that he had arrived at the middle term of life without marrying, and, what is much more remarkable, without once exposing himself, from eighteen to eight-and-thirty, to the genial imputation of ever having had a sweetheart.

When he was out of service he lived alone with his widowed mother. Mrs Scatchard was a woman above the average in her lowly station as to capacity and manners. She had seen better days, as the phrase is, but she never referred to them in the presence of curious visitors; and, though perfectly polite to everyone who approached her, never cultivated any intimacies among her neighbours. She contrived to provide, hardly enough, for her simple wants by doing rough work for the tailors, and always managed to keep a decent home for her son to return to whenever his ill-luck drove him out helpless into the world.

One bleak autumn, when Isaac was getting on fast toward forty, and when he was, as usual, out of place through no fault of his own, he set forth from his mother's cottage on a long walk inland to a gentleman's seat where he had heard that a stable-help was required.

It wanted then but two days of his birthday; and Mrs Scatchard, with her usual fondness, made him promise, before he started, that he would be back in time to keep that anniversary with her, in as festive a way as their poor means would allow. It was easy for him to comply with this request, even supposing he slept a night each way on the road.

He was to start from home on Monday morning, and, whether he got the new place or not, he was to be back for his birthday dinner on Wednesday at two o'clock.

Arriving at his destination too late on the Monday night to make application for the stable-helper's place, he slept at the village inn, and in good time on the Tuesday morning presented himself at the gentleman's house to fill the vacant situation. Here again his ill-luck pursued him as inexorably as ever. The excellent written testimonials to his character which he was able to produce availed him nothing; his long walk had been taken in vain: only the day before the stable-helper's place had been given to another man.

Isaac accepted this new disappointment resignedly and as a matter of course. Naturally slow in capacity, he had the bluntness of sensibility and phlegmatic patience of disposition which frequently distinguish men with sluggishly-working mental powers. He thanked the gentleman's steward with his usual quiet civility for granting him an interview, and took his departure with no appearance of unusual depression in his face or manner.

Before starting on his homeward walk, he made some enquiries at the inn, and ascertained that he might save a few miles on his return by following a new road. Furnished with full instructions, several times repeated, as to the various turnings he was to take, he set forth on his homeward journey, and walked on all day with only one stoppage for bread and cheese. Just as it was getting toward dark, the rain came on and the wind began to rise, and he found himself, to make matters worse, in a part of the country with which he was entirely unacquainted, though he knew himself to be some fifteen miles from home. The first house he found to enquire at was a lonely roadside inn, standing on the outskirts of a thick wood. Solitary as the place looked, it was welcome to a lost man who was also hungry, thirsty, footsore, and wet. The landlord was civil and respectable-looking, and the price he asked for a bed was reasonable enough. Isaac therefore decided on stopping comfortably at the inn for that night.

He was constitutionally a temperate man. His supper consisted of two rashers of bacon, a slice of home-made bread, and a pint of ale. He did not go to bed immediately after his moderate meal, but sat up with the landlord, talking about his bad prospects and his long run of ill-luck, and diverging from these topics to the subjects of horse-flesh and racing. Nothing was said either by himself, his host, or the few labourers who strayed into the tap-room, which could, in the slightest degree, excite the very small and very dull imaginative faculty which Isaac Scatchard possessed.

At a little after eleven the house was closed. Isaac went round with the landlord and held the candle while the doors and lower windows were being secured. He noticed with surprise the strength of the bolts and bars, and iron-sheathed shutters.

'You see, we are rather lonely here,' said the landlord. 'We never have had any attempts made to break in yet, but it's always as well to be on the safe side. When nobody is sleeping here, I am the only man in the house. My wife and daughter are timid, and the servant-girl takes after her missusses. Another glass of ale before you turn in? No! Well, how such a sober man as you comes to be out of place is more than I can make out, for one. Here's where you're to sleep. You're our only lodger tonight, and I think you'll say my missus has done her best to make you comfortable. You're quite sure you won't have another glass of ale? Very well. Goodnight.'

It was half past eleven by the clock in the passage as they went upstairs to the bedroom, the window of which looked on to the wood at the back of the house.

Isaac locked the door, set his candle on the chest of drawers, and wearily got ready for bed. The bleak autumn wind was still blowing, and the solemn, monotonous, surging moan of it in the wood was dreary and awful to hear through the night-silence. Isaac felt strangely wakeful. He resolved, as he lay down in bed, to keep the candle alight until he began to grow sleepy, for there was something unendurably depressing in the bare idea of lying awake in the darkness, listening to the dismal, ceaseless moaning of the wind in the wood.

Sleep stole on him before he was aware of it. His eyes closed, and he fell off insensibly to rest without having so much as thought of extinguishing the candle.

The first sensation of which he was conscious after sinking into slumber was a strange shivering that ran through him suddenly from head to foot, and a dreadful sinking pain at the heart, such as he had never felt before. The shivering only disturbed his slumbers; the pain woke him instantly. In one moment he passed from a state of sleep to a state of wakefulness – his eyes wide open – his mental perceptions cleared on a sudden, as if by a miracle.

The candle had burnt down nearly to the last morsel of tallow, but the top of the unsnuffed wick had just fallen off, and the light in the little room was, for the moment, fair and full.

Between the foot of his bed and the closed door there stood a woman with a knife in her hand, looking at him.

He was stricken speechless with terror, but he did not lose the preternatural clearness of his faculties, and he never took his eyes off the woman. She said not a word as they stared each other in the face, but she began to move slowly toward the left-hand side of the bed.

His eyes followed her. She was a fair, fine woman, with yellowish flaxen hair and light grey eyes, with a droop in the left eyelid. He noticed those things and fixed them on his mind before she was round at the side of the bed. Speechless, with no expression in her face, with no noise following her footfall, she came closer and closer – stopped – and slowly raised the knife. He laid his right arm over his throat to save it; but, as he saw the knife coming down, threw his hand across the bed to the right side, and jerked his body over that way just as the knife descended on the mattress within an inch of his shoulder.

His eyes fixed on her arm and hand as she slowly drew her knife out of the bed: a white, well-shaped arm, with a pretty down lying lightly over the fair skin – a delicate lady's hand, with the crowning beauty of a pink flush under and round the fingernails.

She drew the knife out, and passed back again slowly to the foot of the bed; stopped there for a moment looking at him; then came on – still speechless, still with no expression on the blank, beautiful face, still with no sound following the stealthy footfalls – came on to the right side of the bed, where he now lay.

As she approached she raised the knife again, and he drew himself away to the left side. She struck, as before, right into the mattress, with a deliberate, perpendicularly-downward action of the arm. This time his eyes wandered from her to the knife. It was like the large clasp-knives which he had often seen labouring men use to cut their bread and bacon with. Her delicate little fingers did not conceal more than two thirds of the handle: he noticed that it was made of buckhorn, clean and shining as the blade was, and looking like new.

For the second time she drew the knife out, concealed it in the wide sleeve of her gown, then stopped by the bedside, watching him. For an instant he saw her standing in that position, then the wick of the spent candle fell over into the socket; the flame diminished to a little blue point, and the room grew dark.

A moment, or less, if possible, passed so, and then the wick flamed up, smokingly, for the last time. His eyes were still looking eagerly over the right-hand side of the bed when the final flash of light came, but they discerned nothing. The fair woman with the knife was gone.

The conviction that he was alone again weakened the hold of the terror that had struck him dumb up to this time The preternatural sharpness which the very intensity of his panic had mysteriously imparted to his faculties left them suddenly. His brain grew confused – his heart beat wildly – his ears opened for the first time since the appearance of the woman to a sense of the woeful ceaseless moaning of the wind among the trees. With the dreadful conviction of the reality of what he had seen still strong within him, he leaped out of bed, and screaming 'Murder! Wake up, there! Wake up!' dashed headlong through the darkness to the door.

It was fast locked, exactly as he had left it on going to bed.

His cries on starting up had alarmed the house. He heard the terrified, confused exclamations of women; he saw the master of the house approaching along the passage with his burning rush-candle in one hand and his gun in the other.

'What is it?' asked the landlord, breathlessly.

Isaac could only answer in a whisper. 'A woman, with a knife in her hand,' he gasped out. 'In my room – a fair, yellow-haired woman; she jabbed at me with the knife twice over.'

The landlord's pale cheeks grew paler. He looked at Isaac eagerly by the flickering light of his candle, and his face began to get red again; his voice altered, too, as well as his complexion.

'She seems to have missed you twice,' he said.

'I dodged the knife as it came down,' Isaac went on, in the same scared whisper. 'It struck the bed each time.'

The landlord took his candle into the bedroom immediately. In less than a minute he came out again into the passage in a violent passion.

'The devil fly away with you and your woman with the knife! There isn't a mark in the bedclothes anywhere. What do you mean by coming into a man's place, and frightening his family out of their wits about a dream?'

'I'll leave your house,' said Isaac, faintly. 'Better out on the road, in rain and dark, on my road home, than back again in that room, after what I've seen in it. Lend me a light to get my clothes by, and tell me what I'm to pay.'

'Pay!' cried the landlord, leading the way with his light sulkily into the bedroom. 'You'll find your score on the slate when you go downstairs. I wouldn't have taken you in for all the money you've got about you if I'd known your dreaming, screeching ways before-hand. Look at the bed. Where's the cut of a knife in it? Look at the window – is the lock bursted? Look at the door (which I heard you fasten yourself) – is it broke in? A murdering woman with a knife in my house! You ought to be ashamed of yourself!'

Isaac answered not a word. He huddled on his clothes, and then they went down stairs together.

'Nigh on twenty minutes past two!' said the landlord, as they passed the clock. 'A nice time in the morning to frighten honest people out of their wits!'

Isaac paid his bill, and the landlord let him out at the front door, asking, with a grin of contempt, as he undid the strong fastenings, whether 'the murdering woman got in that way'.

They parted without a word on either side. The rain had ceased, but the night was dark, and the wind bleaker than ever. Little did the darkness, or the cold, or the uncertainty about the way home matter to Isaac. If he had been turned out into a wilderness in a thunderstorm, it would have been a relief after what he had suffered in the bedroom of the inn.

What was the fair woman with the knife? The creature of a dream, or that other creature from the unknown world called among men by the name of ghost? He could make nothing of the mystery – had made nothing of it, even when it was midday on Wednesday, and when he stood, at last, after many times missing his road, once more on the doorstep of home.

3

His mother came out eagerly to receive him. His face told her in a moment that something was wrong.

'I've lost the place; but that's my luck. I dreamed an ill dream last night, mother – or maybe I saw a ghost. Take it either way, it scared me out of my senses, and I'm not my own man again yet.'

'Isaac, your face frightens me. Come in to the fire – come in, and tell mother all about it.'

He was as anxious to tell as she was to hear; for it had been his hope, all the way home, that his mother, with her quicker capacity and superior knowledge, might be able to throw some light on the mystery which he could not clear up for himself. His memory of the dream was still mechanically vivid, though his thoughts were entirely confused by it.

His mother's face grew paler and paler as he went on. She never interrupted him by so much as a single word; but when he had done, she moved her chair close to his, put her arm round his neck, and said to him.

'Isaac, you dreamed your ill dream on this Wednesday morning. What time was it when you saw the fair woman with the knife in her hand?'

Isaac reflected on what the landlord had said when they had passed by the clock on his leaving the inn; allowed as nearly as he could for the time that must have elapsed between the unlocking of his bedroom door and the paying of his bill just before going away, and answered.

'Somewhere about two o'clock in the morning.'

His mother suddenly quitted her hold of his neck, and struck her hands together with a gesture of despair.

'This Wednesday is your birthday, Isaac, and two o'clock in the morning was the time when you were born.'

Isaac's capacities were not quick enough to catch the infection of his mother's superstitious dread. He was amazed, and a little startled also, when she suddenly rose from her chair, opened her old writing-desk, took pen, ink, and paper, and then said to him.

'Your memory is but a poor one, Isaac, and, now I'm an old woman, mine's not much better. I want all about this dream of yours to be as well known to both of us, years hence, as it is now. Tell me over again all you told me a minute ago, when you spoke of what the woman with the knife looked like.'

Isaac obeyed, and marvelled much as he saw his mother carefully set down on paper the very words that he was saying.

'Light grey eyes,' she wrote, as they came to the descriptive part, 'with a droop in the left eyelid; flaxen hair, with a gold-yellow streak in it; white arms, with a down upon them; little lady's hand, with a reddish look about the linger nails; clasp-knife with a buckhorn handle, that seemed as good as new.' To these particulars Mrs Scatchard added the year, month, day of the week, and time in the morning when the woman of the dream appeared to her son. She then locked up the paper carefully in her writing-desk.

Neither on that day nor on any day after could her son induce her to return to the matter of the dream. She obstinately kept her thoughts about it to herself, and even refused to refer again to the paper in her writing-desk. Ere long Isaac grew weary of attempting to make her break her resolute silence; and time, which sooner or later wears out all things, gradually wore out the impression produced on him by the dream. He began by thinking of it ceaselessly, and he ended by not thinking of it at all.

The result was the more easily brought about by the advent of some important changes for the better in his prospects which commenced not long after his terrible night's experience at the inn. He reaped at last the reward of his long and patient suffering under adversity by getting an excellent place, keeping it for seven years, and leaving it, on the death of his master, not only with an excellent character, but also with a comfortable annuity bequeathed to him as a reward for saving his mistress's life in a carriage accident. Thus it happened that Isaac Scatchard returned to his old mother, seven years after the time of the dream at the inn, with an annual sum of money at his disposal sufficient to keep them both in ease and independence for the rest of their lives.

The mother, whose health had been bad of late years, profited so much by the care bestowed on her and by freedom from money anxieties, that when Isaac's birthday came round she was able to sit up comfortably at table and dine with him.

On that day, as the evening drew on, Mrs Scatchard discovered that a bottle of tonic medicine which she was accustomed to take, and in which she had fancied that a dose or more was still left, happened to be empty. Isaac immediately volunteered to go to the chemist's and get it filled again. It was as rainy and bleak an autumn night as on the memorable past occasion when he lost his way and slept at the road-side inn.

On going into the chemist's shop he was passed hurriedly by a poorly-dressed woman coming out of it. The glimpse he had of her face struck him, and he looked back after her as she descended the doorsteps.

'You're noticing that woman?' said the chemist's apprentice behind the counter. 'It's my opinion there's something wrong with her. She's been asking for laudanum to put to a bad tooth. Master's out for half an hour, and I told her I wasn't allowed to sell poison to strangers in his absence. She laughed in a queer way, and said she would come back in half an hour. If she expects master to serve her, I think she'll be disappointed. It's a case of suicide, sir, if ever there was one yet.'

These words added immeasurably to the sudden interest in the woman which Isaac had felt at the first sight of her face. After he had got the medicine-bottle filled, he looked about anxiously for her as soon as he was out in the street. She was walking slowly up and down on the opposite side of the road. With his heart, very much to his own surprise, beating fast, Isaac crossed over and spoke to her.

He asked if she was in any distress. She pointed to her torn shawl, her scanty dress, her crushed, dirty bonnet; then moved under a lamp so as to let the light fall on her stern, pale, but still most beautiful face.

'I look like a comfortable, happy woman, don't I?' she said, with a bitter laugh.

She spoke with a purity of intonation which Isaac had never heard before from other than ladies' lips. Her slightest actions seemed to have the easy, negligent grace of a thorough-bred woman. Her skin, for all its poverty-stricken paleness, was as delicate as if her life had been passed in the enjoyment of every social comfort that wealth can purchase. Even her small, finely-shaped hands, gloveless as they were, had not lost their whiteness.

Little by little, in answer to his questions, the sad story of the woman came out. There is no need to relate it here; it is told over and over again in police reports and paragraphs about Attempted Suicides.

'My name is Rebecca Murdoch,' said the woman, as she ended. 'I have ninepence left, and I thought of spending it at the chemist's over the way in securing a passage to the other world. Whatever it is, it can't be worse to me than this, so why should I stop here?'

Besides the natural compassion and sadness moved in his heart by what he heard, Isaac felt within him some mysterious influence at work all the time the woman was speaking which utterly confused his ideas and almost deprived him of his powers of speech. All that he could say in answer to her last reckless words was that he would prevent her from attempting her own life, if he followed her about all night to do it. His rough, trembling earnestness seemed to impress her.

'I won't occasion you that trouble,' she answered, when he repeated his threat. 'You have given me a fancy for living by speaking kindly to me. No need for the mockery of protestations and promises. You may believe me without them. Come to Fuller's Meadow tomorrow at twelve, and you will find me alive, to answer for myself – No! – no money. My ninepence will do to get me as good a night's lodging as I want.'

She nodded and left him. He made no attempt to follow – he felt no suspicion that she was deceiving him.

'It's strange, but I can't help believing her,' he said to himself, and walked away, bewildered, toward home.

On entering the house, his mind was still so completely absorbed by its new subject of interest that he took no notice of what his mother was doing when he came in with the bottle of medicine. She had opened her old writing-desk in his absence, and was now reading a paper attentively that lay inside it. On every birthday of Isaac's since she had written down the particulars of his dream from his own lips, she had been accustomed to read that same paper, and ponder over it in private.

The next day he went to Fuller's Meadow.

He had done only right in believing her so implicitly. She was there, punctual to a minute, to answer for herself. The last-left faint defences in Isaac's heart against the fascination which a word or look from her began inscrutably to exercise over him sank down and vanished before her forever on that memorable morning.

When a man previously insensible to the influence of women forms an attachment in middle life, the instances are rare indeed, let the warning circumstances be what they may, in which he is found capable of freeing himself from the tyranny of the new ruling passion. The charm of being spoken to familiarly, fondly, and gratefully by a woman whose language and manners still retained enough of their early refinement to hint at the high social station that she had lost, would have been a dangerous luxury to a man of Isaac's rank at the age of twenty. But it was far more than that – it was certain ruin to him – now that his heart was opening unworthily to a new influence at that middle time of life when strong feelings of all kinds, once implanted, strike root most stubbornly in a man's moral nature. A few more stolen interviews after that first morning in Fuller's Meadow completed his infatuation. In less than a month from the time when he first met her, Isaac Scatchard had consented to give Rebecca Murdoch a new interest in existence, and a chance of recovering the character she had lost, by promising to make her his wife.

She had taken possession, not of his passions only, but of his faculties as well. All the mind he had he put into her keeping. She directed him on every point – even instructing him how to break the news of his approaching marriage in the safest manner to his mother.

'If you tell her how you met me and who I am at first,' said the cunning woman, 'she will move heaven and earth to prevent our marriage. Say I am the sister of one of your fellow-servants – ask her to see me before you go into any more particulars – and leave it to me to do the rest. I mean to make her love me next best to you, Isaac, before she knows anything of who I really am.'

The motive of the deceit was sufficient to sanctify it to Isaac. The stratagem proposed relieved him of his one great anxiety, and quieted his uneasy conscience on the subject of his mother. Still, there was something wanting to perfect his happiness, something that he could not realise, something mysteriously untraceable, and yet something that perpetually made itself felt; not when he was absent from Rebecca Murdoch, but, strange to say, when he was actually in her presence! She was kindness itself with him. She never made him feel his inferior capacities and inferior manners. She showed the sweetest anxiety to please him in the smallest trifles; but, in spite of all these attractions, he never could feel quite at his ease with her. At their first meeting, there had mingled with his admiration, when he looked in her face, a faint, involuntary feeling of doubt whether that face was entirely strange to him. No after familiarity had the slightest effect on this inexplicable, wearisome uncertainty.

Concealing the truth as he had been directed, he announced his marriage engagement precipitately and confusedly to his mother on the day when he contracted it. Poor Mrs Scatchard showed her perfect confidence in her son by flinging her arms round his neck, and giving him joy of having found at last, in the sister of one of his fellow-servants, a woman to comfort and care for him after his mother was gone. She was all eagerness to see the woman of her son's choice, and the next day was fixed for the introduction.

It was a bright sunny morning, and the little cottage parlour was full of light as Mrs Scatchard, happy and expectant, dressed for the occasion in her Sunday gown, sat waiting for her son and her future daughter-in-law.

Punctual to the appointed time, Isaac hurriedly and nervously led his promised wife into the room. His mother rose to receive her – advanced a few steps, smiling – looked Rebecca full in the eyes, and suddenly stopped. Her face, which had been flushed the moment before, turned white in an instant; her eyes lost their expression of softness and kindness, and assumed a blank look of terror; her outstretched hands fell to her sides, and she staggered back a few steps with a low cry to her son.

'Isaac,' she whispered, clutching him fast by the arm when he asked alarmedly if she was taken ill, 'Isaac, does that woman's face remind you of nothing?'

Before he could answer – before he could look round to where Rebecca stood, astonished and angered by her reception, at the lower end of the room, his mother pointed impatiently to her writing-desk, and gave him the key.

'Open it,' she said, in a quick, breathless whisper.

'What does this mean? Why am I treated as if I had no business here? Does your mother want to insult me?' asked Rebecca, angrily.

'Open it, and give me the paper in the left-hand drawer. Quick! Quick, for Heaven's sake!' said Mrs Scatchard, shrinking farther back in terror.

Isaac gave her the paper. She looked it over eagerly for a moment, then followed Rebecca, who was now turning away haughtily to leave the room, and caught her by the shoulder – abruptly raised the long, loose sleeve of her gown, and glanced at her hand and arm. Something like fear began to steal over the angry expression of

Rebecca's face as she shook herself free from the old woman's grasp. 'Mad!' she said to herself; 'and Isaac never told me.' With these few words she left the room.

Isaac was hastening after her when his mother turned and stopped his farther progress. It wrung his heart to see the misery and terror in her face as she looked at him.

'Light grey eyes,' she said, in low, mournful, awestruck tones, pointing toward the open door; 'a droop in the left eyelid; flaxen hair, with a gold-yellow streak in it; white arms, with a down upon them; little lady's hand, with a reddish look under the finger nails – *The Dream Woman*, Isaac, the Dream Woman!'

That faint cleaving doubt which he had never been able to shake off in Rebecca Murdoch's presence was fatally set at rest forever. He had seen her face, then, before – seven years before, on his birthday, in the bedroom of the lonely inn.

'Be warned! Oh, my son, be warned! Isaac, Isaac, let her go, and do you stop with me!'

Something darkened the parlour window as those words were said. A sudden chill ran through him, and he glanced sidelong at the shadow. Rebecca Murdoch had come back. She was peering in curiously at them over the low window-blind.

'I have promised to marry, mother,' he said, 'and marry I must.'

The tears came into his eyes as he spoke and dimmed his sight, but he could just discern the fatal face outside moving away again from the window.

His mother's head sank lower.

'Are you faint?' he whispered.

'Broken-hearted, Isaac.'

He stooped down and kissed her. The shadow, as he did so, returned to the window, and the fatal face peered in curiously once more.

4

Three weeks after that day Isaac and Rebecca were man and wife. All that was hopelessly dogged and stubborn in the man's moral nature seemed to have closed round his fatal passion, and to have fixed it unassailably in his heart.

After that first interview in the cottage parlour no consideration would induce Mrs Scatchard to see her son's wife again, or even to talk of her when Isaac tried hard to plead her cause after their marriage.

This course of conduct was not in any degree occasioned by a discovery of the degradation in which Rebecca had lived. There was no question of that between mother and son. There was no question of anything but the fearfully-exact resemblance between the living, breathing woman, and the spectre-woman of Isaac's dream.

Rebecca, on her side, neither felt nor expressed the slightest sorrow at the estrangement between herself and her mother-in-law. Isaac, for the sake of peace, had never contradicted her first idea that age and long illness had affected Mrs Scatchard's mind. He even allowed his wife to upbraid him for not having confessed this to her at the time of their marriage engagement, rather than risk anything by hinting at the truth. The sacrifice of his integrity before his one all-mastering delusion seemed but a small thing, and cost his conscience but little after the sacrifices he had already made.

The time of waking from this delusion – the cruel and the rueful time – was not far off. After some quiet months of married life, as the summer was ending, and the year was getting on toward the month of his birthday, Isaac found his wife altering toward him. She grew sullen and contemptuous; she formed acquaintances of the most dangerous kind in defiance of his objections, his entreaties, and his commands; and, worst of all, she learned, ere long, after every fresh difference with her husband, to seek the deadly self-oblivion of drink. Little by little, after the first miserable discovery that his wife was keeping company with drunkards, the shocking certainty forced itself on Isaac that she had grown to be a drunkard herself.

He had been in a sadly desponding state for some time before the occurrence of these domestic calamities. His mother's health, as he could but too plainly discern every time he went to see her at the cottage, was failing fast, and he upbraided himself in secret as the cause of the bodily and mental suffering she endured. When to his remorse on his mother's account was added the shame and misery occasioned by the discovery of his wife's degradation, he sank under the double trial – his face began to alter fast, and he looked what he was, a spirit-broken man.

His mother, still struggling bravely against the illness that was hurrying her to the grave, was the first to notice the sad alteration in him, and the first to hear of his last worst trouble with his wife. She could only weep bitterly on the day when he made his humiliating confession, but on the next occasion when he went to see her she had taken a resolution in reference to his domestic afflictions which astonished and even alarmed him. He found her dressed to go out, and on asking the reason received this answer:

'I am not long for this world, Isaac,' she said, 'and I shall not feel easy on my deathbed unless I have done my best to the last to make my son happy. I mean to put my own fears and my own feelings out of the question, and to go with you to your wife, and try what I can do to reclaim her. Give me your arm, Isaac, and let me do the last thing I can in this world to help my son before it is too late.'

He could not disobey her, and they walked together slowly toward his miserable home.

It was only one o'clock in the afternoon when they reached the cottage where he lived. It was their dinner-hour, and Rebecca was in the kitchen. He was thus able to take his mother quietly into the parlour, and then prepare his wife for the interview. She had fortunately drunk but little at that early hour, and she was less sullen and capricious than usual.

He returned to his mother with his mind tolerably at ease. His wife soon followed him into the parlour, and the meeting between her and Mrs Scatchard passed off better than he had ventured to anticipate, though he observed with secret apprehension that his mother, resolutely as she controlled herself in other respects, could not look his wife in the face when she spoke to her. It was a relief to him, therefore, when Rebecca began to lay the cloth.

She laid the cloth, brought in the bread-tray, and cut a slice from the loaf for her husband, then returned to the kitchen. At that moment, Isaac, still anxiously watching his mother, was startled by seeing the same ghastly change pass over her face which had altered it so awfully on the morning when Rebecca and she first met. Before he could say a word, she whispered, with a look of horror, 'Take me back – home, home again, Isaac. Come with me, and never go back again.'

He was afraid to ask for an explanation; he could only sign to her to be silent, and help her quickly to the door. As they passed the bread-tray on the table she stopped and pointed to it.

'Did you see what your wife cut your bread with?' she asked, in a low whisper.

'No, mother – I was not noticing – what was it?'

'Look!'

He did look. A new clasp-knife, with a buckhorn handle, lay with the loaf in the bread-tray. He stretched out his hand shudderingly to possess himself of it; but, at the same time, there was a noise in the kitchen, and his mother caught at his arm.

'The knife of the dream! Isaac, I'm faint with fear. Take me away before she comes back.'

He was hardly able to support her. The visible, tangible reality of the knife struck him with a panic, and utterly destroyed any faint doubts that he might have entertained up to this time in relation to the mysterious dream-warning of nearly eight years before. By a last desperate effort, he summoned self-possession enough to help his mother out of the house – so quietly that the 'Dream Woman' (he thought of her by that name now) did not hear them departing from the kitchen.

'Don't go back, Isaac – don't go back!' implored Mrs Scatchard, as he turned to go away, after seeing her safely seated again in her own room.

'I must get the knife,' he answered, under his breath. His mother tried to stop him again, but he hurried out without another word.

On his return he found that his wife had discovered their secret departure from the house. She had been drinking, and was in a fury of passion. The dinner in the kitchen was flung under the grate; the cloth was off the parlour table. Where was the knife?

Unwisely, he asked for it. She was only too glad of the opportunity of irritating him which the request afforded her. 'He wanted the knife, did he? Could he give her a reason why? No! Then he should not have it – not if he went down on his knees to ask for it.' Further recriminations elicited the fact that she thought it a bargain, and that she considered it her own especial property. Isaac saw the uselessness of attempting to get the knife by fair means, and determined to search for it, later in the day, in secret. The search was unsuccessful. Night came on, and he left the house to walk about the streets. He was afraid now to sleep in the same room with her.

Three weeks passed. Still sullenly enraged with him, she would not give up the knife; and still that fear of sleeping in the same room with her possessed him. He walked about at night, or dozed in the parlour, or sat watching by his mother's bedside. Before the expiration of the first week in the new month his mother died. It wanted then but ten days of her son's birthday. She had longed to live till that anniversary. Isaac was present at her death, and her last words in this world were addressed to him: 'Don't go back, my son, don't go back!'

He was obliged to go back, if it were only to watch his wife.

Exasperated to the last degree by his distrust of her, she had revengefully sought to add a sting to his grief, during the last days of his mother's illness, by declaring that she would assert her right to attend the funeral. In spite of all that he could do or say, she held with wicked pertinacity to her word, and on the day appointed for the burial forced herself – inflamed and shameless with drink – into her husband's presence, and declared that she would walk in the funeral procession to his mother's grave.

This last worst outrage, accompanied by all that was most insulting in word and look, maddened him for the moment. He struck her.

The instant the blow was dealt he repented it. She crouched down, silent, in a corner of the room, and eyed him steadily; it was a look that cooled his hot blood and made him tremble. But there was no time now to think of a means of making atonement. Nothing remained but to risk the worst till the funeral was over. There was but one way of making sure of her. He locked her into her bedroom.

When he came back some hours after, he found her sitting, very much altered in look and bearing, by the bedside, with a bundle on her lap. She rose, and faced him quietly, and spoke with a strange stillness in her voice, a strange repose in her eyes, a strange composure in her manner.

'No man has ever struck me twice,' she said, 'and my husband shall have no second opportunity. Set the door open and let me go. From this day forth we see each other no more.'

Before he could answer she passed him and left the room. He saw her walk away up the street.

Would she return?

All that night he watched and waited, but no footstep came near the house. The next night, overpowered by fatigue, he lay down in bed in his clothes, with the door locked, the key on the table, and the candle burning. His slumber was not disturbed. The third night, the fourth, the fifth, the sixth passed, and nothing happened. He lay down on the seventh, still in his clothes, still with the door locked, the key on the table, and the candle burning, but easier in his mind.

Easier in his mind, and in perfect health of body when he fell off to sleep. But his rest was disturbed. He woke twice without any sensation of uneasiness. But the third time it was that never-to-be-forgotten shivering of the night at the lonely inn, that dreadful sinking pain at the heart, which once more aroused him in an instant.

His eyes opened toward the left-hand side of the bed, and there stood –

The Dream Woman again? No! His wife; the living reality, with the dream-spectre's face, in the dream-spectre's attitude; the fair arm up, the knife clasped in the delicate white hand.

He sprang upon her almost at the instant of seeing her, and yet not quickly enough to prevent her from hiding the knife. Without a word from him – without a cry from her – he pinioned her in a chair. With one hand he felt up her sleeve, and there, where the Dream Woman had hidden the knife, his wife had hidden it – the knife with the buckhorn handle, that looked like new.

In the despair of that fearful moment his brain was steady, his heart was calm. He looked at her fixedly with the knife in his hand, and said these last words: 'You told me we should see each other no more, and you have come back. It is my turn now to go, and to go forever. I say that we shall see each other no more, and *my* word shall not be broken.'

He left her, and set forth into the night. There was a bleak wind abroad, and the smell of recent rain was in the air. The distant church-clocks chimed the quarter as he walked rapidly beyond the last houses in the suburb. He asked the first policeman he met what hour that was of which the quarter past had just struck.

The man referred sleepily to his watch, and answered, 'Two o'clock.' Two in the morning. What day of the month was this day that had just begun? He reckoned it up from the date of his mother's funeral. The fatal parallel was complete: it was his birthday!

Had he escaped the mortal peril which his dream foretold? Or had he only received a second warning?

As that ominous doubt forced itself on his mind, he stopped, reflected, and turned back again toward the city. He was still resolute to hold to his word, and never to let her see him more; but there was a thought now in his mind of having her watched and followed. The knife was in his possession; the world was before him; but a new distrust of her – a vague, unspeakable, superstitious dread – had overcome him.

'I must know where she goes, now she thinks I have left her,' he said to himself, as he stole back wearily to the precincts of his house.

It was still dark. He had left the candle burning in the bedchamber; but when he looked up to the window of the room now, there was no light in it. He crept cautiously to the house door. On going away, he remembered to have closed it; on trying it now, he found it open.

He waited outside, never losing sight of the house, till daylight. Then he ventured indoors – listened, and heard nothing – looked into kitchen, scullery, parlour, and found nothing; went up, at last, into the bedroom – it was empty. A picklock lay on the floor, betraying how she had gained entrance in the night, and that was the only trace of her.

Whither had she gone? That no mortal tongue could tell him. The darkness had covered her flight; and when the day broke, no man could say where the light found her.

Before leaving the house and the town forever, he gave instructions to a friend and neighbour to sell his furniture for anything that it would fetch, and apply the proceeds to employing the police to trace her. The directions were honestly followed, and the money was all spent, but the enquiries led to nothing. The picklock on the bedroom floor remained the one last useless trace of the Dream Woman.

* * *

At this point of the narrative the landlord paused, and, turning toward the window of the room in which we were sitting, looked in the direction of the stable-yard.

'So far,' he said, 'I tell you what was told to me. The little that remains to be added lies within my own experience. Between two and three months after the events I have just been relating, Isaac Scatchard came to me, withered and old-looking before his time, just as you saw him today. He had his testimonials to character with him, and he asked for employment here. Knowing that my wife and he were distantly related, I gave him a trial in consideration of that relationship, and liked him in spite of his queer habits. He is as sober, honest, and willing a man as there is in England. As for his restlessness at night, and his sleeping away his leisure time in the day, who can wonder at it after hearing his story? Besides, he never objects to being roused up when he's wanted, so there's not much inconvenience to complain of, after all.'

'I suppose he is afraid of a return of that dreadful dream, and of waking out of it in the dark?' said I.

'No,' returned the landlord. 'The dream comes back to him so often that he has got to bear with it by this time resignedly enough. It's his wife keeps him waking at night, as he has often told me.'

'What! Has she never been heard of yet?'

'Never. Isaac himself has the one perpetual thought about her, that she is alive and looking for him. I believe he wouldn't let himself drop off to sleep toward two in the morning for a king's ransom. Two in the morning, he says, is the time she will find him, one of these days. Two in the morning is the time all the year round when he likes to be most certain that he has got that clasp-knife safe about him. He does not mind being alone as long as he is awake, except on the night before his birthday, when he firmly believes himself to be in peril of his life. The birthday has only come round once since he has been here, and then he sat up along with the night-porter. "She's looking for me", is all he says when anybody speaks to him about the one anxiety of his life; "she's looking for me". He may be right. She *may* be looking for him. Who can tell?'

'Who can tell?' said I.

Mrs Zant and the Ghost

I

The course of this narrative describes the return of a disembodied spirit to earth, and leads the reader on new and strange ground.

Not in the obscurity of midnight, but in the searching light of day, did the supernatural influence assert itself. Neither revealed by a vision, nor announced by a voice, it reached mortal knowledge through the sense which is least easily self-deceived: the sense that feels.

The record of this event will of necessity produce conflicting impressions. It will raise, in some minds, the doubt which reason asserts; it will invigorate, in other minds, the hope which faith justifies; and it will leave the terrible question of the destinies of man, where centuries of vain investigation have left it – in the dark.

Having only undertaken in the present narrative to lead the way along a succession of events, the writer declines to follow modern examples by thrusting himself and his opinions on the public view. He returns to the shadow from which he has emerged, and leaves the opposing forces of incredulity and belief to fight the old battle over again, on the old ground.

2

The events happened soon after the first thirty years of the present century had come to an end.

On a fine morning, early in the month of April, a gentleman of middle age (named Rayburn) took his little daughter Lucy out for a walk in the woodland pleasure-ground of Western London, called Kensington Gardens.

The few friends whom he possessed reported of Mr Rayburn (not unkindly) that he was a reserved and solitary man. He might have been more accurately described as a widower devoted to his only surviving child. Although he was not more than forty years of age, the one pleasure which made life enjoyable to Lucy's father was offered by Lucy herself.

Playing with her ball, the child ran on to the southern limit of the Gardens, at that part of it which still remains nearest to the old Palace of Kensington. Observing close at hand one of those spacious covered seats, called in England 'alcoves', Mr Rayburn was reminded that he had the morning's newspaper in his pocket, and that he might do well to rest and read. At that early hour the place was a solitude.

'Go on playing, my dear,' he said; 'but take care to keep where I can see you.'

Lucy tossed up her ball; and Lucy's father opened his newspaper. He had not been reading for more than ten minutes, when he felt a familiar little hand laid on his knee.

'Tired of playing?' he enquired – with his eyes still on the newspaper.

'I'm frightened, papa.'

He looked up directly. The child's pale face startled him. He took her on his knee and kissed her.

'You oughtn't to be frightened, Lucy, when I am with you,' he said, gently. 'What is it?' He looked out of the alcove as he spoke, and saw a little dog among the trees. 'Is it the dog?' he asked.

Lucy answered: 'It's not the dog – it's the lady.'

The lady was not visible from the alcove.

'Has she said anything to you?' Mr Rayburn enquired.

'No.'

'What has she done to frighten you?'

The child put her arms round her father's neck.

'Whisper, papa,' she said; 'I'm afraid of her hearing us. I think she's mad.'

'Why do you think so, Lucy?'

'She came near to me. I thought she was going to say something. She seemed to be ill.'

'Well? And what then?'

'She looked at me.'

There, Lucy found herself at a loss how to express what she had to say next – and took refuge in silence.

'Nothing very wonderful, so far,' her father suggested.

'Yes, papa – but she didn't seem to see me when she looked.'

'Well, and what happened then?'

'The lady was frightened – and that frightened me. I think,' the child repeated positively, 'she's mad.'

It occurred to Mr Rayburn that the lady might be blind. He rose at once to set the doubt at rest.

'Wait here,' he said, 'and I'll come back to you.'

But Lucy clung to him with both hands; Lucy declared that she was afraid to be by herself. They left the alcove together.

The new point of view at once revealed the stranger, leaning against the trunk of a tree. She was dressed in the deep mourning of a widow. The pallor of her face, the glassy stare in her eyes, more than accounted for the child's terror – it excused the alarming conclusion at which she had arrived.

'Go nearer to her,' Lucy whispered.

They advanced a few steps. It was now easy to see that the lady was young, and wasted by illness – but (arriving at a doubtful conclusion perhaps under the present circumstances) apparently possessed of rare personal attractions in happier days. As the father and daughter advanced a little, she discovered them. After some hesitation, she left the tree; approached with an evident intention of speaking; and suddenly paused. A change to astonishment and fear animated her vacant eyes. If it had not been plain before, it was now beyond all doubt that she was not a poor blind creature, deserted and helpless. At the same time, the expression of her face was not easy to understand. She could hardly have looked more amazed and bewildered, if the two strangers who were observing her had suddenly vanished from the place in which they stood.

Mr Rayburn spoke to her with the utmost kindness of voice and manner.

'I am afraid you are not well,' he said. 'Is there anything that I can do – '

The next words were suspended on his lips. It was impossible to realise such a state of things; but the strange impression that she had already produced on him was now confirmed. If he could believe his senses, her face did certainly tell him that he was invisible and inaudible to the woman whom he had just addressed! She moved slowly away with a heavy sigh, like a person disappointed and distressed. Following her with his eyes, he saw the dog once more – a little smooth-coated terrier of the ordinary English breed. The dog showed none of the restless activity of his race. With his head down and his tail depressed, he crouched like a creature paralysed by fear. His mistress roused him by a call. He followed her listlessly as she turned away.

After walking a few paces only, she suddenly stood still.

Mr Rayburn heard her talking to herself.

'Did I feel it again?' she said, as if perplexed by some doubt that awed or grieved her. After a while her arms rose slowly, and opened with a gentle caressing action – an embrace strangely offered to the empty air! 'No,' she said to herself, sadly, after waiting a moment. 'More perhaps when tomorrow comes – no more today.' She looked up at the clear blue sky. 'The beautiful sunlight! The merciful sunlight!' she murmured. 'I should have died if it had happened in the dark.'

Once more she called to the dog; and once more she walked slowly away.

'Is she going home, papa?' the child asked.

'We will try and find out,' the father answered.

He was by this time convinced that the poor creature was in no condition to be permitted to go out without someone to take care of her. From motives of humanity, he was resolved on making the attempt to communicate with her friends.

3

The lady left the Gardens by the nearest gate, stopping to lower her veil before she turned into the busy thoroughfare which leads to Kensington. Advancing a little way along the High Street, she entered a house of respectable appearance, with a card in one of the windows which announced that apartments were to let.

Mr Rayburn waited a minute – then knocked at the door, and asked if he could see the mistress of the house. The servant showed him into a room on the ground floor, neatly but scantily furnished. One little white object varied the grim brown monotony of the empty table. It was a visiting-card.

With a child's unceremonious curiosity Lucy pounced on the card, and spelled the name, letter by letter: 'Z, A, N, T,' she repeated. 'What does that mean ?'

Her father looked at the card, as he took it away from her, and put it back on the table. The name was printed, and the address was added in pencil: 'Mr John Zant, Purley's Hotel.'

The mistress made her appearance. Mr Rayburn heartily wished himself out of the house again, the moment he saw her. The ways in which it is possible to cultivate the social virtues are more numerous and more varied than is generally supposed. This lady's way had apparently accustomed her to meet her fellow-creatures on the hard ground of justice without mercy. Something in her eyes, when she looked at Lucy, said: 'I wonder whether that child gets punished when she deserves it?'

'Do you wish to see the rooms which I have to let?' she began.

Mr Rayburn at once stated the object of his visit – as clearly, as civilly, and as concisely as a man could do it. He was conscious (he added) that he had been guilty perhaps of an act of intrusion.

The manner of the mistress of the house showed that she entirely agreed with him. He suggested, however, that his motive might excuse him. The mistress's manner changed, and asserted a difference of opinion.

'I only know the lady whom you mention,' she said, 'as a person of the highest respectability, in delicate health. She has taken my first-floor apartments, with excellent references; and she gives remarkably little trouble. I have no claim to interfere with her proceedings, and no reason to doubt that she is capable of taking care of herself.'

Mr Rayburn unwisely attempted to say a word in his own defence. 'Allow me to remind you – ' he began.

'Of what, sir?'

'Of what I observed, when I happened to see the lady in Kensington Gardens.'

'I am not responsible for what you observed in Kensington Gardens. If your time is of any value, pray don't let me detain you.'

Dismissed in those terms, Mr Rayburn took Lucy's hand and withdrew. He had just reached the door, when it was opened from the outer side. The Lady of Kensington Gardens stood before him. In the position which he and his daughter now occupied, their backs were toward the window. Would she remember having seen them for a moment in the Gardens?

'Excuse me for intruding on you,' she said to the landlady. 'Your servant tells me my brother-in-law called while I was out. He sometimes leaves a message on his card.'

She looked for the message, and appeared to be disappointed: there was no writing on the card.

Mr Rayburn lingered a little in the doorway on the chance of hearing something more. The landlady's vigilant eyes discovered him.

'Do you know this gentleman?' she said maliciously to her lodger. 'Not that I remember.'

Replying in those words, the lady looked at Mr Rayburn for the first time; and suddenly drew back from him.

'Yes,' she said, correcting herself; 'I think we met – '

Her embarrassment overpowered her; she could say no more.

Mr Rayburn compassionately finished the sentence for her.

'We met accidentally in Kensington Gardens,' he said.

She seemed to be incapable of appreciating the kindness of his motive. After hesitating a little she addressed a proposal to him, which seemed to show distrust of the landlady.

'Will you let me speak to you upstairs in my own rooms?' she asked.

Without waiting for a reply, she led the way to the stairs. Mr Rayburn and Lucy followed. They were just beginning the ascent to the first floor, when the spiteful landlady left the lower room, and called to her lodger over their heads: 'Take care what you say to this man, Mrs Zant! He thinks you're mad.'

Mrs Zant turned round on the landing, and looked at him. Not a word fell from her lips. She suffered, she feared, in silence. Something in the sad submission of her face touched the springs of innocent pity in Lucy's heart. The child burst out crying.

That artless expression of sympathy drew Mrs Zant down the few stairs which separated her from Lucy.

'May I kiss your dear little girl?' she said to Mr Rayburn. The landlady, standing on the mat below, expressed her opinion of the value of caresses, as compared with a sounder method of treating young persons in tears: 'If that child was mine,' she remarked, 'I would give her something to cry for.'

In the meantime, Mrs Zant led the way to her rooms.

The first words she spoke showed that the landlady had succeeded but too well in prejudicing her against Mr Rayburn.

'Will you let me ask your child,' she said to him, 'why you think me mad?'

He met this strange request with a firm answer.

'You don't know yet what I really do think. Will you give me a minute's attention?'

'No,' she said positively. 'The child pities me, I want to speak to the child. What did you see me do in the Gardens, my dear, that surprised you?' Lucy turned uneasily to her father; Mrs Zant persisted. 'I first saw you by yourself, and then I saw you with your father,' she went on. 'When I came nearer to you, did I look very oddly – as if I didn't see you at all?'

Lucy hesitated again; and Mr Rayburn interfered.

'You are confusing my little girl,' he said. 'Allow me to answer your questions – or excuse me if I leave you.'

There was something in his look, or in his tone, that mastered her. She put her hand to her head.

'I don't think I'm fit for it,' she answered vacantly. 'My courage has been sorely tried already. If I can get a little rest and sleep, you may find me a different person. I am left a great deal by myself; and I have reasons for trying to compose my mind. Can I see you tomorrow? Or write to you? Where do you live?'

Mr Rayburn laid his card on the table in silence. She had strongly excited his interest. He honestly desired to be of some service to this forlorn creature – abandoned so cruelly, as it seemed, to her own guidance. But he had no authority to exercise, no sort of claim to direct her actions, even if she consented to accept his advice. As a last resource he ventured on an allusion to the relative of whom she had spoken downstairs.

'When do you expect to see your brother-in-law again?' he said.

'I don't know,' she answered. 'I should like to see him – he is so kind to me.'

She turned aside to take leave of Lucy.

'Good-by, my little friend. If you live to grow up, I hope you will never be such a miserable woman as I am.' She suddenly looked round at Mr Rayburn. 'Have you got a wife at home?' she asked.

'My wife is dead.'

'And *you* have a child to comfort you! Please leave me; you harden my heart. Oh, sir, don't you understand? You make me envy you!'

Mr Rayburn was silent when he and his daughter were out in the street again. Lucy, as became a dutiful child, was silent, too. But there are limits to human endurance – and Lucy's capacity for self-control gave way at last.

'Are you thinking of the lady, papa?' she said.

He only answered by nodding his head. His daughter had interrupted him at that critical moment in a man's reflections, when he is on the point of making up his mind. Before they were at home again Mr Rayburn had arrived at a decision. Mrs Zant's brother-in-law was evidently ignorant of any serious necessity for his interference – or he would have made arrangements for immediately repeating his visit. In this state of things, if any evil happened to Mrs Zant, silence on Mr Rayburn's part might be indirectly to blame for a serious misfortune. Arriving at that conclusion, he decided upon running the risk of being rudely received, for the second time, by another stranger.

Leaving Lucy under the care of her governess, he went at once to the address that had been written on the visiting-card left at the lodging-house, and sent in his name. A courteous message was returned. Mr John Zant was at home, and would be happy to see him.

4

Mr Rayburn was shown into one of the private sitting-rooms of the hotel.

He observed that the customary position of the furniture in a room had been, in some respects, altered. An armchair, a side-table, and a footstool had all been removed to one of the windows, and had been placed as close as possible to the light. On the table lay a large open roll of morocco leather, containing rows of elegant little instruments in steel and ivory. Waiting by the table, stood Mr John Zant. He said 'Good-morning' in a bass voice, so profound and so melodious that those two commonplace words assumed a new importance, coming from his lips. His personal appearance was in harmony with his magnificent voice – he was a tall, finely-made man of dark complexion; with big brilliant black eyes, and a noble curling beard, which hid the whole lower part of his face. Having bowed with a happy mingling of dignity and politeness, the conventional side of this gentleman's character suddenly vanished, and a crazy side, to all appearance, took its place. He dropped on his knees in front of the footstool. Had he forgotten to say his prayers that morning, and was he in such a hurry to remedy the fault that he had no time to spare for consulting appearances? The doubt had hardly suggested itself, before it was set at rest in a most unexpected manner. Mr Zant looked at his visitor with a bland smile, and said: 'Please let me see your feet.'

For the moment, Mr Rayburn lost his presence of mind. He looked at the instruments on the side-table.

'Are you a corn-cutter?' was all he could say.

'Excuse me, sir, ' returned the polite operator, 'the term you use is quite obsolete in our profession.' He rose from his knees, and added modestly: 'I am a Chiropodist.'

'I beg your pardon.'

'Don't mention it! You are not, I imagine, in want of my professional services. To what motive may I attribute the honour of your visit?'

By this time Mr Rayburn had recovered himself.

'I have come here,' he answered, 'under circumstances which require apology as well as explanation.'

Mr Zant's highly polished manner betrayed signs of alarm; his suspicions pointed to a formidable conclusion – a conclusion that shook him to the innermost recesses of the pocket in which he kept his money.

'The numerous demands on me – ' he began.

Mr Rayburn smiled.

'Make your mind easy,' he replied. 'I don't want money. My object is to speak with you on the subject of a lady who is a relation of yours.'

'My sister-in-law!' Mr Zant exclaimed. 'Pray take a seat.'

Doubting if he had chosen a convenient time for his visit, Mr Rayburn hesitated.

'Am I likely to be in the way of persons who wish to consult you?' he asked.

'Certainly not. My morning hours of attendance on my clients are from eleven to one.' The clock on the mantelpiece struck the quarter-past one as he spoke. 'I hope you don't bring me bad news?' he said, very earnestly. 'When I called on Mrs Zant this morning, I heard that she had gone out for a walk. Is it indiscreet to ask how you became acquainted with her?'

Mr Rayburn at once mentioned what he had seen and heard in Kensington Gardens; not forgetting to add a few words, which described his interview afterward with Mrs Zant.

The lady's brother-in-law listened with an interest and sympathy, which offered the strongest possible contrast to the unprovoked rudeness of the mistress of the lodging-house. He declared that he could only do justice to his sense of obligation by following Mr Rayburn's example, and expressing himself as frankly as if he had been speaking to an old friend.

'The sad story of my sister-in-law's life,' he said, 'will, I think, explain certain things which must have naturally perplexed you. My brother was introduced to her at the house of an Australian gentleman, on a visit to England. She was then employed as governess to his daughters. So sincere was the regard felt for her by the family that the parents had, at the entreaty of their children, asked her to accompany them when they returned to the Colony. The governess thankfully accepted the proposal.'

'Had she no relations in England?' Mr Rayburn asked.

'She was literally alone in the world, sir. When I tell you that she had been brought up in the Foundling Hospital, you will understand what I mean. Oh, there is no romance in my sister-in-law's story! She never has known, or will know, who her parents were or why they deserted her. The happiest moment in her life was the moment when she and my brother first met. It was an instance, on both sides, of love at first sight. Though not a rich man, my brother had earned a sufficient income in mercantile pursuits. His character spoke for itself. In a word, he altered all the poor girl's prospects, as we then hoped and believed, for the better. Her employers deferred their return to Australia, so that she might be married from their house. After a happy life of a few weeks only – '

His voice failed him; he paused, and turned his face from the light.

'Pardon me,' he said; 'I am not able, even yet, to speak composedly of my brother's death. Let me only say that the poor young wife was a widow, before the happy days of the honeymoon were over. That dreadful calamity struck her down. Before my brother had been committed to the grave, her life was in danger from brain-fever.'

Those words placed in a new light Mr Rayburn's first fear that her intellect might be deranged. Looking at him attentively, Mr Zant seemed to understand what was passing in the mind of his guest.

'No!' he said. 'If the opinions of the medical men are to be trusted, the result of the illness is injury to her physical strength – not injury to her mind. I have observed in her, no doubt, a certain waywardness of temper since her illness; but that is a trifle. As an example of what I mean, I may tell you that I invited her, on her recovery, to pay me a visit. My house is not in London – the air doesn't agree with me – my place of residence is at St Sallins-on-Sea. I am not myself a married man; but my excellent housekeeper would have received Mrs Zant with the utmost kindness. She was resolved – obstinately resolved, poor thing – to remain in London. It is needless to say that, in her melancholy position, I am attentive to her slightest wishes. I took a lodging for her; and, at her special request, I chose a house which was near Kensington Gardens.

'Is there any association with the Gardens which led Mrs Zant to make that request?'

'Some association, I believe, with the memory of her husband. By the way, I wish to be sure of finding her at home, when I call tomorrow. Did you say (in the course of your interesting statement) that she intended – as you supposed – to return to Kensington Gardens tomorrow? Or has my memory deceived me?'

'Your memory is perfectly accurate.'

'Thank you. I confess I am not only distressed by what you have told me of Mrs Zant – I am at a loss to know how to act for the best. My only idea, at present, is to try change of air and scene. What do you think yourself?'

'I think you are right.'

Mr Zant still hesitated.

'It would not be easy for me, just now,' he said, 'to leave my patients and take her abroad.'

The obvious reply to this occurred to Mr Rayburn. A man of larger worldly experience might have felt certain suspicions, and might have remained silent. Mr Rayburn spoke.

'Why not renew your invitation and take her to your house at the seaside?' he said.

In the perplexed state of Mr Zant's mind, this plain course of action had apparently failed to present itself. His gloomy face brightened directly.

'The very thing!' he said. 'I will certainly take your advice. If the air of St Sallins does nothing else, it will improve her health and help her to recover her good looks. Did she strike you as having been (in happier days) a pretty woman?'

This was a strangely familiar question to ask – almost an indelicate question, under the circumstances A certain furtive expression in Mr Zant's fine dark eyes seemed to imply that it had been put with a purpose. Was it possible that he suspected Mr Rayburn's interest in his sister-in-law to be inspired by any motive which was not perfectly unselfish and perfectly pure? To arrive at such a conclusion as this might be to judge hastily and cruelly of a man who was perhaps only guilty of a want of delicacy of feeling. Mr Rayburn honestly did his best to assume the charitable point of view. At the same time, it is not to be denied that his words, when he answered, were carefully guarded, and that he rose to take his leave.

Mr John Zant hospitably protested.

'Why are you in such a hurry? Must you really go? I shall have the honour of returning your visit tomorrow, when I have made arrangements to profit by that excellent suggestion of yours. Good-bye. God bless you.'

He held out his hand: a hand with a smooth surface and a tawny colour, that fervently squeezed the fingers of a departing friend. 'Is that man a scoundrel?' was Mr Rayburn's first thought, after he had left the hotel. His moral sense set all hesitation at rest – and answered: 'You're a fool if you doubt it.'

5

Disturbed by presentiments, Mr Rayburn returned to his house on foot, by way of trying what exercise would do toward composing his mind.

The experiment failed. He went upstairs and played with Lucy; he drank an extra glass of wine at dinner; he took the child and her governess to a circus in the evening; he ate a little supper, fortified by another glass of wine, before he went to bed – and still those vague forebodings of evil persisted in torturing him. Looking back through his past life, he asked himself if any woman (his late wife of course excepted!) had ever taken the predominant place in his thoughts which Mrs Zant had assumed – without any discernible reason to account for it? If he had ventured to answer his own question, the reply would have been: Never!

All the next day he waited at home, in expectation of Mr John Zant's promised visit, and waited in vain.

Toward evening the parlourmaid appeared at the family tea-table, and presented to her master an unusually large envelope sealed with black wax, and addressed in a strange handwriting. The absence of stamp and postmark showed that it had been left at the house by a messenger.

'Who brought this?' Mr Rayburn asked.

'A lady, sir – in deep mourning.'

'Did she leave any message?'

'No, sir.'

Having drawn the inevitable conclusion, Mr Rayburn shut himself up in his library. He was afraid of Lucy's curiosity and Lucy's questions, if he read Mrs Zant's letter in his daughter's presence.

Looking at the open envelope after he had taken out the leaves of writing which it contained, he noticed these lines traced inside the cover:

My one excuse for troubling you, when I might have consulted my brother-in-law, will be found in the pages which I enclose. To speak plainly, you have been led to fear that I am not in my right senses. For this very reason, I now appeal to you. Your dreadful doubt of me, sir, is my doubt too. Read what I have written about myself – and then tell me, I entreat you, which I am: a person who has been the object of a supernatural revelation? Or an unfortunate creature who is only fit for imprisonment in a madhouse?

Mr Rayburn opened the manuscript. With steady attention, which soon quickened to breathless interest, he read what follows.

6

The Lady's Manuscript

Yesterday morning the sun shone in a clear blue sky – after a succession of cloudy days, counting from the first of the month.

The radiant light had its animating effect on my poor spirits. I had passed the night more peacefully than usual; undisturbed by the dream, so cruelly familiar to me, that my lost husband is still living – the dream from which I always wake in tears. Never, since the dark days of my sorrow, have I been so little troubled by the self-tormenting fancies and fears which beset miserable women, as when I left the house, and turned my steps toward Kensington Gardens – for the first time since my husband's death.

Attended by my only companion, the little dog who had been his favourite as well as mine, I went to the quiet corner of the Gardens which is nearest to Kensington.

On that soft grass, under the shade of those grand trees, we had loitered together in the days of our betrothal. It was his favourite walk; and he had taken me to see it in the early days of our acquaintance. There, he had first asked me to be his wife. There, we had felt the rapture of our first kiss. It was surely natural that I should wish to see once more a place sacred to such memories as these? I am only twenty-three years old; I have no child to comfort me, no companion of my own age, nothing to love but the dumb creature who is so faithfully fond of me.

I went to the tree under which we stood, when my dear one's eyes told his love before he could utter it in words. The sun of that vanished day shone on me again; it was the same noontide hour; the same solitude was around me. I had feared the first effect of the dreadful contrast between past and present. No! I was quiet and resigned. My thoughts, rising higher than earth, dwelt on the better life beyond the grave. Some tears came into my eyes. But I was not unhappy. My memory of all that happened may be trusted, even in trifles which relate only to myself – I was not unhappy.

The first object that I saw, when my eyes were clear again, was the dog. He crouched a few paces away from me, trembling pitiably, but uttering no cry. What had caused the fear that overpowered him?

I was soon to know.

I called to the dog; he remained immovable – conscious of some mysterious coming thing that held him spellbound. I tried to go to the poor creature, and fondle and comfort him.

At the first step forward that I took, something stopped me.

It was not to be seen, and not to be heard. It stopped me.

The still figure of the dog disappeared from my view: the lonely scene round me disappeared – excepting the light from heaven, the tree that sheltered me, and the grass in front of me. A sense of unutterable expectation kept my eyes riveted on the grass. Suddenly, I saw its myriad blades rise erect and shivering. The fear came to me of something passing over them with the invisible swiftness of the wind. The shivering advanced. It was all round me. It crept into the leaves of the tree over my head; they shuddered, without a sound to tell of their agitation; their pleasant natural rustling was struck dumb. The song of the birds had ceased. The cries of the water-fowl on the pond were heard no more. There was a dreadful silence.

But the lovely sunshine poured down on me, as brightly as ever.

In that dazzling light, in that fearful silence, I felt an Invisible Presence near me. It touched me gently.

At the touch, my heart throbbed with an overwhelming joy. Exquisite pleasure thrilled through every nerve in my body. I knew him! From the unseen world – himself unseen – he had returned to me. Oh, I knew him!

And yet, my helpless mortality longed for a sign that might give me assurance of the truth. The yearning in me shaped itself into words. I tried to utter the words. I would have said, if I could have spoken: 'Oh, my angel, give me a token that it is You!' But I was like a person struck dumb – I could only think it.

The Invisible Presence read my thought. I felt my lips touched, as my husband's lips used to touch them when he kissed me. And that was my answer. A thought came to me again. I would have said, if I could have spoken: 'Are you here to take me to the better world?'

I waited. Nothing that I could feel touched me.

I was conscious of thinking once more. I would have said, if I could have spoken: 'Are you here to protect me?'

I felt myself held in a gentle embrace, as my husband's arms used to hold me when he pressed me to his breast. And that was my answer.

The touch that was like the touch of his lips, lingered and was lost; the clasp that was like the clasp of his arms, pressed me and fell away. The garden-scene resumed its natural aspect. I saw a human creature near, a lovely little girl looking at me.

At that moment, when I was my own lonely self again, the sight of the child soothed and attracted me. I advanced, intending to speak to her. To my horror I suddenly ceased to see her. She disappeared as if I had been stricken blind.

And yet I could see the landscape round me; I could see the heaven above me. A time passed – only a few minutes, as I thought – and the child became visible to me again, walking hand-in-hand with her father. I approached them; I was close enough to see that they were looking at me with pity and surprise. My impulse was to ask if they saw anything strange in my face or my manner. Before I could speak, the horrible wonder happened again. They vanished from my view.

Was the Invisible Presence still near? Was it passing between me and my fellow-mortals, forbidding communication in that place and at that time?

It must have been so. When I turned away in my ignorance, with a heavy heart, the dreadful blankness which had twice shut out from me the beings of my own race, was not between me and my dog. The poor little creature filled me with pity; I called him to me. He moved at the sound of my voice, and followed me languidly; not quite awakened yet from the trance of terror that had possessed him.

Before I had retired by more than a few steps, I thought I was conscious of the Presence again. I held out my longing arms to it. I waited in the hope of a touch to tell me that I might return. Perhaps I was answered by indirect means? I only know that a resolution to return to the same place, at the same hour, came to me, and quieted my mind.

The morning of the next day was dull and cloudy; but the rain held off. I set forth again to the Gardens.

My dog ran on before me into the street – and stopped: waiting to see in which direction I might lead the way. When I turned toward the Gardens, he dropped behind me. In a little while I looked back. He was following me no longer; he stood irresolute. I called to him. He advanced a few steps – hesitated – and ran back to the house.

I went on by myself. Shall I confess my superstition? I thought the dog's desertion of me a bad omen.

Arrived at the tree, I placed myself under it. The minutes followed each other uneventfully. The cloudy sky darkened. The dull surface of the grass showed no shuddering consciousness of an unearthly creature passing over it.

I still waited, with an obstinacy which was fast becoming the obstinacy of despair. How long an interval elapsed, while I kept watch on the ground before me, I am not able to say. I only know that a change came.

Under the dull grey light I saw the grass move – but not as it had moved, on the day before. It shrivelled as if a flame had scorched it. No flame appeared. The brown underlying earth showed itself winding onward in a thin strip – which might have been a footpath traced in fire. It frightened me. I longed for the protection of the Invisible Presence. I prayed for a warning of it, if danger was near.

A touch answered me. It was as if a hand unseen had taken my hand – had raised it, little by little – had left it, pointing to the thin brown path that wound toward me under the shrivelled blades of grass.

I looked to the far end of the path.

The unseen hand closed on my hand with a warning pressure: the revelation of the coming danger was near me – I waited for it. I saw it.

The figure of a man appeared, advancing toward me along the thin brown path. I looked in his face as he came nearer. It showed me dimly the face of my husband's brother – John Zant.

The consciousness of myself as a living creature left me. I knew nothing; I felt nothing. I was dead.

When the torture of revival made me open my eyes, I found myself on the grass. Gentle hands raised my head, at the moment when I recovered my senses. Who had brought me to life again? Who was taking care of me?

I looked upward, and saw – bending over me – John Zant.

7

There, the manuscript ended.

Some lines had been added on the last page; but they had been so carefully erased as to be illegible. These words of explanation appeared below the cancelled sentences:

I had begun to write the little that remains to be told, when it struck me that I might, unintentionally, be exercising an unfair influence on your opinion. Let me only remind you that I believe absolutely in the supernatural revelation which I have endeavoured to describe. Remember this – and decide for me what I dare not decide for myself.

There was no serious obstacle in the way of compliance with this request.

Judged from the point of view of the materialist, Mrs Zant might no doubt be the victim of illusions (produced by a diseased state of the nervous system), which have been known to exist – as in the celebrated case of the bookseller, Nicolai, of Berlin – without being accompanied by derangement of the intellectual powers. But Mr Rayburn was not asked to solve any such intricate problem as this. He had been merely instructed to read the manuscript, and to say what impression it had left on him of the mental condition of the writer; whose doubt of herself had been, in all probability, first suggested by remembrance of the illness from which she had suffered – brain-fever.

Under these circumstances, there could be little difficulty in forming an opinion. The memory which had recalled, and the judgement which had arranged, the succession of events related in the narrative, revealed a mind in full possession of its resources.

Having satisfied himself so far, Mr Rayburn abstained from considering the more serious question suggested by what he had read.

At any time his habits of life and his ways of thinking would have rendered him unfit to weigh the arguments which assert or deny supernatural revelation among the creatures of earth. But his mind was now so disturbed by the startling record of experience which he had just read, that he was only conscious of feeling certain impressions – without possessing the capacity to reflect on them. That his anxiety on Mrs Zant's account had been increased, and that his doubts of Mr John Zant had been encouraged, were the only practical results of the confidence placed in him of which he was thus far aware. In the ordinary exigencies of life a man of hesitating disposition, his interest in Mrs Zant's welfare, and his desire to discover what had passed between her brother-in-law and herself, after their meeting in the Gardens, urged him into instant action. In half an hour more, he had arrived at her lodgings. He was at once admitted.

8

Mrs Zant was alone, in an imperfectly lighted room.

'I hope you will excuse the bad light,' she said; 'my head has been burning as if the fever had come back again. Oh, don't go away! After what I have suffered, you don't know how dreadful it is to be alone.'

The tone of her voice told him that she had been crying. He at once tried the best means of setting the poor lady at ease, by telling her of the conclusion at which he had arrived, after reading her manuscript. The happy result showed itself instantly: her face brightened, her manner changed; she was eager to hear more.

'Have I produced any other impression on you?' she asked.

He understood the allusion. Expressing sincere respect for her own convictions, he told her honestly that he was not prepared to enter on the obscure and terrible question of supernatural interposition. Grateful for the tone in which he had answered her, she wisely and delicately changed the subject.

'I must speak to you of my brother-in-law,' she said. 'He has told me of your visit; and I am anxious to know what you think of him. Do you like Mr John Zant?'

Mr Rayburn hesitated.

The careworn look appeared again in her face. 'If you had felt as kindly toward him as he feels toward you,' she said, 'I might have gone to St Sallins with a lighter heart.'

Mr Rayburn thought of the supernatural appearances, described at the close of her narrative. 'You believe in that terrible warning,' he remonstrated; 'and yet, you go to your brother-in-law's house!'

'I believe,' she answered, 'in the spirit of the man who loved me in the days of his earthly bondage. I am under *his* protection. What have I to do but to cast away my fears, and to wait in faith and hope? It might have helped my resolution if a friend had been near to encourage me.' She paused and smiled sadly. 'I must remember,' she resumed, 'that your way of understanding my position is not my way. I ought to have told you that Mr John Zant feels needless anxiety about my health. He declares that he will not lose sight of me until his mind is at ease. It is useless to attempt to alter his opinion. He says my nerves are shattered – and who that sees me can doubt it? He tells me that my only chance of getting better is to try change of air and perfect repose – how can I contradict him? He reminds me that I have no relation but himself, and no house open to me but his own – and God knows he is right!'

She said those last words in accents of melancholy resignation, which grieved the good man whose one merciful purpose was to serve and console her. He spoke impulsively with the freedom of an old friend

'I want to know more of you and Mr John Zant than I know now,' he said. 'My motive is a better one than mere curiosity. Do you believe that I feel a sincere interest in you?'

'With my whole heart.'

That reply encouraged him to proceed with what he had to say. 'When you recovered from your fainting-fit,' he began, 'Mr John Zant asked questions, of course?'

'He asked what could possibly have happened, in such a quiet place as Kensington Gardens, to make me faint.'

'And how did you answer?'

'Answer? I couldn't even look at him!'

'You said nothing?'

'Nothing. I don't know what he thought of me; he might have been surprised, or he might have been offended.'

'Is he easily offended?' Mr Rayburn asked.

'Not in my experience of him.'

'Do you mean your experience of him before your illness?'

'Yes. Since my recovery, his engagements with country patients have kept him away from London. I have not seen him since he took these lodgings for me. But he is always considerate. He has written more than once to beg that I will not think him neglectful, and to tell me (what I knew already through my poor husband) that he has no money of his own, and must live by his profession.'

'In your husband's lifetime, were the two brothers on good terms?'

'Always. The one complaint I ever heard my husband make of John Zant was that he didn't come to see us often enough, after our marriage. Is there some wickedness in him which we have never suspected? It may be – but *how* can it be? I have every reason to be grateful to the man against whom I have been supernaturally warned! His conduct to me has been always perfect. I can't tell you what I owe to his influence in quieting my mind, when a dreadful doubt arose about my husband's death.'

'Do you mean doubt if he died a natural death?'

'Oh, no! No! He was dying of rapid consumption – but his sudden death took the doctors by surprise. One of them thought that he might have taken an overdose of his sleeping drops, by mistake. The other disputed this conclusion, or there might have been an inquest in the house. Oh, don't speak of it any more! Let us talk of something else. Tell me when I shall see you again.'

'I hardly know. When do you and your brother-in-law leave London?'

'Tomorrow.' She looked at Mr Rayburn with a piteous entreaty in her eyes; she said, timidly: 'Do you ever go to the seaside, and take your dear little girl with you?'

The request, at which she had only dared to hint, touched on the idea which was at that moment in Mr Rayburn's mind.

Interpreted by his strong prejudice against John Zant, what she had said of her brother-in-law filled him with forebodings of peril to herself; all the more powerful in their influence, for this reason – that he shrank from distinctly realising them. If another person had been present at the interview, and had said to him afterward: 'That man's reluctance to visit his sister-in-law, while her husband was living, is associated with a secret sense of guilt which her innocence cannot even imagine: he, and he alone, knows the cause of her husband's sudden death: his feigned anxiety about her health is adopted as the safest means of enticing her into his house – if those formidable conclusions had been urged on Mr Rayburn, he would have felt it his duty to reject them, as unjustifiable aspersions on an absent man. And yet, when he took leave that evening of Mrs Zant, he had pledged himself to give Lucy a holiday at the seaside: and he had said, without blushing, that the child really deserved it, as a reward for general good conduct and attention to her lessons!

9

Three days later, the father and daughter arrived toward evening at St Sallins-on-Sea. They found Mrs Zant at the station.

The poor woman's joy, on seeing them, expressed itself like the joy of a child. 'Oh, I am so glad! So glad!' was all she could say when they met. Lucy was half-smothered with kisses, and was made supremely happy by a present of the finest doll she had ever possessed. Mrs Zant accompanied her friends to the rooms which had been secured at the hotel. She was able to speak confidentially to Mr Rayburn, while Lucy was in the balcony hugging her doll, and looking at the sea.

The one event that had happened during Mrs Zant's short residence at St Sallins was the departure of her brother-in-law that morning, for London. He had been called away to operate on the feet of a wealthy patient who knew the value of his time: his housekeeper expected that he would return to dinner.

As to his conduct toward Mrs Zant, he was not only as attentive as ever – he was almost oppressively affectionate in his language and manner. There was no service that a man could render which he had not eagerly offered to her. He declared that he already perceived an improvement in her health; he congratulated her on having decided to stay in his house; and (as a proof, perhaps, of his sincerity) he had repeatedly pressed her hand. 'Have you any idea what all this means?' she said, simply.

Mr Rayburn kept his idea to himself. He professed ignorance; and asked next what sort of person the housekeeper was.

Mrs Zant shook her head ominously.

'Such a strange creature,' she said, 'and in the habit of taking such liberties that I begin to be afraid she is a little crazy.'

'Is she an old woman?'

'No – only middle-aged. This morning, after her master had left the house, she actually asked me what I thought of my brother-in-law! I told her, as coldly as possible, that I thought he was very kind. She was quite insensible to the tone in which I had spoken; she went on from bad to worse. 'Do you call him the sort of man who would take the fancy of a young woman?' was her next question. She actually looked at me (I might have been wrong; and I hope I was) as if the 'young woman' she had in her mind was myself! I said: 'I don't think of such things, and I don't talk about them.' Still, she was not in the least discouraged; she made a personal remark next: 'Excuse me – but you do look wretchedly pale.' I thought she seemed to enjoy the defect in my complexion; I really believe it raised me in her estimation. 'We shall get on better in time,' she said; 'I am beginning to like you.' She walked out humming a tune. Don't you agree with me? Don't you think she's crazy?'

'I can hardly give an opinion until I have seen her. Does she look as if she might have been a pretty woman at one time of her life?'

'Not the sort of pretty woman whom I admire!'

Mr Rayburn smiled. 'I was thinking,' he resumed, 'that this person's odd conduct may perhaps be accounted for. She is probably jealous of any young lady who is invited to her master's house – and (till she noticed your complexion) she began by being jealous of you.'

Innocently at a loss to understand how *she* could become an object of the housekeeper's jealousy, Mrs Zant looked at Mr Rayburn in astonishment. Before she could give expression to her feeling of surprise, there was an interruption – a welcome interruption. A waiter entered the room, and announced a visitor; described as 'a gentleman'.

Mrs Zant at once rose to retire.

'Who is the gentleman?' Mr Rayburn asked – detaining Mrs Zant as he spoke.

A voice which they both recognised answered gaily, from the outer side of the door: 'A friend from London.'

10

'Welcome to St Sallins!' cried Mr John Zant. 'I knew that you were expected, my dear sir, and I took my chance of finding you at the hotel.' He turned to his sister-in-law, and kissed her hand with an elaborate gallantry worthy of Sir Charles Grandison himself. 'When

I reached home, my dear, and heard that you had gone out, I guessed that your object was to receive our excellent friend. You have not felt lonely while I have been away? That's right! That's right!' he looked toward the balcony, and discovered Lucy at the open window, staring at the magnificent stranger. 'Your little daughter, Mr Rayburn? Dear child! Come and kiss me.'

Lucy answered in one positive word: 'No.'

Mr John Zant was not easily discouraged.

'Show me your doll, darling,' he said. 'Sit on my knee.'

Lucy answered in two positive words – 'I won't.'

Her father approached the window to administer the necessary reproof. Mr John Zant interfered in the cause of mercy with his best grace. He held up his hands in cordial entreaty. 'Dear Mr Rayburn! The fairies are sometimes shy; and *this* little fairy doesn't take to strangers at first sight. Dear child! All in good time. And what stay do you make at St Sallins? May we hope that our poor attractions will tempt you to prolong your visit?'

He put his flattering little question with an ease of manner which was rather too plainly assumed; and he looked at Mr Rayburn with a watchfulness which appeared to attach undue importance to the reply. When he said: 'What stay do you make at St Sallins?' did he really mean: 'How soon do you leave us?' Inclining to adopt this conclusion, Mr Rayburn answered cautiously that his stay at the seaside would depend on circumstances. Mr John Zant looked at his sister-in-law, sitting silent in a corner with Lucy on her lap. 'Exert your attractions,' he said; 'make the circumstances agreeable to our good friend. Will you dine with us today, my dear sir, and bring your little fairy with you?'

Lucy was far from receiving this complimentary allusion in the spirit in which it had been offered. 'I'm not a fairy,' she declared. 'I'm a child.'

'And a naughty child,' her father added, with all the severity that he could assume.

'I can't help it, papa; the man with the big beard puts me out.'

The man with the big beard was amused – amiably, paternally amused – by Lucy's plain speaking. He repeated his invitation to dinner; and he did his best to look disappointed when Mr Rayburn made the necessary excuses.

'Another day,' he said (without, however, fixing the day). 'I think you will find my house comfortable. My housekeeper may perhaps be eccentric – but in all essentials a woman in a thousand. Do you feel the change from London already? Our air at St Sallins is really worthy of its reputation. Invalids who come here are cured as if by magic. What do you think of Mrs Zant? How does she look?'

Mr Rayburn was evidently expected to say that she looked better. He said it. Mr John Zant seemed to have anticipated a stronger expression of opinion.

'Surprisingly better!' he pronounced. 'Infinitely better! We ought both to be grateful. Pray believe that we *are* grateful.'

'If you mean grateful to me,' Mr Rayburn remarked, 'I don't quite understand – '

'You don't quite understand? Is it possible that you have forgotten our conversation when I first had the honour of receiving you? Look at Mrs Zant again.'

Mr Rayburn looked; and Mrs Zant's brother-in-law explained himself.

'You notice the return of her colour, the healthy brightness of her eyes. (No, my dear, I am not paying you idle compliments; I am stating plain facts.) For that happy result, Mr Rayburn, we are indebted to you.'

'Surely not?'

'Surely yes! It was at your valuable suggestion that I thought of inviting my sister-in-law to visit me at St Sallins. Ah, you remember it now. Forgive me if I look at my watch; the dinner hour is on my mind. Not, as your dear little daughter there seems to think, because I am greedy, but because I am always punctual, in justice to the cook. Shall we see you tomorrow? Call early, and you will find us at home.'

He gave Mrs Zant his arm, and bowed and smiled, and kissed his hand to Lucy, and left the room. Recalling their interview at the hotel in London, Mr Rayburn now understood John Zant's object (on that occasion) in assuming the character of a helpless man in need of a sensible suggestion. If Mrs Zant's residence under his roof became associated with evil consequences, he could declare that she would never have entered the house but for Mr Rayburn's advice.

With the next day came the hateful necessity of returning this man's visit.

Mr Rayburn was placed between two alternatives. In Mrs Zant's interests he must remain, no matter at what sacrifice of his own inclinations, on good terms with her brother-in-law – or he must return to London, and leave the poor woman to her fate. His choice, it is needless to say, was never a matter of doubt. He called at the house, and did his innocent best – without in the least deceiving Mr

John Zant – to make himself agreeable during the short duration of his visit. Descending the stairs on his way out, accompanied by Mrs Zant, he was surprised to see a middle-aged woman in the hall, who looked as if she was waiting there expressly to attract notice.

'The housekeeper,' Mrs Zant whispered. 'She is impudent enough to try to make acquaintance with you.'

This was exactly what the housekeeper was waiting in the hall to do.

'I hope you like our watering-place, sir,' she began. 'If I can be of service to you, pray command me. Any friend of this lady's has a claim on me – and you are an old friend, no doubt. I am only the housekeeper; but I presume to take a sincere interest in Mrs Zant; and I am indeed glad to see you here. We none of us know – do we? – how soon we may want a friend. No offence, I hope? Thank you, sir. Good-morning.'

There was nothing in the woman's eyes which indicated an unsettled mind; nothing in the appearance of her lips which suggested habits of intoxication. That her strange outburst of familiarity proceeded from some strong motive seemed to be more than probable. Putting together what Mrs Zant had already told him, and what he had himself observed, Mr Rayburn suspected that the motive might be found in the housekeeper's jealousy of her master.

II

Reflecting in the solitude of his own room, Mr Rayburn felt that the one prudent course to take would be to persuade Mrs Zant to leave St Sallins. He tried to prepare her for this strong proceeding, when she came the next day to take Lucy out for a walk.

'If you still regret having forced yourself to accept your brother-in-law's invitation,' was all he ventured to say, 'don't forget that you are perfect mistress of your own actions. You have only to come to me at the hotel, and I will take you back to London by the next train.'

She positively refused to entertain the idea.

'I should be a thankless creature, indeed,' she said, 'if I accepted your proposal. Do you think I am ungrateful enough to involve you in a personal quarrel with John Zant? No! If I find myself forced to leave the house, I will go away alone.'

There was no moving her from this resolution. When she and Lucy had gone out together, Mr Rayburn remained at the hotel, with a mind ill at ease. A man of readier mental resources might have felt at a loss how to act for the best, in the emergency that now confronted him. While he was still as far as ever from arriving at a decision, some person knocked at the door.

Had Mrs Zant returned? He looked up as the door was opened, and saw to his astonishment – Mr John Zant's housekeeper.

'Don't let me alarm you, sir,' the woman said. 'Mrs Zant has been taken a little faint, at the door of our house. My master is attending to her.'

'Where is the child?' Mr Rayburn asked.

'I was bringing her back to you, sir, when we met a lady and her little girl at the door of the hotel. They were on their way to the beach – and Miss Lucy begged hard to be allowed to go with them. The lady said the two children were playfellows, and she was sure you would not object.'

'The lady is quite right. Mrs Zant's illness is not serious, I hope?'

'I think not, sir. But I should like to say something in her interests. May I? Thank you.' She advanced a step nearer to him, and spoke her next words in a whisper. 'Take Mrs Zant away from this place, and lose no time in doing it.'

Mr Rayburn was on his guard. He merely asked: 'Why?'

The housekeeper answered in a curiously indirect manner – partly in jest, as it seemed, and partly in earnest.

'When a man has lost his wife,' she said, 'there's some difference of opinion in Parliament, as I hear, whether he does right or wrong, if he marries his wife's sister. Wait a bit! I'm coming to the point. My master is one who has a long head on his shoulders; he sees consequences which escape the notice of people like me. In his way of thinking, if one man may marry his wife's sister, and no harm done, where's the objection if another man pays a compliment to the family, and marries his brother's widow? My master, if you please, is that other man. Take the widow away before she marries him.'

This was beyond endurance.

'You insult Mrs Zant,' Mr Rayburn answered, 'if you suppose that such a thing is possible!'

'Oh! I insult her, do I? Listen to me. One of three things will happen. She will be entrapped into consenting to it – or frightened into consenting to it – or drugged into consenting to it – '

Mr Rayburn was too indignant to let her go on.

'You are talking nonsense,' he said. 'There can be no marriage; the law forbids it.'

'Are you one of the people who see no further than their noses?'
she asked insolently. 'Won't the law take his money? Is he obliged to
mention that he is related to her by marriage, when he buys the
licence?' She paused; her humour changed; she stamped furiously on
the floor. The true motive that animated her showed itself in her
next words, and warned Mr Rayburn to grant a more favourable
hearing than he had accorded to her yet. 'If you won't stop it,' she
burst out, 'I will! If he marries anybody, he is bound to marry
me. Will you take her away? I ask you, for the last time – *will* you
take her away?'

The tone in which she made that final appeal to him had its effect.

'I will go back with you to John Zant's house,' he said, 'and judge
for myself.'

She laid her hand on his arm: 'I must go first – or you may not
be let in. Follow me in five minutes; and don't knock at the
street door.'

On the point of leaving him, she abruptly returned.

'We have forgotten something,' she said. 'Suppose my master
refuses to see you. His temper might get the better of him; he
might make it so unpleasant for you that you would be obliged
to go.'

'*My* temper might get the better of *me*,' Mr Rayburn replied;
'and – if I thought it was in Mrs Zant's interests – I might refuse to
leave the house unless she accompanied me.'

'That will never do, sir.'

'Why not?'

'Because I should be the person to suffer.'

'In what way?'

'In this way. If you picked a quarrel with my master, I should be
blamed for it because I showed you upstairs. Besides, think of the
lady. You might frighten her out of her senses, if it came to a struggle
between you two men.'

The language was exaggerated; but there was a force in this last
objection which Mr Rayburn was obliged to acknowledge.

'And, after all,' the housekeeper continued, 'he has more right
over her than you have. He is related to her, and you are only
her friend.'

Mr Rayburn declined to let himself be influenced by this consideration, 'Mr John Zant is only related to her by marriage,' he said.
'If she prefers trusting in me – come what may of it, I will be worthy
of her confidence.'

The housekeeper shook her head.

'That only means another quarrel,' she answered. 'The wise way, with a man like my master, is the peaceable way. We must manage to deceive him.'

'I don't like deceit.'

'In that case, sir, I'll wish you goodbye. We will leave Mrs Zant to do the best she can for herself.'

Mr Rayburn was unreasonable. He positively refused to adopt this alternative.

'Will you hear what I have got to say?' the housekeeper asked.

'There can be no harm in that,' he admitted. 'Go on.'

She took him at his word.

'When you called at our house,' she began, 'did you notice the doors in the passage, on the first floor? Very well. One of them is the door of the drawing-room, and the other is the door of the library. Do you remember the drawing-room, sir?'

'I thought it a large well-lighted room,' Mr Rayburn answered. 'And I noticed a doorway in the wall, with a handsome curtain hanging over it.'

'That's enough for our purpose,' the housekeeper resumed. 'On the other side of the curtain, if you had looked in, you would have found the library. Suppose my master is as polite as usual, and begs to be excused for not receiving you, because it is an inconvenient time. And suppose you are polite on your side and take yourself off by the drawing-room door. You will find me waiting downstairs, on the first landing. Do you see it now?'

'I can't say I do.'

'You surprise me, sir. What is to prevent us from getting back softly into the library, by the door in the passage? And why shouldn't we use that second way into the library as a means of discovering what may be going on in the drawing-room? Safe behind the curtain, you will see him if he behaves uncivilly to Mrs Zant, or you will hear her if she calls for help. In either case, you may be as rough and ready with my master as you find needful; it will be he who has frightened her, and not you. And who can blame the poor housekeeper because Mr Rayburn did his duty, and protected a helpless woman? There is my plan, sir. Is it worth trying?'

He answered, sharply enough: 'I don't like it.'

The housekeeper opened the door again, and wished him goodbye. If Mr Rayburn had felt no more than an ordinary interest in Mrs

Zant, he would have let the woman go. As it was, he stopped her; and, after some further protest (which proved to be useless), he ended in giving way.

'You promise to follow my directions?' she stipulated.

He gave the promise. She smiled, nodded, and left him. True to his instructions, Mr Rayburn reckoned five minutes by his watch, before he followed her.

12

The housekeeper was waiting for him, with the street-door ajar.

'They are both in the drawing-room,' she whispered, leading the way upstairs. 'Step softly, and take him by surprise.'

A table of oblong shape stood midway between the drawing-room walls. At the end of it which was nearest to the window, Mrs Zant was pacing to and fro across the breadth of the room. At the opposite end of the table, John Zant was seated. Taken completely by surprise, he showed himself in his true character. He started to his feet, and protested with an oath against the intrusion which had been committed on him.

Heedless of his action and his language, Mr Rayburn could look at nothing, could think of nothing, but Mrs Zant. She was still walking slowly to and fro, unconscious of the words of sympathy which he addressed to her, insensible even as it seemed to the presence of other persons in the room.

John Zant's voice broke the silence. His temper was under control again: he had his reasons for still remaining on friendly terms with Mr Rayburn.

'I am sorry I forgot myself just now,' he said.

Mr Rayburn's interest was concentrated on Mrs Zant; he took no notice of the apology.

'When did this happen?' he asked.

'About a quarter of an hour ago. I was fortunately at home. Without speaking to me, without noticing me, she walked upstairs like a person in a dream.'

Mr Rayburn suddenly pointed to Mrs Zant.

'Look at her!' he said. 'There's a change!'

All restlessness in her movements had come to an end. She was standing at the further end of the table, which was nearest to the window, in the full flow of sunlight pouring at that moment over her face. Her eyes looked out straight before her – void of all expression.

Her lips were a little parted: her head drooped slightly toward her shoulder, in an attitude which suggested listening for something or waiting for something. In the warm brilliant light, she stood before the two men, a living creature self-isolated in a stillness like the stillness of death.

John Zant was ready with the expression of his opinion.

'A nervous seizure,' he said. 'Something resembling catalepsy, as you see.'

'Have you sent for a doctor?'

'A doctor is not wanted.'

'I beg your pardon. It seems to me that medical help is absolutely necessary.'

'Be so good as to remember,' Mr John Zant answered, 'that the decision rests with me, as the lady's relative. I am sensible of the honour which your visit confers on me. But the time has been unhappily chosen. Forgive me if I suggest that you will do well to retire.'

Mr Rayburn had not forgotten the housekeeper's advice, or the promise which she had exacted from him. But the expression in John Zant's face was a serious trial to his self-control. He hesitated, and looked back at Mrs Zant.

If he provoked a quarrel by remaining in the room, the one alternative would be the removal of her by force. Fear of the consequences to herself, if she was suddenly and roughly roused from her trance, was the one consideration which reconciled him to submission. He withdrew.

The housekeeper was waiting for him below, on the first landing. When the door of the drawing-room had been closed again, she signed to him to follow her, and returned up the stairs. After another struggle with himself, he obeyed. They entered the library from the corridor – and placed themselves behind the closed curtain which hung over the doorway. It was easy so to arrange the edge of the drapery as to observe, without exciting suspicion, whatever was going on in the next room.

Mrs Zant's brother-in-law was approaching her at the time when Mr Rayburn saw him again.

In the instant afterward, she moved – before he had completely passed over the space between them. Her still figure began to tremble. She lifted her drooping head. For a moment there was a shrinking in her – as if she had been touched by something. She seemed to recognise the touch: she was still again.

John Zant watched the change. It suggested to him that she was beginning to recover her senses. He tried the experiment of speaking to her.

'My love, my sweet angel, come to the heart that adores you!'

He advanced again; he passed into the flood of sunlight pouring over her.

'Rouse yourself!' he said.

She still remained in the same position; apparently at his mercy, neither hearing him nor seeing him.

'Rouse yourself!' he repeated. 'My darling, come to me!'

At the instant when he attempted to embrace her – at the instant when Mr Rayburn rushed into the room – John Zant's arms, suddenly turning rigid, remained outstretched. With a shriek of horror, he struggled to draw them back – struggled, in the empty brightness of the sunshine, as if some invisible grip had seized him.

'What has got me?' the wretch screamed. 'Who is holding my hands? Oh, the cold of it! The cold of it!'

His features became convulsed; his eyes turned upward until only the white eyeballs were visible. He fell prostrate with a crash that shook the room.

The housekeeper ran in. She knelt by her master's body. With one hand she loosened his cravat. With the other she pointed to the end of the table.

Mrs Zant still kept her place; but there was another change. Little by little, her eyes recovered their natural living expression – then slowly closed. She tottered backward from the table, and lifted her hands wildly, as if to grasp at something which might support her. Mr Rayburn hurried to her before she fell – lifted her in his arms – and carried her out of the room.

One of the servants met them in the hall. He sent her for a carriage. In a quarter of an hour more, Mrs Zant was safe under his care at the hotel.

13

That night a note, written by the housekeeper, was delivered to Mrs Zant.

The doctors give little hope. The paralytic stroke is spreading upward to his face. If death spares him, he will live a helpless man. I shall take care of him to the last. As for you – forget him.

Mrs Zant gave the note to Mr Rayburn. 'Read it, and destroy it,' she said. 'It is written in ignorance of the terrible truth.'

He obeyed – and looked at her in silence, waiting to hear more. She hid her face. The few words she had addressed to him, after a struggle with herself, fell slowly and reluctantly from her lips.

She said: 'No mortal hand held the hands of John Zant. The guardian spirit was with me. The promised protection was with me. I know it. I wish to know no more.'

Having spoken, she rose to retire. He opened the door for her, seeing that she needed rest in her own room.

Left by himself, he began to consider the prospect that was before him in the future. How was he to regard the woman who had just left him? As a poor creature weakened by disease, the victim of her own nervous delusion? Or as the chosen object of a supernatural revelation – unparalleled by any similar revelation that he had heard of, or had found recorded in books? His first discovery of the place that she really held in his estimation dawned on his mind, when he felt himself recoiling from the conclusion which presented her to his pity, and yielding to the nobler conviction which felt with her faith, and raised her to a place apart among other women.

14

They left St Sallins the next day.

Arrived at the end of the journey, Lucy held fast by Mrs Zant's hand. Tears were rising in the child's eyes.

'Are we to bid her goodbye?' she said sadly to her father.

He seemed to be unwilling to trust himself to speak; he only said: 'My dear, ask her yourself.'

But the result justified him. Lucy was happy again.

A Terribly Strange Bed

Shortly after my education at college was finished, I happened to be staying at Paris with an English friend. We were both young men then, and lived, I am afraid, rather a wild life, in the delightful city of our sojourn. One night we were idling about the neighbourhood of the Palais Royal, doubtful to what amusement we should next betake ourselves. My friend proposed a visit to Frascati's; but his suggestion was not to my taste. I knew Frascati's, as the French saying is, by heart; had lost and won plenty of five-franc pieces there, merely for amusement's sake, until it was amusement no longer, and was thoroughly tired, in fact, of all the ghastly respectabilities of such a social anomaly as a respectable gambling-house. 'For Heaven's sake,' said I to my friend, 'let us go somewhere where we can see a little genuine, blackguard, poverty-stricken gaming with no false ginger-bread glitter thrown over it all. Let us get away from fashionable Frascati's, to a house where they don't mind letting in a man with a ragged coat, or a man with no coat, ragged or otherwise.' 'Very well,' said my friend, 'we needn't go out of the Palais Royal to find the sort of company you want. Here's the place just before us; as blackguard a place, by all report, as you could possibly wish to see.' In another minute we arrived at the door and entered the house.

When we got upstairs, and had left our hats and sticks with the doorkeeper, we were admitted into the chief gambling-room. We did not find many people assembled there. But, few as the men were who looked up at us on our entrance, they were all types – lamentably true types – of their respective classes.

We had come to see blackguards; but these men were some-thing worse. There is a comic side, more or less appreciable, in all blackguardism – here there was nothing but tragedy – mute, weird tragedy. The quiet in the room was horrible. The thin, haggard, long-haired young man, whose sunken eyes fiercely watched the turning up of the cards, never spoke; the flabby, fat-faced, pimply player, who pricked his piece of pasteboard perseveringly, to register how often black won, and how often red – never spoke; the dirty, wrinkled old man, with the vulture eyes and the darned greatcoat, who had lost his last *sou*, and still looked on desperately, after he could play no longer – never spoke. Even the voice of the croupier sounded as if it were strangely dulled and thickened in the atmosphere of the room. I had entered the place to laugh, but the spectacle before me was something to weep over. I soon found it necessary to take refuge in excitement from the depression of spirits which was fast stealing on me. Unfortunately I sought the nearest excitement, by going to the table and beginning to play. Still more unfortunately, as the event will show, I won – won prodigiously; won incredibly; won at such a rate that the regular players at the table crowded round me; and staring at my stakes with hungry, superstitious eyes, whispered to one another that the English stranger was going to break the bank.

The game was *Rouge et Noir*. I had played at it in every city in Europe, without, however, the care or the wish to study the Theory of Chances – that philosopher's stone of all gamblers! And a gambler, in the strict sense of the word, I had never been. I was heart-whole from the corroding passion for play. My gaming was a mere idle amusement. I never resorted to it by necessity, because I never knew what it was to want money. I never practised it so incessantly as to lose more than I could afford, or to gain more than I could coolly pocket without being thrown off my balance by my good luck. In short, I had hitherto frequented gambling-tables – just as I frequented ballrooms and opera-houses – because they amused me, and because I had nothing better to do with my leisure hours.

But on this occasion it was very different – now, for the first time in my life, I felt what the passion for play really was. My success first bewildered, and then, in the most literal meaning of the word, intoxicated me. Incredible as it may appear, it is nevertheless true, that I only lost when I attempted to estimate chances, and played according to previous calculation. If I left everything to luck, and staked without any care or consideration, I was sure to win – to win in the face of every recognised probability in favour of the bank. At first some of the men present ventured their money safely enough on my colour; but I speedily increased my stakes to sums which they dared not risk. One after another they left off playing, and breathlessly looked on at my game.

Still, time after time, I staked higher and higher, and still won. The excitement in the room rose to fever pitch. The silence was interrupted by a deep-muttered chorus of oaths and exclamations in different languages, every time the gold was shovelled across to my side of the table – even the imperturbable croupier dashed his rake on the floor in a (French) fury of astonishment at my success. But one man present preserved his self-possession, and that man was my friend. He came to my side, and whispering in English, begged me to leave the place, satisfied with what I had already gained. I must do him the justice to say that he repeated his warnings and entreaties several times, and only left me and went away after I had rejected his advice (I was to all intents and purposes gambling drunk) in terms which rendered it impossible for him to address me again that night.

Shortly after he had gone, a hoarse voice behind me cried: 'Permit me, my dear sir – permit me to restore to their proper place two napoleons which you have dropped. Wonderful luck, sir! I pledge you my word of honour, as an old soldier, in the course of my long experience in this sort of thing, I never saw such luck as yours – never! Go on, sir – *Sacre mille bombes!* Go on boldly, and break the bank!'

I turned round and saw, nodding and smiling at me with inveterate civility, a tall man, dressed in a frogged and braided surtout.

If I had been in my senses, I should have considered him, personally, as being rather a suspicious specimen of an old soldier. He had goggling bloodshot eyes, mangy moustaches, and a broken nose. His voice betrayed a barrack-room intonation of the worst order, and he had the dirtiest pair of hands I ever saw – even in France. These little personal peculiarities exercised, however, no repelling influence on me. In the mad excitement, the reckless triumph of that moment, I was ready to 'fraternise' with anybody who encouraged me in my game. I accepted the old soldier's offered pinch of snuff; clapped him on the back, and swore he was the honestest fellow in the world – the most glorious relic of the Grand Army that I had ever met with. 'Go on!' cried my military friend, snapping his fingers in ecstasy – 'Go on, and win! Break the bank – *Mille tonnerres!* My gallant English comrade, break the bank!'

And I *did* go on – went on at such a rate, that in another quarter of an hour the croupier called out, 'Gentlemen, the bank has discontinued for tonight.' All the notes, and all the gold in that 'bank', now lay in a heap under my hands; the whole floating capital of the gambling-house was waiting to pour into my pockets!

'Tie up the money in your pocket-handkerchief, my worthy sir,' said the old soldier, as I wildly plunged my hands into my heap of gold. 'Tie it up, as we used to tie up a bit of dinner in the Grand

Army; your winnings are too heavy for any breeches-pockets that ever were sewed. There! That's it – shovel them in, notes and all! *Credie!* What luck! Stop! Another napoleon on the floor! *Ah! Sacre petit polisson de Napoleon!* Have I found thee at last? Now then, sir – two tight double knots each way with your honourable permission, and the money's safe. Feel it! Feel it, fortunate sir! Hard and round as a cannon-ball – *Ah, bah!* If they had only fired such cannon-balls at us at Austerlitz – *nom d'une pipe!* If they only had! And now, as an ancient grenadier, as an ex-brave of the French army, what remains for me to do? I ask what? Simply this: to entreat my valued English friend to drink a bottle of champagne with me, and toast the goddess Fortune in foaming goblets before we part!'

'Excellent ex-brave! Convivial ancient grenadier! Champagne by all means! An English cheer for an old soldier! Hurrah! Hurrah! Another English cheer for the goddess Fortune! Hurrah! Hurrah! Hurrah!'

'Bravo! The Englishman; the amiable, gracious Englishman, in whose veins circulates the vivacious blood of France! Another glass? *Ah, bah!* – the bottle is empty! Never mind! *Vive le vin!* I, the old soldier, order another bottle, and half a pound of *bonbons* with it!'

'No, no, ex-brave; never – ancient grenadier! *Your* bottle last time; *my* bottle this. Behold it! Toast away! The French Army! The great Napoleon! The present company! The croupier! The honest croupier's wife and daughters – if he has any! The Ladies generally! Everybody in the world!'

By the time the second bottle of champagne was emptied, I felt as if I had been drinking liquid fire – my brain seemed all aflame. No excess in wine had ever had this effect on me before in my life. Was it the result of a stimulant acting upon my system when I was in a highly excited state? Was my stomach in a particularly disordered condition? Or was the champagne amazingly strong?

'Ex-brave of the French Army!' cried I, in a mad state of exhilaration, '*I* am on fire! How are *you*? You have set me on fire. Do you hear, my hero of Austerlitz? Let us have a third bottle of champagne to put the flame out!'

The old soldier wagged his head, rolled his goggle-eyes, until I expected to see them slip out of their sockets; placed his dirty forefinger by the side of his broken nose; solemnly ejaculated 'Coffee!' and immediately ran off into an inner room.

The word pronounced by the eccentric veteran seemed to have a magical effect on the rest of the company present. With one accord they all rose to depart. Probably they had expected to profit by my intoxication; but finding that my new friend was benevolently bent on preventing me from getting dead drunk, had now abandoned all hope of thriving pleasantly on my winnings. Whatever their motive might be, at any rate they went away in a body. When the old soldier returned, and sat down again opposite to me at the table, we had the room to ourselves. I could see the croupier, in a sort of vestibule which opened out of it, eating his supper in solitude. The silence was now deeper than ever.

A sudden change, too, had come over the 'ex-brave'. He assumed a portentously solemn look; and when he spoke to me again, his speech was ornamented by no oaths, enforced by no finger-snapping, enlivened by no apostrophes or exclamations.

'Listen, my dear sir,' said he, in mysteriously confidential tones – 'listen to an old soldier's advice. I have been to the mistress of the house (a very charming woman, with a genius for cookery!) to impress on her the necessity of making us some particularly strong and good coffee. You must drink this coffee in order to get rid of your little amiable exaltation of spirits before you think of going home – you *must*, my good and gracious friend! With all that money to take home tonight, it is a sacred duty to yourself to have your wits about you. You are known to be a winner to an enormous extent by several gentlemen present tonight, who, in a certain point of view, are very worthy and excellent fellows; but they are mortal men, my dear sir, and they have their amiable weaknesses. Need I say more? Ah, no, no! You understand me! Now, this is what you must do – send for a cabriolet when you feel quite well again – draw up all the windows when you get into it – and tell the driver to take you home only through the large and well-lighted thoroughfares. Do this; and you and your money will be safe. Do this; and tomorrow you will thank an old soldier for giving you a word of honest advice.'

Just as the ex-brave ended his oration in very lachrymose tones, the coffee came in, ready poured out in two cups. My attentive friend handed me one of the cups with a bow. I was parched with thirst, and drank it off at a draught. Almost instantly afterwards, I was seized with a fit of giddiness, and felt more completely intoxicated than ever. The room whirled round and round furiously; the old soldier seemed to be regularly bobbing up and down before me like the piston of a steam-engine. I was half deafened by a violent singing in my ears; a feeling of utter bewilderment, helplessness, idiocy, overcame me. I rose from my chair, holding on by the table to keep my balance; and stammered out that I felt dreadfully unwell – so unwell that I did not know how I was to get home.

'My dear friend,' answered the old soldier – and even his voice seemed to be bobbing up and down as he spoke – 'my dear friend, it would be madness to go home in *your* state; you would be sure to lose your money; you might be robbed and murdered with the greatest ease. *I* am going to sleep here; do *you* sleep here, too – they make up capital beds in this house – take one; sleep off the effects of the wine, and go home safely with your winnings tomorrow – tomorrow, in broad daylight.'

I had but two ideas left: one, that I must never let go hold of my handkerchief full of money; the other, that I must lie down somewhere immediately, and fall off into a comfortable sleep. So I agreed to the proposal about the bed, and took the offered arm of the old soldier, carrying my money with my disengaged hand. Preceded by the croupier, we passed along some passages and up a flight of stairs into the bedroom which I was to occupy. The ex-brave shook me warmly by the hand, proposed that we should breakfast together, and then, followed by the croupier, left me for the night.

I ran to the wash-hand stand; drank some of the water in my jug; poured the rest out, and plunged my face into it; then sat down in a chair and tried to compose myself. I soon felt better. The change for my lungs, from the fetid atmosphere of the gambling-room to the cool air of the apartment I now occupied, the almost equally refreshing change for my eyes, from the glaring gaslights of the 'salon' to the dim, quiet flicker of one bedroom-candle, aided wonderfully the restorative effects of cold water. The giddiness left me, and I began to feel a little like a reasonable being again. My first thought was of the risk of sleeping all night in a gambling-house; my second, of the still greater risk of trying to get out after the house was closed, and of going home alone at night through the streets of Paris with a large sum of money about me. I had slept in worse places than this on my travels; so I determined to lock, bolt, and barricade my door, and take my chance till the next morning.

Accordingly, I secured myself against all intrusion; looked under the bed, and into the cupboard; tried the fastening of the window; and then, satisfied that I had taken every proper precaution, pulled off my upper clothing, put my light, which was a dim one, on the hearth among a feathery litter of wood-ashes, and got into bed, with the handkerchief full of money under my pillow.

I soon felt not only that I could not go to sleep, but that I could not even close my eyes. I was wide awake, and in a high fever. Every nerve in my body trembled – every one of my senses seemed to be preternaturally sharpened. I tossed and rolled, and tried every kind of position, and perseveringly sought out the cold corners of the bed, and all to no purpose. Now I thrust my arms over the clothes; now I poked them under the clothes; now I violently shot my legs straight out down to the bottom of the bed; now I convulsively coiled them up as near my chin as they would go; now I shook out my crumpled pillow, changed it to the cool side, patted it flat, and lay down quietly on my back; now I fiercely doubled it in two, set it up on end, thrust it against the board of the bed, and tried a sitting posture. Every effort was in vain; I groaned with vexation as I felt that I was in for a sleepless night.

What could I do? I had no book to read. And yet, unless I found out some method of diverting my mind, I felt certain that I was in the condition to imagine all sorts of horrors; to rack my brain with forebodings of every possible and impossible danger; in short, to pass the night in suffering all conceivable varieties of nervous terror.

I raised myself on my elbow, and looked about the room – which was brightened by a lovely moonlight pouring straight through the window – to see if it contained any pictures or ornaments that I could at all clearly distinguish. While my eyes wandered from wall to wall, a remembrance of Le Maistre's delightful little book, *Voyage autour de ma Chambre*, occurred to me. I resolved to imitate the French author, and find occupation and amusement enough to relieve the tedium of my wakefulness, by making a mental inventory of every article of furniture I could see, and by following up to their sources the multitude of associations which even a chair, a table, or a wash-hand stand may be made to call forth.

In the nervous unsettled state of my mind at that moment, I found it much easier to make my inventory than to make my reflections, and thereupon soon gave up all hope of thinking in Le Maistre's fanciful track – or, indeed, of thinking at all. I looked about the room at the different articles of furniture, and did nothing more.

There was, first, the bed I was lying in; a four-post bed, of all things in the world to meet with in Paris – yes, a thorough clumsy British four-poster, with the regular top lined with chintz – the regular fringed valance all round – the regular stifling, unwhole-some curtains, which I remembered having mechanically drawn back against the posts without particularly noticing the bed when I first got into the room. Then there was the marble-topped wash-hand stand, from which the water I had spilled, in my hurry to pour it out, was still dripping, slowly and more slowly, on to the brick floor. Then two small chairs, with my coat, waistcoat, and trousers flung on them. Then a large elbow-chair covered with dirty-white dimity, with my cravat and shirt collar thrown over the back. Then a chest of drawers with two of the brass handles off, and a tawdry, broken china inkstand placed on it by way of ornament for the top. Then the dressing-table, adorned by a very small looking-glass, and a very large pincushion. Then the window – an unusually large window. Then a dark old picture, which the feeble candle dimly showed me. It was a picture of a fellow in a high Spanish hat, crowned with a plume of towering feathers. A swarthy, sinister ruffian, looking upward, shading his eyes with his hand, and looking intently upward – it might be at some tall gallows at which he was going to be hanged. At any rate, he had the appearance of thoroughly deserving it.

This picture put a kind of constraint upon me to look upward too – at the top of the bed. It was a gloomy and not an interesting object, and I looked back at the picture. I counted the feathers in the man's hat – they stood out in relief – three white, two green. I observed the crown of his hat, which was of conical shape, according to the fashion supposed to have been favoured by Guido Fawkes. I wondered what he was looking up at. It couldn't be at the stars; such a desperado was neither astrologer nor astronomer. It must be at the high gallows, and he was going to be hanged presently. Would the executioner come into possession of his conical crowned hat and plume of feathers? I counted the feathers again – three white, two green.

While I still lingered over this very improving and intellectual employment, my thoughts insensibly began to wander. The moonlight shining into the room reminded me of a certain moonlight night in England – the night after a picnic party in a Welsh valley. Every incident of the drive homeward, through lovely scenery, which the moonlight made lovelier than ever, came back to my remembrance, though I had never given the picnic a thought for years; though, if I had *tried* to recollect it, I could certainly have recalled little or nothing of that scene long past. Of all the wonderful faculties that help to tell us we are immortal, which speaks the sublime truth more eloquently than memory? Here was I, in a strange house of the most suspicious character, in a situation of uncertainty, and even of peril, which might seem to make the cool exercise of my recollection almost out of the question; nevertheless remembering, quite involuntarily, places, people, conversations, minute circumstances of every kind, which I had thought forgotten for ever; which I could not possibly have recalled at will, even under the most favourable auspices. And what cause had produced in a moment the whole of this strange, complicated, mysterious effect? Nothing but some rays of moonlight shining in at my bedroom window.

I was still thinking of the picnic – of our merriment on the drive home – of the sentimental young lady who *would* quote 'Childe Harold' because it was moonlight. I was absorbed by these past scenes and past amusements, when, in an instant, the thread on which my memories hung snapped asunder; my attention immediately came back to present things more vividly than ever, and I found myself, I neither knew why nor wherefore, looking hard at the picture again.

Looking for what?

Good God! The man had pulled his hat down on his brows! No! The hat itself was gone! Where was the conical crown? Where the feathers – three white, two green? Not there! In place of the hat and feathers, what dusky object was it that now hid his forehead, his eyes, his shading hand?

Was the bed moving?

I turned on my back and looked up. Was I mad? Drunk? Dreaming? Giddy again? Or was the top of the bed really moving down – sinking slowly, regularly, silently, horribly, right down throughout the whole of its length and breadth – right down upon me, as I lay underneath?

My blood seemed to stand still. A deadly paralysing coldness stole all over me as I turned my head round on the pillow and determined to test whether the bed-top was really moving or not, by keeping my eye on the man in the picture.

The next look in that direction was enough. The dull, black, frowzy outline of the valance above me was within an inch of being parallel with his waist. I still looked breathlessly. And steadily and slowly – very slowly – I saw the figure, and the line of frame below the figure, vanish, as the valance moved down before it.

I am, constitutionally, anything but timid. I have been on more than one occasion in peril of my life, and have not lost my self-possession for an instant; but when the conviction first settled on my mind that the bed-top was really moving, was steadily and continuously sinking down upon me, I looked up shuddering, helpless, panic-stricken, beneath the hideous machinery for murder, which was advancing closer and closer to suffocate me where I lay.

I looked up, motionless, speechless, breathless. The candle, fully spent, went out; but the moonlight still brightened the room. Down and down, without pausing and without sounding, came the bed-top, and still my panic-terror seemed to bind me faster and faster to the mattress on which I lay – down and down it sank, till the dusty odour from the lining of the canopy came stealing into my nostrils.

At that final moment the instinct of self-preservation startled me out of my trance, and I moved at last. There was just room for me to roll myself sidewise off the bed. As I dropped noiselessly to the floor, the edge of the murderous canopy touched me on the shoulder.

Without stopping to draw my breath, without wiping the cold sweat from my face, I rose instantly on my knees to watch the bed-top. I was literally spellbound by it. If I had heard footsteps behind me, I could not have turned round; if a means of escape had been miraculously provided for me, I could not have moved to take advantage of it. The whole life in me was, at that moment, concentrated in my eyes.

It descended – the whole canopy, with the fringe round it, came down – down – close down; so close that there was not room now to squeeze my finger between the bed-top and the bed. I felt at the sides, and discovered that what had appeared to me from beneath to be the ordinary light canopy of a four-post bed was in reality a thick, broad mattress, the substance of which was concealed by the valance and its fringe. I looked up and saw the four posts rising hideously bare. In the middle of the bed-top was a huge wooden screw that had evidently worked it down through a hole in the ceiling, just as ordinary presses are worked down on the substance selected for compression. The frightful apparatus moved without making the faintest noise. There had been no creaking as it came down; there was now not the faintest sound from the room above. Amid a dead and awful silence I beheld before me – in the nineteenth century, and in the civilised capital of France – such a machine for secret murder by suffocation as might have existed in the worst days of the Inquisition, in the lonely inns among the Hartz Mountains, in the mysterious tribunals of Westphalia! Still, as I looked on it, I could not move, I could hardly breathe, but I began to recover the power of thinking, and in a moment I discovered the murderous conspiracy framed against me in all its horror.

My cup of coffee had been drugged, and drugged too strongly. I had been saved from being smothered by having taken an overdose of some narcotic. How I had chafed and fretted at the fever-fit which had preserved my life by keeping me awake! How recklessly I had confided myself to the two wretches who had led me into this room, determined, for the sake of my winnings, to kill me in my sleep by the surest and most horrible contrivance for secretly accomplishing my destruction! How many men, winners like me, had slept, as I had proposed to sleep, in that bed, and had never been seen or heard of more! I shuddered at the bare idea of it.

But, ere long, all thought was again suspended by the sight of the murderous canopy moving once more. After it had remained on the bed – as nearly as I could guess – about ten minutes, it began to move up again. The villains who worked it from above evidently believed that their purpose was now accomplished. Slowly and silently, as it had descended, that horrible bed-top rose towards its former place. When it reached the upper extremities of the four posts, it reached the ceiling, too. Neither hole nor screw could be seen; the bed became in appearance an ordinary bed again – the canopy an ordinary canopy – even to the most suspicious eyes.

Now, for the first time, I was able to move – to rise from my knees – to dress myself in my upper clothing – and to consider how I should escape. If I betrayed by the smallest noise that the attempt to suffocate me had failed, I was certain to be murdered. Had I made any noise already? I listened intently, looking towards the door.

No! No footsteps in the passage outside – no sound of a tread, light or heavy, in the room above – absolute silence everywhere. Besides locking and bolting my door, I had moved an old wooden chest against it, which I had found under the bed. To remove this chest (my blood ran cold as I thought of what its contents *might* be!) without making some disturbance was impossible; and, moreover, to think of escaping through the house, now barred up for the night, was sheer insanity. Only one chance was left me – the window. I stole to it on tiptoe.

My bedroom was on the first floor, above an *entresol*, and looked into a back street. I raised my hand to open the window, knowing that on that action hung, by the merest hair-breadth, my chance of safety. They keep vigilant watch in a House of Murder. If any part of the frame cracked, if the hinge creaked, I was a lost man! It must have occupied me at least five minutes, reckoning by time – five *hours*, reckoning by suspense – to open that window. I succeeded in doing it silently – in doing it with all the dexterity of a house-breaker – and then looked down into the street. To leap the distance beneath me would be almost certain destruction! Next, I looked round at the sides of the house. Down the left side ran a thick water-pipe – it passed close by the outer edge of the window. The moment I saw the pipe I knew I was saved. My breath came and went freely for the first time since I had seen the canopy of the bed moving down upon me!

To some men the means of escape which I had discovered might have seemed difficult and dangerous enough – to *me* the prospect of slipping down the pipe into the street did not suggest even a thought of peril. I had always been accustomed, by the practice of gymnastics, to keep up my schoolboy powers as a daring and expert climber; and knew that my head, hands, and feet would serve me faithfully in any hazards of ascent or descent. I had already got one leg over the window-sill, when I remembered the handkerchief filled with money under my pillow. I could well have afforded to leave it behind me, but I was revengefully determined that the miscreants of the gambling-house should miss their plunder as well as their victim. So I went back to the bed and tied the heavy handkerchief at my back by my cravat.

Just as I had made it tight and fixed it in a comfortable place, I thought I heard a sound of breathing outside the door. The chill feeling of horror ran through me again as I listened. No! Dead silence still in the passage – I had only heard the night air blowing softly into the room. The next moment I was on the window-sill – and the next I had a firm grip on the water-pipe with my hands and knees.

I slid down into the street easily and quietly, as I thought I should, and immediately set off at the top of my speed to a branch 'Prefecture' of Police, which I knew was situated in the immediate neighbourhood. A 'Sub-prefect', and several picked men among his subordinates, happened to be up, maturing, I believe, some scheme for discovering the perpetrator of a mysterious murder which all Paris was talking of just then. When I began my story, in a breathless hurry and in very bad French, I could see that the Sub-prefect suspected me of being a drunken Englishman who had robbed somebody; but he soon altered his opinion as I went on, and before I had anything like concluded, he shoved all the papers before him into a drawer, put on his hat, supplied me with another (for I was bareheaded), ordered a file of soldiers, desired his expert followers to get ready all sorts of tools for breaking open doors and ripping up brick flooring, and took my arm, in the most friendly and familiar manner possible, to lead me with him out of the house. I will venture to say that when the Sub-prefect was a little boy, and was taken for the first time to the play, he was not half as much pleased as he was now at the job in prospect for him at the gambling-house!

Away we went through the streets, the Sub-prefect cross-examining and congratulating me in the same breath as we marched at the head of our formidable *posse comitatus*. Sentinels were placed at the back and front of the house the moment we got to it; a tremendous battery of knocks was directed against the door; a light appeared at a window; I was told to conceal myself behind the police – then came more knocks and a cry of 'Open in the name of the law!' At that terrible summons bolts and locks gave way before an invisible hand, and the moment after the Sub-prefect was in the passage, confronting a waiter half-dressed and ghastly pale. This was the short dialogue which immediately took place:

'We want to see the Englishman who is sleeping in this house.'

'He went away hours ago.'

'He did no such thing. His friend went away; *he* remained. Show us to his bedroom!'

'I swear to you, Monsieur le Sous-Préfect, he is not here! He – '

'I swear to you, Monsieur le Garcon, he is. He slept here – he didn't find your bed comfortable – he came to us to complain of it – here he is among my men – and here am I ready to look for a flea or two in his bedstead. Renaudin!' calling to one of the subordinates, and pointing to the waiter – 'collar that man and tie his hands behind him. Now, then, gentlemen, let us walk upstairs!'

Every man and woman in the house was secured – the 'Old Soldier' the first. Then I identified the bed in which I had slept, and then we went into the room above.

No object that was at all extraordinary appeared in any part of it. The Sub-prefect looked round the place, commanded everybody to be silent, stamped twice on the floor, called for a candle, looked attentively at the spot he had stamped on, and ordered the flooring there to be carefully taken up. This was done in no time. Lights were produced, and we saw a deep raftered cavity between the floor of this room and the ceiling of the room beneath. Through this cavity there ran perpendicularly a sort of case of iron thickly greased; and inside the case appeared the screw, which communicated with the bed-top below. Extra lengths of screw, freshly oiled; levers covered with felt;

all the complete upper works of a heavy press – constructed with infernal ingenuity so as to join the fixtures below, and when taken to pieces again, to go into the smallest possible compass – were next discovered and pulled out on the floor. After some little difficulty the Sub-prefect succeeded in putting the machinery together, and, leaving his men to work it, descended with me to the bedroom. The smothering canopy was then lowered, but not so noiselessly as I had seen it lowered. When I mentioned this to the Sub-prefect, his answer, simple as it was, had a terrible significance. 'My men,' said he, 'are working down the bed-top for the first time – the men whose money you won were in better practice.'

We left the house in the sole possession of two police agents – every one of the inmates being removed to prison on the spot. The Sub-prefect, after taking down my *procès-verbal* in his office, returned with me to my hotel to get my passport. 'Do you think,' I asked, as I gave it to him, 'that any men have really been smothered in that bed, as they tried to smother *me*?'

'I have seen dozens of drowned men laid out at the Morgue,' answered the Sub-prefect, 'in whose pocketbooks were found letters stating that they had committed suicide in the Seine, because they had lost everything at the gaming table. Do I know how many of those men entered the same gambling-house that *you* entered? Won as *you* won? Took that bed as *you* took it? Slept in it? Were smothered in it? And were privately thrown into the river, with a letter of explanation written by the murderers and placed in their pocket-books? No man can say how many or how few have suffered the fate from which you have escaped. The people of the gambling-house kept their bedstead machinery a secret from *us* – even from the police! The dead kept the rest of the secret for them. Good night, or rather good-morning, Monsieur Faulkner! Be at my office again at nine o'clock – in the meantime, *au revoir!*'

The rest of my story is soon told. I was examined and re-examined; the gambling-house was strictly searched all through from top to bottom; the prisoners were separately interrogated; and two of the less guilty among them made a confession. I discovered that the Old Soldier was the master of the gambling-house – *justice* discovered that he had been drummed out of the army as a vagabond years ago; that he had been guilty of all sorts of villainies since; that he was in possession of stolen property, which the owners identified; and that he, the croupier, another accomplice, and the woman who had made my cup of coffee, were all in the secret of the bedstead. There appeared some reason to doubt whether the inferior persons attached to the house knew anything of the suffocating machinery; and they received the benefit of that doubt, by being treated simply as thieves and vagabonds. As for the Old Soldier and his two head myrmidons, they went to the galleys; the woman who had drugged my coffee was imprisoned for I forget how many years; the regular attendants at the gambling-house were considered 'suspicious' and placed under 'surveillance'; and I became, for one whole week (which is a long time) the head 'lion' in Parisian society. My adventure was dramatised by three illustrious playmakers, but never saw theatrical daylight; for the censorship forbade the introduction on the stage of a correct copy of the gambling-house bedstead.

One good result was produced by my adventure, which any censorship must have approved: it cured me of ever again trying *Rouge et Noir* as an amusement. The sight of a green cloth, with packs of cards and heaps of money on it, will henceforth be for ever associated in my mind with the sight of a bed canopy descending to suffocate me in the silence and darkness of the night.

Miss Jéromette and the Clergyman

I

My brother, the clergyman, looked over my shoulder before I was aware of him, and discovered that the volume which completely absorbed my attention was a collection of famous Trials, published in a new edition and in a popular form.

He laid his finger on the Trial which I happened to be reading at the moment. I looked up at him; his face startled me. He had turned pale. His eyes were fixed on the open page of the book with an expression which puzzled and alarmed me.

'My dear fellow,' I said, 'what in the world is the matter with you?'

He answered in an odd absent manner, still keeping his finger on the open page.

'I had almost forgotten,' he said. 'And this reminds me.'

'Reminds you of what?' I asked. 'You don't mean to say you know anything about the Trial?'

'I know this,' he said. 'The prisoner was guilty.'

'Guilty?' I repeated. 'Why, the man was acquitted by the jury, with the full approval of the judge! What call you possibly mean?'

'There are circumstances connected with that Trial,' my brother answered, 'which were never communicated to the judge or the jury – which were never so much as hinted or whispered in court. *I* know them – of my own knowledge, by my own personal experience. They are very sad, very strange, very terrible. I have mentioned them to no mortal creature. I have done my best to forget them. You – quite innocently – have brought them back to my mind. They oppress, they distress me. I wish I had found you reading any book in your library, except *that* book!'

My curiosity was now strongly excited. I spoke out plainly.

'Surely,' I suggested, 'you might tell your brother what you are unwilling to mention to persons less nearly related to you. We have followed different professions, and have lived in different countries, since we were boys at school. But you know you can trust me.'

He considered a little with himself.

'Yes,' he said. 'I know I can trust you.' He waited a moment, and then he surprised me by a strange question.

'Do you believe,' he asked, 'that the spirits of the dead can return to earth, and show themselves to the living?'

I answered cautiously – adopting as my own the words of a great English writer, touching the subject of ghosts.

'You ask me a question,' I said, 'which, after five thousand years, is yet undecided. On that account alone, it is a question not to be trifled with.'

My reply seemed to satisfy him.

'Promise me,' he resumed, 'that you will keep what I tell you a secret as long as I live. After my death I care little what happens. Let the story of my strange experience be added to the published experience of those other men who have seen what I have seen, and who believe what I believe. The world will not be the worse, and may be the better, for knowing one day what I am now about to trust to your ear alone.'

My brother never again alluded to the narrative which he had confided to me, until the later time when I was sitting by his death-bed. He asked if I still remembered the story of Jéromette. 'Tell it to others,' he said, 'as I have told it to you.'

I repeat it after his death – as nearly as I can in his own words.

2

On a fine summer evening, many years since, I left my chambers in the Temple, to meet a fellow-student, who had proposed to me a night's amusement in the public gardens at Cremorne.

You were then on your way to India; and I had taken my degree at Oxford. I had sadly disappointed my father by choosing the Law as my profession, in preference to the Church. At that time, to own the truth, I had no serious intention of following any special vocation. I simply wanted an excuse for enjoying the pleasures of a London life. The study of the Law supplied me with that excuse. And I chose the Law as my profession accordingly.

On reaching the place at which we had arranged to meet, I found that my friend had not kept his appointment. After waiting vainly for ten minutes, my patience gave way and I went into the Gardens by myself.

I took two or three turns round the platform devoted to the

dancers without discovering my fellow-student, and without seeing any other person with whom I happened to be acquainted at
that time.

For some reason which I cannot now remember, I was not in my
usual good spirits that evening. The noisy music jarred on my nerves,
the sight of the gaping crowd round the platform irritated me, the
blandishments of the painted ladies of the profession of pleasure
saddened and disgusted me. I opened my cigar-case, and turned aside
into one of the quiet by-walks of the Gardens.

A man who is habitually careful in choosing his cigar has this
advantage over a man who is habitually careless. He can always count
on smoking the best cigar in his case, down to the last. I was still
absorbed in choosing *my* cigar, when I heard these words behind
me – spoken in a foreign accent and in a woman's voice: 'Leave me
directly, sir! I wish to have nothing to say to you.'

I turned round and discovered a little lady very simply and taste-
fully dressed, who looked both angry and alarmed as she rapidly
passed me on her way to the more frequented part of the Gardens. A
man (evidently the worse for the wine he had drunk in the course of
the evening) was following her, and was pressing his tipsy attentions
on her with the coarsest insolence of speech and manner. She was
young and pretty, and she cast one entreating look at me as she went
by, which it was not in manhood – perhaps I ought to say, in young-
manhood – to resist.

I instantly stepped forward to protect her, careless whether I involved myself in a discreditable quarrel with a blackguard or not. As
a matter of course, the fellow resented my interference, and my
temper gave way. Fortunately for me, just as I lifted my hand to
knock him down, a policeman appeared who had noticed that he
was drunk, and who settled the dispute officially by turning him out
of the Gardens.

I led her away from the crowd that had collected. She was evidently frightened – I felt her hand trembling on my arm – but she had
one great merit; she made no fuss about it.

'If I can sit down for a few minutes,' she said in her pretty foreign
accent, 'I shall soon be myself again, and I shall not trespass any
further on your kindness. I thank you very much, sir, for taking care
of me.'

We sat down on a bench in a retired part of the Gardens, near
a little fountain. A row of lighted lamps ran round the outer rim of
the basin. I could see her plainly.

I have said that she was 'a little lady'. I could not have described her more correctly in three words.

Her figure was slight and small: she was a well-made miniature of a woman from head to foot. Her hair and her eyes were both dark. The hair curled naturally; the expression of the eyes was quiet, and rather sad; the complexion, as I then saw it, very pale; the little mouth perfectly charming. I was especially attracted, I remembered, by the carriage of her head; it was strikingly graceful and spirited; it distinguished her, little as she was and quiet as she was, among the thousands of other women in the Gardens, as a creature apart. Even the one marked defect in her – a slight 'cast' in the left eye – seemed to add, in some strange way, to the quaint attractiveness of her face. I have already spoken of the tasteful simplicity of her dress. I ought now to add that it was not made of any costly material, and that she wore no jewels or ornaments of any sort. My little lady was not rich; even a man's eye could see that.

She was perfectly unembarrassed and unaffected. We fell as easily into talk as if we had been friends instead of strangers.

I asked how it was that she had no companion to take care of her. 'You are too young and too pretty,' I said in my blunt English way, 'to trust yourself alone in such a place as this.'

She took no notice of the compliment. She calmly put it away from her as if it had not reached her ears.

'I have no friend to take care of me,' she said simply. 'I was sad and sorry this evening, all by myself, and I thought I would go to the Gardens and hear the music, just to amuse me. It is not much to pay at the gate; only a shilling.'

'No friend to take care of you?' I repeated. 'Surely there must be one happy man who might have been here with you tonight?'

'What man do you mean?' she asked.

'The man,' I answered thoughtlessly, 'whom we call, in England, a Sweetheart.'

I would have given worlds to have recalled those foolish words the moment they passed my lips. I felt that I had taken a vulgar liberty with her. Her face saddened; her eyes dropped to the ground. I begged her pardon.

'There is no need to beg my pardon,' she said. 'If you wish to know, sir – yes, I had once a sweetheart, as you call it in England. He has gone away and left me. No more of him, if you please. I am rested now. I will thank you again, and go home.'

She rose to leave me.

I was determined not to part with her in that way. I begged to be allowed to see her safely back to her own door. She hesitated. I took a man's unfair advantage of her, by appealing to her fears. I said, 'Suppose the blackguard who annoyed you should be waiting outside the gates?' That decided her. She took my arm. We went away together by the bank of the Thames, in the balmy summer night.

A walk of half an hour brought us to the house in which she lodged – a shabby little house in a by-street, inhabited evidently by very poor people.

She held out her hand at the door, and wished me good-night. I was too much interested in her to consent to leave my little foreign lady without the hope of seeing her again. I asked permission to call on her the next day. We were standing under the light of the street-lamp. She studied my face with a grave and steady attention before she made any reply.

'Yes,' she said at last. 'I think I do know a gentleman when I see him. You may come, sir, if you please, and call upon me tomorrow.'

So we parted. So I entered – doubting nothing, foreboding nothing – on a scene in my life which I now look back on with unfeigned repentance and regret.

3

I am speaking at this later time in the position of a clergyman, and in the character of a man of mature age. Remember that; and you will understand why I pass as rapidly as possible over the events of the next year of my life – why I say as little as I can of the errors and the delusions of my youth.

I called on her the next day. I repeated my visits during the days and weeks that followed, until the shabby little house in the by-street had become a second and (I say it with shame and self-reproach) a dearer home to me.

All of herself and her story which she thought fit to confide to me under these circumstances may be repeated to you in few words.

The name by which letters were addressed to her was 'Mademoiselle Jéromette'. Among the ignorant people of the house and the small tradesmen of the neighbourhood – who found her name not easy of pronunciation by the average English tongue – she was known by the friendly nickname of 'The French Miss'. When I knew her, she was resigned to her lonely life among strangers. Some years had elapsed since she had lost her parents, and had left France.

Possessing a small, very small, income of her own, she added to it by colouring miniatures for the photographers. She had relatives still living in France; but she had long since ceased to correspond with them. 'Ask me nothing more about my family,' she used to say. 'I am as good as dead in my own country and among my own people.'

This was all – literally all – that she told me of herself. I have never discovered more of her sad story from that day to this.

She never mentioned her family name – never even told me what part of France she came from or how long she had lived in England. That she was by birth and breeding a lady, I could entertain no doubt; her manners, her accomplishments, her ways of thinking and speaking, all proved it. Looking below the surface, her character showed itself in aspects not common among young women in these days. In her quiet way she was an incurable fatalist, and a firm believer in the ghostly reality of apparitions from the dead. Then again in the matter of money, she had strange views of her own. Whenever my purse was in my hand, she held me resolutely at a distance from first to last. She refused to move into better apartments; the shabby little house was clean inside, and the poor people who lived in it were kind to her – and that was enough. The most expensive present that she ever permitted me to offer her was a little enamelled ring, the plainest and cheapest thing of the kind in the jeweller's shop. In all relations with me she was sincerity itself. On all occasions, and under all circumstances, she spoke her mind (as the phrase is) with the same uncompromising plainness.

'I like you,' she said to me; 'I respect you; I shall always be faithful to you while you are faithful to me. But my love has gone from me. There is another man who has taken it away with him, I know not where.'

Who was the other man?

She refused to tell me. She kept his rank and his name strict secrets from me. I never discovered how he had met with her, or why he had left her, or whether the guilt was his of making of her an exile from her country and her friends. She despised herself for still loving him; but the passion was too strong for her – she owned it and lamented it with the frankness which was so pre-eminently a part of her character. More than this, she plainly told me, in the early days of our acquaintance, that she believed he would return to her. It might be tomorrow, or it might be years hence. Even if he failed to repent of his own cruel conduct, the man would still miss her, as something lost out of his life; and, sooner or later, he would come back.

'And will you receive him if he does come back?' I asked.

'I shall receive him,' she replied, 'against my own better judge-ment – in spite of my own firm persuasion that the day of his return to me will bring with it the darkest days of my life.'

I tried to remonstrate with her.

'You have a will of your own,' I said. 'Exert it if he attempts to return to you.'

'I have no will of my own,' she answered quietly, 'where *he* is concerned. It is my misfortune to love him.' Her eyes rested for a moment on mine, with the utter self-abandonment of despair. 'We have said enough about this,' she added abruptly. 'Let us say no more.'

From that time we never spoke again of the unknown man. During the year that followed our first meeting, she heard nothing of him directly or indirectly. He might be living, or he might be dead. There came no word of him, or from him. I was fond enough of her to be satisfied with this – he never disturbed us.

4

The year passed – and the end came. Not the end as you may have anticipated it, or as I might have foreboded it.

You remember the time when your letters from home informed you of the fatal termination of our mother's illness? It is the time of which I am now speaking. A few hours only before she breathed her last, she called me to her bedside, and desired that we might be left together alone. Reminding me that her death was near, she spoke of my prospects in life; she noticed my want of interest in the studies which were then supposed to be engaging my attention, and she ended by entreating me to reconsider my refusal to enter the Church.

'Your father's heart is set upon it,' she said. 'Do what I ask of you, my dear, and you will help to comfort him when I am gone.'

Her strength failed her: she could say no more. Could I refuse the last request she would ever make to me? I knelt at the bedside, and took her wasted hand in mine, and solemnly promised her the respect which a son owes to his mother's last wishes.

Having bound myself by this sacred engagement, I had no choice but to accept the sacrifice which it imperatively exacted from me. The time had come when I must tear myself free from all unworthy associations. No matter what the effort cost me, I must separate myself at once and forever from the unhappy woman who was not, who never could be, my wife.

At the close of a dull foggy day I set forth with a heavy heart to say the words which were to part us forever.

Her lodging was not far from the banks of the Thames. As I drew near the place the darkness was gathering, and the broad surface of the river was hidden from me in a chill white mist. I stood for a while, with my eyes fixed on the vaporous shroud that brooded over the flowing water – I stood and asked myself in despair the one dreary question: 'What am I to say to her?'

The mist chilled me to the bones. I turned from the river-bank, and made my way to her lodgings hard by. 'It must be done!' I said to myself, as I took out my key and opened the house door.

She was not at her work, as usual, when I entered her little sitting-room. She was standing by the fire, with her head down and with an open letter in her hand.

The instant she turned to meet me, I saw in her face that something was wrong. Her ordinary manner was the manner of an unusually placid and self-restrained person. Her temperament had little of the liveliness which we associate in England with the French nature. She was not ready with her laugh; and in all my previous experience, I had never yet known her to cry. Now, for the first time, I saw the quiet face disturbed; I saw tears in the pretty brown eyes. She ran to meet me, and laid her head on my breast, and burst into a passionate fit of weeping that shook her from head to foot.

Could she by any human possibility have heard of the coming change in my life? Was she aware, before I had opened my lips, of the hard necessity which had brought me to the house?

It was simply impossible; the thing could not be.

I waited until her first burst of emotion had worn itself out. Then I asked – with an uneasy conscience, with a sinking heart – what had happened to distress her.

She drew herself away from me, sighing heavily, and gave me the open letter which I had seen in her hand.

'Read that,' she said. 'And remember I told you what might happen when we first met.'

I read the letter.

It was signed in initials only; but the writer plainly revealed himself as the man who had deserted her. He had repented; he had returned to her. In proof of his penitence he was willing to do her the justice which he had hitherto refused – he was willing to marry her, on the condition that she would engage to keep the marriage a secret, so long as his parents lived. Submitting this proposal, he waited to know whether she would consent, on her side, to forgive and forget.

I gave her back the letter in silence. This unknown rival had done me the service of paving the way for our separation. In offering her the atonement of marriage, he had made it, on my part, a matter of duty to *her*, as well as to myself, to say the parting words. I felt this instantly. And yet, I hated him for helping me.

She took my hand, and led me to the sofa. We sat down, side by side. Her face was composed to a sad tranquillity. She was quiet; she was herself again.

'I have refused to see him, she said, 'until I had first spoken to you. You have read his letter. What do you say?'

I could make but one answer. It was my duty to tell her what my own position was in the plainest terms. I did my duty – leaving her free to decide on the future for herself. Those sad words said, it was useless to prolong the wretchedness of our separation. I rose, and took her hand for the last time.

I see her again now, at that final moment, as plainly as if it had happened yesterday. She had been suffering from an affection of the throat; and she had a white silk handkerchief tied loosely round her neck. She wore a simple dress of purple merino, with a black silk apron over it. Her face was deadly pale; her fingers felt icily cold as they closed round my hand.

'Promise me one thing,' I said, 'before I go. While I live, I am your friend – if I am nothing more. If you are ever in trouble, promise that you will let me know it.'

She started, and drew back from me as if I had struck her with a sudden terror.

'Strange!' she said, speaking to herself. '*He* feels as I feel. He is afraid of what may happen to me, in my life to come.'

I attempted to reassure her. I tried to tell her what was indeed the truth – that I had only been thinking of the ordinary chances and changes of life, when I spoke.

She paid no heed to me; she came back and put her hands on my shoulders and thoughtfully and sadly looked up in my face.

'My mind is not your mind in this matter,' she said. 'I once owned to you that I had my forebodings, when we first spoke of this man's return. I may tell you now, more than I told you then. I believe I shall die young, and die miserably. If I am right, have you interest enough still left in me to wish to hear of it?'

She paused, shuddering – and added these startling words: 'You *shall* hear of it.'

The tone of steady conviction in which she spoke alarmed and distressed me. My face showed her how deeply and how painfully I was affected.

'There, there!' she said, returning to her natural manner; 'don't take what I say too seriously. A poor girl who has led a lonely life like mine thinks strangely and talks strangely – sometimes. Yes; I give you my promise. If I am ever in trouble, I will let you know it. God bless you – you have been very kind to me – goodbye!'

A tear dropped on my face as she kissed me. The door closed between us. The dark street received me.

It was raining heavily. I looked up at her window, through the drifting shower. The curtains were parted: she was standing in the gap, dimly lit by the lamp on the table behind her, waiting for our last look at each other. Slowly lifting her hand, she waved her farewell at the window, with the unsought native grace which had charmed me on the night when we first met. The curtain fell again – she disappeared – nothing was before me, nothing was round me, but the darkness and the night.

5

In two years from that time, I had redeemed the promise given to my mother on her deathbed. I had entered the Church.

My father's interest made my first step in my new profession an easy one. After serving my preliminary apprenticeship as a curate, I was appointed, before I was thirty years of age, to a living in the West of England.

My new benefice offered me every advantage that I could possibly desire – with the one exception of a sufficient income. Although my wants were few, and although I was still an unmarried man, I found it desirable, on many accounts, to add to my resources. Following the example of other young clergymen in my position, I determined to receive pupils who might stand in need of preparation for a career at the Universities. My relatives exerted themselves; and my good fortune still befriended me. I obtained two pupils to start with. A third would complete the number which I was at present prepared to receive. In course of time, this third pupil made his appearance, under circumstances sufficiently remarkable to merit being mentioned in detail.

It was the summer vacation; and my two pupils had gone home. Thanks to a neighbouring clergyman, who kindly undertook to perform my duties for me, I too obtained a fortnight's holiday, which I spent at my father's house in London.

During my sojourn in the metropolis, I was offered an opportunity of preaching in a church, made famous by the eloquence of one of the popular pulpit-orators of our time. In accepting the proposal, I felt naturally anxious to do my best, before the unusually large and unusually intelligent congregation which would be assembled to hear me.

At the period of which I am now speaking, all England had been startled by the discovery of a terrible crime, perpetrated under circumstances of extreme provocation. I chose this crime as the main subject of my sermon. Admitting that the best among us were frail mortal creatures, subject to evil promptings and provocations like the worst among us, my object was to show how a Christian man may find his certain refuge from temptation in the safeguards of his religion. I dwelt minutely on the hardship of the Christian's first struggle to resist the evil influence – on the help which his Christianity inexhaustibly held out to him in the worst relapses of the weaker and viler part of his nature – on the steady and certain gain which was the ultimate reward of his faith and his firmness – and on the blessed sense of peace and happiness which accompanied the final triumph. Preaching to this effect, with the fervent conviction which I really felt, I may say for myself, at least, that I did no discredit to the choice which had placed me in the pulpit. I held the attention of my congregation, from the first word to the last.

While I was resting in the vestry on the conclusion of the service, a note was brought to me written in pencil. A member of my congregation – a gentleman – wished to see me, on a matter of considerable importance to himself. He would call on me at any place, and at any hour, which I might choose to appoint. If I wished to be satisfied of his respectability, he would beg leave to refer me to his father, with whose name I might possibly be acquainted.

The name given in the reference was undoubtedly familiar to me, as the name of a man of some celebrity and influence in the world of London. I sent back my card, appointing an hour for the visit of my correspondent on the afternoon of the next day.

6

The stranger made his appearance punctually. I guessed him to be some two or three years younger than myself. He was undeniably handsome; his manners were the manners of a gentleman – and yet, without knowing why, I felt a strong dislike to him the moment he entered the room.

After the first preliminary words of politeness had been exchanged between us, my visitor informed me as follows of the object which he had in view.

'I believe you live in the country, sir?' he began.

'I live in the West of England,' I answered.

'Do you make a long stay in London?'

'No. I go back to my rectory tomorrow.'

'May I ask if you take pupils?'

'Yes.'

'Have you any vacancy?'

'I have one vacancy.'

'Would you object to let me go back with you tomorrow, as your pupil?'

The abruptness of the proposal took me by surprise. I hesitated.

In the first place (as I have already said), I disliked him. In the second place, he was too old to be a fit companion for my other two pupils – both lads in their teens. In the third place, he had asked me to receive him at least three weeks before the vacation came to an end. I had my own pursuits and amusements in prospect during that interval, and saw no reason why I should inconvenience myself by setting them aside.

He noticed my hesitation, and did not conceal from me that I had disappointed him.

'I have it very much at heart,' he said, 'to repair without delay the time that I have lost. My age is against me, I know. The truth is – I have wasted my opportunities since I left school, and I am anxious, honestly anxious, to mend my ways, before it is too late. I wish to prepare myself for one of the Universities – I wish to show, if I can, that I am not quite unworthy to inherit my father's famous name. You are the man to help me, if I can only persuade you to do it. I was struck by your sermon yesterday; and, if I may venture to make the confession in your presence, I took a strong liking to you. Will you see my father, before you decide to say No? He will be able to explain whatever may seem strange in my present application; and he will be happy to see you this afternoon, if you can spare the time. As to the question of terms, I am quite sure it can be settled to your entire satisfaction.'

He was evidently in earnest – gravely, vehemently in earnest. I unwillingly consented to see his father.

Our interview was a long one. All my questions were answered fully and frankly.

The young man had led an idle and desultory life. He was weary of it, and ashamed of it. His disposition was a peculiar one. He stood sorely in need of a guide, a teacher, and a friend, in whom he was disposed to confide. If I disappointed the hopes which he had centred in me, he would be discouraged, and he would relapse into the aimless and indolent existence of which he was now ashamed. Any terms for which I might stipulate were at my disposal if I would consent to receive him, for three months to begin with, on trial.

Still hesitating, I consulted my father and my friends.

They were all of opinion (and justly of opinion so far) that the new connection would be an excellent one for me. They all reproached me for taking a purely capricious dislike to a well-born and well-bred young man, and for permitting it to influence me, at the outset of my career, against my own interests. Pressed by these considerations, I allowed myself to be persuaded to give the new pupil a fair trial. He accompanied me, the next day, on my way back to the rectory.

7

Let me be careful to do justice to a man whom I personally disliked. My senior pupil began well: he produced a decidedly favourable impression on the persons attached to my little household.

The women, especially, admired his beautiful light hair, his crisply-curling beard, his delicate complexion, his clear blue eyes, and his finely shaped hands and feet. Even the inveterate reserve in his manner, and the downcast, almost sullen, look which had prejudiced *me* against him, aroused a common feeling of romantic enthusiasm in my servants' hall. It was decided, on the high authority of the housekeeper herself, that 'the new gentleman' was in love – and, more interesting still, that he was the victim of an unhappy attachment which had driven him away from his friends and his home.

For myself, I tried hard, and tried vainly, to get over my first dislike to the senior pupil.

I could find no fault with him. All his habits were quiet and regular; and he devoted himself conscientiously to his reading. But, little by little, I became satisfied that his heart was not in his studies. More than this, I had my reasons for suspecting that he was concealing something from me, and that he felt painfully the reserve on his own part which he could not, or dared not, break through. There were moments when I almost doubted whether he had not chosen my remote country rectory as a safe place of refuge from some person or persons of whom he stood in dread.

For example, his ordinary course of proceeding, in the matter of his correspondence, was, to say the least of it, strange.

He received no letters at my house. They waited for him at the village post office. He invariably called for them himself, and invariably forbore to trust any of my servants with his own letters for the post. Again, when we were out walking together, I more than once caught him looking furtively over his shoulder, as if he suspected some person of following him, for some evil purpose. Being constitutionally a hater of mysteries, I determined, at an early stage of our intercourse, on making an effort to clear matters up. There might be just a chance of my winning the senior pupil's confidence, if I spoke to him while the last days of the summer vacation still left us alone together in the house.

'Excuse me for noticing it,' I said to him one morning, while we were engaged over our books – 'I cannot help observing that you appear to have some trouble on your mind. Is it indiscreet, on my part, to ask if I can be of any use to you?'

He changed colour – looked up at me quickly – looked down again at his book – struggled hard with some secret fear or secret reluctance that was in him – and suddenly burst out with this extraordinary question: 'I suppose you were in earnest when you preached that sermon in London?'

'I am astonished that you should doubt it,' I replied.

He paused again; struggled with himself again; and startled me by a second outbreak, even stranger than the first.

'I am one of the people you preached at in your sermon,' he said. 'That's the true reason why I asked you to take me for your pupil. Don't turn me out! When you talked to your congregation of tortured and tempted people, you talked of Me.'

I was so astonished by the confession, that I lost my presence of mind. For the moment, I was unable to answer him.

'Don't turn me out!' he repeated. 'Help me against myself. I am telling you the truth. As God is my witness, I am telling you the truth!'

'Tell me the *whole* truth,' I said; 'and rely on my consoling and helping you – rely on my being your friend.'

In the fervour of the moment, I took his hand. It lay cold and still in mine; it mutely warned me that I had a sullen and a secret nature to deal with.

'There must be no concealment between us,' I resumed. 'You have entered my house, by your own confession, under false pretences. It is your duty to me, and your duty to yourself, to speak out.'

The man's inveterate reserve – cast off for the moment only – renewed its hold on him. He considered, carefully considered, his next words before he permitted them to pass his lips.

'A person is in the way of my prospects in life,' he began slowly, with his eyes cast down on his book. 'A person provokes me horribly. I feel dreadful temptations (like the man you spoke of in your sermon) when I am in the person's company. Teach me to resist temptation. I am afraid of myself, if I see the person again. You are the only man who can help me. Do it while you can.'

He stopped, and passed his handkerchief over his forehead.

'Will that do?' he asked – still with his eyes on his book.

'It will *not* do,' I answered. 'You are so far from really opening your heart to me, that you won't even let me know whether it is a man or a woman who stands in the way of your prospects in life. You used the word "person", over and over again – rather than say "he" or "she" when you speak of the provocation which is trying you. How can I help a man who has so little confidence in me as that?'

My reply evidently found him at the end of his resources. He tried, tried desperately, to say more than he had said yet. No! The words seemed to stick in his throat. Not one of them would pass his lips.

'Give me time,' he pleaded piteously. 'I can't bring myself to it, all at once. I mean well. Upon my soul, I mean well. But I am slow at this sort of thing. Wait till tomorrow.'

Tomorrow came – and again he put it off.

'One more day!' he said. 'You don't know how hard it is to speak plainly. I am half afraid; I am half ashamed. Give me one more day.'

I had hitherto only disliked him. Try as I might (and did) to make merciful allowance for his reserve, I began to despise him now.

8

The day of the deferred confession came, and brought an event with it, for which both he and I were alike unprepared. Would he really have confided in me but for that event? He must either have done it, or have abandoned the purpose which had led him into my house.

We met as usual at the breakfast-table. My housekeeper brought in my letters of the morning. To my surprise, instead of leaving the room again as usual, she walked round to the other side of the table, and laid a letter before my senior pupil – the first letter, since his residence with me, which had been delivered to him under my roof.

He started, and took up the letter. He looked at the address. A spasm of suppressed fury passed across his face; his breath came quickly; his hand trembled as it held the letter. So far, I said nothing. I waited to see whether he would open the envelope in my presence or not.

He was afraid to open it in my presence. He got on his feet; he said, in tones so low that I could barely hear him: 'Please excuse me for a minute' – and left the room.

I waited for half an hour – for a quarter of an hour after that – and then I sent to ask if he had forgotten his breakfast.

In a minute more, I heard his footstep in the hall. He opened the breakfast-room door, and stood on the threshold, with a small travelling-bag in his hand.

'I beg your pardon,' he said, still standing at the door. 'I must ask for leave of absence for a day or two. Business in London.'

'Can I be of any use?' I asked. 'I am afraid your letter has brought you bad news?'

'Yes,' he said shortly. 'Bad news. I have no time for breakfast.'

'Wait a few minutes,' I urged. 'Wait long enough to treat me like your friend – to tell me what your trouble is before you go.'

He made no reply. He stepped into the hall and closed the door – then opened it again a little way, without showing himself.

'Business in London,' he repeated – as if he thought it highly important to inform me of the nature of his errand. The door closed for the second time. He was gone.

I went into my study, and carefully considered what had happened.

The result of my reflections is easily described. I determined on discontinuing my relations with my senior pupil. In writing to his father (which I did, with all due courtesy and respect, by that day's post), I mentioned as my reason for arriving at this decision – First, that I had found it impossible to win the confidence of his son. Secondly, that his son had that morning suddenly and mysteriously left my house for London, and that I must decline accepting any further responsibility toward him, as the necessary consequence.

I had put my letter in the post-bag, and was beginning to feel a little easier after having written it, when my housekeeper appeared in the study, with a very grave face, and with something hidden apparently in her closed hand.

'Would you please look, sir, at what we have found in the gentleman's bedroom, since he went away this morning?'

I knew the housekeeper to possess a woman's full share of that amicable weakness of the sex which goes by the name of 'Curiosity'. I had also, in various indirect ways, become aware that my senior pupil's strange departure had largely increased the disposition among the women of my household to regard him as the victim of an unhappy attachment. The time was ripe, as it seemed to me, for checking any further gossip about him, and any renewed attempts at prying into his affairs in his absence.

'Your only business in my pupil's bedroom,' I said to the housekeeper, 'is to see that it is kept clean, and that it is properly aired. There must be no interference, if you please, with his letters, or his papers, or with anything else that he has left behind him. Put back directly whatever you may have found in his room.'

The housekeeper had her full share of a woman's temper as well as of a woman's curiosity. She listened to me with a rising colour, and a just perceptible toss of the head.

'Must I put it back, sir, on the floor, between the bed and the wall?' she enquired, with an ironical assumption of the humblest deference to my wishes. '*That's* where the girl found it when she was sweeping the room. Anybody can see for themselves,' pursued the housekeeper indignantly, 'that the poor gentleman has gone away broken-hearted. And there, in my opinion, is the hussy who is the cause of it!'

With those words, she made me a low curtsey, and laid a small photographic portrait on the desk at which I was sitting.

I looked at the photograph.

In an instant, my heart was beating wildly – my head turned giddy – the housekeeper, the furniture, the walls of the room, all swayed and whirled round me.

The portrait that had been found in my senior pupil's bedroom was the portrait of Jéromette!

9

I had sent the housekeeper out of my study. I was alone, with the photograph of the Frenchwoman on my desk.

There could surely be little doubt about the discovery that had burst upon me. The man who had stolen his way into my house, driven by the terror of a temptation that he dared not reveal, and the man who had been my unknown rival in the bygone time, were one and the same!

Recovering self-possession enough to realise this plain truth, the inferences that followed forced their way into my mind as a matter of course. The unnamed person who was the obstacle to my pupil's prospects in life, the unnamed person in whose company he was assailed by temptations which made him tremble for himself, stood revealed to me now as being, in all human probability, no other than Jéromette. Had she bound him in the fetters of the marriage which he had himself proposed? Had she discovered his place of refuge in my house? And was the letter that had been delivered to him of her writing? Assuming these questions to be answered in the affirmative, what, in that case, was his 'business in London'? I remembered how he had spoken to me of his temptations, I recalled the expression that had crossed his face when he recognised the handwriting on the letter – and the conclusion that followed literally shook me to the soul. Ordering my horse to be saddled, I rode instantly to the railway-station.

The train by which he had travelled to London had reached the terminus nearly an hour since. The one useful course that I could take, by way of quieting the dreadful misgivings crowding one after another on my mind, was to telegraph to Jéromette at the address at which I had last seen her. I sent the subjoined message – prepaying the reply:

IF YOU ARE IN ANY TROUBLE, TELEGRAPH TO ME. I WILL BE WITH YOU BY THE FIRST TRAIN. ANSWER, IN ANY CASE.

There was nothing in the way of the immediate dispatch of my message. And yet the hours passed, and no answer was received. By the advice of the clerk, I sent a second telegram to the London office, requesting an explanation. The reply came back in these terms:

IMPROVEMENTS IN STREET. HOUSES PULLED DOWN. NO TRACE OF PERSON NAMED IN TELEGRAM.

I mounted my horse, and rode back slowly to the rectory.

'The day of his return to me will bring with it the darkest days of my life.' ... 'I shall die young, and die miserably. Have you interest enough still left in me to wish to hear of it?' ... 'You *shall* hear of it.' Those words were in my memory while I rode home in the cloudless moonlight night. They were so vividly present to me that I could hear again her pretty foreign accent, her quiet clear tones, as she spoke them. For the rest, the emotions of that memorable day had worn me out. The answer from the telegraph office had struck me with a strange and stony despair. My mind was a blank. I had no thoughts. I had no tears.

I was about halfway on my road home, and I had just heard the clock of a village church strike ten, when I became conscious, little by little, of a chilly sensation slowly creeping through and through me to the bones. The warm, balmy air of a summer night was abroad. It was the month of July. In the month of July, was it possible that any living creature (in good health) could feel cold? It was *not* possible – and yet, the chilly sensation still crept through and through me to the bones.

I looked up. I looked all round me.

My horse was walking along an open highroad. Neither trees nor waters were near me. On either side, the flat fields stretched away bright and broad in the moonlight.

I stopped my horse, and looked round me again.

Yes: I saw it. With my own eyes I saw it. A pillar of white mist – between five and six feet high, as well as I could judge – was moving beside me at the edge of the road, on my left hand. When I stopped, the white mist stopped. When I went on, the white mist went on. I pushed my horse to a trot – the pillar of mist was with me. I urged him to a gallop – the pillar of mist was with me. I stopped him again – the pillar of mist stood still.

The white colour of it was the white colour of the fog which I had seen over the river – on the night when I had gone to bid her farewell. And the chill which had then crept through me to the bones was the chill that was creeping through me now.

I went on again slowly. The white mist went on again slowly – with the clear bright night all round it.

I was awed rather than frightened. There was one moment, and one only, when the fear came to me that my reason might be shaken. I caught myself keeping time to the slow tramp of the horse's feet with the slow utterances of these words, repeated over and over again: 'Jéromette is dead. Jéromette is dead.' But my will was still my own: I was able to control myself, to impose silence on my own muttering lips. And I rode on quietly. And the pillar of mist went quietly with me.

My groom was waiting for my return at the rectory gate. I pointed to the mist, passing through the gate with me.

'Do you see anything there?' I said.

The man looked at me in astonishment.

I entered the rectory. The housekeeper met me in the hall. I pointed to the mist, entering with me.

'Do you see anything at my side?' I asked.

The housekeeper looked at me as the groom had looked at me.

'I am afraid you are not well, sir,' she said. 'Your colour is all gone – you are shivering. Let me get you a glass of wine. '

I went into my study, on the ground-floor, and took the chair at my desk. The photograph still lay where I had left it. The pillar of mist floated round the table, and stopped opposite to me, behind the photograph.

The housekeeper brought in the wine. I put the glass to my lips, and set it down again. The chill of the mist was in the wine. There was no taste, no reviving spirit in it. The presence of the housekeeper oppressed me. My dog had followed her into the room. The presence of the animal oppressed me. I said to the woman: 'Leave me by myself, and take the dog with you.'

They went out, and left me alone in the room.

I sat looking at the pillar of mist, hovering opposite to me.

It lengthened slowly, until it reached to the ceiling. As it lengthened, it grew bright and luminous. A time passed, and a shadowy appearance showed itself in the centre of the light. Little by little, the shadowy appearance took the outline of a human form. Soft brown eyes, tender and melancholy, looked at me through the unearthly light in the mist. The head and the rest of the face broke next slowly on my view. Then the figure gradually revealed itself, moment by moment, downward and downward to the feet. She stood before me as I had last seen her, in her purple-merino dress, with the black-silk apron, with the white handkerchief tied loosely round her neck. She stood before me, in the gentle beauty that I remembered so well; and looked at me as she had looked when she gave me her last kiss – when her tears had dropped on my cheek.

I fell on my knees at the table. I stretched out my hands to her imploringly. I said: 'Speak to me – O, once again speak to me, Jéromette.'

Her eyes rested on me with a divine compassion in them. She lifted her hand, and pointed to the photograph on my desk, with a gesture which bade me turn the card. I turned it. The name of the man who had left my house that morning was inscribed on it, in her own handwriting.

I looked up at her again, when I had read it. She lifted her hand once more, and pointed to the handkerchief round her neck. As I looked at it, the fair white silk changed horribly in colour – the fair white silk became darkened and drenched in blood.

A moment more – and the vision of her began to grow dim. By slow degrees, the figure, then the face, faded back into the shadowy appearance that I had first seen. The luminous inner light died out in the white mist. The mist itself dropped slowly downward – floated a moment in airy circles on the floor – vanished. Nothing was before me but the familiar wall of the room, and the photograph lying face downward on my desk.

10

The next day, the newspapers reported the discovery of a murder in London. A Frenchwoman was the victim. She had been killed by a wound in the throat. The crime had been discovered between ten and eleven o'clock on the previous night.

I leave you to draw your conclusion from what I have related. My own faith in the reality of the apparition is immovable. I say, and believe, that Jéromette kept her word with me. She died young, and died miserably. And I heard of it from herself.

Take up the Trial again, and look at the circumstances that were revealed during the investigation in court. His motive for murdering her is there.

You will see that she did indeed marry him privately; that they lived together contentedly, until the fatal day when she discovered that his fancy had been caught by another woman; that violent quarrels took place between them, from that time to the time when my sermon showed him his own deadly hatred toward her, reflected in the case of another man; that she discovered his place of retreat in my house, and threatened him by letter with the public assertion of her conjugal rights; lastly, that a man, variously described by different witnesses, was seen leaving the door of her lodgings on the night of the murder. The Law – advancing no further than this – may have discovered circumstances of suspicion, but no certainty. The

Law, in default of direct evidence to convict the prisoner, may have rightly decided in letting him go free.

But *I* persisted in believing that the man was guilty. *I* declare that he, and he alone, was the murderer of Jéromette. And now, you know why.

The Dead Hand

When this present nineteenth century was younger by a good many years than it is now, a certain friend of mine, named Arthur Holliday, happened to arrive in the town of Doncaster exactly in the middle of the race-week, or, in other words, in the middle of the month of September.

He was one of those reckless, rattlepated, openhearted, and open-mouthed young gentlemen who possess the gift of familiarity in its highest perfection, and who scramble carelessly along the journey of life, making friends, as the phrase is, wherever they go. His father was a rich manufacturer, and had bought landed property enough in one of the midland counties to make all the born squires in his neighbourhood thoroughly envious of him. Arthur was his only son, possessor in prospect of the great estate and the great business after his father's death; well supplied with money, and not too rigidly looked after, during his father's lifetime. Report, or scandal, whichever you please, said that the old gentleman had been rather wild in his youthful days, and that, unlike most parents, he was not disposed to be violently indignant when he found that his son took after him. This may be true or not. I myself only knew the elder Mr Holliday when he was getting on in years, and then he was as quiet and as respectable a gentleman as ever I met with.

Well, one September, as I told you, young Arthur comes to Doncaster, having suddenly decided, in his harebrained way, that he would go to the races. He did not reach the town till towards the close of evening, and he went at once to see about his dinner and bed at the principal hotel. Dinner they were ready enough to give him; but as for a bed, they laughed when he mentioned it. In the race week at Doncaster, it is no uncommon thing for visitors who have not bespoken apartments to pass the night in their carriages at the inn doors. As for the lower sort of strangers, I myself have often seen them, at that full time, sleeping out on the doorsteps for want of a covered place to creep under. Rich as he was, Arthur's chance of getting a night's lodging (seeing that he had not written beforehand to secure one) was more than doubtful. He tried the second hotel, and the third hotel, and two of the inferior inns after that; and was met everywhere with the same form of answer. No accommodation for the night of any sort was left. All the bright golden sovereigns in his pocket would not buy him a bed at Doncaster in the race-week.

To a young fellow of Arthur's temperament, the novelty of being turned away into the street like a penniless vagabond, at every house where he asked for a lodging, presented itself in the light of a new and highly amusing piece of experience. He went on with his carpet-bag in his hand, applying for a bed at every place of entertainment for travellers that he could find in Doncaster, until he wandered into the outskirts of the town.

By this time the last glimmer of twilight had faded out, the moon was rising dimly in a mist, the wind was getting cold, the clouds were gathering heavily, and there was every prospect that it was soon going to rain.

The look of the night had rather a lowering effect on young Holliday's good spirits. He began to contemplate the houseless situation in which he was placed from the serious rather than the humorous point of view; and he looked about him for another public-house to enquire at, with something very like downright anxiety in his mind on the subject of a lodging for the night.

The suburban part of the town towards which he had now strayed was hardly lighted at all, and he could see nothing of the houses as he passed them, except that they got progressively smaller and dirtier the farther he went. Down the winding road before him shone the dull gleam of an oil lamp, the one faint lonely light that struggled ineffectually with the foggy darkness all round him. He resolved to go on as far as this lamp; and then, if it showed him nothing in the shape of an inn, to return to the central part of the town, and to try if he could not at least secure a chair to sit down on, through the night, at one of the principal hotels.

As he got near the lamp, he heard voices; and, walking close under it, found that it lighted the entrance to a narrow court, on the wall of which was painted a long hand in faded flesh colour, pointing, with a lean forefinger, to this inscription:

THE TWO ROBINS

Arthur turned into the court without hesitation, to see what The Two Robins could do for him. Four or five men were standing together round the door of the house, which was at the bottom of the court, facing the entrance from the street. The men were all listening to one other man, better dressed than the rest, who was telling his audience something, in a low voice, in which they were apparently very much interested.

On entering the passage, Arthur was passed by a stranger with a knapsack in his hand, who was evidently leaving the house.

'No,' said the traveller with the knapsack, turning round and addressing himself cheerfully to a fat, sly-looking, bald-headed man, with a dirty white apron on, who had followed him down the passage. 'No, Mr Landlord, I am not easily scared by trifles; but I don't mind confessing that I can't quite stand *that*.'

It occurred to young Holliday, the moment he heard these words, that the stranger had been asked an exorbitant price for a bed at The Two Robins; and that he was unable, or unwilling to pay it. The moment his back was turned, Arthur, comfortably conscious of his own well-filled pockets, addressed himself in a great hurry, for fear any other benighted traveller should slip in and forestall him, to the sly-looking landlord with the dirty apron and the bald head.

'If you have got a bed to let,' he said, 'and if that gentleman who has just gone out won't pay your price for it, I will.'

The sly landlord looked hard at Arthur.

'Will you, sir?' he asked, in a meditative, doubtful way.

'Name your price,' said young Holliday; thinking that the landlord's hesitation sprang from some boorish distrust of him. 'Name your price, and I'll give you the money at once, if you like.'

'Are you game for five shillings?' enquired the landlord, rubbing his stubbly double chin, and looking up thoughtfully at the ceiling above him.

Arthur nearly laughed in the man's face; but thinking it prudent to control himself, offered the five shillings as seriously as he could. The sly landlord held out his hand, then suddenly drew it back again.

'You're acting all fair and above-board by me, he said; 'and, before I take your money, I'll do the same by you. Look here, this is how it stands. You can have a bed all to yourself for five shillings; but you can't have more than a half share of the room it stands in. Do you see what I mean, young gentleman?'

'Of course I do,' returned Arthur, a little irritably. 'You mean that it is a double-bedded room, and that one of the beds is occupied?'

The landlord nodded his head, and rubbed his double chin harder than even. Arthur hesitated, and mechanically moved back a step or two towards the door. The idea of sleeping in the same room with a total stranger did not present an attractive prospect to him. He felt more than half inclined to drop his five shillings into his pocket, and to go out into the street once more.

'Is it yes, or no?' asked the landlord. 'Settle it as quick as you can, because there's lots of people wanting a bed at Doncaster, tonight, besides you.'

Arthur looked towards the court, and heard the rain falling heavily in the street outside. He thought he would ask a question or two before he rashly decided on leaving the shelter of The Two Robins.

'What sort of man is it who has got the other bed?' he enquired. 'Is he a gentleman? I mean is he a quiet, well-behaved person?'

'The quietest man I ever came across,' said the landlord, rubbing his fat hands stealthily one over the other. 'As sober as a judge, and as regular as clockwork in his habits. It hasn't struck nine, not ten minutes ago, and he's in his bed already. I don't know whether that comes up to your notion of a quiet man: it goes a long way ahead of mine, I can tell you.'

'Is he asleep, do you think?' asked Arthur.

'I know he's asleep,' returned the landlord. 'And what's more, he's gone off so fast, that I'll warrant you don't wake him. This way, sir,' said the landlord, speaking over young Holliday's shoulder, as if he was addressing some new guest who was approaching the house.

'Here you are,' said Arthur, determined to be beforehand with the stranger, whoever he might be. 'I'll take the bed.' And he handed the five shillings to the landlord, who nodded, dropped the money carelessly into his waistcoat-pocket, and lighted a candle.

'Come up and see the room,' said the host of The Two Robins, leading the way to the staircase quite briskly, considering how fat he was.

They mounted to the second floor of the house. The landlord half opened a door, fronting the landing, then stopped, and turned round to Arthur.

'It's a fair bargain, mind, on my side as well as on yours,' he said. 'You give me five shillings; I will give you in return a clean, comfortable bed; and I warrant, beforehand, that you won't be interfered with, or annoyed in any way, by the man who sleeps in the same room with you.' Saying those words, he looked hard, for a moment, in young Holliday's face, and then led the way into the room.

It was larger and cleaner than Arthur expected it would be. The two beds stood parallel with each other – a space of about six feet intervening between them. They were both of the same medium size, and both had the same plain white curtains, made to draw, if necessary, all round them.

The occupied bed was the bed nearest the window. The curtains were all drawn round it, except the half curtain at the bottom, on the side of the bed farthest from the window. Arthur saw the feet of the sleeping man raising the scanty clothes into a sharp little eminence, as if he were lying flat on his back. He took the candle, and advanced softly to draw the curtain – stopped half way, and listened for a moment – then turned to the landlord.

'He is a very quiet sleeper,' said Arthur.

'Yes,' said the landlord, 'very quiet.'

Young Holliday advanced with the candle, arid looked in at the man cautiously.

'How pale he is,' said Arthur.

'Yes,' returned the landlord, 'pale enough, isn't he?'

Arthur looked closer at the man. The bedclothes were drawn up to his chin, and they lay perfectly still over the region of his chest. Surprised and vaguely startled, as he noticed this, Arthur stooped down closer over the stranger; looked at his ashy, parted lips; listened breathlessly for an instant; looked again at the still face, and the motionless lips and chest; and turned round suddenly on the landlord, with his own cheeks as pale, for the moment, as the hollow cheeks of the man on the bed.

'Come here,' he whispered, under his breath. 'Come here, for God's sake! The man's not asleep – he is dead.'

'You have found that out sooner than I thought you would, ' said the landlord composedly. 'Yes, he's dead, sure enough. He died at five o'clock today.'

'How did he die? Who is he?' asked Arthur, staggered for the moment by the audacious coolness of the answer.

'As to who he is,' rejoined the landlord, 'I know no more about him than you do. There are his books and letters and things, all sealed up in that brown paper parcel, for the Coroner's inquest to open tomorrow or next day. He's been here a week, paying his way fairly enough, and stopping indoors, for the most part, as if he was ailing. My girl brought up his tea at five today, and as he was pouring of it out, he fell down in a faint, or a fit, or a compound of both, for anything I know. We couldn't bring him to – and I said he was dead. And the doctor couldn't bring him to – and the doctor said he was dead. And there he is. And the Coroner's inquest's coming as soon as it can. And that's as much as I know about it.'

Arthur held the candle close to the man's lips. The flame still burnt straight up, as steadily as ever. There was a moment of silence; and the rain pattered drearily through it against the panes of the window.

'If you haven't got nothing more to say to me,' continued the landlord, 'I suppose I may go. You don't expect your five shillings back, do you? There's the bed I promised you, clean and comfortable. There's the man I warranted not to disturb you, quiet in this world for ever. If you're frightened to stop alone with him, that's not my lookout. I've kept my part of the bargain, and I mean to keep the money. I'm not Yorkshire myself, young gentleman; but I've lived long enough in these parts to have my wits sharpened; and I shouldn't wonder if you found out the way to brighten up yours, next time you come among us.'

With those words, the landlord turned towards the door, and laughed to himself softly, in high satisfaction at his own sharpness.

Startled and shocked as he was, Arthur had by this time sufficiently recovered himself to feel indignant at the trick that had been played on him, and at the insolent manner in which the landlord exulted in it.

'Don't laugh, till you are quite sure you have got the laugh against me,' he said sharply. 'You shan't have the five shillings for nothing, my man. I'll keep the bed.'

'Will you?' said the landlord. 'Then I wish you a good night's rest.' With that brief farewell, he went out, and shut the door after him.

A good night's rest! The words had hardly been spoken, the door had hardly been closed, before Arthur half repented the hasty words that had just escaped him. Though not naturally over-sensitive, and not wanting in courage of the moral as well as the physical sort, the presence of the dead man had an instantaneously chilling effect on his mind when he found himself alone in the room – alone, and bound by his own rash words to stay there till the next morning. An older man would have thought nothing of those words, and would have acted without reference to them, as his calmer sense suggested. But Arthur was too young to treat the ridicule, even of his inferiors, with contempt – too young not to fear the momentary humiliation of falsifying his own foolish boast, more than he feared the trial of watching out the long night in the same chamber with the dead.

'It is but a few hours,' he thought to himself, 'and I can get away the first thing in the morning.'

He was looking towards the occupied bed, as that idea passed through his mind, and the sharp angular eminence made in the clothes by the dead man's upturned feet again caught his eye. He advanced and drew the curtains, purposely abstaining, as he did so, from looking at the face of the corpse, lest he might unnerve himself at the outset by fastening some ghastly impression of it on his mind. He drew the curtain very gently, and sighed involuntarily as he closed it.

'Poor fellow!' he said, almost as sadly as if he had known the man. 'Ah, poor fellow!'

He went next to the window. The night was black and he could see nothing from it. The rain still pattered heavily against the glass. He inferred, from hearing it, that the window was at the back of the house; remembering that the front was sheltered from the weather by the court and the buildings over it.

While he was still standing at the window – for even the dreary rain was a relief, because of the sound it made; a relief, also, because it moved, and had some faint suggestion, in consequence, of life and companionship in it – while he was standing at the window, and looking vacantly into the black darkness outside, he heard a distant church clock strike ten. Only ten! How was he to pass the time till the house was astir the next morning?

Under any other circumstances, he would have gone down to the public-house parlour, would have called for his grog, and would have laughed and talked with the company assembled as familiarly as if he had known them all his life. But the very thought of whiling away the time in this manner was now distasteful to him. The new situation in which he was placed seemed to have altered him to himself already. Thus far, his life had been the common, trifling, prosaic surface-life of a prosperous young man, with no troubles to conquer, and no trials to face. He had lost no relation whom he loved, no friend whom he treasured. Till this night, what share he had of the immortal inheritance that is divided amongst us all, had lain dormant with him. Till this night, Death and he had not once met, even in thought.

He took a few turns up and down the room – then stopped. The noise made by his boots on the poorly carpeted floor jarred on his ear. He hesitated a little, and ended by taking the boots off, and walking backwards and forwards noiselessly.

All desire to sleep or to rest had left him. The bare thought of lying down on the unoccupied bed, instantly drew the picture on his mind of a dreadful mimicry of the position of the dead man. Who was he? What was the story of his past life? Poor he must have been, or he would not have is stopped at such a place as The Two Robins Inn – and weakened, probably, by long illness, or he could hardly have died in the manner which the landlord had described. Poor, ill, lonely – dead in a strange place; dead, with nobody but a stranger to pity him. A sad story: truly, on the mere face of it, a very sad story.

While these thoughts were passing through his mind, he had stopped insensibly at the window, close to which stood the foot of the bed with the closed curtains. At first he looked at it absently; then he became conscious that his eyes were fixed on it; and then, a perverse desire took possession of him to do the very thing which he had resolved not to do, up to this time – to look at the dead man.

He stretched out his hand towards the curtains; but checked himself in the very act of undrawing them, turned his back sharply on the bed, and walked towards the chimney-piece, to see what things were placed on it, and to try if he could keep the dead man out of his mind that way.

There was a pewter inkstand on the chimney-piece, with some mildewed remains of ink in the bottle. There were two coarse china ornaments of the commonest kind; and there was a square of embossed card, dirty and fly-blown, with a collection of wretched riddles printed on it, in all sorts of zigzag directions, and in variously coloured inks. He took the card and went away to read it at the table on which the candle was placed, sitting down with his back resolutely turned to the curtained bed.

He read the first riddle, the second, the third, all in one corner of the card – then turned it round impatiently to look at another. Before he could begin reading the riddles printed here, the sound of the church clock stopped him.

Eleven.

He had got through an hour of the time, in the room with the dead man.

Once more he looked at the card. It was not easy to make out the letters printed on it, in consequence of the dimness of the light which the landlord had left him – a common tallow candle, furnished with a pair of heavy old-fashioned steel snuffers. Up to this time, his mind had been too much occupied to think of the light. He had left the wick of the candle unsnuffed, till it had risen higher than the flame, and had burnt into an odd penthouse shape at the top, from which morsels of the charred cotton fell off, from time to time, in little flakes. He took up the snuffers now, and trimmed the wick. The light brightened directly, and the room became less dismal.

Again he turned to the riddles; reading them doggedly and resolutely, now in one corner of the card, now in another. All his efforts, however, could not fix his attention on them. He pursued his occupation mechanically, deriving no sort of impression from what he was reading. It was as if a shadow from the curtained bed had got between his mind and the gaily printed letters – a shadow that nothing could dispel. At last, he gave up the struggle, threw the card from him impatiently, and took to walking softly up and down the room again.

The dead man, the dead man, the *hidden* dead man on the bed!

There was the one persistent idea still haunting him. Hidden! Was it only the body being there – or was it the body being there, *concealed*, that was preying on his mind? He stopped at the window, with that doubt in him; once more listening to the pattering rain, once more looking out into the black darkness.

Still the dead man!

The darkness forced his mind back upon itself, and set his memory at work, reviving, with a painfully vivid distinctness, the momentary impression it had received from his first sight of the corpse. Before long, the face seemed to be hovering out in the middle of the rain and darkness, confronting him through the window, with the paleness whiter, with the dreadful dull line of light between the imperfectly closed eyelids broader than he had seen it – with the parted lips slowly dropping farther and is farther away from each other – with the features growing larger and moving closer, till they seemed to fill the window, and silence the rain, and shut out the night.

The sound of a voice shouting below stairs woke him suddenly from the dream of his own distempered fancy. He recognised it as the voice of the landlord.

'Shut up at twelve, Ben,' he heard it say. 'I'm off to bed.'

He wiped away the damp that had gathered on his forehead, reasoned with himself for a little while, and resolved to shake his mind free of the ghastly counterfeit which still clung to it, by forcing himself to confront, if it was only for a moment, the solemn reality. Without allowing himself an instant to hesitate, he parted the curtains at the s foot of the bed, and looked through.

There was the sad, peaceful, white face, with the awful mystery of stillness on it, laid back upon the pillow. No stir, no change there!

He only looked at it for a moment before he closed the curtains again; but that moment steadied him, calmed him, restored him – mind and body – to himself.

He returned to his old occupation of walking up and down the room, persevering in it this time till the clock struck again.

Twelve.

As the sound of the clock bell died away, it was succeeded by the confused noise, downstairs, of the drinkers in the tap-room leaving the house. The next sound, after an interval of silence, was caused by the barring of the door, and the closing of the shutters at the back of the inn. Then the silence followed again, and was disturbed no more.

He was alone now – absolutely, hopelessly alone with the dead man, till the next morning.

The wick of the candle wanted trimming again. He took up the snuffers – but paused suddenly on the very point of using them, and looked attentively at the candle – then back, over his shoulder, at the curtained bed – then again at the candle. It had been lighted, for the first time, to show him the way upstairs, and three parts of it, at least, were already consumed. In another hour it would be burnt out. In another hour – unless he called at once to the man who had shut up the inn, for a fresh candle – he would be left in the dark.

Strongly as his mind had been affected since he had entered the room, his unreasonable dread of encountering ridicule, and of exposing his courage to suspicion, had not altogether lost its influence over him yet.

He lingered irresolutely by the table, waiting till he could prevail on himself to open the door, and call from the landing to the man who had shut up the inn. In his present hesitating frame of mind, it was a kind of relief to gain a few moments only by engaging in the trifling occupation of snuffing the candle. His hand trembled a little, and the snuffers were heavy and awkward to use. When he closed them on the wick, he closed them a hair's breadth too low. In an instant the candle was out, and the room was plunged in pitch darkness.

The one impression which the absence of light immediately produced on his mind, was distrust of the curtained bed – distrust which shaped itself into no distinct idea, but which was powerful enough, in its very vagueness, to bind him down to his chair, to make his heart beat fast, and to set him listening intently. No sound stirred in the room but the familiar sound of the rain against the window, louder and sharper now than he had heard it yet.

Still the vague distrust, the inexpressible dread, possessed him, and kept him in his chair. He had put his carpet-bag on the table when he first entered the room; and he now took the key from his pocket, reached out his hand softly, opened the bag, and groped in it for his travelling writing-case, in which he knew that there was a small store of matches. When he had got one of the matches, he waited before he struck it on the coarse wooden table, and listened intently again, without knowing why. Still there was no sound in the room but the steady, ceaseless, rattling sound of the rain.

He lighted the candle again, without another moment of delay; and, on the instant of its burning up, the first object in the room that his eyes sought for was the curtained bed.

Just before the light had been put out, he had looked in that direction, and had seen no change, no disarrangement of any sort, in the folds of the closely-drawn curtains.

When he looked at the bed now, he saw, hanging over the side of it – a long white hand.

It lay perfectly motionless, midway on the side of the bed, where the curtain at the head and the curtain at the foot met. Nothing more was visible. The clinging curtains hid everything but the long white hand.

He stood looking at it, unable to stir, unable to call out; feeling nothing, knowing nothing; every faculty he possessed gathered up and lost in the one seeing faculty. How long that first panic held him, he never could tell afterwards. It might have been only for a moment; it might have been for many minutes together. How he got to the bed – whether he ran to it headlong, or whether he approached it slowly – how he wrought himself up to unclose the curtains and look in, he never has remembered, and never will remember, to his dying day. It is enough that he did go to the bed, and that he did look inside the curtains.

The man had moved. One of his arms was outside the clothes; his face was turned a little on the pillow; his eyelids were wide open. Changed as to position, and as to one of the features, the face was otherwise fearfully and wonderfully unaltered. The dead paleness and the dead quiet were on it still.

One glance showed Arthur this – one glance before he flew breathlessly to the door, and alarmed the house.

The man whom the landlord called 'Ben' was the first to appear on the stairs. In three words, Arthur told him what had happened, and sent him for the nearest doctor.

I, who tell you this story, was then staying with a medical friend of mine, in practice at Doncaster, taking care of his patients for him during his absence in London; and I, for the time being, was the nearest doctor. They had sent for me from the inn, when the stranger was taken ill in the afternoon; but I was not at home, and medical assistance was sought for elsewhere. When the man from The Two Robins rang the night-bell, I was just thinking of going to bed. Naturally enough, I did not believe a word of his story about 'a dead man who had come to life again'. However, I put on my hat, armed myself with one or two bottles of restorative medicine, and ran to the inn, expecting to find nothing more remarkable, when I got there, than a patient in a fit.

My surprise at finding that the man had spoken the literal truth was almost, if not quite, equalled by my astonishment at finding myself face to face with Arthur Holliday as soon as I entered the bedroom. It was no time then for giving or seeking explanations. We just shook hands amazedly; and then I ordered everybody but Arthur out of the room, and hurried to the man on the bed.

The kitchen fire had not been long out. There was plenty of hot water in the boiler, and plenty of flannel to be had. With these, with my medicines, and with such help as Arthur could render under my direction, I dragged the man, literally, out of the jaws of death. In less than an hour from the s time when I had been called in, he was alive and talking, in the bed on which he had been laid out to wait for the coroner's inquest.

You will naturally ask me what had been the matter with him; and I might treat you, in reply, to a long theory, plentifully sprinkled with what the children call hard words. I prefer telling you that, in this case, cause and effect could not be satisfactorily joined together by any theory whatever. There are mysteries in life, and in the conditions of it, is which human science has not fathomed yet; and I candidly confess to you that, in bringing that man back to existence, I was, morally speaking, groping haphazard in the dark. I know (from the testimony of the doctor who attended him in the afternoon) that the vital machinery, so far as its action is appreciable by our senses, had, in this case, unquestionably stopped; and I am equally certain (seeing that I recovered him) that the vital principle was not extinct. When I add that he had suffered from a long and complicated illness, and that his whole nervous system was utterly deranged, I have told you all I really know of the physical condition of my dead-alive patient at The Two Robins Inn.

When he 'came to', as the phrase goes, he was a startling object to look at, with his colourless face, his sunken cheeks, his wild black eyes, and his long black hair. The first question he asked me about himself, when he could speak, made me suspect that I had been called in to a man in my own profession. I mentioned to him my surmise, and he told me that I was right.

He said he had come last from Paris, where he had been attached to a hospital. That he had lately returned to England, on his way to Edinburgh, to continue his studies; that he had been taken ill on the journey; and that he had stopped to rest and recover himself at Doncaster. He did not add a word about his name, or who he was, and of course I did not question him on the subject. All I enquired, when he ceased speaking, was what branch of the profession he intended to follow.

'Any branch,' he said, bitterly, 'which will put bread into the mouth of a poor man.'

At this, Arthur, who had been hitherto watching him in silent curiosity, burst out impetuously in his usual good-humoured way: 'My dear fellow!' (everybody was 'my dear fellow' with Arthur) 'now you have come to life again, don't begin by being downhearted about your prospects. I'll answer for it, I can help you to some capital thing in the medical line – or, if I can t, I know my father can.'

The medical student looked at him steadily. 'Thank you,' he said coldly; then added, 'May I ask who your father is?'

'He's well enough known all about this part of the country,' replied Arthur. 'He is a great manufacturer, and his name is Holliday.'

My hand was on the man's wrist during this brief conversation. The instant the name of Holliday was pronounced, I felt the pulse under my fingers flutter, stop, go on suddenly with a bound, and beat afterwards for a minute or two at the fever rate.

'How did you come here?' asked the stranger, quickly, excitably, passionately almost.

Arthur related briefly what had happened from the time of his first taking the bed at the inn.

'I am indebted to Mr Holliday's son, then, for the help that has saved my life,' said the medical student, speaking to himself, with a singular sarcasm in his voice. Come here!'

He held out, as he spoke, his long, white, bony right hand.

'With all my heart,' said Arthur, taking his hand cordially. 'I may confess it now,' he continued, laughing; 'upon my honour you almost frightened me out of my wits.'

The stranger did not seem to listen. His wild black eyes were fixed with a look of eager interest on Arthur's face, and his long bony fingers kept tight hold of Arthur's hand. Young Holliday, on his side, returned the gaze, amazed and puzzled by the medical student's odd language and manners. The two faces were close together; I looked at them; and, to my amazement, I was suddenly impressed by the sense of a likeness between them – not in features or complexion, but solely in expression. It must have been a strong likeness, or I should certainly not have found it out, for I am naturally slow at detecting resemblances between faces.

'You have saved my life,' said the strange man, still looking hard in Arthur's face, still holding tightly by his hand. 'If you had been my own brother, you could not have done more for me than that.'

He laid a singularly strong emphasis on those three words, 'my own brother', and a change passed over his face as he pronounced them – a change that no language of mine is competent to describe.

'I hope I have not done being of service to you yet,' said Arthur. 'I'll speak to my father as soon as I get home.'

'You seem to be fond and proud of your father,' said the medical student. 'I suppose, in return, he is fond and proud of you?'

'Of course he is,' answered Arthur, laughing. 'Is there anything wonderful in that? Isn't *your* father fond – '

The stranger suddenly dropped young Holliday's hand, and turned his face away.

'I beg your pardon.' said Arthur. 'I hope I have not unintentionally pained you. I hope you have not lost your father?'

'I can't well lose what I have never had,' retorted the medical student, with a harsh mocking laugh.

'What you have never had!'

The strange man suddenly caught Arthur's hand again, suddenly looked once more hard in his face.

'Yes,' he said, with a repetition of the bitter laugh. 'You have brought a poor devil back into the world, who has no business there. Do I astonish you? Well! I have a fancy of my own for telling you what men in my situation generally keep a secret. I have no name and no father. The merciful law of Society tells me I am Nobody's son! Ask your father if he will be my father too, and help me on in life with the family name.'

Arthur looked at me more puzzled than ever.

I signed to him to say nothing, and then laid my fingers again on the man's wrist. No! In spite of the extraordinary speech that he had just made, he was not, as I had been disposed to suspect, beginning to get light-headed. His pulse, by this time, had fallen back to a quiet, slow beat, and his skin was moist and cool. Not a symptom of fever or agitation about him.

Finding that neither of us answered him, he turned to me, and began talking of the extraordinary nature of his case, and asking my advice about the future course of medical treatment to which he ought to subject himself. I said the matter required careful thinking over, and suggested that I should send him a prescription a little later. He told me to write it at once, as he would, most likely, be leaving Doncaster in the morning before I was up. It was quite useless to represent to him the folly and danger of such a proceeding as this. He heard me politely and patiently, but held to his resolution, without offering any reasons or explanations, and repeated to me, that if I wished to give him a chance of seeing my prescription, I must write it at once.

Hearing this, Arthur volunteered the loan of a travelling writing-case, which, he said, he had with him; and, bringing it to the bed, shook the notepaper out of the pocket of the case forthwith in his usual careless way. With the paper, there fell out, on the counter-pane of the bed, a small packet of sticking-plaster and a little water-colour drawing of a landscape.

The medical student took up the drawing and looked at it. His eye fell on some initials, neatly written in cipher, in one corner. He started, and trembled; his pale face grew whiter than ever; his wild black eyes turned on Arthur, and looked through and through him.

'A pretty drawing,' he said, in a remarkably quiet tone of voice.

'Ah! and done by such a pretty girl,' said Arthur. 'Oh, such a pretty girl! I wish it was not a landscape – I wish it was a portrait of her!'

'You admire her very much?'

Arthur, half in jest, half in earnest, kissed his hand for answer.

'Love at first sight,' said young Holliday, putting the drawing away again. 'But the course of it doesn't run smooth. It's the old story. She's monopolised, as usual. Trammelled by a rash engagement to some poor man who is never likely to get money enough to marry her. It was lucky I heard of it in time, or I should certainly have risked a declaration when she gave me that drawing. Here, doctor. Here is pen, ink and paper, all ready for you.'

'When she gave you that drawing! Gave it. Gave it.'

He repeated the words slowly to himself, and suddenly closed his eyes. A momentary distortion passed across his face, and I saw one of his hands clutch up the bedclothes and squeeze them hard. I thought he was going to be ill again, and begged that there might be no more talking. He opened his eyes when I spoke, fixed them once more, searchingly, on Arthur, and said, slowly and distinctly: 'You like her, and she likes you. The poor man may die out of your way. Who can tell that she may not give you herself as well as her drawing, after all?'

Before young Holliday could answer, he turned to me, and said in a whisper, 'Now for the prescription.' From that time, though he spoke to Arthur again, he never looked at him more.

When I had written the prescription, he examined it, approved of it, and then astonished us both by abruptly wishing us good night. I offered to sit up with him, and he shook his head. Arthur offered to sit up with him, and he said, shortly, with his face turned away, 'No.' I insisted on having somebody left to watch him. He gave way when he found I was determined, and said he would accept the services of the waiter at the inn.

'Thank you both,' he said, as we rose to go. 'I have one last favour to ask – not of you, doctor, for I leave you to exercise your professional discretion – but of Mr Holliday.' His eyes, while he spoke, still rested steadily on me, and never once turned towards Arthur. 'I beg that Mr Holliday will not mention to anyone – least of all to his father – the events that have occurred, and the words that have passed, in this room. I entreat him to bury me in his memory, as, but for him, I might have been buried in my grave. I cannot give my reasons for making this strange request. I can only implore him to grant it.'

His voice faltered for the first time, and he hid his face on the pillow. Arthur, completely bewildered, gave the required pledge. I took young Holliday away with me, immediately afterwards, to the house of my friend; determining to go back to the inn, and to see the medical student again before he had left in the morning.

I returned to the inn at eight o'clock, purposely abstaining from waking Arthur, who was sleeping off the past night's excitement on one of my friend's sofas. A suspicion had occurred to me, as soon as I was alone in my bedroom, which made me resolve that Holliday and the stranger whose life he had saved should not meet again, if I could prevent it.

I have already alluded to certain reports, or scandals, which I knew of, relating to the early life of Arthur's father. While I was thinking, in my bed, of what had passed at the inn – of the change in the student's pulse when he heard the name of Holliday; of the resemblance of expression that I had discovered between his face and Arthur's; of the emphasis he had laid on those three words, 'my own brother'; and of his incomprehensible acknowledgment of his own illegitimacy – while I was thinking of these things, the reports I have mentioned suddenly flew into my mind, and linked themselves fast to the chain of my previous reflections. Something within me whispered, 'It is best that those two young men should not meet again.' I felt it before I slept; I felt it when I woke; and I went, as I told you, alone to the inn the next morning.

I had missed my only opportunity of seeing my nameless patient again. He had been gone nearly an hour when I enquired for him.

I have now told you everything that I know for certain, in relation to the man whom I brought back to life in the double-bedded room of the inn at Doncaster. What I have next to add is matter for inference and surmise, and is not, strictly speaking, matter of fact.

I have to tell you, first, that the medical student turned out to be strangely and unaccountably right in assuming it as more than probable that Arthur Holliday would marry the young lady who had given him the watercolour drawing of the landscape. That marriage took place a little more than a year after the events occurred which I have just been relating.

The young couple came to live in the neighbourhood in which I was then established in practice. I was present at the wedding, and was rather surprised to find that Arthur was singularly reserved with me, both before and after his marriage, on the subject of the young lady's prior engagement. He only referred to it once, when we were alone, merely telling me, on that occasion, that his wife had done all that honour and duty required of her in the matter, and that the engagement had been is broken off with the full approval of her parents. I never heard more from him than this. For three years he and his wife lived together happily. At the expiration of that time, the symptoms of a serious illness first declared themselves in Mrs Arthur Holliday. It turned out to be a long, lingering, hopeless malady. I attended her throughout. We had been great friends when she was well, and we became more attached to each other than ever when she was ill. I had many long and interesting conversations with her in the intervals when she suffered least. The result of one of those conversations I may briefly relate, leaving you to draw any inferences from it that you please.

The interview to which I refer, occurred shortly before her death.

I called one evening, as usual, and found her alone, with a look in her eyes which told me she had been crying. She only informed me, at first, that she had been depressed in spirits; but, by little and little, she became more communicative. and confessed to me that she had been looking over some old letters, which had been addressed to her, before she had seen Arthur, by a man to whom she had been engaged to be married. I asked her how the engagement came to be broken off. She replied that it had not been broken off, but that it had died out in a very mysterious manner. The person to whom she was engaged – her first love, she called him – was poor, and there was no immediate prospect of their being married. He followed my profession, and went abroad to study. They had corresponded regularly, until the time when, as she believed, he had returned to England. From that period she heard no more of him. He was of a fretful, sensitive temperament; and she feared that she might have inadvertently done or said something to offend him. However that might be, he had never written to her again; and, after waiting a year, she had married Arthur. I asked when the first estrangement had begun, and found that the time at which she ceased to hear anything of her first lover, exactly corresponded with the time at which I had been called in to my mysterious patient at The Two Robins Inn.

A fortnight after that conversation, she died. In course of time Arthur married again. Of late years, he has lived principally in London, and I have seen little or nothing of him.

I have some years to pass over before I can approach to anything like a conclusion of this fragmentary narrative. And even when that later period is reached, the little that I have to say will not occupy your attention for more than a few minutes.

One rainy autumn evening, while I was still practising as a country doctor, I was sitting alone, thinking over a case then under my charge which sorely perplexed me, when I heard a low knock at the door of my room.

'Come in,' I cried, looking up curiously to see who wanted me.

After a momentary delay, the lock moved, and a long, white, bony hand stole round the door as it opened, gently pushing it over a fold in the carpet which hindered it from working freely on the hinges. The hand was followed by a man whose face instantly struck me with a very strange sensation. There was something familiar to me in the look of him, and yet it was also something that suggested the idea of change.

He quietly introduced himself as 'Mr Lorn'; presented to me some excellent professional recommendations; and proposed to fill the place, then vacant, of my assistant. While he was speaking, I noticed it as singular that we did not appear to be meeting each other like strangers; and that, while I was certainly startled at seeing him, he did not appear to be at all startled at seeing me.

It was on the tip of my tongue to say that I thought I had met with him before. But there was something in his face, and something in my recollections – I can hardly say what – which unaccountably restrained me from speaking, and which, as unaccountably, attracted me to him at once, and made me feel ready and glad to accept his proposal.

He took my assistant's place on that very day. We got on together as if we had been old friends from the first; but, throughout the whole time of his residence in my house, he never volunteered any confidences on the subject of his past life; and I never approached the forbidden topic except by hints, which he resolutely refused to understand.

I had long had a notion that my patient at the inn might have been a natural son of the elder Mr Holliday's, and that he might also have been the man who was engaged to Arthur's first wife. And now, another idea occurred to me, that Mr Lorn was the only person in existence who could, if he chose, enlighten me on both those doubtful points. But he never did choose – and I was never enlightened. He remained with me till I removed to London to try my fortune there, as a physician, for the second time; and then he went his way, and I went mine, and we have never seen one another since.

I can add no more. I may have been right in my suspicion, or I may have been wrong. All I know is that, in those days of my country practice, when I came home late, and found my assistant asleep, and woke him, he used to look, in coming to, wonderfully like the stranger at Doncaster, as he raised himself in the bed on that memorable night.

Blow Up with the Brig!

I have got an alarming confession to make. I am haunted by a Ghost.

If you were to guess for a hundred years, you would never guess what my ghost is. I shall make you laugh to begin with – and afterward I shall make your flesh creep. My Ghost is the ghost of a Bedroom Candlestick.

Yes, a bedroom candlestick and candle, or a flat candlestick and candle – put it which way you like – that is what haunts me. I wish it was something pleasanter and more out of the common way; a beautiful lady, or a mine of gold and silver, or a cellar of wine and a coach and horses, and suchlike. But, being what it is, I must take it for what it is, and make the best of it; and I shall thank you kindly if you will help me out by doing the same.

I am not a scholar myself, but I make bold to believe that the haunting of any man with anything under the sun begins with the frightening of him. At any rate, the haunting of me with a bedroom candlestick and candle began with the frightening of me with a bedroom candlestick and candle – the frightening of me half out of my life; and, for the time being, the frightening of me altogether out of my wits. That not a very pleasant thing to confess before stating the particulars; but perhaps you will be the readier to believe that I am not a downright coward, because you find me bold enough to make a clean breast it already, to my own great disadvantage so far.

Here are the particulars, as well as I can put them: I was apprenticed to the sea when I was about as tall as my own walking-stick; and I made good enough use of my time to be fit for a mate's berth at the age of twenty-five years.

It was in the year eighteen hundred and eighteen, or nineteen, I am not quite certain which, that I reached the before-mentioned age of twenty-five. You will please to excuse my memory not being very good for dates, names, numbers, places, and such like. No fear, though, about the particulars I have undertaken to tell you of; I have got them all shipshape in my recollection; I can see them, at this moment, as clear as noonday in my own mind. But there is a mist over what went before, and, for the matter of that, a mist likewise over much that came after – and it's not very likely to lift at my time of life, is it?

Well, in eighteen hundred and eighteen, or nineteen, when there was peace in our part of the world – and not before it was wanted, you will say – there was fighting, of a certain scampering, scrambling kind, going on in that old battlefield which we seafaring men know by the name of the Spanish Main.

The possessions that belonged to the Spaniards in South America had broken into open mutiny and declared for themselves years before. There was plenty of bloodshed between the new Government and the old; but the new had got the best of it, for the most part, under one General Bolivar – a famous man in his time, though he seems to have dropped out of people's memories now. Englishmen and Irishmen with a turn for fighting, and nothing particular to do at home, joined the general as volunteers; and some of our merchants here found it a good venture to send supplies across the ocean to the popular side. There was risk enough, of course, in doing this; but where one speculation of the kind succeeded, it made up for two, at the least, that failed. And that's the true principle of trade, wherever I have met with it, all the world over.

Among the Englishmen who were concerned in this Spanish-American business, I, your humble servant, happened, in a small way, to be one.

I was then mate of a brig belonging to a certain firm in the City, which drove a sort of general trade, mostly in queer out-of-the-way places, as far from home as possible; and which freighted the brig, in the year I am speaking of, with a cargo of gunpowder for General Bolivar and his volunteers. Nobody knew anything about our instructions, when we sailed, except the captain; and he didn't half seem to like them. I can't rightly say how many barrels of powder we had on board, or how much each barrel held – I only know we had no other cargo. The name of the brig was the Good Intent – a queer name enough, you will tell me, for a vessel laden with gunpowder, and sent to help a revolution. And as far as this particular voyage was concerned, so it was. I mean that for a joke, and I hope you will encourage me by laughing at it.

The *Good Intent* was the craziest tub of a vessel I ever went to sea in, and the worst found in all respects. She was two hundred and thirty or two hundred and eighty tons burden, I forget which; and she had a crew of eight, all told – nothing like as many as we ought by rights to have had to work the brig. However, we were well and honestly paid our wages; and we had to set that against the chance of foundering at sea, and, on this occasion, likewise the chance of being blown up into the bargain.

In consideration of the nature of our cargo, we were harassed with new regulations, which we didn't at all like, relative to smoking our pipes and lighting our lanterns; and, as usual in such cases, the captain, who made the regulations, preached what he didn't practise. Not a man of us was allowed to have a bit of lighted candle in his hand when he went below – except the skipper; and he used his light, when he turned in, or when he looked over his charts on the cabin table, just as usual.

This light was a common kitchen candle or 'dip', and it stood in an old battered flat candlestick, with all the japan worn and melted off, and all the tin showing through. It would have been more seamanlike and suitable in every respect if he had had a lamp or a lantern; but he stuck to his old candlestick; and that same old candlestick has ever afterward stuck to *me*. That's another joke, if you please, and a better one than the first, in my opinion.

Well (I said 'well' before, but it's a word that helps a man on like), we sailed in the brig, and shaped our course, first, for the Virgin Islands, in the West Indies; and, after sighting them, we made for the Leeward Islands next, and then stood on due south, till the lookout at the masthead hailed the deck and said he saw land. That land was the coast of South America. We had had a wonderful voyage so far. We had lost none of our spars or sails, and not a man of us had been harassed to death at the pumps. It wasn't often the *Good Intent* made such a voyage as that, I can tell you.

I was sent aloft to make sure about the land, and I did make sure of it.

When I reported the same to the skipper, he went below, and had a look at his letter of instructions and the chart. When he came on deck again, he altered our course a trifle to the eastward – I forget the point on the compass, but that don't matter. What I do remember is, that it was dark before we closed in with the land. We kept the lead going, and hove the brig to in from four to five fathoms water, or it might be six – I can't say for certain. I kept a sharp eye to the drift of the vessel, none of us knowing how the currents ran on that coast. We all wondered why the skipper didn't anchor; but he said No, he must first show a light at the foretopmast-head, and wait for an answering light on shore. We did wait, and nothing of the sort appeared. It was starlight and calm. What little wind there was came in puffs off the land. I suppose we waited, drifting a little to the westward, as I made it out, the best part of an hour before anything happened – and then, instead of seeing the light on shore, we saw a boat coming toward us, rowed by two men only.

We hailed them, and they answered 'Friends!' and hailed us by our name. They came on board. One of them was an Irishman, and the other was a coffee-coloured native pilot, who jabbered a little English.

The Irishman handed a note to our skipper, who showed it to me. It informed us that the part of the coast we were off was not over-safe for discharging our cargo, seeing that spies of the enemy (that is to say, of the old Government) had been taken and shot in the neighbourhood the day before. We might trust the brig to the native pilot; and he had his instructions to take us to another part of the coast. The note was signed by the proper parties; so we let the Irishman go back alone in the boat, and allowed the pilot to exercise his lawful authority over the brig. He kept us stretching off from the land till noon the next day – his instructions, seemingly, ordering him to keep up well out of sight of the shore. We only altered our course in the afternoon, so as to close in with the land again a little before midnight.

This same pilot was about as ill-looking a vagabond as ever I saw; a skinny, cowardly, quarrelsome mongrel, who swore at the men in the vilest broken English, till they were every one of them ready to pitch him overboard. The skipper kept them quiet, and I kept them quiet; for the pilot being given us by our instructions, we were bound to make the best of him. Near nightfall, however, with the best will in the world to avoid it, I was unlucky enough to quarrel with him.

He wanted to go below with his pipe, and I stopped him, of course, because it was contrary to orders. Upon that he tried to hustle by me, and I put him away with my hand. I never meant to push him down; but somehow I did. He picked himself up as quick as lightning, and pulled out his knife. I snatched it out of his hand, slapped his murderous face for him, and threw his weapon overboard. He gave me one ugly look, and walked aft. I didn't think much of the look then, but I remembered it a little too well afterward.

We were close in with the land again, just as the wind failed us, between eleven and twelve that night, and dropped our anchor by the pilot's directions.

It was pitch-dark, and a dead, airless calm. The skipper was on deck, with two of our best men for watch. The rest were below, except the pilot, who coiled himself up, more like a snake than a man, on the forecastle. It was not my watch till four in the morning. But I didn't like the look of the night, or the pilot, or the state of things generally, and I shook myself down on deck to get my nap there, and be ready for anything at a moment's notice. The last I remember was the skipper whispering to me that he didn't like the look of things either, and that he would go below and consult his instructions again. That is the last I remember, before the slow, heavy, regular roll of the old brig on the ground-swell rocked me off to sleep.

I was awoke by a scuffle on the forecastle and a gag in my mouth. There was a man on my breast and a man on my legs, and I was bound hand and foot in half a minute.

The brig was in the hands of the Spaniards. They were swarming all over her. I heard six heavy splashes in the water, one after another. I saw the captain stabbed to the heart as he came running up the companion, and I heard a seventh splash in the water. Except myself, every soul of us on board had been murdered and thrown into the sea. Why I was left, I couldn't think, till I saw the pilot stoop over me with a lantern and look, to make sure of who I was. There was a devilish grin on his face, and he nodded his head at me, as much as to say: you were the man who hustled me down and slapped my face, and I mean to play the game of cat and mouse with you in return for it!

I could neither move nor speak, but I could see the Spaniards take off the main hatch and rig the purchases for getting up the cargo. A quarter of an hour afterward I heard the sweeps of a schooner, or other small vessel, in the water. The strange craft was laid alongside of us, and the Spaniards set to work to discharge our cargo into her. They all worked hard except the pilot; and he came from time to time, with his lantern, to have another look at me, and to grin and nod always in the same devilish way. I am old enough now not to be ashamed of confessing the truth, and I don't mind acknowledging that the pilot frightened me.

The fright, and the bonds, and the gag, and the not being able to stir hand or foot, had pretty nigh worn me out by the time the Spaniards gave over work. This was just as the dawn broke. They had shifted a good part of our cargo on board their vessel, but nothing like all of it, and they were sharp enough to be off with what they had got before daylight.

I need hardly say that I had made up my mind by this time to the worst I could think of. The pilot, it was clear enough, was one of the spies of the enemy, who had wormed himself into the confidence of our consignees without being suspected. He, or more likely his employers, had got knowledge enough of us to suspect what our cargo was; we had been anchored for the night in the safest berth for them to surprise us in; and we had paid the penalty of having a small crew, and consequently an insufficient watch. All this was clear enough – but what did the pilot mean to do with me?

On the word of a man, it makes my flesh creep now, only to tell you what he did with me.

After all the rest of them were out of the brig, except the pilot and two Spanish seamen, these last took me up, bound and gagged as I was, lowered me into the hold of the vessel, and laid me along on the floor, lashing me to it with ropes' ends, so that I could just turn from one side to the other, but could not roll myself fairly over, so as to change my place. They then left me. Both of them were the worse for liquor; but the devil of a pilot was sober – mind that! – as sober as I am at the present moment.

I lay in the dark for a little while, with my heart thumping as if it was going to jump out of me. I lay about five minutes or so when the pilot came down into the hold alone.

He had the captain's cursed flat candlestick and a carpenter's awl in one hand, and a long thin twist of cotton-yarn, well oiled, in the other. He put the candlestick, with a new 'dip' candle lighted in it, down on the floor about two feet from my face, and close against the side of the vessel. The light was feeble enough; but it was sufficient to show a dozen barrels of gunpowder or more left all round me in the hold of the brig. I began to suspect what he was after the moment I noticed the barrels. The horrors laid hold of me from head to foot, and the sweat poured off my face like water.

I saw him go next to one of the barrels of powder standing against the side of the vessel in a line with the candle, and about three feet, or rather better, away from it. He bored a hole in the side of the barrel with his awl, and the horrid powder came trickling out, as black as hell, and dripped into the hollow of his hand, which he held to catch it. When he had got a good handful, he stopped up the hole by jamming one end of his oiled twist of cotton-yarn fast into it, and he then rubbed the powder into the whole length of the yarn till he had blackened every hair-breadth of it.

The next thing he did – as true as I sit here, as true as the heaven above us all – the next thing he did was to carry the free end of his long, lean, black, frightful slow-match to the lighted candle alongside my face. He tied it (the bloody-minded villain!) in several folds round the tallow dip, about a third of the distance down, measuring from the flame of the wick to the lip of the candlestick. He did that; he looked to see that my lashings were all safe; and then he put his face close to mine, and whispered in my ear, 'Blow up with the brig!'

He was on deck again the moment after, and he and the two others shoved the hatch on over me. At the farthest end from where I lay they had not fitted it down quite true, and I saw a blink of daylight glimmering in when I looked in that direction. I heard the sweeps of the schooner fall into the water – splash! splash! fainter and fainter, as they swept the vessel out in the dead calm, to be ready for the wind in the offing. Fainter and fainter, splash, splash! for a quarter of an hour or more.

While those receding sounds were in my ears, my eyes were fixed on the candle.

It had been freshly lighted. If left to itself, it would bum for between six and seven hours. The slow-match was twisted round it about a third of the way down, and therefore the flame would be about two hours reaching it. There I lay, gagged, bound, lashed to the floor, seeing my own life burning down with the candle by my side – there I lay, alone on the sea, doomed to be blown to atoms, and to see that doom drawing on, nearer and nearer with every fresh second of time, through nigh on two hours to come; powerless to help myself, and speechless to call for help to others. The wonder to me is that I didn't cheat the flame, the slow-match, and the powder, and die of the horror of my situation before my first half-hour was out in the hold of the brig.

I can't exactly say how long I kept the command of my senses after I had ceased to hear the splash of the schooner's sweeps in the water. I can trace back everything I did and everything I thought, up to a certain point; but, once past that, I get all abroad, and lose myself in my memory now, much as I lost myself in my own feelings at the time.

The moment the hatch was covered over me, I began, as every other man would have begun in my place, with a frantic effort to free my hands. In the mad panic I was in, I cut my flesh with the lashings as if they had been knife-blades, but I never stirred them. There was less chance still of freeing my legs, or of tearing myself from the fastenings that held me to the floor. I gave in when I was all but suffocated for want of breath. The gag, you will please to remember, was a terrible enemy to me; I could only breathe freely through my nose – and that is but a poor vent when a man is straining his strength as far as ever it will go.

I gave in and lay quiet, and got my breath again, my eyes glaring and straining at the candle all the time.

While I was staring at it, the notion struck me of trying to blow out the flame by pumping a long breath at it suddenly through my nostrils. It was too high above me, and too far away from me, to be reached in that fashion. I tried, and tried, and tried; and then I gave in again, and lay quiet again, always with my eyes glaring at the candle, and the candle glaring at me. The splash of the schooner's sweeps was very faint by this time. I could only just hear them in the morning stillness. Splash! splash! – fainter and fainter – splash! splash!

Without exactly feeling my mind going, I began to feel it getting queer as early as this. The snuff of the candle was growing taller and taller, and the length of tallow between the flame and the slow-match, which was the length of my life, was getting shorter and shorter. I calculated that I had rather less than an hour and a half to live.

An hour and a half! Was there a chance in that time of a boat pulling off to the brig from shore? Whether the land near which the vessel was anchored was in possession of our side, or in possession of the enemy's side, I made out that they must, sooner or later, send to hail the brig merely because she was a stranger in those parts. The question for me was, how soon? The sun had not risen yet, as I could tell by looking through the chink in the hatch. There was no coast village near us, as we all knew, before the brig was seized, by seeing no lights on shore. There was no wind, as I could tell by listening, to bring any strange vessel near. If I had had six hours to live, there might have been a chance for me, reckoning from sunrise to noon. But with an hour and a half, which had dwindled to an hour and a quarter by this time – or, in other words, with the earliness of the morning, the uninhabited coast, and the dead calm all against me – there was not the ghost of a chance. As I felt that, I had another struggle – the last – with my bonds, and only cut myself the deeper for my pains.

I gave in once more, and lay quiet, and listened for the splash of the sweeps.

Gone! Not a sound could I hear but the blowing of a fish now and then on the surface of the sea, and the creak of the brig's crazy old spars, as she rolled gently from side to side with the little swell there was on the quiet water.

An hour and a quarter. The wick grew terribly as the quarter slipped away, and the charred top of it began to thicken and spread out mushroom-shape. It would fall off soon. Would it fall off red-hot, and would the swing of the brig cant it over the side of the candle and let it down on the slow-match? If it would, I had about ten minutes to live instead of an hour.

This discovery set my mind for a minute on a new tack altogether. I began to ponder with myself what sort of a death blowing up might be. Painful! Well, it would be, surely, too sudden for that. Perhaps just one crash inside me, or outside me, or both; and nothing more! Perhaps not even a crash; that and death and the scattering of this living body of mine into millions of fiery sparks, might all happen in the same instant! I couldn't make it out; I couldn't settle how it would be. The minute of calmness in my mind left it before I had half done thinking; and I got all abroad again.

When I came back to my thoughts, or when they came back to me (I can't say which), the wick was awfully tall, the flame was burning with a smoke above it, the charred top was broad and red, and heavily spreading out to its fall.

My despair and horror at seeing it took me in a new way, which was good and right, at any rate, for my poor soul. I tried to pray – in my own heart, you will understand, for the gag put all lip-praying out of my power. I tried, but the candle seemed to burn it up in me. I struggled hard to force my eyes from the slow, murdering flame, and to look up through the chink in the hatch at the blessed daylight. I tried once, tried twice; and gave it up. I next tried only to shut my eyes, and keep them shut – once – twice – and the second time I did it. 'God bless old mother, and sister Lizzie; God keep them both, and forgive me.' That was all I had time to say, in my own heart, before my eyes opened again, in spite of me, and the flame of the candle flew into them, flew all over me, and burned up the rest of my thoughts in an instant.

I couldn't hear the fish blowing now; I couldn't hear the creak of the spars; I couldn't think; I couldn't feel the sweat of my own death agony on my face – I could only look at the heavy, charred top of the wick. It swelled, tottered, bent over to one side, dropped – red-hot at the moment of its fall – black and harmless, even before the swing of the brig had canted it over into the bottom of the candlestick.

I caught myself laughing.

Yes! laughing at the safe fall of the bit of wick. But for the gag, I should have screamed with laughing. As it was, I shook with it inside me – shook till the blood was in my head, and I was all but suffocated for want of breath. I had just sense enough left to feel that my own horrid laughter at that awful moment was a sign of my brain going at last. I had just sense enough left to make another struggle before my mind broke loose like a frightened horse, and ran away with me.

One comforting look at the blink of daylight through the hatch was what I tried for once more. The fight to force my eyes from the candle and to get that one look at the daylight was the hardest I had had yet; and I lost the fight. The flame had hold of my eyes as fast as the lashings had hold of my hands. I couldn't look away from it. I couldn't even shut my eyes, when I tried that next, for the second time. There was the wick growing tall once more. There was the space of unburned candle between the light and the slow-match shortened to an inch or less.

How much life did that inch leave me? Three-quarters of an hour? Half an hour? Fifty minutes? Twenty minutes? Steady! An inch of tallow-candle would burn longer than twenty minutes. An inch of tallow! The notion of a man's body and soul being kept together by an inch of tallow! Wonderful! Why, the greatest king that sits on a throne can't keep a man's body and soul together; and here's an inch of tallow that can do what the king can't! There's something to tell mother when I get home which will surprise her more than all the rest of my voyages put together. I laughed inwardly again at the thought of that, and shook and swelled and suffocated myself, till the light of the candle leaped in through my eyes, and licked up the laughter, and burned it out of me, and made me all empty and cold and quiet once more.

Mother and Lizzie. I don't know when they came back; but they did come back – not, as it seemed to me, into my mind this time, but right down bodily before me, in the hold of the brig.

Yes: sure enough, there was Lizzie, just as light-hearted as usual, laughing at me. Laughing? Well, why not? Who is to blame Lizzie for thinking I'm lying on my back, drunk in the cellar, with the beer-barrels all round me? Steady! she's crying now – spinning round and round in a fiery mist, wringing her hands, screeching out for help – fainter and fainter, like the splash of the schooner's sweeps. Gone – burned up in the fiery mist! Mist? fire? No, neither one nor the other. It's mother makes the light – mother knitting, with ten flaming points at the ends of her fingers and thumbs, and slow-matches hanging in bunches all round her face instead of her own grey hair. Mother in her old armchair, and the pilot's long skinny hands hanging over the back of the chair, dripping with gunpowder. No! No gunpowder, no chair, no mother – nothing but the pilot's face, shining red-hot, like a sun, in the fiery mist; turning upside down in the fiery mist; running backward and forward along the slow-match, in the fiery mist; spinning millions of miles in a minute, in the fiery mist – spinning itself smaller and smaller into one tiny point, and that point darting on a sudden straight into my head – and then, all fire and all mist – no hearing, no seeing, no thinking, no feeling – the brig, the sea, my own self, the whole world, all gone together!

After what I've just told you, I know nothing and remember nothing, till I woke up (as it seemed to me) in a comfortable bed, with two rough-and-ready men like myself sitting on each side of my pillow, and a gentleman standing watching me at the foot of the bed. It was about seven in the morning. My sleep (or what seemed like my sleep to me) had lasted better than eight months – I was among my own countrymen in the island of Trinidad – the men at each side of my pillow were my keepers, turn and turn about – and the gentleman standing at the foot of the bed was the doctor. What I said and did in those eight months, I never have known, and never shall. I woke out of it as if it had been one long sleep – that's all I know.

It was another two months or more before the doctor thought it safe to answer the questions I asked him.

The brig had been anchored, just as I had supposed, off a part of the coast which was lonely enough to make the Spaniards pretty sure of no interruption, so long as they managed their murderous work quietly under cover of night.

My life had not been saved from the shore, but from the sea. An American vessel, becalmed in the offing, had made out the brig as the sun rose; and the captain having his time on his hands in consequence of the calm, and seeing a vessel anchored where no vessel had any reason to be, had manned one of his boats and sent his mate with it, to look a little closer into the matter, and bring back a report of what he saw.

What he saw, when he and his men found the brig deserted and boarded her, was a gleam of candlelight through the chink in the hatchway. The flame was within about a thread's breadth of the slow-match when he lowered himself into the hold; and if he had not had the sense and coolness to cut the match in two with his knife before he touched the candle, he and his men might have been blown up along with the brig as well as me. The match caught, and turned into sputtering red fire, in the very act of putting the candle out; and if the communication with the powder-barrel had not been cut off, the Lord only knows what might have happened.

What became of the Spanish schooner and the pilot, I have never heard from that day to this. As for the brig, the Yankees took her, as they took me, to Trinidad, and claimed their salvage, and got it, I hope, for their own sakes. I was landed just in the same state as when they rescued me from the brig – that is to say, clean out of my senses. But please to remember, it was a long time ago; and, take my word for it, I was discharged cured, as I have told you. Bless your hearts, I'm all right now, as you may see. I'm a little shaken by telling the story, as is only natural – a little shaken, my good friends, that's all.

Nine O'Clock!

The night of the 30th of June, 1793, is memorable in the prison annals of Paris, as the last night in confinement of the leaders of the famous Girondin party in the first French revolution. On the morning of the 31st, the twenty-one deputies who represented the department of the Gironde were guillotined to make way for Robespierre and the Reign of Terror.

With these men fell the last revolutionists of that period who shrank from founding a republic on massacre; who recoiled from substituting for a monarchy of corruption, a monarchy of bloodshed. The elements of their defeat lay as much in themselves as in the events of their time. They were not, as a party, true to their own convictions; they temporised; they fatally attempted to take a middle course amid the terrible emergencies of a terrible epoch, and they fell – fell before worse men, because those men were in earnest.

Condemned to die, the Girondins submitted nobly to their fate; their great glory was the glory of their deaths. The speech of one of them on hearing his sentence pronounced, was a prophecy of the future, fulfilled to the letter.

'I die,' he said to the Jacobin judges, the creatures of Robespierre, who tried him. 'I die at a time when the people have lost their reason; you will die on the day when they recover it.' Valazé was the only member of the condemned party who displayed a momentary weakness; he stabbed himself on hearing his sentence pronounced. But the blow was not mortal – he died on the scaffold, and died bravely with the rest.

On the night of the 30th the Girondins held their famous banquet in the prison; celebrated, with the ferocious stoicism of the time, their last social meeting before the morning on which they were to die. Other men, besides the twenty-one, were present at this supper of the condemned. They were prisoners who held Girondin opinions, but whose names were not illustrious enough for history to preserve. Though sentenced to confinement they were not sentenced to death. Some of their number, who had protested most boldly against the condemnation of the deputies, were ordered to witness the execution on the morrow, as a timely example to terrify them into submission. More than this, Robespierre and his colleagues did not, as yet, venture to attempt: the Reign of Terror was a cautious reign at starting.

The supper-table of the prison was spread; the guests, twenty-one of their number stamped already with the seal of death, were congregated at the last Girondin banquet; toast followed toast; the Marseillaise was sung; the desperate triumph of the feast was rising fast to its climax, when a new and ominous subject of conversation was started at the lower end of the table, and spread electrically, almost in a moment , to the top.

This subject (by whom originated no one knew) was simply a question as to the hour in the morning at which the execution was to take place. Every one of the prisoners appeared to be in ignorance on this point; and the gaolers either could not, or would not, enlighten them. Until the cart for the condemned rolled into the prison-yard, not one of the Girondins could tell whether he was to be called out to the guillotine soon after sunrise, or not till near noon.

This uncertainty was made a topic for discussion, or for jesting on all sides. It was eagerly seized on as a pretext for raising to the highest pitch the ghastly animation and hilarity of the evening. In some quarters, the recognised hour of former executions was quoted as precedent sure to be followed by the executioners of the morrow; in others, it was asserted that Robespierre and his party would purposely depart from established customs in this, as in previous instances. Dozens of wild schemes were suggested for guessing the hour by fortune-telling rules on the cards; bets were offered and accepted among the prisoners who were not condemned to death, and witnessed in stoical mockery by the prisoners who were. Jests were exchanged about early rising and hurried toilets; in short, every man contributed an assertion, with one solitary exception. That exception was the Girondin, Duprat, one of the deputies who was sentenced to die by the guillotine.

He was a younger man than the majority of his brethren, and was personally remarkable by his pale, handsome, melancholy face, and his reserved yet gentle manners. Throughout the evening, he had spoken but rarely; there was something of the silence and serenity of a martyr in his demeanour. That he feared death as little as any of his companions was plainly visible in his bright, steady eye; in his unchanging complexion; in his firm, calm voice, when he occasionally addressed those who happened to be near him. But he was evidently out of place at the banquet; his temperament was reflective, his disposition serious; feasts were at no time a sphere in which he was calculated to shine.

His taciturnity, while the hour of the execution was under discussion, had separated him from most of those with whom he sat, at the lower end of the table. They edged up towards the top, where the conversation was most general and most animated. One of his friends, however, still kept his place by Duprat's side, and thus questioned him anxiously, but in low tones, on the cause of his immovable silence:

'Are you the only man of the company, Duprat, who has neither a guess nor a joke to make about the time of the execution?'

'I never joke, Marginy,' was the answer, given with a slight smile which had something of the sarcastic in it; 'and as for guessing at the time of the execution, I never guess at things which I know.'

'Know! You know the hour of the execution! Then why not communicate your knowledge to your friends around you?'

'Because not one of them would believe what I said.'

'But, surely, you could prove it. Somebody must have told you.'

'Nobody has told me.'

'You have seen some private letter, then; or you have managed to get sight of the execution-order; or – '

'Spare your conjectures, Marginy. I have not read, as I have not been told, what is the hour at which we are to die tomorrow.'

'Then how on earth can you possibly know it?'

'I do not know when the execution will begin, or when it will end. I only know that it will be going on at nine o'clock tomorrow morning. Out of the twenty-one who are to suffer death, one will be guillotined exactly at that hour. Whether he will be the first whose head falls, or the last, I cannot tell.'

'And pray who may this man be, who is going to die exactly at nine o'clock? Of course, prophetically knowing so much, you know that!'

'I do know it. I am the man whose death by the guillotine will take place exactly at the hour I have mentioned.'

'You said just now, Duprat, that you never joked. Do you expect me to believe that what you have just spoken is spoken in earnest?'

'I repeat that I never joke; and I answer that I expect you to believe me. I know the hour at which my death will take place tomorrow, just as certainly as I know the fact of my own existence tonight.'

'But how? My dear friend, can you really lay claim to supernatural intuition, in this eighteenth century of the world, in this renowned Age of reason?'

'No two men, Marginy, understand that word, supernatural, exactly in the same sense; you and I differ about its meaning, or, in other words, differ about the real distinction between the doubtful and the true. We will not discuss the subject: I wish to be understood, at the outset, as laying claim to no superior intuitions whatever; but I tell you, at the same time, that even in this Age of Reason, I have reason for what I have said. My father and my brother both died at nine o'clock in the morning, and were both warned very strangely of their deaths. I am the last of my family; I was warned last night, as they were warned; and I shall die by the guillotine, as they died in their beds, at the fatal hour of nine.'

'But, Duprat, why have I never heard of this before? As your oldest and, I am sure, your dearest friend, I thought you had long since trusted me with all your secrets.'

'And you shall know this secret; I only kept it from you till the time when I would be certain that my death would substantiate my words, to the very letter. Come! You are as bad supper-company as I am; let us slip away from the table unperceived, while our friends are all engaged in conversation. Yonder end of the hall is dark and quiet – we can speak there uninterruptedly, for some hours to come,'

He led the way from the supper-table, followed by Marginy. Arrived at one of the darkest and most retired corners of the great hall of the prison, Duprat spoke again:

'I believe, Marginy,' he said, 'that you are one of those who have been ordered by our tyrants to witness my execution, and the execution of my brethren, as a warning spectacle for an enemy to the Jacobin cause?'

'My dear, dear friend! It is too true; I am ordered to witness the butchery which I cannot prevent – our last awful parting will be at the foot of the scaffold. I am among the victims who are spared – mercilessly spared – for a little while yet.'

'Say the martyrs! We die as martyrs, calmly, hopefully, innocently. When I am placed under the guillotine tomorrow morning, listen, my friend, for the striking of the church clocks; listen for the hour while you look your last on me. Until that time, suspend your judgement on the strange chapter of family history which I am now about to relate.'

Marginy took his friend's hand, and promised compliance with the request. Duprat then began as follows.

'You knew my brother Alfred, when he was quite a youth, and you knew something of what people flippantly termed the eccentricities of his character. He was three years my junior; but from childhood, he showed far less of a child's innate levity and happiness than his elder brother. He was noted for his seriousness and thoughtfulness as a boy; showed little inclination for a boy's usual lessons, and less still for a boy's usual recreations, – in short, he was considered by everybody (my father included) as deficient in intellect; as a vacant dreamer, and an inveterate idler, whom it was hopeless to improve. our tutor tried to lead him to various studies, and tried in vain. It was the same when the cultivation of his mind was given up, and the cultivation of his body was next attempted. The fencing-master could make nothing of him; and the dancing-master, after the first three lessons, resigned in despair. Seeing that it was useless to set others to teach him, my father made a virtue of necessity, and left him, if he chose, to teach himself.

'To the astonishment of everyone, he had not been long consigned to his own guidance, when he was discovered in the library, reading every old treatise on astrology which he could lay his hands on. He had rejected all useful knowledge for the most obsolete of obsolete sciences – the old, abandoned delusion of divination by stars! My father laughed heartily over the strange study to which his idle son had at last applied himself, but made no attempt to oppose his new caprice, and sarcastically presented him with a telescope on his next birthday. I should remind you here, of what you may perhaps have forgotten, that my father was a philosopher of the Voltaire school, who believed that the summit of human wisdom was to arrive at the power of sneering at all enthusiasms, and doubting of all truths. Apart from his philosophy, he was a kind-hearted, easy man, of quick, rather than profound intelligence. He could see nothing in my brother's new occupation but the evidence of a new idleness, a fresh caprice which would be abandoned in a few months. My father was not the man to appreciate those yearnings towards the poetical and the spiritual, which were part of Alfred's temperament, and which gave to his peculiar studies of the stars and their influences, a certain charm altogether unconnected with the more practical attractions of scientific investigation.

'This idle caprice of my brother's, as my father insisted on terming it, had lasted more than a twelvemonth, when there occurred the first of a series of mysterious and – as I consider them – supernatural events, with all of which Alfred was very remarkably connected. I was myself a witness of the strange circumstance, which I am now about to relate to you.

'One day – my brother being then sixteen years of age – I happened to go into my father's study, during his absence, and found Alfred there, standing close to a window which looked into the garden. I walked up to him, and observed a curious expression of vacancy and rigidity in his face, especially in his eyes. Although I knew him to be subject to what are called fits of absence, I still thought it rather extraordinary that he never moved, and never noticed me when I was close to him. I took his hand, and asked if he was unwell. His flesh felt quite cold; neither my touch nor my voice produced the smallest sensation in him. Almost at the same moment when I noticed this, I happened to be looking accidentally towards the garden. There was my father walking along one of the paths, and there, by his side, walking with him, was another Alfred! – Another, yet exactly the same as the Alfred by whose side I was standing, whose hand I still held in mine!

'Thoroughly panic-stricken, I dropped his hand, and uttered a cry of terror. At the loud sound of my voice, the statue-like presence before me immediately began to show signs of animation. I looked round again at the garden. The figure of my brother, which I had beheld there, was gone, and I saw to my horror, that my father was looking for it – looking in all directions for the companion (spectre, or human being?) of his walk!

'When I turned towards Alfred once more, he had (if I may so express it) come to life again, and was asking, with his usual gentleness of manner and kindness of voice, why I was looking so pale? I evaded the question by making some excuse, and in my turn enquired of him, how long he had been in my father's study.

' "Surely you ought to know best," he answered with a laugh, "for you must have been here before me. It is not many minutes ago since I was walking in the garden with – "

'Before he could complete the sentence my father entered the room.

' "Oh! here you are, Master Alfred," said he. "May I ask for what purpose you took it into your wise head to vanish in that extraordinary manner? Why, you slipped away from me in an instant, while I was picking a flower! On my word, sir, you're a better player at hide-and-seek than your brother – he would only have run into the shrubbery, you have managed to run in here, though how you did it in the time passes my poor comprehension. I was not a moment picking the flower, yet in that moment you were gone!"

'Alfred glanced suddenly and searchingly at me; his face became deadly pale, and, without speaking a word, he hurried from the room.

' "Can you explain this?" said my father, looking very much astonished.

'I hesitated a moment, and then told him what I had seen. He took a pinch of snuff – a favourite habit with him when he was going to be sarcastic, in imitation of Voltaire.

' "One visionary in a family is enough," said he; "I recommend you not to turn yourself into a bad imitation of your brother Alfred! Send your ghost after me, my good boy! I am going back into the garden, and should like to see him again!"

'Ridicule, even much sharper than this, would have had little effect on me. If I was certain of anything in the world, I was certain that I had seen my brother in the study – nay, more, had touched him – and equally certain that I had seen his double – his exact similitude, in the garden. As far as any man could know that he was in possession of his own senses, I knew myself to be in possession of mine. Left alone to think over what I had beheld, I felt a supernatural terror creeping through me – a terror which increased, when I recollected that on one or two occasions friends had said they had seen Alfred out of doors, when we all knew him to be at home. These statements, which my father had laughed at, and had taught me to laugh at, either as a trick, or a delusion on the part of others, now recurred to my memory as startling corroborations of what I had just seen myself. The solitude of the study oppressed me in a manner which I cannot describe. I left the apartment to seek Alfred, determined to question him, with all possible caution, on the subject of his strange trance, and his sensations at the moment when I had awakened him from it.

'I found him in his bedroom, still pale, and now very thoughtful. As the first words in reference to the scene in the study passed my lips, he started violently, and entreated me, with very unusual warmth of speech and manner, never to speak to him on that subject again – never, if I had any love or regard for him! Of course, I complied with his request. The mystery, however, was not destined to end here.

'About two months after the event which I have just related, we had arranged, one evening, to go to the theatre. My father had insisted that Alfred should be of the party, otherwise he would certainly have declined accompanying us; for he had no inclination whatever for public amusements of any kind. However, with his usual docility, he prepared to obey my father's desire, by going upstairs to put on his evening dress. It was winter-time, so he was obliged to take a candle with him.

'We waited in the drawing-room for his return a very long time, so long, that my father was on the point of sending upstairs to remind him of the lateness of the hour, when Alfred reappeared without the candle which he had taken with him from the room. The ghostly alteration over his face – the hideous death-look that distorted his features I shall never forget – I shall see it tomorrow on the scaffold!

'Before either my father or I could utter a word, my brother said: "I have been taken suddenly ill; but I am better now. Do you still wish me to go to the theatre?"

' "Certainly not, my dear Alfred," answered my father; "we must send for the doctor immediately."

' "Pray do not call in the doctor, sir; he would be of no use. I will tell you why, if you will let me speak to you alone."

'My father, looking seriously alarmed, signed to me to leave the room. For more than half an hour I remained absent, suffering almost unendurable suspense and anxiety on my brother's account. When I was recalled, I observed that Alfred was quite calm, though still deadly pale. My father's manner displayed an agitation which I had never observed in it before. He rose from his chair when I re-entered the room, and left me alone with my brother.

' "Promise me," said Alfred, in answer to my entreaties to know what had happened, "promise that you will not ask me to tell you more than my father has permitted me to tell. It is his desire that I should keep certain things a secret from you."

'I gave the required promise, but gave it most unwillingly. Alfred then proceeded.

' "When I left you to go and dress for the theatre, I felt a sense of oppression all over me, which I cannot describe. As soon as I was alone, it seemed as if some part of the life within me was slowly wasting away. I could hardly breathe the air around me, big drops of perspiration burst out on my forehead, and then a feeling of terror seized me which I was utterly unable to control. Some of those strange fancies of seeing my mother's spirit, which used to influence me at the time of her death, came back again to my mind. I ascended the stairs slowly and painfully, not daring to look behind me, for I heard – yes, heard! – something following me. When I got into my room, and had shut the door, I began to recover my self-possession a little. But the sense of oppression was still as heavy on me as ever, when I approached the wardrobe to get out my clothes. Just as I stretched forth my hand to turn the key, I saw, to my horror, the two doors of the wardrobe opening of themselves, opening slowly and silently. The candle went out at the same moment, and the whole inside of the wardrobe became to me like a great mirror, with a bright light shining in the middle of it. Out of that light there came a figure, the exact counterpart of myself. Over its breast hung an open scroll, and on that I read the warning of my own death, and a revelation of the destinies of my father and his race. Do not ask me what were the words on the scroll, I have given my promise not to tell you. I may only say that, as soon as I had read all, the room grew dark, and the vision disappeared."

'Forgetful of my promise, I entreated Alfred to repeat to me the words on the scroll. He smiled sadly, and refused to speak on the subject any more. I next sought out my father, and begged him to divulge the secret. Still sceptical to the last, he answered that one diseased imagination in the family was enough, and that he would not permit me to run the risk of being infected by Alfred's mental malady. I passed the whole of that day and the next in a state of agitation and alarm which nothing could tranquillise. The sight I had seen in the study gave a terrible significance to the little that my brother had told me. I was uneasy if he was a moment out of my sight. There was something in his expression – calm and even cheerful as it was – which made me dread the worst.

'On the morning of the third day after the occurrence I have just related, I rose very early, after a sleepless night, and went into Alfred's bedroom. He was awake, and welcomed me with more than usual affection and kindness. As I drew a chair to his bedside, he asked me to get pen, ink, and paper, and write down something from his dictation. I obeyed, and found to my terror and distress, that the idea of death was more present to his imagination than ever. He employed me in writing a statement of his wishes in regard to the disposal of all his own little possessions, as keepsakes to be given, after he was no more, to my father, myself, the house-servants, and one or two of his own most intimate friends. Over and over again I entreated him to tell me whether he really believed that his death was near. He invariably replied that I should soon know, and then led the conversation to indifferent topics. As the morning advanced, he asked to see my father, who came, accompanied by the doctor, the latter having been in attendance for the last two days.

'Alfred took my father's hand, and begged his forgiveness of any offence, any disobedience of which he had ever been guilty. Then, reaching out his other hand, and taking mine, as I stood on the opposite side of the bed, he asked what the time was. A clock was placed on the mantel-piece of the room, but not in a position in which he could see it, as he now lay. I turned round to look at the dial, and answered that, it was just on the stroke of nine.

' "Farewell!" said Alfred, calmly; "in this world, farewell for ever!"

'The next instant the clock struck. I felt his fingers tremble in mine, then grow quite still. The doctor seized a hand-mirror that lay on the table, and held it over his lips. He was dead – dead, as the last chime of the hour echoed through the awful silence of the room!

'I pass over the first days of our affliction. You, who have suffered the loss of a beloved sister, can well imagine their misery. I pass over these days, and pause for a moment at the time when we could speak with some calmness and resignation on the subject of our bereavement. On the arrival of that period, I ventured, in conversation with my father, to refer to the vision which had been seen by our dear Alfred in his bedroom, and to the prophecy which he described himself as having read upon the supernatural scroll.

'Even yet my father persisted in his scepticism; but now, as it seemed to me, more because he was afraid, than because he was unwilling, to believe. I again recalled to his memory what I myself had seen in the study. I asked him to recollect how certain Alfred had been beforehand, and how fatally right, about the day and hour of his death. Still I could get but one answer; my brother had died of a nervous disorder (the doctor said so); his imagination had been diseased from his childhood; there was only one way of treating the vision which he described himself as having seen, and that was, not to speak of it again between ourselves; never to speak of it at all to our friends.

'We were sitting in the study during this conversation. It was evening. As my father uttered the last words of his reply to me, I saw his eye turn suddenly and uneasily towards the further end of the room. In dead silence, I looked in the same direction, and saw the door opening of itself. the vacant space beyond was filled with a bright, steady glow, which hid all outer objects in the hall, and which I cannot describe to you by likening it to any light that we are accustomed to behold either by day or night. In my terror, I caught my father by the arm, and asked him, in a whisper, whether he did not see something extraordinary in the direction of the doorway?

' "Yes," he answered, in tones as low as mine, "I see, or fancy I see, a strange light. The subject on which we have been speaking has impressed our feelings as it should not. Our nerves are still unstrung by the shock of the bereavement we have suffered: our senses are deluding us. Let us look away towards the garden."

' "But the opening of the door, father; remember the opening of the door!"

' "Ours is not the first door which has accidentally flown open of itself."

' "Then why not shut it again?"

' "Why not, indeed. I will close it at once." He rose, advanced a few paces, then stopped, and came back to his place. "It is a warm evening," he said, avoiding my eyes, which were eagerly fixed on him, "the room will be all the cooler, if the door is suffered to remain open."

'His face grew quite pale as he spoke. The light lasted for a few minutes longer, then suddenly disappeared. For the rest of the evening my father's manner was very much altered. He was silent and thoughtful, and complained of a feeling of oppression and languor, which he tried to persuade himself was produced by the heat of the weather. At an unusually early hour he retired to his room.

'The next morning, when I got downstairs, I found, to my astonishment, that the servants were engaged in preparations for the departure of somebody from the house. I made enquiries of one of them who was hurriedly packing a trunk. "My master, sir, starts for Lyons the first thing this morning," was the reply. I immediately repaired to my father's room, and found him there with an open letter in his hand, which he was reading. His face, as he looked up at me on my entrance, expressed the most violent emotions of apprehension and despair.

' "I hardly know whether I am awake or dreaming; whether I am the dupe of a terrible delusion, or the victim of a supernatural reality more terrible still," he said in low awe-struck tones as I approached him. "One of the prophecies which Alfred told me in private that he had read upon the scroll, has come true! He predicted the loss of the bulk of my fortune – here is the letter, which informs me that the merchant at Lyons in whose hands my money was placed, has become bankrupt. Can the occurrence of this ruinous calamity be the chance fulfilment of a mere guess? Or was the doom of my family really revealed to my dead son? I go to Lyons immediately to know the truth: this letter may have been written under false information; it may be the work of an impostor. And yet, Alfred's prediction – I shudder to think of it!"

' "The light, father!" I exclaimed, "the light we saw last night in the study!"

' "Hush! Don't speak of it! Alfred said that I should be warned of the truth of the prophecy, and of its immediate fulfilment, by the shining of the same supernatural light that he had seen – I tried to disbelieve what I beheld last night – I hardly know whether I dare believe it even now! This prophecy is not the last: there are others yet to be fulfilled – but let us not speak, let us not think of them! I must start at once for Lyons; I must be on the spot, if this horrible news is true, to save what I can from the wreck. The letter – give me back the letter! – I must go directly!"

'He hurried back from the room. I followed him; and, with some difficulty, obtained permission to be the companion of his momentous journey. When we arrived at Lyons, we found that the statement in the letter was true. My father's fortune was gone: a mere pittance, derived from a small estate that had belonged to my mother, was all that was left to us.

'My father's health gave way under this misfortune. He never referred again to Alfred's prediction, and I was afraid to mention the subject; but I saw that it was affecting his mind quite as painfully as the loss of his property. Over and over again, he checked himself very strangely when he was on the point of speaking to me about my brother. I saw that there was some secret pressing heavily on his mind, which he was afraid to disclose to me. It was useless to ask for his confidence. His temper had become irritable under disaster; perhaps, also, under the dread uncertainties which were now evidently tormenting him in secret. My situation was a very sad and a very dreary one, at that time: I had no remembrances of the past that were not mournful and affrighting remembrances; I had no hopes for the future that were not darkened by a vague presentiment of troubles and perils to come; and I was expressly forbidden by my father to say a word about the terrible events which had cast an unnatural gloom over my youthful career, to any of the friends (yourself included) whose counsel and whose sympathy might have guided and sustained me in the day of trial.

'We returned to Paris; sold our house there; and retired to live on the small estate, to which I have referred as the last possession left us. We had not been many days in our new abode, when my father imprudently exposed himself to a heavy shower of rain, and suffered in consequence from a violent attack of cold. This temporary malady was not dreaded by the medical attendant; but it was soon aggravated by a fever, produced as much by the anxiety and distress of mind from which he continued to suffer, as by any other cause. Still the doctor gave hope; but still he grew daily worse – so much worse, that I removed my bed into his room, and never quitted him night or day.

'One night I had fallen asleep, overpowered by fatigue and anxiety, when I was awakened by a cry from my father. I instantly trimmed the light, and ran to his side. He was sitting up in bed, with his eyes fixed on the door, which had been left ajar to ventilate the room. I saw nothing in that direction, and asked what was the matter. He murmured some expressions of affection towards me, and begged me to sit by his bedside till the morning; but gave no definite answer to my question. Once or twice, I thought he wandered a little; and I observed that he occasionally moved his hand under the pillow, as if searching for something there. However, when the morning came, he appeared to be calm and self-possessed. The doctor arrived; and pronouncing him to be better, retired to the dressing-room to write a prescription. The moment his back was turned, my father laid his weak hand on my arm, and whispered faintly: "Last night I saw the supernatural light again – the second prediction – true, true – my death this time – the same hour as Alfred's – nine – nine o'clock, this morning." He paused a moment through weakness; then added: "Take that sealed paper – under the pillow – when I am dead, read it – now go into the dressing-room – my watch is there – I have heard the church clock strike eight; let me see how long it is now till nine – go – go quickly!"

'Horror-stricken, moving and acting like a man in a trance, I silently obeyed him. The doctor was still in the dressing-room: despair made me catch eagerly at any chance of saving my father; I told his medical attendant what I had just heard, and entreated advice and assistance without delay.

' "He is a little delirious," said the doctor – "don't be alarmed: we can cheat him out of his dangerous idea, and so perhaps save his life. Where is the watch?" (I produced it) – "See: it is ten minutes to nine. I will put back the hands one hour; that will give good time for a composing draught to operate. There! Take him the watch, and let him see the false time with his own eyes. He will be comfortably asleep before the hour hand gets round again to nine."

'I went back with the watch to my father's bed-side. "Too slow," he murmured, as he looked at the dial – "too slow by an hour – the church clock – I counted eight."

' "Father! Dear father! You are mistaken," I cried, "I counted also: it was only seven."

' "Only seven!" he echoed faintly, "another hour then – another hour to live!" He evidently believed what I had said to him. In spite of the fatal experiences of the past, I now ventured to hope the best for our stratagem, as I resumed my place by his side.

'The doctor came in; but my father never noticed him. He kept his eyes fixed on the watch, which lay between us, on the coverlet. When the minute hand was within a few seconds of indicating the false hour of eight, he looked round at me, murmured very feebly and doubtingly, "another hour to live!" and then gently closed his eyes. I looked at the watch, and saw that it was just eight o'clock, according to our alteration of the right time. At the same moment, I heard the doctor, whose hand had been on my father's pulse, exclaim, "My God! It's stopped! He has died at nine o'clock!"

'The fatality, which no human stratagem or human science could turn aside, was accomplished! I was alone in the world!

'In the solitude of our little cottage, on the day of my father's burial, I opened the sealed letter, which he had told me to take from the pillow of his deathbed. In preparing to read it, I knew that I was preparing for the knowledge of my own doom; but I neither trembled nor wept. I was beyond grief: despair such as mine was then, is calm and self-possessed to the last.

'The letter ran thus: "After your father and brother have fallen under the fatality that pursues our house, it is right, my dear son, that you should be warned how you are included in the last of the predictions which still remains unaccomplished. Know then, that the final lines read by our dear Alfred on the scroll, prophesied that you should die, as we have died, at the fatal hour of nine; but by a bloody and violent death, the day of which was not foretold. My beloved boy! You know not, you never will know, what I suffered in the possession of this terrible secret, as the truth of the former prophecies forced itself more and more plainly on my mind! Even now, as I write, I hope against all hope, believe vainly and desperately against all experience, that this last, worst doom may be avoided. Be cautious; be patient; look well before you at each step of your career. The fatality by which you are threatened is terrible; but there is a Power above fatality, and before that Power my spirit and my child's spirit now pray for you. Remember this when your heart is heavy, your path through life grows dark. Remember that the better world is still before you, the world where we shall all meet! Farewell!"

'When I first read those lines, I read them with the gloomy, immovable resignation of the Eastern fatalists; and that resignation never left me afterwards. Here, in this prison, I feel it, calm as ever. I bowed patiently to my doom, when it was only predicted: I bow to it as patiently now, when it is on the eve of accomplishment. You have often wondered, my friend, at the tranquil, equable sadness of my manner: after what I have just told you, can you wonder any longer?

'But let me return for a moment to the past. Though I had no hope of escaping the fatality which had overtaken my father and my brother, my life, after my double bereavement, was the existence of all others which might seem most likely to evade the accomplishment of my predicted doom. Yourself and one other friend excepted, I saw no society; my walks were limited to the cottage garden and the neighbouring fields, and my everyday, unvarying occupation was confined to that hard and resolute course of study, by which alone I could hope to prevent my mind from dwelling on what I had suffered in the past, or on what I might still be condemned to suffer in the future. Never was there a life more quiet and more uneventful than mine!

'You know how I awoke to an ambition, which irresistibly impelled me to change this mode of existence. News from Paris penetrated even to my obscure retreat, and disturbed my self-imposed tranquillity. I heard of the last errors and weaknesses of Louis the Sixteenth; I heard of the assembling of the States-General; and I knew that the French Revolution had begun. The tremendous emergencies of that epoch drew men of all characters from private to public pursuits, and made politics the necessity rather than the choice of every Frenchman's life. The great change preparing for the country acted universally on individuals, even to the humblest, and it acted on me.

'I was elected a deputy, more for the sake of the name I bore, than on account of any little influence which my acquirements and my character might have exercised in the neighbourhood of my country abode. I removed to Paris, and took my seat in the Chamber, little thinking at that time, of the crime and the bloodshed to which our revolution, so moderate in its beginning, would lead; little thinking that I had taken the first, irretrievable steps towards the bloody and violent death which was lying in store for me.

'Need I go on? You know how warmly I joined the Girondin party; you know how we have been sacrificed; you know what the death is which I and my brethren are to suffer tomorrow. On now ending, I repeat what I said at beginning: judge not of my narrative till you have seen with your own eyes what really takes place in the morning. I have carefully abstained from all comment, I have simply related events as they happened, forbearing to add my own views of their significance, my own ideas on the explanation of which they admit. You may believe us to have been a family of nervous visionaries, witnesses of certain remarkable contingencies; victims of curious, but not impossible chances, which we have fancifully and falsely interpreted into supernatural events. I leave you undisturbed in this conviction (if you really feel it); tomorrow you will think differently; tomorrow you will be an altered man. In the meantime, remember what I now say, as you would remember my dying words: last night I saw the supernatural radiance which warned my father and my brother; and which warns me, that, whatever the time when the execution begins, whatever the order in which the twenty-one Girondins are chosen for death, I shall be the man who kneels under the guillotine, as the clock strikes nine!'

* * *

It was morning. Of the ghastly festivities of the night no sign remained. The prison-hall wore an altered look, as the twenty-one condemned men (followed by those who were ordered to witness their execution) were marched out to the carts appointed to take them from the dungeon to the scaffold.

The sky was cloudless, the sun warm and brilliant, as the Girondin leaders and their companions were drawn slowly through the streets to the place of execution. Duprat and Marginy were placed in separate vehicles: the contrast in their demeanour at that awful moment was strongly marked. The features of the doomed man still preserved their noble and melancholy repose; his glance was steady; his colour never changed. The face of Marginy, on the contrary, displayed the strongest agitation; he was pale even to his lips. The terrible narrative he had heard, the anticipation of the final and appalling proof by which its truth was now to be tested, had robbed him, for the first time in his life, of all his self-possession. Duprat had predicted truly; the morrow had come, and he was an altered man already.

The carts drew up at the foot of the scaffold which was soon to be stained with the blood of twenty-one human beings. The condemned deputies mounted it; and ranged themselves at the end opposite the guillotine. The prisoners who were to behold the execution remained in their cart. Before Duprat ascended the steps, he held his friend's hand for the last time: 'Farewell!' he said, calmly. 'Farewell! I go to my father, and my brother! Remember my words of last night.'

With straining eyes, and bloodless cheeks, Marginy saw Duprat take his position in the middle row of his companions, who stood in three ranks of seven each. Then the awful spectacle of the execution began. After the first seven deputies had suffered there was a pause; the horrible traces of the judicial massacre were being removed. When the execution proceeded, Duprat was the third taken from the middle rank of the condemned. As he came forward, he stood for an instant erect under the guillotine, he looked with a smile on his friend, and repeated in a clear voice the word, 'Remember!' – then bowed himself on the block. The blood stood still at Marginy's heart, as he looked and listened, during the moment of silence that followed. That moment past, the church clocks of Paris struck. He dropped down in the cart, and covered his face with his hands; for through the heavy beat of the hour he heard the fall of the fatal steel.

'Pray, sir, was it nine or ten that struck just now?' said one of Marginy's fellow-prisoners to an officer of the guard who stood near the cart.

The person addressed referred to his watch, and answered –
'*Nine o'clock!*'

The Devil's Spectacles

I

Memoirs of an Arctic Voyager

He says, sir, he thinks he's nigh to his latter end, and he would like, if convenient, to see you before he goes.'

'Do you mean before he dies?'

'That's about it, sir.'

I was in no humour (for reasons to be hereafter mentioned) for seeing anybody under disastrous circumstances of any sort; but the person who had sent me word that he was 'nigh to his latter end' had special claims on my consideration.

He was an old sailor, who had first seen blue water under the protection of my father, then a post-captain in the navy. Born on our estate, and the only male survivor of our head gamekeeper's family of seven children, he had received a good education through my father's kindness, and he ought to have got on well in the world; but he was one of those born vagabonds who set education at defiance. His term of service having expired, he disappeared for many years. During part of the time he was supposed to have been employed in the merchant navy. At the end of that long interval he turned up one day at our country house, an invalided man, without a penny in his pocket. My good father, then nearing the end of his life, was invalided too. Whether he had a fellow-feeling for the helpless creature whom he had once befriended, or whether he only took counsel of his own generous nature, it is now needless to enquire. He appointed Septimus Notman to be lodge-keeper at the second of our two park gates, and he recommended Septimus to my personal care on his deathbed. 'I'm afraid he's an old scoundrel,' my father confessed; 'but somebody must look after him as long as he lasts, and if you don't take his part, Alfred, nobody else will.' After this Septimus kept his place at the gate while we were in the country. When we returned to our London house the second gate was closed. The old sailor was lodged (by a strong exertion of my influence) in a room over a disused stable, which our coachman had proposed to turn into a hayloft. Everybody disliked Septimus Notman. He was said to be mad; to be a liar, a hypocrite, a vicious wretch, and a disagreeable brute. There were people who even reported that he had been a pirate during the time when we lost sight of him and who declared, when they were asked for their proof, that his crimes were written in his face. He was not in the least affected by the opinions of his neighbours; he chewed his tobacco and drank his grog, and, in the words of the old song, 'He cared for nobody, no, not he!' Well had my poor father said, that if I didn't take his part nobody else would. And shall I tell you a secret? Though I strictly carried out my father's wishes, and though Septimus was disposed in his own rough way to be grateful to me, I didn't like him either.

So I went to the room over the stables (we were in London at the time) with dry eyes and I sat down by his bed and cut up a cake of tobacco for him, and said, 'Well, what's the matter?' as coolly as if he had sent me word that he thought he had caught a cold in the head. 'I'm called away,' Septimus answered, 'and before I go I've got a confession to make, and something useful to offer you. It's reported among the servants, Mr Alfred, that you're in trouble just now between two ladies. You may see your way clear in that matter, sir, if death spares me long enough to say a few last words.'

'Never mind me, Septimus. Has a doctor seen you?'

'The doctor knows no more about me than I know myself. The doctor be – !'

'Have you any last wishes I can attend to?'

'None, sir.'

'Shall I send for a clergyman?'

Septimus Notman looked at me as directly as he could – he was afflicted with a terrible squint. Otherwise he was a fine, stoutly-built man, with a ruddy face profusely encircled by white hair and whiskers, a hoarse, heavy voice, and the biggest hands I ever saw. He put one of these enormous hands under his pillow before he answered me.

'If you think,' he said, 'that a clergyman will come to a man who has got the Devil's Spectacles here, under his pillow, and who has only to put those Spectacles on to see through that clergyman's clothes, flesh, and whatnot, and read everything that's written in his secret mind as plain as print, fetch him, Master Alfred – fetch him!'

I thought the clergyman might not like this, and withdrew my suggestion accordingly. The least I could do, as a matter of common politeness, after giving up the clergyman, was to ask if I might look at the Devil's Spectacles.

'Hear how I came by them first!' said Septimus.

'Will it take long?' I enquired.

'It will take long, and it will make your flesh creep.'

I remembered my promise to my father, and placed myself and my flesh at the mercy of Septimus Notman. But he was not ready to begin yet.

'Do you see that white jug?' he said, pointing to the wash-stand.

'Yes. Do you want water?'

'I want grog. There's grog in the white jug. And there's a pewter mug on the chimney-piece. I must be strung up, Master Alfred – I must be strung up.'

The white jug contained at least half a gallon of rum and water, roughly calculated. I strung him up. In the case of any other dying person I might have hesitated. But a man who possessed the Devil's Spectacles was surely an exception to ordinary rules, and might finish his career and finish his grog at one and the same time.

'Now I'm ready,' he said, 'What do you think I was up to in the time when you all lost sight of me? The latter part of that time, I mean?'

'They say you were a pirate,' I replied.

'Worse than that. Guess again.'

I tried to persuade myself that there might be such a human anomaly as a merciful pirate, and guessed once more.

'A murderer,' I suggested.

'Worse than that. Guess again.'

I declined to guess again. 'Tell me yourself what you have been,' I said.

He answered without the least appearance of discomposure, 'I've been a cannibal.'

Perhaps it was weak of me – but I did certainly start to my feet and make for the door.

'Hear the circumstances,' said Septimus. 'You know the proverb, sir? Circumstances alter cases.'

There was no disputing the proverb. I sat down again. I was a young and tender man, which, in my present position, was certainly against me. But I had very little flesh on my bones and that was in my favour.

'It happened when I went out with the Arctic expedition,' Septimus proceeded. 'I've forgotten all my learning, and lost my memory for dates. The year escapes me, and the latitude and longitude escape me. But I can tell you the rest of it. We were an exploring party, you must know, with sledges. It was getting close to the end of the summer months in those parts, and we were nigher than any of them have ever got since to the North Pole. We should have found our way there – don't you doubt it – but for three of our best men who fell sick of the scurvy. The second lieutenant, who was in command, called a halt, as the soldiers say. "With this loss of strength," says he, "it's my duty to take you back to the ships. We must let the North Pole be, and pray God that we may have no more invalided men to carry. I give you half an hour's rest before we turn back." The carpenter was one of our sound men. He spoke next. He reported one of the two sledges not fit for service. "How long will you be making it fit?" says the lieutenant. "In a decent climate," says the carpenter, " I should say two or three hours, sir. Here, double that time, at least." You may say why not do without the sledge? I'll tell you why. On account of the sick men to be carried. "Be as quick about it as you can," says the lieutenant: "time means life in our predicament." Most of the men were glad enough to rest. Only two of us murmured at not going on. One was a boatswain's mate; t'other was me. "Do you think the North Pole's the other side of that rising ground there?" says the lieutenant. The boatswain's mate was young and self-conceited. "I should like to try, sir," he says, "if any other man has pluck enough to go along with me." He looked at me when he said that. I wasn't going to have my courage called in question publicly by a slip of a lad; and, moreover, I had a fancy to try for the North Pole, too. I volunteered to go along with him. Our notion, you will understand, was to take a compass and some grub with us; to try what we could find in a couple hours' march forward; and to get back in good time for our duty on the return journey. The lieutenant wouldn't hear of it. "I'm responsible for every man in my charge," says he. "You're a couple of fools. Stay where you are." We were a couple of fools. We watched our opportunity, while they were all unloading the broken-down sledge; and slipped off to try our luck, and get the reward for discovering the North Pole.'

There he stopped, and pointed to the grog. 'Dry work, talking,' he said. 'Give us a drop more.'

I filled the pewter mug again. And again Septimus Notman emptied it.

'We set our course northwest by north,' he went on; 'and after a while (seeing the ground favoured us) we altered it again to due north. I can't tell you how long we walked (we neither of us had watches) – but this I'll swear to. Just as the last of the daylight was dying out, we got to the top of a hillock; and there we saw the glimmer of the open Polar Sea! No! Not the Sound that enters Kennedy's Channel, which has been mistaken for it, I know – but the real thing, the still and lonesome Polar Sea! What would you have done in our place? I'll tell you what we did. We sat down on some nice dry snow, and took out our biscuits and grog. Freezing work, do you say? You'll find it in the books, if you don't believe me – the further north you get in those parts, the less cold there is, and the more open water you find. Ask Captain M'Clure what sort of a bed he slept upon, on the night of October thirtieth, 'fifty-one. Well, and what do you think we did when we had eaten and drunk? Lit our pipes. And what next? Fell fast asleep, after our long walk, on our nice dry snow. And what sort of prospect met us when we woke? Darkness and drizzle and mist. I had the compass, and I tried to set our course on the way back. I could no more see the compass than if I had been blind. We had no means of striking a light, except my match-box. I had left it on the snow by my side when I fell asleep. Not a match would light. As for help of any sort, it was not to be thought of. We couldn't have been less than five miles distant from the place where we had left our messmates. So there we were, the boatswain's mate and me, alone in the desert, lost at the North Pole.'

I began to feel interested. 'You tried to get back, I suppose, dark as it was?' I said.

'We walked till we dropped,' Septimus answered; 'and then we yelled and shouted till we had no voices left; and then we hollowed out a hole in the snow, and waited for daylight.'

'What did you expect when daylight came?'

'I expected nothing, Master Alfred. The boatswain's mate (beginning to get a little light-headed, you know) expected the lieutenant to send in search of us, or wait till we returned. A likely thing for an officer in charge to do, with the lives of the sledging party depending on his getting them back to the ships, and only two men missing, who had broken orders and deserted their duty. A good riddance of bad rubbish – that's what he said of us when we were reported missing, I'll be bound. When the light came we tried to get back; and we did set our course cleverly enough. But, bless you, we had nothing left to eat or drink! When the light failed us again we were done up. We dropped on the snow, under the lee of a rock, and gave out. The boatswain's mate said his prayers, and I said Amen. Not the least use! On the contrary, as the night advanced it got colder and colder. We were both close together, to keep each other warm. I don't know how long it was, I only know it was still pitch dark, when I heard the boatswain's mate give a little flutter of a sigh, and no more. I opened his clothes, and put my hand on his heart. Dead, of cold and exhaustion, and no mistake. I shouldn't have been long after him but for my own presence of mind.'

'Your presence of mind? What did you do?'

'Stripped every rag of clothes off him, and put them all on myself. What are you shivering about? He couldn't feel it, could he? I tell you, he'd have been frozen stiff before the next day's light came – but for my presence of mind again. As well as my failing strength would let me, I buried him under the snow. Virtue, they say, Master Alfred, is its own reward. That good action proved to be the saving of my life.'

'What do you mean?'

'Didn't I tell you I buried him?'

'Well!'

'Well, in that freezing air, the burying of him kept him eatable. Don't you see?'

'You wretch!'

'Put yourself in my place, and don't call names. I held out till I was mad with hunger. And then I did open my knife with my teeth. And I did burrow down in the snow till I felt him –'

I could hear no more of it. 'Get on to the end! I said. 'Why didn't you die at the North Pole?'

'Because somebody helped me to get away.'

'Who helped you?'

'The Devil.'

He showed his yellow old teeth in a horrible grin. I could draw but one conclusion – his mind was failing him before death. Anything that spared me his hideous confession of cannibalism was welcome. I asked how the supernatural rescue happened.

'More grog first,' he said. 'The horrors come on me when I think of it.' He was evidently sinking. Without the grog I doubt if he could have said much more.

'I can't tell you how many days passed,' he went on; 'I only know that the time was nigh when it was all dark and no light. The darker it got, the deeper I scooped the sort of cavern I'd made for myself under the snow. Whether it was night, or whether it was day I know no more than you do. On a sudden, in the awful silence and solitude, I heard a voice, high up, as it were, on the rock behind me. It was a cheering and a pleasant voice, and it said, "Well, Septimus Notman, is there much left of the boatswain's mate by this time? Did he eat short while he lasted?" I cried out in fright, "Who the devil – ?" The voice stopped me before I could say the rest. "You've hit it," says the voice, "I am that person; and it's about time the Devil helped you out of this." "No," says I, "I'd rather perish by cold than fire any day." "Make your mind easy," says he, taking the point, "I don't want you in my place yet. I expect you to do a deal more in the way of degrading your humanity before you come to me, and I offer you a safe passage back to the nearest settlement. Friend Septimus, you're a man after my own heart." "As how, sir?" says I.

"Because you're such a complete beast," says he. "A human being who elevates himself, and rises higher and higher to his immortal destiny, is a creature I hate. He gets above me, even in his earthly lifetime. But you have dropped – you dear good fellow – to the level of a famished wolf. You have gobbled up your dead companion; and if you ever had such a thing as a soul – ha, Septimus! – it parted company with you at the first morsel you tasted of the Boatswain's mate. Do you think I'll leave such a prime specimen of the Animal Man as you are, deserted at the North Pole? No, no; I grant you a free pass by my railway; darkness and distance are no obstacles to Me. Are you ready?" You may not believe me; but I felt myself being lifted up, as it were, against my own will. "Give us a light," I says, "I can't travel in the dark." "Take my spectacles," says he, "they'll help you to see more than you bargain for. Look through them at your fellow mortals, and you'll see the inmost thoughts of their hearts as plain as I do, and, considering your nature, Septimus, that will drop you even below the level of a wolf." "Suppose I don't want to look," says I, "may I throw the spectacles away?" "They'll come back to you," says he. "May I smash them up?" "They'll put themselves together again." "What am I to do with them?" "Give them to another man. Now then! One, two, three – and away!" You may not believe me again; I lost my senses, Master Alfred. Hold me up; I'm losing them now. More grog – that's right – more grog. I came to myself at Upernavik, with the Devil's Spectacles in my pocket. Take them, sir. And read those two ladies' hearts. And act accordingly. Hush! I hear him speaking to me again. Behind my pillow. Just as he spoke on the rock. Most polite and cheering. Calling to me, as it were, "Come, cannibal – come!" Like a song, isn't it? "Come, cannibal – come!" '

He sang the last words faintly, and died with a smile on his face. Delirium or lies? With the Spectacles actually in my hands, I was inclined to think lies. They were of the old-fashioned sort, with big, circular glasses, and stout tortoiseshell frames; they smelt musty, but not sulphurous. I possess a sense of humour, I am happy to say. When they were thoroughly cleaned, I determined to try the Devil's Spectacles on the two ladies, and submit to the consequences, whatever they might be.

2

Memoirs of Myself

Who were the two ladies?

They were both young and unmarried. As a matter of delicacy, I ask permission to mention them by their Christian names only. Zilla, aged seventeen. Cecilia, aged two and twenty.

And what was my position between them?

I was the same age as Cecilia. She was my mother's companion and reader; handsome, well-born and poor. I had made her a proposal, and had been accepted. There were no money difficulties in the way of our marriage, in spite of my sweetheart's empty purse. I was an only child, and I had inherited, excepting my mother's jointure, the whole of the large property that my father left at his death. In social rank Cecilia was more than my equal; we were therefore not ill-matched from the worldly point of view. Nevertheless, there was an obstacle to our union, and a person interested in making the most of it. The obstacle was Zilla. The person interested was my mother. Zilla was her niece – her elder brother's daughter. The girl's parents had died in India, and she had been sent to school in England, under the care of her uncle and guardian. I had never seen her, and had hardly heard of her, until there was a question of her spending the Christmas holidays (in the year when Septimus Notman died) at our house.

'Her uncle has no objection,' my mother said; 'and I shall be more than glad to see her. A most interesting creature, as I hear. So lovely, and so good, that they call her The Angel, at school. I say nothing about her nice little fortune or the high military rank that her poor father possessed. You don't care for these things. But, oh, Alfred, it would make me so happy if you fell in love with Zilla and married her!'

Three days before, I had made my proposal to Cecilia, and had been accepted – subject to my mother's approval. I thought this a good opportunity of stating my case plainly; and I spoke out. Never before had I seen my mother so outraged and disappointed – enraged with Cecilia; disappointed with me. 'A woman without a farthing of a dowry; a woman who was as old as I was; a woman who had taken advantage of her position in the house to mislead and delude me!' and so on. Cecilia would certainly have been sent away if I had not declared that I should feel it my duty, in that event, to marry her immediately. My mother knew my temper, and refrained from giving Cecilia any cause of offence. Cecilia, on her side, showed what is called a proper pride; she declined to become my wife until my mother approved of her. She considered herself to be a martyr; and I considered myself to be an abominably treated man. Between us, I am afraid we made our good mother's life unendurable – she was obliged to be the first who gave way. It was understood that we were to be married in the spring. It was also understood that Zilla was bitterly disappointed at having her holiday visit to us put off. 'She was so anxious to see you, poor child,' my mother said to me; 'but I really daren't ask her here under present circumstances. She is so fresh, so innocent, so infinitely superior in personal attractions to Cecilia, that I don't know what might happen if you saw her now. You are the soul of honour, Alfred; but you and Zilla had better remain strangers to each other – you might repent your rash engagement.' After this, it is needless to say that I was dying to see Zilla; while, at the same time, I never for an instant swerved from my fidelity to Cecilia.

Such was my position, on the memorable day when Septimus Notman died, leaving me possessor of the Devil's Spectacles.

3
The Test of the Spectacles

The first person whom I encountered on returning to the house was the butler. He met me in the hall, with a receipted account in his hand which I had sent him to pay. The amount was close on a hundred pounds, and I had paid it immediately. 'Is there no discount?' I asked, looking at the receipt.

'The parties expect cash, sir, and charge accordingly.'

He looked so respectable when he made this answer, he had served us for so many years, that I felt an irresistible temptation to try the

Devil's Spectacles on the butler, before I ventured to look through them at the ladies of my family. Our honest old servant would be such an excellent test.

'I am afraid my sight is failing me,' I said.

With this exceedingly simple explanation I put on the spectacles and looked at the butler.

The hall whirled round with me; on my word of honour I tremble and turn cold while I write of it now. Septimus Notman had spoken the truth!

In an instant the butler's heart became hideously visible – a fat organ seen through the medium of the infernal glasses. The thought in him was plainly legible to me in these words: 'Does my master think I'm going to give him the five per cent off the bill? Beastly meanness, interfering with the butler's perquisites.'

I took off my spectacles and put them in my pocket.

'You are a thief,' I said to the butler. 'You have got the discount money on this bill – five pounds all but a shilling or two – in your pocket. Send in your accounts; you leave my service.'

'Tomorrow, sir, if you like!' answered the butler, indignantly. 'After serving your family for five-and-twenty years, to be called a thief for only taking my perquisites is an insult, Mr Alfred, that I have not deserved.' He put his handkerchief to his eyes and left me.

It was true that he had served us for a quarter of a century; it was also true that he had taken his perquisite and told a fib about it. But he had his compensating virtues. When I was a child he had given me many a ride on his knee and many a stolen drink of wine and water. His cellar-book had always been honestly kept; and his wife herself admitted that he was a model husband. At other times I should have remembered this, I should have felt that I had been hasty, and have asked his pardon. At this time I failed to feel the slightest compassion for him, and never faltered for a moment in my resolution to send him away. What change had passed over me?

The library door opened, and an old schoolfellow and college friend of mine looked out. 'I thought I heard your voice in the hall,' he said; 'I have been waiting an hour for you.'

'Anything very important,' I asked, leading the way back to the library.

'Nothing of the least importance to you,' he replied, modestly.

I wanted no further explanation. More than once already I had lent him money, and, sooner or later, he had always repaid me. 'Another little loan?' I enquired, smiling pleasantly.

'I am really ashamed to ask you again, Alfred. But if you could lend me fifty pounds – just look at that letter?'

He made some joke, suggested by the quaint appearance of the Spectacles. I was too closely occupied to appreciate his sense of humour. What had he just said to me? He had said. 'I am ashamed to ask you again.' And what had he thought while he was speaking? He had thought. 'When one has a milch cow at one's disposal, who but a fool would fail to take advantage of it?'

I handed him back the letter (from a lawyer, threatening 'proceedings') and I said, in my hardest tones, 'It's not convenient to oblige you this time.'

He stared at me like a man thunderstruck. 'Is this a joke, Alfred?' he asked.

'Do I look as if I was joking?'

He took up his hat. 'There is but one excuse for you,' he said. 'Your social position is too much for your weak brain – your money has got into your head. Good morning.'

I had been indebted to him for all sorts of kind services at school and college. He was an honourable man, and a faithful friend. If the galling sense of his own narrow means made him unjustly contemptuous towards rich people, it was a fault (in my case, an exasperating fault), no doubt. But who is perfect? And what are fifty pounds to me? This is what I should once have felt, before he could have found time enough to get to the door. As things were, I let him go, and thought myself well rid of a mean hanger-on who only valued me for my money.

Being now free to visit the ladies, I rang the bell and asked if my mother was at home. She was in her boudoir. And where was Miss Cecilia? In the boudoir, too.

On entering the room I found visitors in the way, and put off the trial of the Spectacles until they had taken their leave. Just as they were going a thundering knock at the door announced more visitors. This time, fortunately, we escaped with no worse consequences than the delivery of cards. We actually had two minutes to ourselves. I seized the opportunity of reminding my mother that I was constitutionally inaccessible to the claims of Society, and that I thought we might as well have our house to ourselves for half an hour or so. 'Send word downstairs,' I said, 'that you are not at home.'

My mother – magnificent in her old lace, her admirably-dressed grey hair, and her finely falling robe of purple-silk – looked across the fireplace at Cecilia – tall, and lazy, and beautiful, with lovely brown eyes, luxuriant black hair, a warmly-pale complexion, and an amber-coloured dress – and said to me, 'You forget Cecilia. She likes Society.'

Cecilia looked at my mother with an air of languid surprise. 'What an extraordinary mistake!' she answered. 'I hate Society.'

My mother smiled – rang the bell – and gave the order – Not at home. I produced my spectacles. There was an outcry at the hideous ugliness of them. I laid blame on 'my oculist', and waited for what was to follow between the two ladies. My mother spoke. Consequently I looked at my mother.

[I present her words first, and her thoughts next, in parenthesis.]

'So you hate society, my dear? Surely you have changed your opinion lately?' ('She doesn't mind how she lies as long as she can curry favour with Alfred. False creature.')

[I report Cecilia's answer on the same plan.]

'Pardon me; I haven't in the least changed my opinion – I was only afraid to express it. I hope I have not given offence by expressing it now.' ('She can't exist without gossip, and then she tries to lay it on me. Worldly old wretch!')

What I began to think of my mother, I am ashamed to record. What I thought of Cecilia may be stated in two words. I was more eager than ever to see 'The Angel of the school', the good and lovely Zilla.

My mother stopped the further progress of my investigations. 'Take off those hideous Spectacles, Alfred, or leave us to our visitors. I don't say your sight may not be failing; I only say change your oculist.'

I took off the Spectacles, all the more willingly that I began to be really afraid of them. The talk between the ladies went on.

'Yours is a strange confession, my dear,' my mother said to Cecilia. 'May I ask what motive so young a lady can have for hating Society?'

'Only the motive of wanting to improve myself,' Cecilia answered. 'If I knew a little more of modern languages, and if I could be something better than a feeble amateur when I paint in watercolours, you might think me worthier to be Alfred's wife. But Society is always in the way when I open my book or take up my brushes. In London I have no time to myself, and, I really can't disguise it, the frivolous life I lead is not to my taste.'

I thought this – (my Spectacles being in my pocket, remember) – very well and very prettily said. My mother looked at me. 'I quite agree with Cecilia,' I said, answering the look. 'We cannot count on having five minutes to ourselves in London from morning to night.'

Another knock at the street door contributed its noisy support to my views as I spoke. 'We daren't even look out of the window,' I remarked, 'for fear Society may look up at the same moment, and see that we are at home.'

My mother smiled. 'You are certainly two remarkable young people,' she said, with an air of satirical indulgence – and paused for a moment, as if an idea had occurred to her which was more than usually worthy of consideration. If her eye had not been on me at the moment, I believe I should have taken my Spectacles out of my pocket. 'You are both so thoroughly agreed in disliking Society and despising London,' she resumed, 'that I feel it my duty, as a good mother, to make your lives a little more in harmony with your tastes, if I can. You complain, Alfred, that you can never count on having five minutes to yourself with Cecilia, Cecilia complains that she is perpetually interrupted in the laudable effort to improve her mind. I offer you both the whole day to yourselves, week after week, for the next three months. We will spend the winter at Long Fallas.'

Long Fallas was our country seat. There was no hunting; the shooting was let; the place was seven miles from Timbercombe town and station; and our nearest neighbour was a young Ritualistic clergyman, popularly reported in the village to be starving himself to death. I declined my mother's extraordinary proposal without a moment's hesitation. Cecilia, with the readiest and sweetest submission, accepted it.

This was our first open difference of opinion. Even without the Spectacles I could see that my mother hailed it as a good sign. She had consented to our marriage in the spring, without in the least altering her opinion that the angelic Zilla was the right wife for me. 'Settle it between yourselves, my dears,' she said, and left her chair to look for her work. Cecilia rose immediately to save her the trouble.

The instant their backs were turned on me I put on the terrible glasses. Is there such a thing in anatomy as a back view of the heart? There is such a thing assuredly when you look through the Devil's Spectacles. My mother's private sentiments presented themselves to me, as follows: 'If they don't get thoroughly sick of each other in a winter at Long Fallas I give up all knowledge of human nature. He shall marry Zilla yet.' Cecilia's motives asserted themselves with transparent simplicity in these words, 'His mother fully expects me to say "No". Horrible as the prospect is, I'll disappoint her by saying "Yes".'

'Horrible as the prospect is' was to my mind a very revolting expression, considering that I was personally included in the prospect. My mother's mischievous test of our affection for each other now presented itself to me in the light of a sensible proceeding. In the solitude of Long Fallas, I should surely discover whether Cecilia was about to marry me for my money or for myself. I concealed my Spectacles, and said nothing at the time. But later, when my mother entered the drawing-room dressed to go out for dinner, I waylaid her, quite willing to go to Long Fallas. Cecilia came in dressed for dinner also. She had never looked so irresistibly lovely as when she was informed of my change of opinion. 'What a happy time we shall have,' she said, and smiled as if she really meant it?

They went away to their party. I was in the library when they returned. Hearing the carriage stop at the door I went out into the hall, and was suddenly checked on my way to the ladies by the sound of a man's voice: 'Many thanks; I am close to home now.' My mother's voice followed: 'I will let you know if we go to the country, Sir John. You will ride over and see us?' 'With the greatest pleasure. Good-night, Miss Cecilia.' There was no mistaking the tone in which those last four words were spoken. Sir John's accent expressed indescribable tenderness. I retired again to the library.

My mother came in, followed by her charming companion.

'Here is a new complication,' she said. 'Cecilia doesn't want to go to Long Fallas.' I asked why. Cecilia answered, without looking at me, 'Oh, I have changed my mind.' She turned aside to relieve my mother of her fur cloak. I instantly consulted my Spectacles, and obtained my information in these mysterious terms: 'Sir John goes to Timbercombe.'

Very short, and yet suggestive of more than one interpretation. A little enquiry made the facts more clear. Sir John had been one of the guests at the dinner, and he and Cecilia had shaken hands like old friends. At my mother's request, he had been presented to her. He had produced such an excellent impression that she had taken him in her carriage part of his way home. She had also discovered that he was about to visit a relative living at Timbercombe (already mentioned, I think, as our nearest town). Another momentary opportunity with the Spectacles completed my discoveries. Sir John had proposed marriage (unsuccessfully) to Cecilia, and being still persistently in love with her, only wanted a favourable opportunity to propose again. The excellent impression which he had produced on my mother was perfectly intelligible now.

In feeling reluctant to give her rejected lover that other opportunity, was Cecilia afraid of Sir John, or afraid of herself? My Spectacles informed me that she deliberately declined to face that question, even in her thoughts.

Under these circumstances, the test of a dreary winter residence at Long Fallas became, to my mind, more valuable than ever. Single-handed, Cecilia might successfully keep up appearances and deceive other people, though she might not deceive me. But, in combination with Sir John, there was a chance that she might openly betray the true state of her feelings. If I was really the favoured man, she would, of course, be dearer to me than ever. If not (with more producible proof than the Devil's Spectacles to justify me), I need not hesitate to break off the engagement.

'Second thoughts are not always best, dear Cecilia,' I said. 'Do me a favour. Let us try Long Fallas, and if we find the place quite unendurable, let us return to London.'

Cecilia looked at me and hesitated – looked at my mother, and submitted to Long Fallas in the sweetest manner. The more they were secretly at variance, the better the two ladies appeared to understand each other.

We did not start for the country until three days afterward. The packing up was a serious matter to begin with, and my mother prolonged the delay by paying a visit to her niece at the school in the country. She kept the visit a secret from Cecilia, of course. But even when we were alone, and when I asked about Zilla, I was only favoured with a very brief reply. She merely lifted her eyes to Heaven, and said, 'Perfectly charming!'

4

The Test of Long Fallas

We had had a week of it. If we had told each other the truth we should have said, 'Let us go back to London.'

Thus far there had been no signs of Sir John. The Spectacles informed me that he had arrived at Timbercombe, and that Cecilia had written to him. But, strangely enough, they failed to disclose what she had said. Has she forgotten it already, or was there some defect, hitherto unsuspected, in my supernatural glasses?

Christmas Day was near at hand. The weather was, so far, almost invariably misty and wet. Cecilia began to yawn over her favourite intellectual resources. My mother waited with superhuman patience for events. As for myself, having literally nothing else to amuse me, I took to gratifying an improper curiosity in the outlying regions of the family circle. In plain English, I discovered a nice little needlewoman, who was employed at Long Fallas. Her name was Miss Peskey. When nobody was looking, I amused myself with Miss Peskey.

Let no person of strict principles be alarmed. It was an innocent flirtation, on my side; and the nice little needlewoman rigidly refused to give me the smallest encouragement. Quite a young girl, Miss Peskey had the self-possession of a mature woman. She allowed me time to see that she had a trim little figure, soft blue eyes, and glossy golden hair; and then, in the sweetest of voices, respectfully requested me to leave her to her work. If I tried to persuade her to let me stay a little longer, she rose meekly, and said 'I shall, most unwillingly, be compelled to place myself under the protection of the housekeeper.' Once I attempted to take her hand. She put her handkerchief to her eyes and said, 'Is it manly, sir, to insult a defenceless girl?' In one word, Miss Peskey foiled me at every point. For the first week I never even got the chance of looking at her through the Devil's Spectacles.

On the first day of the new week the weather cleared up wonderfully; spring seemed to have come to us in the middle of winter.

Cecilia and I went out riding. On our return, having nothing better to do, I accompanied the horses back to the stables, and naturally offended the groom, who thought I was 'watching him'. Returning toward the house, I passed the window of the ground-floor room, at the back of the building, devoted to the needlewoman. A railed yard kept me at a respectful distance, but at the same time gave me a view of the interior of the room. Miss Peskey was not alone; my mother was with her. They were evidently talking, but not a word reached my ears. It mattered nothing. While I could see them through my Spectacles, their thoughts were visible to me before they found their way into words.

My mother was speaking – 'Well, my dear, have you formed your opinion of him yet?'

Miss Peskey replied, 'Not quite yet.'

'You are wonderfully cautious in arriving at a conclusion. How much longer is this clever contrivance of yours to last?'

'Give me two days more, dear madam; I can't decide until Sir John helps me.'

'Is Sir John really coming here?'

'I think so.'

'And have you managed it?'

'If you will kindly excuse me, I would rather not answer just yet.'

The housekeeper entered the room, and called my mother away on some domestic business. As she walked to the door, I had time to read her thought before she went out – 'Very extraordinary to find such resources of clever invention in such a young girl!'

Miss Peskey, left in maiden meditation with her work on her lap, smiled to herself. I turned the glasses on her, and made a discovery that petrified me. To put it plainly, the charming needlewoman was deceiving us all (with the one exception of my mother) under an assumed name and vocation in life. Miss Peskey was no other than my cousin Zilla, 'the Angel of the school'!

Let me do my poor mother justice. She was guilty of the consenting to the deception, and of no more. The invention of the trick, and the entire responsibility of carrying it out, rested wholly and exclusively with Miss Zilla, aged seventeen.

I followed the train of thought which my mother's questions had set going in the mind of this young person. To justify my own conduct, I must report the result as briefly as I can. Have you heard of 'fasting' girls? Have you heard of 'mesmeric' girls? Have you heard of girls (in the newspapers) who have invented the most infamous charges against innocent men? Then don't accuse my Spectacles of seeing impossible sights!

My report of Miss Zilla's thoughts, as they succeeded each other, begins as follows:

First Thought: 'My small fortune is all very well; but I want to be mistress of a great establishment, and get away from school. Alfred, dear fellow, is reported to have fifteen thousand a year. Is his mother's companion to be allowed to catch this rich fish, without the least opposition? Not if I know it!'

Second Thought: 'How very simple old people are! His mother visits me, invites me to Long Fallas, and expects me to cut out Cecilia. Men are such fools (the writing master has fallen in love with me) that she would only have to burst out crying, and keep him to herself. I have proposed a better way than fair fighting for Alfred, suggested by a play I read the other day. The old mother consents, with conditions. "I am sure you will do nothing, my dear, unbecoming to a young lady. Win him, as Miss Hardcastle won Mr Marlow in *She Stoops to Conquer*, if you like; but do nothing to forfeit your self-respect." What astonishing simplicity! Where did she go to school when she was young?'

Third Thought: 'How amazingly lucky that Cecilia's maid is lazy, and that the needlewoman dines in the servants' hall! The maid had the prospect of getting up before six in the morning, to be ready to go in the chaise-car with the servant who does the household errands at Timbercombe – and for what? To take a note from her mistress to Sir John, and wait for an answer. The good little needlewoman hears this, smiles, and says, "I don't mind how early I get up; I'll take it for you, and bring back the answer." '

Fourth Thought: 'What a blessing it is to have blue eyes and golden hair! Sir John was quite struck with me. I thought at the time he would do instead of Alfred. Fortunately I have since asked the simple old mother about him. He is a poor baronet. Not to be thought of for an instant. "My Lady" – without a corresponding establishment! Too dreadful! But I didn't throw away my fascinations. I saw him wince when he read the letter. "No bad news, I hope, sir," I ventured to say. He shook his head solemnly. "Your mistress" (he took me, of course, for Cecilia's maid) forbids me to call at Long Fallas." I thought to myself what a hypocrite Cecilia must be, as I said modestly to Sir John, to keep up appearances. Our private arrangement is that he is to ride over to Long Fallas tomorrow, and wait in the shrubbery at half-past two. If it rains or snows he is to try the next fine day. In either case the poor needlewoman will ask for a half-holiday, and will induce Miss Cecilia to take a little walk in the right direction. Sir John gave me two sovereigns and a kiss at parting. I accepted both tributes with the most becoming humility. He shall have his money's worth, though he is a poor baronet; he shall meet his young lady in the shrubbery. And I may catch the rich fish, after all!'

Fifth Thought: 'Bother this horrid work! It is all very well to be clever with one's needle, but how it disfigures one's forefinger! No matter, I must play my part while it lasts, or I shall be reported lazy by the most detestable woman I ever met with – the housekeeper at Long Fallas.'

She threaded her needle, and I put my Spectacles in my pocket.

I don't think I suspected it at the time; but I am now well aware that Septimus Notman's diabolical gift was exerting an influence over me. I was wickedly cool, under circumstances which would have roused my righteous indignation in the days before my Spectacles. Sir John and the Angel; my mother and her family interests; Cecilia and her unacknowledged lover – what a network of conspiracy and deception was wound about me! And what a perfectly fiendish pleasure I felt in planning to match them on their own ground! The method of obtaining this object presented itself to me in the simplest form. I had only to take my mother for a walk in the near neighbourhood of the shrubbery – and the exposure would be complete! That night I studied the barometer with unutterable anxiety. The prospect of the weather was all that I could wish.

5
The Truth in the Shrubbery

On the next day, the friendly sun shone, the balmy air invited everybody to go out. I made no further use of the Spectacles that morning: my purpose was to keep them in my pocket until the interview in the shrubbery was over. Shall I own the motive? It was simply fear – fear of making further discoveries, and of losing the masterly self-control on which the whole success of my project depended.

We lunched at one o'clock. Had Cecilia and Zilla come to a private understanding on the subject of the interview in the shrubbery? By way of ascertaining this, I asked Cecilia if she would like to go out riding in the afternoon. She declined the proposal – she wanted to finish a sketch. I was sufficiently answered.

'Cecilia complains that your manner has grown cold toward her lately,' mother said, when we were left together.

My mind was dwelling on Cecilia's letter to Sir John. Would any man have so easily adopted Zilla's suggestion not to take Cecilia at her word, unless there had been something to encourage him? I could only trust myself to answer my mother very briefly. 'Cecilia is changed towards me' – was all my reply.

My mother was evidently gratified by this prospect of a misunderstanding between us. 'Ah!' she said, 'if Cecilia only had Zilla's sweet temper.'

This was a little too much to endure – but I did endure it. 'Will you come out with me, mamma, for a walk in the grounds?' I asked.

My mother accepted the invitation so gladly, that I really think I should have felt ashamed of myself – if I had not had the contaminating Spectacles in my pocket. We had just settled to start soon after two o'clock, when there was a timid knock at the door. The angelic needlewoman appeared to ask for her half-holiday. My mother actually blushed! Old habits will cling to the members of the past generation. 'What is it?' she said, in low uncertain tones. 'Might I go to the village, ma'am, to buy some little things?' 'Certainly.' The door closed again. 'Now for the shrubbery!' I thought. 'Make haste, mamma,' I said, 'the best of the day is going. And mind one thing – put on your thickest boots!'

On one side of the shrubbery were the gardens. The other side was bounded by a wooden fence. A footpath, running part of the way beside the fence, crossed the grass beyond, and made a short cut between the nearest park gate and the servants' offices. This was the safe place that I had chosen. We could hear perfectly – though the closely-planted evergreens might prevent the exercise of sight. I had recommended 'thick boots' because there was no help but to muffle the sound of our footsteps by walking on the wet grass. At its further end, the shrubbery joined the carriage road up to the house.

My mother's surprise at the place that I had chosen for our walk would have been expressed in words, as well as by looks, if I had not stopped her by a whispered warning. 'Keep perfectly quiet,' I said, 'and listen. I have a motive for bringing you here.'

The words had hardly passed my lips, before we heard the voices of Cecilia and the needlewoman in the shrubbery.

'Wait a minute,' said Cecilia; 'you must be a little more explicit, before I consent to go any farther. How came you to take my letter to Sir John, instead of my maid?'

'Only to oblige her, Miss. She was not very well, and she didn't fancy going all the way to Timbercombe. I can buy no good needles in the village, and I was glad of the opportunity of getting to the town.'

There was a pause. Cecilia was reflecting, as I supposed. My mother began to turn pale.

Cecilia resumed. 'There is nothing in Sir John's answer to my letter,' she said, ' that leads me to suppose he can be guilty of an act of rudeness. I have always believed him to be a gentleman. No gentleman would force his way into my presence, when I wrote expressly to ask him to spare me. Pray how did you know he was determined only to take his dismissal from my lips?'

'Gentlemen's feelings sometimes get the better of them, Miss. Sir John was very much distressed – '

Cecilia interrupted her. 'There was nothing in my letter to distress him,' she said.

'He was distressed, Miss; and he did say, "I cannot take my answer this way – I must and will see her." And then he asked me to get you to walk out today, and to say nothing so that he might take you by surprise. He is so madly in love with you, Miss, that he is all but beside himself. I am really afraid of what might happen, if you don't soften his disappointment to him in some way. How any lady can treat such a handsome gentleman so cruelly, passes my poor judgement!'

Cecilia instantly resented the familiarity implied in those last words. 'You are not called upon to exercise your judgement,' she said. 'You can go back to the house.'

'Hadn't I better see Sir John first, Miss?'

'Certainly not! You and Sir John have seen quite enough of each other already.'

There was another pause. My mother stood holding by my arm, pale and trembling. We could neither of us speak. My own mind was strangely agitated. Either Cecilia was a monster of deceit, or she had thus far spoken and acted as became a true and highly-bred woman. The distant sound of horses' hoofs on the park road, told us both that the critical moment was at hand. In another minute, the sound ceased. Sir John had probably dismounted, and tied up his horse at the entrance of the shrubbery. After an interval, we heard Cecilia's voice again, farther away from us. We followed the voice. The interview which was to decide my future destiny in life had begun.

'No, Sir John; I must have my question answered first. Is there anything in my letter – was there anything in my conduct, when we met in London – which justifies this?'

'Love justifies everything, Cecilia!'

'You are not to call me Cecilia, if you please. Have you no plainer answer to give me?'

'Have you no mercy on a man, who cannot live without you? Is there really nothing in myself and my title to set against the perfectly obscure person, to whom you have so rashly engaged yourself? It would be an insult to suppose that his wealth has tempted you. What can be his merit in your eyes? His own friends can say no more in his favour than that he is a good-natured fool. I don't blame you; women often drift into engagements that they repent of afterwards. Do yourself justice! Be true to the nobility of character – and be the angel who makes our two lives happy, before it is too late!'

'Have you done, Sir John?'

There was a moment of silence. It was impossible to mistake her tone – Sir John's flow of eloquence came to a full stop.

'Before I answer you,' Cecilia proceeded, 'I have something to say first. The girl who took my letter to you was not my maid, as you may have supposed. She is a stranger to me; and I suspect her of being a false creature with some purpose of her own to serve. I find a difficulty in attributing to a person in your rank of life the mean deceit which answers my letter in terms that lead me to trust you, and then takes me by surprise in this way. My messenger (as I believe) is quite insolent enough to have suggested this course to you. Am I right? I expect a reply, Sir John, that is worthy in its entire truthfulness of you and your title. Am I right?'

'You are right, Miss Cecilia. Pray don't despise me. The temptation to plead with you once more –'

'I will speak to you, Sir John, as candidly as you have spoken to me. You are entirely wrong in supposing it possible for me to repent of my marriage engagement. The man, whose false friends have depreciated him in your estimation, is the only man I love, and the only man I will marry. And I beg you to understand, if he lost the whole of his fortune tomorrow, I would marry him the next day, if he asked me. Must I say more? Or will you treat me with the delicacy of a gentleman, and take your leave?'

I don't remember whether he said anything or not, before he left her. I only know that they parted. Don't ask me to confess what I felt. Don't ask me to describe what my mother felt. Let the scene be changed, and the narrative be resumed at a later hour of the day.

6

The End of the Spectacles

I asked myself a question, which I beg to repeat here. What did I owe to the Devil's Spectacles?

In the first place, I was indebted to my glasses for seeing all the faults, and none of the merits, in the persons about me. In the second place, I arrived at the discovery that, if we are to live usefully and happily with our fellow-creatures, we must take them at their best, and not at their worst. Having reached these conclusions, I trusted my own unassisted insight, and set myself to ascertain what the Devil had not helped me to discover in the two persons who were dearest to me – my mother and Cecilia.

I began with Cecilia, leaving my mother time to recover after the shock that had fallen on her.

It was impossible to acknowledge what I had seen through the Spectacles, or what I had heard at the shrubbery fence. In speaking to Cecilia, I could only attribute my coldness of manner to jealousy of the mere name of 'Sir John', and ask to be pardoned for even a momentary distrust of the most constant and charming of women. There was something, I suppose, in my contrite consciousness of having wronged her, that expressed itself in my looks and in my tones. We were sitting together on the sofa. For the first time since our engagement, she put her arm around my neck, and kissed me, without waiting to be kissed first.

I am not very demonstrative,' she said, softly; 'and I don't think, Alfred, you have ever known how fond I am of you. My dear, when Sir John and I met again at that dinner party, I was too faithful to you to even allow myself to think of him. Your poor mother irritated me by seeming to doubt whether I could trust myself within reach of Timbercombe, or I should never have consented to go to Long Fallas. You remember that she invited Sir John to ride over and see us. I wrote to him, informing him of my engagement to you, and telling him, in the plainest words, that if he did call at this house, nothing would induce me to see him. I had every reason to suppose that he would understand and respect my motives – '

She paused. The rich colour rose in her lovely face. I refused to let her distress herself by saying a word of what had happened in the shrubbery. Look back, if you have forgotten it, and see how completely the Spectacles failed to show me the higher and nobler motives that had animated her. The little superficial irritabilities and distrusts, they exhibited to perfection; but the true regard for each other, hidden below the surface in my mother and in my promised wife, was completely beyond them.

'Shall we go back to London, tomorrow?' I asked.

'Are you tired of being here with me, Alfred?'

'I am tired of waiting till the spring, my angel. I will live with you wherever you like, if you will only consent to hasten the transformation which makes you my wife. Will you consent?'

'If your mother asks me. Don't hurry her, Alfred.'

But I did hurry her. After what we had heard in the shrubbery I could look into my mother's heart (without assistance), and feel sure that the nobler part of her nature would justify my confidence in it. She was not only ready to 'ask Cecilia', then and there – she was eager, poor soul, to confess how completely she had been misled by her natural interest in her brother's child. Being firmly resolved to keep the secret of my discovery of her niece, I refused to hear her, as I had refused to hear Cecilia. Did I not know, without being told, what child's play it would be to Zilla to dazzle and delude my innocent mother? I merely asked if 'the needlewoman was still in the house'. The answer was thoroughly explicit: 'She is at the railway station by this time, and she will never enter any house of mine again.'

I had a moment's private talk with the station-master at Timbercombe. Sir John had left his friends at the town, on the previous day. He and Zilla had met on the platform, waiting for the London train. She had followed him into the smoking-carriage. Just as the station-master was going to start the train, Sir John opened the door, with a strong expression of disgust, and took refuge in another carriage. She had tried the baronet as a last resource, and he had slipped through her fingers too. What did it matter to Zilla? She had plenty of time before her, and she belonged to the order of persons who never fail to make the most of her advantages. The other day I saw the announcement of her marriage to a great ironmaster, a man worth millions of money, with establishments to correspond. Bravo, Zilla! No need to look for your nobler motives with the naked eye.

A few days before I became a married man I was a guest at the dinner table of a bachelor friend, and I met Sir John. It would have been ridiculous to leave the room; I merely charged my host to keep my name concealed. I sat next to the baronet, and he doesn't know, to this day, who his 'very agreeable neighbour' was.

Instead of spending our honeymoon abroad, Cecilia and I went back to Long Fallas. We found the place delightful, even in the winter time.

Did I take the Devil's Spectacles back with me?

No.

Did I throw them away or smash them into small morsels?

Neither. I remembered what Septimus Notman had told me. The one way of getting rid of them was to give them to some other man.

And to what other man did I give them?

I had not forgotten what my rival had said of me in the shrubbery. I gave the Devil's Spectacles to Sir John.

7

Between the Reader and the Editor

Are we to have no satisfactory explanation of the supernatural element in the story? How did it come into the Editor's hands? Was there neither name or address on the manuscript?

There was an address, if you must know. But I decline to mention it.

Suppose I guess that the address was at a lunatic asylum? What would you say to that?

I should say I suspected you of being a critic, and I should have the honour of wishing you good-morning.